Murder Most

FELINE

Murder Most FELINE

Cunning Tales of Cats and Crime

Edited by

ED GORMAN, MARTIN H. GREENBERG, AND LARRY SEGRIFF

Cumberland House
Nashville, Tennessee

Published by
Cumberland House Publishing, Inc.
431 Harding Industrial Drive
Nashville, TN 37211
www.cumberlandhouse.com

Cover design: Gore Studio, Inc.
Text design: Mary Sanford

Library of Congress Cataloging-in-Publication Data
Murder most feline : cunning tales of cats and crime / edited by Ed Gorman, Martin H. Greenberg, Larry Segriff.
      p. cm.
   ISBN 1-58182-215-4 (alk. paper)
   1. Cats—Fiction. 2. Legal stories, American. 3. Detective and mystery stories, American. I. Gorman, Edward II. Greenberg, Martin Harry. III. Segriff, Larry.

   PS648.C38 M87 2001
   813'.08723629752—dc21

                                                                    2001042459

Printed in the United States of America
1 2 3 4 5 6 7—06 05 04 03 02 01

CONTENTS

INTRODUCTION

Oyez! Oyez! Oyez! The court is now in session!

On the surface, one would think that cats and the court system do not have much in common. After all, most people consider the modern legal system to be a slow, massive, unwieldy (possibly even out-of-control) institution where injustices are perpetrated on a daily basis while the rights of the innocents are overlooked. Cats, on the other hand, are living symbols of grace and dignity, quick to deal out their own idea of justice in the form of a claw or bite when necessary, and only occasionally ignoring the rights of their innocent owners.

But upon closer examination, there are several similarities between felines and the American legal system. For example, the justice system (when it works) is reputed to be impartial, and often is, deciding good and evil without regard for race, social status, or gender. Cat owners know that a cat is impartial in many ways, deciding who is worthy of his or her affection also without regard to race, status, or gender, but according to some mysterious private agenda only the cat knows. When the court's attention is brought to bear on a person or event, the scrutiny can be overwhelming, causing many to break down under the all-encompassing eye of the law. The feeling is very much like being stared at by a cat who wants something you have, that inscrutable feline gaze which, if one is not careful, may lead to the confession of all kinds of sins or to the surrender of whatever item that will take those all-knowing eyes off their target. Finally, there has been a recent trend in the judicial system of turning the participants—from the alleged criminals and/or victims to the legal teams on both sides of the case—into celebrities, raising them to an exalted (or sometimes lowering them to a reviled) position in the nation's consciousness. And anybody who has ever owned a cat knows the type of star treatment they expect to receive—and the punishment that may occur if they don't get it.

With these similarities in mind, it seems only natural to combine cats, crime, and the courts and see what the verdict is. The results are the seventeen stories collected here, all of which make jurisprudence more fun than any televised trial could ever be. From a private detective who goes to bat for a cat's inheritance to a feline companion who is a crucial, albeit unknowing, witness in a courtroom unlike any other, cats take the stand in their own defense to catch criminals, provide evidence, and turn the legal system on its collective ear—all in the name of justice.

The jury has returned, the bailiff is calling the court to order, and the judge is entering the courtroom. So sit back on the courtroom bench and get ready to watch law meet paw in these cases of cats and crime.

—The Editors

Murder Most
FELINE

The Witness Cat

Parnell Hall

Steve Winslow was having a bad day. It started off with a witness giving him fits and ended up with his secretary not speaking to him.

Steve was getting nowhere with this witness. The more he cross-examined, the worse it got. Russ Overmeyer sat on the witness stand, smug, self-satisfied, fielding all his questions and turning them back against his client. And this was the key witness. If Steve Winslow couldn't shake Overmeyer's testimony, the defendant was sunk.

Steve Winslow glanced over at the defense table where his client sat. A wizened old man with a stubborn streak and an irascible nature, Clinton Hobbs was glaring at him with cranky eyes. Which was not surprising. Steve Winslow was Mr. Hobbs's court-appointed lawyer, assigned because the defendant was indigent and could not afford to hire an attorney for himself. And Mr. Hobbs could not have been less happy with the choice. With long hair, blue jeans, and corduroy jacket, Steve Winslow looked like a leftover from the sixties. That, coupled with the fact he was much too young to actually be from the sixties, did not exactly inspire Mr. Hobbs with confidence. Steve Winslow was acting as his attorney only because the judge would not allow him to choose another.

Which had to be rather frustrating for someone accused of murder.

Steve Winslow pushed the hair out of his eyes and cocked his head at the witness. "Well, then, Mr. Overmeyer. Getting back to the night in question when you claim you saw my client leaving the bedroom of the decedent—"

The prosecutor, Assistant District Attorney Harvey Beerbaum, was on his feet. "Objection to the word *claim,* Your Honor. The witness isn't claiming anything, he's stating what he saw."

Judge Judith Weston banged the gavel. A tough, no-nonsense jurist, Judge Weston did not take kindly to technical objections. "Overruled," she snapped. "I have confidence the witness can take care of himself. And I would thank you to state your objections at the sidebar, not in front of the jury."

"Yes, Your Honor," A.D.A. Beerbaum said.

"Would the court reporter read back the question?"

"Actually, I believe I was interrupted *before* I asked the question," Steve Winslow said.

"Then ask it now," Judge Weston said irritably.

"Yes, Your Honor." Steve Winslow glanced at the prosecutor. Their eyes met, and Steve smiled. It dawned on A.D.A. Beerbaum that Steve Winslow had deliberately goaded him into annoying the judge.

"Now then, Mr. Overmeyer," Steve Winslow continued. "On the night in question, the night your uncle was killed, the night you claim you saw the defendant coming from his room—just what time did this supposedly happen?"

Russ Overmeyer had a round face, shiny bald head, and twinkling eyes. "It was 9:35."

"Really? How do you fix the time?"

"By television. I was watching a nine o'clock sitcom. It had just ended, and I was on my way to the kitchen to make myself a sandwich."

"Where were you watching television?"

"In my bedroom."

"Were you alone at the time?"

"Yes, I was."

"And where was your bedroom with relation to the decedent's?"

"It's in another wing."

"Another wing?"

"Yes. My uncle's mansion has thirty-four rooms. His bedroom is part of a suite of rooms on the east wing of the second floor. My bedroom is a single room in the west wing. I should explain I do not live in the house.

I have an apartment in Manhattan. When I'm out on Long Island, I often stay over."

"And this was one of those nights?"

"That's right."

"So you were in your bedroom watching television. The show ended, and you went to the kitchen to make a sandwich. And just what happened then?"

"As I say, I saw the defendant, Clinton Hobbs, come out of my uncle's bedroom."

"You're certain it was the defendant you saw?"

"Yes, I am."

"You know him well?"

"Of course. He's been the caretaker for years."

"Do you know him personally? Have you ever spoken to him?"

"I have spoken to him. As to knowing him personally, he's not an easy person to get to know. But I certainly know who he is."

"Did you speak to him on this occasion?"

"No, I did not. And I wouldn't have wanted to."

Steve Winslow frowned. The witness had thrown it out tauntingly, daring him to ask. If he didn't, he'd lose considerable points with the jury. If he did, it would probably be worse.

Steve Winslow took a breath. "Why wouldn't you have wanted to speak to him?"

"Because of his manner. He was irritated, angry, and upset. As if he'd just gone through some emotional trauma."

Steve Winslow didn't object, just nodded thoughtfully. "That's how you would characterize it?"

"That's right."

"You had reason to be concerned?"

"Of course."

"Because you'd seen him coming from your uncle's room?"

"That's right."

"So you rushed to your uncle's room to see what had happened."

"No, I didn't."

"You didn't?"

"No."

"Why not? If you were so concerned, why didn't you check on your uncle?"

"It didn't occur to me."

"It didn't occur to you to check on him?"

"No."

"So you weren't concerned about him, were you?"

"I was concerned. I knew that they'd had a fight. But it never occurred to me that Clinton had killed him."

"You find that hard to believe?"

"Actually, I do. Mr. Hobbs had been the caretaker of my uncle's house for more than twenty years. I knew he was a difficult man with a violent temper. But I did not know he would stoop to murder."

"And you don't know it now, do you?"

Russ Overmeyer smirked. "No, I don't. Because I didn't actually see him do it. I am concluding he did it from the circumstantial evidence. From the fact I saw him leaving the room. From the fact he had a fight with my uncle. From the fact I saw him return the murder weapon to the tool shed."

Steve Winslow raised his finger. "Now, that's the other point I wanted to take up with you. You say you saw the defendant storm out of your uncle's bedroom and down the stairs. And this was while you were on your way to the kitchen to make a sandwich. And Mr. Hobbs was so agitated you decided to follow him instead?"

"I didn't decide to follow him. I just looked out the window to see where he went."

"You looked out the window?"

"Yes, I did."

"And where was the window?"

"Downstairs," Russ Overmeyer said. "If I may say so, this was actually on my way to the kitchen. So, it's not as you say that I decided to follow the defendant. My attention was attracted to him by his agitated manner, so when I followed him downstairs on my way to the kitchen and heard him slam the back door, I did look out the window to see where he went."

"And where was that?"

"He went right to the tool shed behind the house. Where the police found the murder weapon."

"Move to strike," Steve Winslow said.

"Granted," Judge Weston said. "It will go out. Mr. Overmeyer, just testify to what you personally saw."

"That's what I'm doing."

"No, it is not," Judge Weston said. "Unless you were personally present when the police found the murder weapon, don't testify to them finding it. And call me 'Your Honor.'"

"Yes, Your Honor."

"You saw the defendant go into the tool shed," Steve Winslow continued. "Did you see him come out?"

"Yes, I did."

"How soon was that?"

"Right away."

"You mean he just stuck his head in the door?"

"Well, longer than that."

"How much longer?"

"Long enough to have left something there."

Clinton Hobbs's eyes blazed. "That's a lie," he snarled.

Judge Weston banged the gavel. "Silence. Order in the court."

"But he's lying, Your Honor. I never went near that shed."

Judge Weston banged the gavel again. "That will do. Counselor, control your client or I'll have him removed."

Steve Winslow turned to the defendant. "Hang on, Mr. Hobbs," he said. "It's their turn at bat. Don't worry, you'll get your chance." He turned back to the witness. "Now, Mr. Overmeyer, after the defendant left the tool shed, what did he do?"

"He headed in the direction of his cabin."

"His cabin?"

"That's what we call it. It's a little outbuilding near the garage where he lives."

"Mr. Hobbs went back to his cabin?"

"He went in that direction. I didn't watch to see where he went."

"What did you do?"

"I went to the kitchen and made myself a sandwich. Which is what I'd been intending all along."

"Then you weren't concerned about what you'd just seen."

"No, I was not. I knew there'd been an altercation. I didn't know there'd been a murder."

"What changed your mind?"

"On my way upstairs, I noticed my uncle's door was ajar. That was strange. He always kept it closed. I went to the door and stuck my head in. I could see at once something was wrong. The bedclothes were mussed, and my uncle was lying half in and half out of the bed. And his head. It was awful. The blood."

"Yes, you described the scene quite vividly on direct examination. Did you notice anything else at the time?"

"At the time?"

"Yes."

"No, I didn't. All I could see was my uncle."

"And what did you do?"

"Picked up the phone and called the police."

"The phone in the bedroom?"

"Yes."

"It didn't occur to you that you shouldn't touch it?"

"At a time like that? It certainly didn't. I ran to the phone and made the call."

"You were there when the police arrived?"

"Yes, I was."

"You took them to your uncle's room."

"Yes, I did."

"Now, on direct examination you testified that your uncle's jewelry box was open."

"That's right."

"Who noticed that?"

"I beg your pardon?"

"Did the police discover that, or did you point it out to them?"

"I think I may have pointed it out."

"You think?"

"Well, they didn't know what it was. I did. I appreciated the significance of it being opened."

"Which you pointed out to the police?"

"That's right."

"So the police didn't discover the jewelry box until you pointed it out to them."

Overmeyer frowned. "I suppose that's right."

"When did you notice the jewelry box was open?"

"Almost at once."

"Really? Your uncle's lying there dying, and the first thing you see is the jewelry box?"

"Yes, well, after overhearing the conversation."

"Ah, yes, the famous conversation," Steve Winslow said. "Would you tell me again just how you happened to overhear that?"

"It wasn't hard," Overmeyer said. "They were talking very loud."

"Where did this conversation take place?"

"In the study."

"Your uncle's study?"

"That's right."

"Would that be on the ground floor?"

"It would."

"And how did you happen to overhear this conversation? Aside from the fact that it was rather loud."

"I was on my way to the kitchen."

"Again?"

Several of the jurors smiled. Overmeyer was rather pudgy, and the inference was obvious.

Overmeyer looked at Steve Winslow coldly. "This was before the other incident."

"Yes, of course," Steve Winslow said. "At any rate, you overheard the conversation. Now could you tell us again just what was said?"

"Mr. Hobbs was furious. He was shouting at my uncle, calling him names. A thief and a liar."

"And what was that all about?"

"It was over the cufflinks."

"The cufflinks?"

"Yes. As I said before, my grandfather had a pair of diamond-studded cufflinks. Apparently, he promised them to Mr. Hobbs. At least Mr. Hobbs seems to think so."

"He sure did," Hobbs said.

Judge Weston scowled. "Mr. Hobbs, I'm not going to warn you again. The next time you speak out of turn, you will be removed from the court-room. Proceed, Mr. Winslow."

"Yes, Your Honor," Steve said. "Now, Mr. Overmeyer, you say your grandfather had a pair of diamond-studded cufflinks?"

"Yes. According to Mr. Hobbs, they were promised to him. Be that as it may, they were not mentioned in his will. Instead, everything went to his son. My uncle. The decedent."

"Your father is deceased?"

"Yes, or he would have inherited. He was the older brother."

"Uh-huh. Who inherits under your uncle's will?"

"I have no idea."

"Are you his closest living relative?"

"I am."

"Then can we assume—"

"Objection, Your Honor."

"Sustained," Judge Weston said. "You may not assume, Mr. Winslow. You may question as to fact."

"Yes, Your Honor. Mr. Overmeyer, is it not a fact that in your own mind you consider yourself your uncle's closest living relative and expect to inherit the majority of his estate?"

"Objection, Your Honor. That's not a fact at all. That's sheer speculation."

"Goes to bias, Your Honor."

"Exactly," Judge Weston said. She turned to the jurors. "Ladies and gentlemen of the jury, you are instructed that this question is being asked not to establish a fact but merely to establish the witness' interest in the case which might affect his testimony. You are to consider it only for that purpose. Proceed, Mr. Winslow."

"Thank you, Your Honor. Mr. Overmeyer, do you expect to inherit your uncle's estate?"

"I would think it is likely. Though I am not familiar with the contents of his will."

"Thank you. Now, with regard to your grandfather's will—the one that neglected to mention these diamond-studded cufflinks—you claim that that is what the argument you overheard was about?"

"Yes, it was."

"Specifically, what was said?"

"Mr. Hobbs wanted the cufflinks. He was yelling at my uncle, cursing him. Specifically, he said, 'They're mine'; 'You have no right to keep them'; and 'You'll pay for this.'"

"'You'll pay for this'?"

"That's right."

"You're certain he said, 'You'll pay for this'?"

"Yes, he did."

"Little melodramatic, don't you think?"

"Well, he's your client."

Several of the jurors smiled at this.

"Yes, he is," Steve Winslow said. "But it's your testimony. And your testimony alone. Isn't that right? When you say the defendant told your uncle 'You'll pay for this,' we only have your word for it."

"That's not true. Because I mentioned the conversation to the cook, and she'd heard it too."

"Uh-huh," Steve Winslow said. He put his hand to his head and paused for a moment, as if thinking up the next question. Actually, he was taking a standing nine-count. Someone else had overheard the argument? That was news to him. He needed time to recover.

Steve Winslow glanced around the courtroom. Behind the defense table, just outside the rail, his young secretary, Tracy Garvin, waved her hands to attract his attention.

Steve Winslow said, "One moment, please," walked over to her, and bent down. "What is it?" he whispered.

Tracy Garvin pulled off her large-framed glasses, pushed the blonde hair out of her eyes, and leaned in to whisper back. "I have a woman who wants to see you right away. Says it's urgent."

"Who is it?"

"Her name's Margorie Wilkins. She's a friend of the defendant."

"What does she want?"

"She wouldn't say except it's very important."

"Fine," he said. "At the moment I'll take anything I can get."

Steve Winslow straightened up, turned to the judge. "Your Honor, a matter has arisen which requires my immediate attention. I would ask for an adjournment."

A.D.A. Beerbaum was on his feet. "May I ask if you have completed your cross-examination?"

"No, I have not."

"Then I would object to an adjournment at this time. Let counsel complete his cross-examination."

"I have a matter to attend to first," Steve Winslow said.

Judge Weston frowned. "Sidebar," she snapped.

The judge came down to the side of the bench, where she conferred with the attorneys in low tones.

"Now, what is this all about?"

"I have just been informed that a woman needs to see me right away. She says it's urgent. I don't know the details, but it has something to do with the case, and it is my duty to check it out."

"Oh, for goodness sakes," Beerbaum said.

Judge Weston turned to him. "You have a problem with that?"

"I most certainly do. Don't you see what's happening here? He's losing. The witness has corroborating testimony, he's unhappy to hear it, so he turned around and signaled his secretary, some sort of secret sign or distress call, to which she responded. Then he pretends she's the one who signaled him, goes over, confers with her, and announces he needs an adjournment to talk to a witness. In all probability what he said was,

'I need an adjournment; find anyone I can talk to as a pretext to get one.'"

"Your Honor, in the first place, that's not true. However, I am struck by Mr. Beerbaum's statement that I was surprised to find there was a corroborating witness. I most certainly was. In light of discovery, I hardly expected to find the prosecution had an additional witness."

"Not an additional witness, Your Honor. You will find the cook, Gretchen Rudall, has been on the witness list from day one."

"Yes, with regard to finding the body. I don't recall any reference to her having heard this conversation in her testimony before the grand jury."

"Come, come, Counselor, we don't present everything to the grand jury, just enough to get an indictment."

"That will do," Judge Weston said. "Mr. Winslow, the prosecution contends that you are merely stalling. I would like some assurance that is not true. Who is this woman who needs to see you so urgently?"

"Her name is Margorie Wilkins, Your Honor."

"And where is this Margorie Wilkins?"

"I understand she's right outside."

"Then an adjournment is unnecessary. A short recess should suffice."

Judge Weston returned to the bench and announced that the court would stand in recess for half an hour.

As the jurors filed out and the court officer led the defendant away, Steve Winslow hurried to Tracy Garvin. "This better be good, Tracy. I'm in real trouble here."

"It's not that bad, is it?"

"Yes, it is. Not that there's a witness. That I didn't know it. It's a court-appointed case, and I didn't do my homework. I feel awful. It's like I'm letting my client down because he can't pay."

"How can you say that? You hired Mark Taylor to work on this case out of your own pocket."

"I put up the money. That doesn't mean I don't have to do my job. Where's this woman?"

"Right outside."

"Well, she better have something to help."

Steve Winslow and Tracy Garvin came out the back door of the courtroom. The corridor was mobbed with people. Steve Winslow looked around. "Where is she?"

"I left her sitting on a bench."

"Where?"

"Over there."

Steve Winslow followed Tracy Garvin down the hallway.

Sitting on a bench was an elderly woman in a gingham dress. She wore too much perfume and too much costume jewelry, including several strands of large pearls which were obviously fake. Next to her on the bench was a huge fur coat, also obviously fake, though what actual fur it was attempting to represent Steve couldn't even begin to guess. The woman had a broad face, accentuated by cat's-eye glasses, made of blue plastic with embedded glitter. She wore slightly more eye shadow than a vampire, slightly less lipstick than Bozo the Clown.

Steve Winslow grimaced. *This* was the witness he was pinning his hopes on? He glanced at Tracy Garvin as if asking her to tell him it wasn't so.

But Tracy Garvin turned to the woman and said, "Miss Wilkins, this is Mr. Winslow."

Margorie Wilkins raised her head and batted her eyes. She looked anything but pleased. "Well," she said. "It's about time."

Steve Winslow smiled. "Sorry to keep you waiting, Miss Wilkins, but I was in court."

"So they tell me. You're Mr. Hobbs's lawyer?"

"That's right."

"When is he going to get out of jail?"

"I was hoping you could help me with that."

Her eyes widened in surprise. "Me? What do you mean, me?"

"Well, do you have some information that might help?"

"Information? What sort of information?"

"That would prove he didn't commit the crime."

"Commit the crime? Of course he didn't commit the crime. Mr. Hobbs wouldn't hurt a fly."

"Which is just what I'm attempting to prove, Miss Wilkins. Now, do you think you could help me with that?"

"No, I don't," she said irritably. "And it's the second time you've asked me. That's not my job. That's your job. Now, when are you going to get him out of jail?"

Steve Winslow frowned. "I don't know how long the trial will last."

"Well, will it be this afternoon?"

"I can almost assure you it won't."

Miss Wilkins snorted. "Well, then that's enough for me."

"I beg your pardon?"

"In that case, I wash my hands of the whole affair. I mean, a favor is a favor. But there are limits. I mean, did he think I would keep her forever?"

"I beg your pardon?" Steve Winslow repeated.

"No, sir, she's yours," Margorie Wilkins said.

She reached under the bench and pulled out a large, brown carrying case. It had a handle on the top and air holes in the sides. She lifted it up on the bench, opened the top, and reached in and pulled out the biggest, blackest cat Steve Winslow had ever seen.

"Oh, what a sweetheart!" Tracy Garvin said.

"Isn't she?" Margorie Wilkins said. "This is Molly, Mr. Hobbs's cat. He asked me to look after her when they took him away. Then he didn't come back. Now what do you think of that?"

Steve Winslow didn't know what to think of that. He was gawking at the cat, which was staring at him with large green eyes, as if recognizing him as the new master and challenging his authority. *Oh yeah,* Molly seemed to say. *You just think you're in charge. Well, think again.*

"Miss Wilkins," Steve Winslow said, "I know nothing about cats."

"What's to know? You feed her when she's hungry—Molly makes her wishes known. And you let her run around your apartment. Don't worry, she'll make herself right at home. Here, you want to hold her?"

Steve Winslow blinked. He had never had much luck with cats. He wouldn't want to hold one under normal circumstances, even if he weren't in the middle of a murder trial. But he couldn't be out and out rude to the woman. He found himself lifting his hands to receive Molly.

It didn't happen. Before he could take the cat, Molly bared her teeth, hissed, snaked out an enormous paw, and raked him across the wrist.

Steve Winslow flinched, then gawked at the cat. "Good lord," he said. "That's the biggest paw I've ever seen."

Margorie Wilkins actually smiled. "Yes," she said. "Molly has double paws."

"Double paws?"

"Yes. Some cats are born that way. She has ten toes on her feet. It makes her paws very big."

"And gives her a lot of claws," Steve Winslow observed, examining the scratches on his wrist. "I'm sorry, Miss Wilkins. I'm afraid this cat doesn't like me."

"Oh, she just doesn't know you," Margorie Wilkins said. "You reach for her, she sees it as a threatening gesture. Here now, you sit down on the bench. There, that's right. Sit right down, and I'll put Molly on your lap. Here, Molly, sit on the nice man's lap."

Steve Winslow's whole body tensed as Margorie Wilkins lowered the cat onto him, particularly since Molly didn't lie down but instead stood on his lap with her enormous paws. She swiveled her neck around and looked up at his face. Satisfied, she turned back and began to tread on his lap.

Steve Winslow nearly jumped off the bench, but Margorie Wilkins put her hand on his shoulder.

"It's all right. She likes you, and she's going to lie down."

Sure enough, after tromping on his legs, Molly swiveled around in a one eighty, curled up on his lap, and began to purr.

Margorie Wilkins beamed. "See," she said, "she likes you."

"I'm flattered," Steve Winslow said. "Look here, Miss Wilkins. I'm not prepared to handle a cat."

"Really?" she said. She stroked the cat and patted Winslow on the cheek. "Then you'd better get your client off."

With that, she smiled at him and walked away.

Steve Winslow looked up at Tracy Garvin. "Tracy—"

"Don't look at me," Tracy said. "I don't have room for a cat."

"You think I do?" Steve Winslow ran his hand over his head. "Good lord, what a position to be in. If I can't get my client off, I'm stuck with her."

"Well, here's Mark Taylor," Tracy said. "Maybe he's got something to help."

The private detective approached them hurriedly. "Hi, Steve. Tracy. What you got there?"

"Clinton Hobbs's cat," Steve Winslow said. "If I can't get him off, she's mine."

"Then you better start buying cat food," Mark Taylor said. "'Cause I got nothing good. Everyone I question says the same thing: Clinton Hobbs had it in for the decedent, felt he'd dorked him out of a pair of cufflinks. Hobbs was obsessed with it, talked about it to everyone he'd meet. In short, nothing contradicts Overmeyer's story, and everything supports it." Mark Taylor ran his fingers through his curly, red hair. "Didn't the police find those cufflinks under your client's bed?"

"Under the mattress."

Mark Taylor grimaced, shook his head. "I don't want to tell you your business, Steve, but if I were you, I'd plead him out."

"I can't plead him out, Mark. I'm stuck with the cat."

"What?"

"I'm kidding, of course," Steve Winslow said. "But Clinton Hobbs says he didn't do it, and if he didn't do it, I can't plead him out."

"It's an assigned case, Steve. You're not making a dime."

"That's got nothing to do with it."

"Well, you're payin' me out of your own pocket. I'm billin' you at cost, but still."

"Bill me at your regular rates, Mark. Mr. Hobbs isn't entitled to anything less just because he can't pay. Now, did you get me anything, anything at all I can use?"

The P.I. frowned, shook his head. "No."

"Great," Steve Winslow said. He scratched Molly under her chin. "Looks like I'm stuck with a cat."

When court reconvened, Steve Winslow took a seat next to his client.

"So?" Clinton Hobbs demanded. "Did you get anything?"

"Frankly, nothing that helps."

"Helps?" Clinton Hobbs said. "The witness is lying. What more do you need?"

"It would help to prove it."

"So prove it," Clinton Hobbs said. "The man says I went into the shed and planted the murder weapon. I didn't do it, I didn't go near the shed, the man is lying."

"But you did have the argument?"

"Yes, I had the argument. That afternoon. But I didn't go to his room that night, I didn't go to the shed, and I didn't steal a pair of cufflinks and hide 'em in my bunk. I mean, how stupid do they think I am?"

"And where were you all that time?"

"I told you where. Sitting down by the boat dock cooling off."

"And having a little drink?"

"So I was drinking. So what?"

"Anyone see you there?"

"You think I wouldn't have mentioned that?"

"No, I'm sure you would. As I recall, it was just you and your cat. Is that right?"

"Yeah, that's right. You gonna put my cat on the stand?"

"That's not what I have in mind," Steve Winslow said.

"Yeah, well what do you have in mind? Listening to your cross-examination, I would say not much. I suppose that doesn't matter to you since I'm the one going to jail."

Steve Winslow sighed. Clinton Hobbs was cranky and irascible, just like his cat. They were certainly well suited for each other. It was up to him to keep them together.

Judge Weston called the court to order. "Mr. Overmeyer, I remind you you are still under oath. Mr. Winslow, you may proceed with your cross-examination."

"Thank you, Your Honor." Steve Winslow approached the witness and smiled. "Now, Mr. Overmeyer. When we left off, I believe you had just testified that the cook had also overheard the conversation between your uncle and my client."

"That's right. She did."

"This was the conversation where they argued over the cufflinks?"

"That's right."

"You heard my client threaten your uncle?"

"Yes, I did."

"And as a result of this conversation, you had reason to notice the jewelry box was open when you entered your uncle's room. That's why you pointed it out to the police. Now, were you present when the police subsequently made a search of my client's cabin?"

"Yes, I was."

"Can you tell us what they found?"

A.D.A. Beerbaum was on his feet. "Your Honor, the officers will speak for themselves."

"If he knows, he may tell," Judge Weston ruled. "Provided he was personally present."

"I was," Overmeyer said. "I directed the police to Clinton Hobbs's cabin. I watched them search it. I was there when they found the cufflinks."

"The cufflinks that were missing from your uncle's jewelry box?"

"That's right."

"Is it, Mr. Overmeyer? I ask you, is it possible that you were mistaken in any part of your testimony?"

"No, it is not."

"Your entire testimony is true?"

"Yes, it is."

"If any portion of your testimony is untrue, is it possible your entire testimony is untrue?"

"Objection, Your Honor."

"I'll withdraw it," Steve Winslow said. "Mr. Overmeyer, you have testified that you saw my client, the defendant, enter the tool shed where the murder weapon was found on the night in question."

"That's right."

"Are you aware of the fact he denies going anywhere near that shed?"

"I know that's what he claims."

"How do you account for that?"

"He's lying."

"Because his statement contradicts yours?"

"Because he's testifying to something I know isn't true."

"Well, that would certainly seem to be the case," Steve Winslow said. "He says one thing, you say the other. These things are diametrically opposed, therefore one of you is lying. I put it to you, Mr. Overmeyer, that the one who is lying is you. Is it not a fact that my client never went anywhere near the tool shed? Is it not a fact that you yourself put the murder weapon in the tool shed after you used it to kill your uncle?"

"No, it is not a fact. And I resent the insinuation."

"It's more than an insinuation," Steve Winslow said. "It's a direct accusation. Did you or did you not kill your uncle?"

"Oh, Your Honor," A.D.A. Beerbaum said.

"Goes to bias," Steve Winslow said.

"I'll allow it," Judge Weston said. "But under very narrow grounds."

"Did you kill your uncle?"

"No, I did not."

"Thank you," Steve Winslow said. "Now, Mr. Overmeyer. You say you were present when the police searched the defendant's cabin and found the cufflinks?"

"Yes, I was."

"Did you tell them where to search?"

"No, I just told them where the defendant lived."

"And they proceeded to search his cabin?"

"That's right."

"And you were present during the search?"

"Yes, I was."

"And did you direct the officers to search any portion of the cabin in particular?"

"No, I did not."

"And where were the cufflinks discovered?"

"Under the mattress."

"Under the defendant's mattress?"

"That's right."

"By under the mattress you mean . . . ?"

"Between the mattress and the box spring. The defendant had a small single bed, but it did consist of a mattress and a box spring."

"Was that one of the first places the police searched?"

"Not really. They went through his dresser drawers. His bathroom things. His kitchen alcove."

"And you never directed them to the mattress?"

"No, I did not."

"But you knew the cufflinks were under the mattress, didn't you?"

"No, I didn't."

"Sure you did. You knew they were there because you planted them there after you killed your uncle and placed the murder weapon in the tool shed."

"I did none of those things."

"None of them?"

"That's right."

Steve Winslow frowned. "That's what bothers me, Mr. Overmeyer. See, my feeling is if you did one of them, you did them all."

"Objection, Your Honor."

"Sustained. Mr. Winslow, this is not the time for an argument."

"Yes, Your Honor. Mr. Overmeyer, I cannot prove you killed your uncle, and I cannot prove you placed the murder weapon in the tool shed. But I can prove you planted those cufflinks under my client's mattress. Would it change your story to know I have a witness?"

"Objection, Your Honor."

"Overruled. The witness may answer."

"No, it would not. You can't have a witness because what you say isn't true."

"Is that so, Mr. Overmeyer? Before you answer any more questions, I'm telling you now that I have a witness who saw you on the night in question enter Mr. Hobbs's cabin, lift up his mattress, and place something under it. In light of that, would you like to change your testimony?"

"No, I would not."

"Is that so?" Steve Winslow looked at the judge. "One moment, Your Honor."

He turned and walked back to the defense table. But he walked right on by and went out through the gate.

"Mr. Winslow," Judge Weston said. "Are you leaving the court?"

"No, I'm not, Your Honor," Steve Winslow answered.

He stopped next to Tracy Garvin, who was sitting in the first row. He bent down and unsnapped the top of the cat case.

"Nice kitty," he said. "Now, Molly, it's time for you to be a very nice cat. Easy does it. Come here, sweetie."

Steve Winslow couldn't see the cat, just the green eyes glowing in the dark. They fixed on him. He heard the hiss, saw the paw snake out.

"Not yet, Molly. Not yet. Come on, now. There's a good girl."

Steve Winslow got his hands under the cat, managed to lift her out of the box. Cradling her in his arms, he pushed his way back through the gate.

"Here's the witness," Steve Winslow said. "Molly, Mr. Hobbs's cat. She was in the cabin that night. She saw you come in, she saw you lift the mattress, and she saw you plant the cufflinks. She knows you did it, and she will identify you now. Molly, where's the man you don't like? The man who was in your master's cabin where he shouldn't have been?"

Steve Winslow marched up to the witness stand, holding the cat.

Molly's head swiveled around. Her eyes fastened on the witness. Suddenly she yowled and her huge, double paw reached out and batted the witness across the face.

Overmeyer shrieked and half rose from his chair.

A.D.A Beerbaum lunged to his feet, spouting objections.

Steve Winslow, paying no attention, bore in on Overmeyer. "The cat identifies the witness as the man who was in her master's cabin that night."

"It's a lie," Overmeyer cried. "It means nothing of the sort. It's a trick. The cat wasn't even there."

Steve Winslow turned from the witness stand, a huge smile on his face. "That's right, Mr. Overmeyer. The cat wasn't there. But you were. That's how you know she wasn't. The cat wasn't there when you planted the cufflinks. She's accused you falsely. She may be guilty of perjury." Steve Winslow smiled and chucked Molly under the chin. "Just like you, Mr. Overmeyer. Just like you."

With that, Steve Winslow turned his back on the disconcerted witness, walked to the defense table, handed the cat to his client, and sat down.

Mark Taylor was duly impressed. "I've got to hand it to you, Steve," he said later that afternoon in the lawyer's office after the cranky Mr. Hobbs had departed with his cranky cat. "I mean, getting the charges dismissed. You sure pulled off a miracle this time."

"Well, I had to," Steve Winslow said. "I have a small studio apartment. Where am I going to keep a cat?"

"Don't let him kid you, Mark," Tracy said. "He'd do anything for a client."

"Don't I know it," Mark Taylor said. "But tell me how. I mean, this was brilliant stage managing on your part. You got the cat up there, you got the witness on the stand, and right on cue the cat lashes out and rakes him across the face. I mean, you couldn't have staged it any better."

"I guess not."

"So how did you do it? I mean, if what the witness said was true, if the cat wasn't there that night, why would Molly hate Overmeyer?"

"She's a cranky cat," Steve Winslow said. "She doesn't like anybody very much."

"Yes, but right on cue," Mark Taylor said. "She swiped the guy's face right on cue. When you lifted her out of the box, you had her all calmed down and everything, so how did you get her to do that?"

"Professional secret," Steve Winslow said.

"Don't give me that," Mark Taylor said. "I've seen you do some crazy things in court, but this takes the cake, having a cat accuse a witness. So how did you get her to do it?"

Steve Winslow stole a look at Tracy Garvin and bit his lip. "Ah, gee, Mark . . ."

"Come on. What did you do?"

"Well," Steve Winslow said, "when I held her up to Overmeyer, I had her cradled in my arms. And my right hand was underneath her."

"And?"

Tracy Garvin's eyes widened. "And?"

Steve Winslow exhaled. "I pulled her tail."

Which is why Tracy Garvin wasn't speaking to him.

Justice Knows No Paws

Jon L. Breen

The judge asked the fourteen citizens seated in the jury box all the expected questions. Did they know the plaintiff, Iris Stapleton Goodhew? (Of course they must have heard of her—she's a celebrity; but it was doubtful they had the pleasure of knowing her personally as I do.) Did they know the defendant, Elmo Gruntz? (Some of the cruder looking male members of the panel might have been acquainted with that low creature and his work, but most of them looked far too civilized.) Did they know the lawyers on either side of the action, the lovely and highly capable Andrea Frost for the plaintiff, the slickly unpleasant Forrest Milhaus for the defendant? Had they or any of their family members ever sued someone or been sued in this overly litigious society? Had they ever worked in the publishing field? Had they ever written anything for publication? Had they ever been party to a plagiarism case? Had they read about the case of Goodhew versus Gruntz in the newspapers? Were there any for whom serving more than a week as a juror would be a hardship?

Then the judge got to the really important question, or at least, judging from the smirk on his face, the one that seemed to give him the most pleasure to ask. "Are any of you allergic to cats?"

That question was indignity number three for me in the sessions leading up to the trial. What, I ask you, could be more prejudicial than to ask the jurors, "Are you allergic to the plaintiff?"

Yes, I realize that, technically, a cat doesn't have status as a plaintiff in a human court. That had been explained to Iris and me at length by our lawyer before we even entered a courtroom. But in-court indignity number one had come a few days earlier when my mere *presence* in the courtroom was questioned by Gruntz and his sleazy lawyer. After a lot of wrangling and some superbly well-reasoned arguments by Andrea, I was allowed to sit in (or sometimes lie or slink in) on the proceedings.

I suppose I must introduce myself, in the unlikely event you don't know me already. I am Whiskers McGuffin. Yes, yes, *the* Whiskers McGuffin. You have undoubtedly seen my name and photograph on numerous dust jackets, even seen and heard me on the TV talk show circuit, as co-author of a very successful series of detective novels with my longtime human companion, Iris Stapleton Goodhew. If you are a true collector, you may also have acquired an autographed copy with my distinctive paw print on the flyleaf. They are called novels, but in truth they are only lightly fictionalized accounts of my real-life exploits as a feline detective. While I, in the tradition established by Ellery Queen, appear in the novels under my own name, Iris adopts an alias as the younger, slimmer, but no more beautiful and charming, Winona Fleming.

The dubious question to the jury also reminded me of indignity number two. Though Iris, via Andrea, successfully insisted that as a full collaborator on the books, I had the right, nay the duty, to be present, there was some talk of requiring me to stay in a cage on or under the counsel table, as if I were some kind of wild animal whose freedom to wander the courtroom would somehow endanger human life or otherwise subvert the cause of justice. No sooner was that battle won than the defendant, Elmo Gruntz, asked for similar rights for his own animal companion, Fang, a huge and fierce German shepherd on whom he said the attack dog Rip in his novels was closely modeled. That led to a long legal confab as well, precipitated by the possibility that Fang really could be a danger to others in the courtroom, though Gruntz claimed he only ripped the flesh of drug lords, child molesters, and other human scum, leaving the pure of heart alone.

What weighed most heavily in the decision that I could attend the trial and Fang could not was the fact that I actually had a collaborative byline on the novels in which I appeared and Fang did not. Either Gruntz was less prone to share credit or, more likely, members of the canine species lack the necessary intelligence for literary achievement. I hope you won't take that as an instance of dog-bashing. Dogs have many fine qualities, and in some respects may even be superior to cats. I don't think a dog could commit premeditated murder, do you? But I'm sure a cat could.

Anyway, back to the courtroom. I'll leap forward, though. A lot of trial action really is boring; in fact, I don't know how people can sit still for it all. At least I could wander around the room and explore without missing anything important. Once the jury had been seated and opening arguments presented, Andrea Frost called to the stand the expert witness who would lay out the basics of our case against Elmo Gruntz. He was the renowned crime fiction critic and historian Merv Glickman, a kind and cheerful man who seemed to know every author, every title, and every continuing character in the history of the form.

I confess I had been dubious about making Merv Glickman our major witness. He is on record as not loving cat mysteries, though he seems reasonably fond of cats, and some of the points he would make in his testimony would not be wholly complimentary to our work. But Andrea assured us that his obvious objectivity could only make our case more persuasive, and Iris seemed to agree.

Andrea spent some twenty minutes establishing Merv's credentials: the publications he'd reviewed for, the books he'd written or edited, the university courses he'd taught, the awards he'd won. Had I been less keyed up, I might have catnapped through much of this. Then Andrea got to the key questions.

"Mr. Glickman, are you familiar with the works of Iris Stapleton Goodhew and Whiskers McGuffin?"

"Yes, I am."

"And are you also familiar with the works of Elmo Gruntz?"

"Yes."

"Did I ask you to make a close study of one novel from each of these, uh, bylines?"

"Yes, you did."

"And what were those two novels?"

"*Cat on a Hatpin Pouffe* by Goodhew and McGuffin, published in 1997 by Conundrum Press, and *Devour* by Elmo Gruntz, published in 1999 by St. Patrick's Press."

"Did you find any points of similarity in the two novels?"

"I found many."

"Could you summarize them for us?"

"Certainly. I'll begin with the more superficial. Each of the books has a title that fits in with a pattern the author has established to create brand recognition. Each of the books has exactly 450 pages and 26 chapters. Of those chapters, in each case half are told from the point of view of an animal character. Every other chapter of *Cat on a Hatpin Pouffe* is narrated by the animal companion of the heroine, free-lance journalist Winona Fleming. That, of course, is Whiskers McGuffin." Merv smiled in my direction, and I meowed in gratitude at his politically correct choice of words.

"Every other chapter of *Devour*," he went on, "is told from the viewpoint of Rip, the dog belonging to unlicensed homeless private eye Abel Durfee." I knew, of course, that the distasteful imputation of animal ownership embodied in this second identification was no accident. Gruntz and his character would naturally think in terms of ownership, master and slave, rather than equality.

"While the chapters about Rip follow his thoughts," Merv went on, "they are not actually written in his voice but from an omniscient narrator. Third dog rather than first dog, you might say.

"Both novels are, of course, whodunits. And in each novel, about twenty of the 450 pages are devoted to advancing the plot."

Andrea raised a disingenuous eyebrow at that. "Twenty pages out of 450? What did the two authors do with the other 430 pages?"

"Well, in the case of *Cat on a Hatpin Pouffe,* there is much attention to descriptions of the scenes, how the various characters are dressed, landscaping, interior decoration, meals, including recipes for selected dishes, things like that. And of course everything must be described twice, once from the viewpoint of a human character and once from the quite different and distinctive, and I might add frequently entertaining, viewpoint of Whiskers McGuffin."

Frequently entertaining? I bristled at the faint praise.

"The approach in *Devour*," Merv went on, "is quite a bit different, with much of the needed page-filling provided by descriptions of physical action: fistfights, car chases, menaces in parking garages, sex, torture, rape—and of course the vengeance finally taken on the baddies by Durfee and Rip is described in loving detail, without a cracking bone or a bleeding wound neglected. Also, Gruntz can go on for pages of monosyllabic, macho posturing dialogue between Durfee and one or more of the villains. Enough speeches of one word to a paragraph and those 450 pages fill up fast."

Forrest Milhaus made some kind of an objection to the slighting tone of Merv's description of Gruntz's repellent novels. Really quite mild, I thought, and he *had* been accepted as an expert witness.

"Please go on, Mr. Glickman," Andrea said, after the judge had, quite appropriately, overruled the objection.

"In both books, there are several chapters made up of the detective summarizing the previous action, all of it well known to the reader, for the benefit of another character. And of course each series has a number of continuing characters who must recur in every book, even if they don't really have anything to do with the story."

"How many continuing characters are there in the series about Winona Fleming and Whiskers McGuffin?"

"May I refer to my notes?"

"Certainly."

Merv drew out a vest-pocket notebook and flipped a few pages. "Seventeen," he replied. "That's not counting Winona and Whiskers."

"That seems like a considerable number."

"They do mount up."

"And how many continuing characters are there in the Abel Durfee and Rip series?"

"Remarkably enough, the same number, seventeen, apart from Durfee and Rip."

"Could you briefly list them for us?"

"From both series, you mean?"

"If you would."

"Well, in the Goodhew/McGuffin series, you have, of course, Winona Fleming's police contact and on-and-off boyfriend Detective Lieutenant Brent Hooper; her upstairs neighbor and best girlfriend Adele Washington; her elderly protective landlord Iggy Lamplighter; veterinarian and on-and-off boyfriend Dr. Curt Hamilton; gossiping hairdresser–cum–cat groomer Sadie McCready; Winona's loving but eccentric parents Hank and Minerva Fleming; her somewhat wild sister Stacy Fleming Tracy; her sister's abusive ex-husband Lester Tracy; her lovable but troubled teenage niece Morning Tracy; her priest brother Father Phil Fleming; her sometime editor and former boyfriend Axel Maxwell; the demented cat psychiatrist Dr. Ephraim Entwhistle; cat food manufacturer Ingo Dominguez and his domestic partner, cat sculptor Fred von Richtofen, who also, by the way, is Brent Hooper's police partner; wealthy and snobbish cat breeder Muffin Esterbrook; and nosy neighborhood druggist Pops Werfel."

"And in the Abel and Rip series?"

"Let's see now. There's Abel's main police contacts, good cop Lieutenant Al Corelli and bad cop Captain Ed McBride; his social worker and sometime girlfriend Estelle Magdalini; his crazy Vietnam-vet sidekick Thorn; local newspaper columnist Manny Graves; good rackets boss Claude Willis; Reggie and Pedro, Claude's two enforcers; bad rackets boss Itchy McAllister; Grog and Amadeus, Itchy's two enforcers; Livia Gravel, local madame and Abel's off-and-on girlfriend; Abel' s sociologist brother, Dr. Max Durfee; his naïve and danger-prone niece Megan Durfee; bartender and A.A. advocate Clancy Esposito; lawyer Sholem 'the Shyster' Schuster; alcoholic unlicensed veterinarian Dr. William 'Carver' McTweed; punchdrunk newsy and ex-boxer Bobby 'the Bandaid' Whistler; and—did I miss anybody? No, I think that's seventeen."

"And all seventeen have to appear in each and every book?"

Merv shrugged. "As I say, when there are 450 pages to fill . . ."

"Could you now briefly summarize the plot of *Cat on a Hatpin Pouffe* for us?"

"Yes. Winona and Whiskers are visiting Sadie McCready to get their respective fur done. Sadie says a friend of hers, fleeing an abusive husband, needs a place to stay. Sensitive to the situation because of her sister's experiences, Winona quickly offers her guest room, though Whiskers is dubious. When their boarder is found strangled with a distinctive designer necktie, suspicion falls on the victim's husband, who sells that line of necktie at an exclusive men's shop he owns. But the detective work of the human-feline team eventually pins the crime on the husband's business partner, whose amatory advances had been rejected by the victim. In the last chapter, Whiskers comes to Winona's rescue by upsetting a poisoned cup of tea served her by the murderer."

"Now tell us the plot of *Devour.*"

"Abel Durfee hears from bartender Clancy that a friend fleeing out-of-town loan sharks needs a place to crash. Abel helps the man vanish into the homeless community, though Rip is suspicious. When the fleeing man is found carved to death with a broken Thunderbird bottle, the cops arrest one of Claude Willis's enforcers, who they think was working for the out-of-town loan sharks. Abel finds out the real murderer was the loan shark's apparently legitimate business partner. He had started a child forced-labor and prostitution ring. The victim had found out, and the killer had come after him. In the last chapter, Rip rescues Abel, who is being force-fed cheap vodka preparatory to being sent over the cliff in his car to an explosive death, and pretty much devours the killer."

"Would you say that is the same plot, Mr. Glickman?"

"I'd have to say it's pretty similar."

"I have no further questions. Your witness."

Forrest Milhaus, who had been smirking through much of Merv's testimony, rose to cross-examine. As he approached the witness chair his shoe grazed my fur, and I scurried under the defense table. He apologized, but I was not fooled, nor, I think, were Iris and Andrea. That had been no accident.

"Mr. Glickman, may we look at some of the supposed similarities between my client's work and the plaintiff's?"

"Certainly."

"You referred to a title pattern to establish brand loyalty. I don't see many similarities between Ms. Goodhew's titles and Mr. Gruntz's."

"Their titles aren't similar. It's the use of a title pattern that is similar."

"Perhaps you could explain. What is Ms. Goodhew's title pattern?"

"Punning versions of famous titles or phrases including the word *cat* or a related word. For example, when Winona and Whiskers invaded Steinbeck country, the title was *The Cat and the Cannery*. A novel with a computer industry background was called *Cat and Mouse*. Their Florida novel offered a slight variation, *Kitten on the Keys*. And of course, the book at issue here is *Cat on a Hatpin Pouffe*."

"Do those strike you as good puns, Mr. Glickman?"

"Maybe some of them are rather strained, but that's not the point, is it?"

"The lawyer asks the questions, Mr. Glickman. And what is my client's continuing title pattern?"

"One word titles, as short as possible. The first in the series was *Rip*, named of course for the dog character. The others referred to what Rip and/or Abel Durfee do to the unfortunate villains. *Tear, Shred, Cut, Flay, Slice, Slash, Gouge, Gash,* and of course *Devour*."

"Not so similar to Ms. Goodhew's titles, are they?"

"Only in that they are title patterns. That wasn't one of my major points."

"No, I suppose not. Shall we move on then? Have you heard of the designations *tough* and *cozy* referring to mystery fiction?"

"Certainly."

"What do they represent?"

"Differing approaches to the crime story, or you might say different schools of mystery writing. I think the terms are self-explanatory."

"Do my client and Ms. Goodhew take the same approach or belong to the same school?"

Merv smiled at that. "Not at all."

"Would Ms. Goodhew be classified as a cozy?"

"Cozy as you can get, yes."

"And would Mr. Gruntz be a tough?"

"None tougher."

"Ms. Goodhew and Mr. Gruntz begin to sound more and more dissimilar."

Andrea was on her feet, and about time. "Objection. Counsel should ask questions, not comment." I had hoped she would call Milhaus on his continuing refusal to include my name as co-author of the books, but I supposed she knew what she was doing.

"Comment withdrawn, your honor." Milhaus picked up from the clerk's table the copies of the two books Andrea had entered into evidence. "Mr. Glickman, I am handing you a copy of *Cat on a Hatpin Pouffe.* I direct your attention to the photograph on the back of the dust jacket."

"Yes, that's a photograph of Ms. Goodhew and of Whiskers." Better of her than me, I always thought, but they don't give me jacket approval.

"What is that object that Ms. Goodhew is holding up to the camera so proudly?"

"That's a Martini."

"Really! It doesn't look like a drink."

"It's an award," Merv explained. "A sculpture of a cat named Martini."

"And what does this award honor?"

"The best cat mystery of the year."

"Why the unusual name?"

"They wanted to call it the Macavity, but that was already taken, so they named it after one of Mr. and Mrs. North's cats."

"And what organization grants this award?"

"The FCC. No, not the one you think. The Feline Crime Consortium. It's an organization of people who write cat mysteries."

"Why did they need such an organization and such an award?"

"Lack of respect accorded cat mysteries. The writers didn't feel that cat mysteries were getting sufficient attention from the other crime fic-tion awards. They didn't expect much of the Edgar, but the more cozy-oriented fan-voted awards like the Anthony and the Agatha were ignoring them, too. So they formed their own organization and came up with their own award."

"And Ms. Goodhew has won this award?"

"She and Whiskers"—thank you, I meowed—"have won three of them. They have been nominated nearly every year."

"Is it true the same four writers are nominated nearly every year?"

"With minor variations, yes, that's true."

"Now I'd like to hand you this copy of Mr. Gruntz's novel *Devour,* the other work we are considering in this trial. And again I direct your attention to the author photo on the back of the jacket."

"Yes, there's Elmo Gruntz and his dog Fang."

"And what is Mr. Gruntz holding in his hand?"

Merv smirked. "As the caption to the photograph explains, that's called a Baskerville, ostensibly an award for the best dog mystery of the year."

"Why do you say ostensibly, Mr. Glickman?"

"Because it's a gag. There is no such award. Your client made it up and awarded it to himself because he thought it would be a funny joke on the cat ladies."

"Ordinarily, I would object to your apparent ability to read my client's thoughts, Mr. Glickman, but let's say you're correct, that the similarity between the two jacket photographs is intentional and satirical in nature. Would you call that an example of plagiarism?"

"No, of course not. But you'll have noticed that wasn't one of the similarities I pointed out in my direct testimony."

"So noted. Now tell me, Mr. Glickman, to your knowledge is Mr. Elmo Gruntz himself a member of the Feline Cat Consortium?"

"Yes."

"Does he come to their conventions?"

"Never misses one."

"Was there some controversy over his membership?"

"To put it mildly. They didn't want to accept him for membership, thought he only wanted to join to make fun of them, make them uncomfortable. But he was able to point to cat characters in several of his books. According to their own rules, they had to let him in."

"Mr. Glickman, are you aware of the relative commercial success of Ms. Goodhew and Mr. Gruntz?"

"It's about a tossup. Goodhew and Whiskers have probably sold more copies overall, including paperback, but Gruntz makes the hardcover bestseller lists and they don't."

"Would you say that Iris Stapleton Goodhew has many reasons for personal rancor against my client that might explain this incredibly frivolous lawsuit?"

Andrea was on her feet. "Objection, your honor. Argumentative. Prejudicial. Calls for speculation." Why couldn't she have said "incompetent, irrelevant, and immaterial"? I always liked that objection. Anyway, the damage was done.

There's no need to describe the rest of the proceedings in detail. Truthfully, it's too painful. Merv Glickman was undoubtedly the key witness, though both Iris (extremely impressive) and Elmo Gruntz (egregiously offensive) were called as witnesses. I'm not sure whether Elmo Gruntz was technically a plagiarist, but the jury let him off. Andrea explained to us afterwards how very difficult it was to bring a successful plagiarism action without copied passages you could compare side by side with the originals. Gruntz was far too clever to leave tracks of that kind. It bothered me that there was so little I could do to help, apart from providing the occasional encouraging nuzzle to the ankles of those I favored. Murder cases are my métier, not civil trials.

Yes, that was a depressing ending, but we're not quite done yet. As you know if you've ever read one, you never close the book on my stories at the end. You always are treated to a preview of what is to come, an abridged version of the first chapter or two of the next book in the series. Now, I know this isn't a book but a short story, but it's very important you get the teaser anyway. Call it crass commercialism, if you must.

Now, an advance look at the next Winona Fleming/Whiskers McGuffin mystery, Curio City Called the Cat, *by Iris Stapleton Goodhew and Whiskers McGuffin, coming to bookstores this spring.*

Chapter One

Fred von Richtofen was in a bad mood. He had been interrupted at a crucial point in the creation of an unusually original and beautiful piece, one that would probably double his price at the gallery he regularly supplied with cat images in clay, bronze, papier-mâché, and other media. But it wasn't the art but the police work that paid his half of the bills, and unless he was prepared to live off Ingo's salary as CEO of the Purrfect Cat Food Company, he had to answer Brent Hooper's call.

"What took you so long?" Brent demanded, as his partner appeared at the front door of the large imposing mansion.

"It's the traffic headed for that damn antique show up the block at the fairgrounds." Fred had been out to his partner for years, but he still affected what he took to be a macho posture. In truth, he'd rather have been at the antique show than here.

As they stood over the body lying at the foot of a tall bookcase, Fred looked at a bloodstained trophy with the figure of a dog lying near a wound in the dead man's head. Shoddy work, his artist's eye told him, but he didn't think Brent would appreciate aesthetic observations at a murder scene.

Brent said, "This is a strange one, Fred."

"Murder, Lieutenant?"

"Has to be. I climbed up the ladder to look at the top of the bookshelf above where the victim is lying. There's a circle of dust where this big dog trophy stood up there. That's a heavy piece, Fred. It couldn't have fallen off by accident, unless there was a 6.0 earthquake this morning we didn't feel or hear about. And I don't think the guy could have brained himself with it, do you?"

"But who could have swung it at him with sufficient force with him just standing there? It must have been pushed off, but how from that height? Who could have got up there to do it without him knowing and being suspicious? And what is the thing anyway? Some kind of award?"

Brent squinted at the part of the lettering that was visible. "I think it says basketball, but we better not move it till the scene-of-crime boys and girls have been here. Wasn't this guy kind of short for a basketball player?"

"Writer, wasn't he? Elmer Fudd, something like that."

Chapter Two
(from the memoirs of Whiskers McGuffin)

The massive antique tent show called Curio City must have covered two acres of the fairgrounds. I like to wander into various nooks and crannies where humans can't go and follow moving things people aren't interested in, so it was to be expected I would get separated from Winona for a while. She was working on a piece about antiques for Axel Maxwell's magazine. As she questioned a man selling art deco lamps, I reestablished contact, rubbing against her ankle and purring. She looked down at me with more love in her eyes than she ever directed toward Brent or Axel or even that Hugh Grant–look-alike vet. I felt relaxed and secure. I knew if she was asked, she'd swear I'd been at her side all morning.

It's in the Bag

Bill Crider

Marilyn Crane had always thought there was something fishy about Roland Bland.

It wasn't just that he was a defense attorney. For one thing, he smelled like fish. Marilyn got the impression that he carried tuna fish sandwiches around in his briefcase, which looked old enough to have been one of Alexander the Great's saddlebags. It was cracking and flaking and coming apart at the seams, and one day when Bland flopped it down on the defense table, a horde of roaches scuttled frantically out of a gaping hole in one corner.

Several people, clearly possessing little fondness for certain creatures of the insect persuasion, had fled screaming in terror and disgust from the Executive Office for Immigration Review, better known as Immigration Court. Bland watched them go and didn't even turn a hair.

"Must have left it in the garage last night," he said, smiling his oily smile as he caressed his ancient briefcase and cooly contemplated the stampeding pests.

Marilyn had stood her ground against the roaches, too, though it hadn't been easy not to run like the others. And she usually held her own against Bland as well, which was why the Ramirez case bothered her so much.

"It's not bad enough that Bland calls me names," Marilyn told her friend Emma, who was also an INS attorney, one evening while they were having a frappuccino at the Starbuck's in the Rice Village. "It's that Judge Whittington seems to bend over backwards to give his clients the benefit of the doubt."

"Bland doesn't call you names," Emma said, seizing, as she always did, on the weakest part of the argument.

"He called me a 'Barbie,'" Marilyn said, looking out at the traffic passing by on University Boulevard through narrowed eyes.

"Not exactly," said Emma, who was short, stout, and had very black hair. *She* looked nothing at all like a Barbie. "What he said was, 'Who's that mean Barbie at the prosecution table?' And he only said it because you beat him pretty badly in your first appearance in court."

Marilyn remembered how nervous she'd been and how good it had felt to win. But she still resented the Barbie bit.

And she resented how easily Bland's latest client, Francisco (Frankie) Ramirez, was getting off.

"You know that Ramirez should have been deported years ago," she told Emma. "I don't know how he's managed to avoid it this long."

Emma knew: "He has a good lawyer."

As much as Marilyn hated to admit it, Emma had a point. Bland was good, all right. But she couldn't let it go.

"I think he has something on Whittington."

"No way. Whittington is as clean as they come."

Emma had a point. Again. Which annoyed Marilyn more than it should have, mainly because Emma was right. Probably Judge Whittington was just inclined to be a little sympathetic to aliens. She didn't hold that against him.

"What about the cat?" she said.

It was known to everyone that Whittington was completely nutty about his cat, whose name was Oliver Wendell Holmes and who slept every day in a towel-lined basket in Whittington's chambers while the judge presided over the court. At the end of the day, Oliver Wendell Holmes would still be asleep in his little basket, at which time Whittington would gently carry him out to his antiquated Volkswagen bus and drive him home.

What happened after that, no one knew—the judge didn't have any friends among the lawyers—but Marilyn assumed that the cat continued to sleep in the basket until the next day, when it would come to court and sleep some more. Cats, in Marilyn's experience, were really, really good at sleeping. They were almost as good at that as they were at ignoring people who called them.

"The cat has nothing to do with anything," Emma said, and Marilyn knew that her friend was right. As usual. But it didn't make her feel any better.

🐪 🐪 🐪

The reason that Marilyn felt a bit of hostility toward both the judge and the attorney was that she truly believed that Francisco (Frankie) Ramirez should never have been allowed to remain in the U.S.

Ramirez had admitted in court that he'd entered the country illegally by stowing away on a boat from his native Colombia and then jumping ship when it came into port. Besides that, he'd gotten married to Maria Calderon, a U.S. citizen, during a long delay in his hearing, a result of his first lawyer abruptly leaving the case. To Marilyn the marriage was a transparent attempt to legitimize his own status, but Frankie didn't see it that way at all.

"Maria and me, we lived together for a long time before that, Your Honor," he said at the hearing. "We truly loved each other. It was like we had a marriage already, you know? A marriage of the heart."

When Marilyn questioned him, he'd been unable to recall the addresses where he and his wife had lived prior to their marriage or even the names of the streets they had supposedly lived on. He couldn't remember what she wore to bed or what her pet name for him was. But he did at least remember that they'd lived for a while with a friend of Maria's named Jorge.

"Jorge Galindo?" Marilyn asked.

"That's him."

"And he was a friend of your wife's?"

"That's right."

"Isn't it true that he was your wife's brother?"

Ramirez looked genuinely surprised. "He was?"

"He was," Marilyn said. "Funny that no one ever mentioned that to you."

Frankie shook his head in astonishment.

"Well, no one ever did," he said, looking guilelessly at Judge Whittington with his big black eyes open wide. "Maybe nobody thought about it."

Marilyn had been sure she had him then, but she had yet another shot to fire.

"Do you and Maria have any children?" she asked.

Frankie's dark eyes grew sad. "No," he said. "We have not been blessed."

"But you *do* have a child, don't you?"

Frankie's eyes narrowed, but he knew enough to be aware that he had to answer the question.

"Yes," he said.

"In fact, you have a son in Colombia, born just a week after your marriage, isn't that right?"

Frankie looked furtive. It was clear that he didn't like the question, but he answered it anyway.

"I guess so."

"But I thought you were living with Maria and that you truly loved her at the time this child was conceived. You and Maria had a marriage of the heart, I believe. Didn't you tell us that?"

Frankie's mouth had an ugly twist now. "I don't know this *conceived*."

The interpreter started to explain, but Frankie waved her off. He wasn't really interested in definitions.

At this point, Roland Bland stood up, smiled greasily, and said, "We'll stipulate that Mr. Ramirez has a child in Colombia and that the child was born during the time he was living with Mrs. Ramirez."

Ramirez nodded as if he'd been coached and went on to say that his wife knew all about the child and had forgiven her husband for his momentary indiscretion, committed while he was visiting his parents in his home country. Mrs. Ramirez, her husband haltingly explained, understood that such things happened. Emotions ran high when a man returned to the country of his birth after a long absence.

Naturally, Mrs. Ramirez had testified to exactly the same thing, although not quite as eloquently, gazing lovingly at her wayward husband all the while, much to Marilyn's disgust.

To Marilyn's even greater chagrin, Judge Whittington was apparently ready to rule that because of his perfectly legitimate marriage to a U.S. citizen, Francisco (Frankie) Ramirez was entitled to remain in the United States. The only thing that stopped him was that they were running out of time for the day, which was a Friday, so the judge continued the hearing until the following Monday.

And that was too bad for Ramirez, because that weekend drug money was found in Ramirez's car.

🐱 🐱 🐱

It began as a routine traffic stop for erratic driving out on Interstate 10, just over the line into Texas from Louisiana, but it became more than routine when the state trooper, John Colby, asked for and was given permission to search Ramirez's car. Colby had become suspicious because of the strong odor of alcohol that emanated from Ramirez, his wife, and the other passenger, a Mr. Gomez. And because of the numerous beer cans that were scattered throughout the vehicle: on the floor, in the seats, and on the package rack over the back seat.

The trooper called for back-up, and when it arrived, the two men searched the car while Gomez and the Ramirezes stood and sweated disconsolately on the shoulder of the road under the blistering Texas sun.

The troopers found a little over six thousand dollars in a paper bag lying on the front floorboard. They also found another bag, this one containing nearly fifty thousand dollars, in the right rear door panel.

Knowing more than a little about the kind of people who carried large sums in small bills and traveled Interstate 10 with depressing regularity, the troopers concluded with little hesitation that Ramirez was a drug trafficker. Besides, as they said in their report, the money smelled so strongly of marijuana that the odor was detectable in the outdoors. They didn't even need a lab analysis.

Ramirez claimed that the money in the front seat was his but that the money in the back belonged to Mr. Gomez. And of course it had nothing to do with drugs. When asked where all that loose cash had come from if not from drug transactions, Ramirez said that he and Gomez had won it playing blackjack at a casino in Louisiana, where they'd gone to celebrate his practically guaranteed new status as a Permanent Legal Resident.

Of course the troopers didn't believe a word of it. They arrested Ramirez for driving under the influence and confiscated the money.

When she heard about the arrest, Marilyn was sure she had Ramirez. If he'd committed a criminal act, like drug trafficking, his staged marriage wouldn't save him. He'd be going home.

🐈 🐈 🐈

Marilyn was already seated at the prosecution's table when Roland Bland came in, the odor of fish wafting along in front of him. Ramirez was beside him as he plopped his practically prehistoric briefcase down on the defense table. No roaches fled its interior, for which Marilyn was grateful.

"Good morning," Bland said, and smiled at Marilyn, revealing tiny white teeth with sharp little canines. He and his client remained standing since the clerk had entered the courtroom.

"All rise," the clerk said, and Marilyn stood up along with the interpreter.

Judge Whittington came in. As usual he cut quite a figure. He was at least six and a half feet tall, and skinnier than Ally McBeal after a week of serious purging. His lank hair hung nearly to his shoulders. It had once been entirely black, but now it was thickly streaked with gray. His cadaverous face was unsmiling, and he carried a little basket in one hand.

Marilyn couldn't see what was in the basket because it was covered with a towel. But she had a sneaking suspicion that she knew exactly what was in there.

"Oliver Wendell Holmes," she said under her breath, meaning, of course, the judge's cat and not the famous jurist for whom the cat had been named.

This time, Marilyn thought, the judge's affection for his cat had led him to go too far. She didn't know whether there was any law against having a cat in the courtroom, but she felt it was far outside the accepted bounds of decorum. She could almost hear the wheels clicking as they turned in Bland's head. If Marilyn won the case, Bland would find a way to have it thrown out because of the stupid cat. She just knew he would.

But was she going to call Judge Whittington's hand? She most certainly was not. Elephants were supposed to have long memories, but they were nothing compared to a judge with a grudge.

So Judge Whittington slipped the basket underneath the bench, and everyone was seated without a word.

There were no spectators today, and all the witnesses were outside the courtroom. Judge Whittington looked around the room, turned on the tape recorder and said, "We're going on the record now."

Immigration court did not use court reporters. All the sessions were taped, and the tapes were transcribed later. When the judge turned on the tape, the hearing had officially begun.

Marilyn felt that she did a pretty good job with the defense witnesses, especially when she caught Ramirez in a contradiction.

"And you say the money in the front seat was yours?" she said.

"No," he said, much to Marilyn's surprise. "The money in the front seat belongs to Mr. Gomez. The money in the back seat is mine."

"I don't believe that's what you told Lieutenant Colby," she said. She looked at her notes. "You said that the money in the front seat was yours."

Ramirez appeared flustered, and he looked toward Bland for help.

"My client is just confused, Your Honor," Bland said smoothly. "You can imagine the fear he must have felt after being stopped on the highway by the minions of the law."

Minions of the law, Marilyn thought. *What a load of crap.*

"Objection, Your Honor," she said. "Mr. Bland is offering testimony for the defendant."

"Sustained," Judge Whittington said, though Marilyn was almost certain he had already taken Bland's words to heart.

"I have no further questions, Your Honor," she said.

Bland tried to repair the damage by getting Ramirez to testify as to how confused and worried he had been when arrested and how confused and worried he was even now, a stranger and afraid in this new country.

Judge Whittington did not look impressed, but Marilyn knew better than to let that get her hopes up. Judge Whittington never looked impressed.

The truth was that Marilyn didn't really care about Ramirez's little slip. What mattered was the police report on the drug money. Unfortunately, according to Judge Whittington when he examined the report, it hadn't been properly signed.

Marilyn asked for a continuance, which was granted. Judge Whittington wanted to hear from the officer. He gave Marilyn a week to set things up.

🫎 🫎 🫎

Colby waddled into the courtroom, looking like the antithesis of Judge Whittington. He was as squat, thick, and solid as a chopping block. He was smiling, and he had a crew cut so short that his pink scalp showed through.

After establishing his credentials, Marilyn said, "Lieutenant Colby, have you had much experience with drug dealers?"

"You better believe it," Colby said in a gravelly voice. "I've worked out there on I-10 for eight years, and I've encountered all sorts of drugs and drug dealers. And traffickers."

"When you stopped Mr. Ramirez, did you have reason to think he might be trafficking in drugs?"

"I was suspicious," Colby said. "But I wasn't sure till I found all that money."

"Objection," Bland said. "We know my client got that money at a casino, not in a drug deal."

"There's no proof the money came from a casino," Marilyn said.

"Or that it's drug money," Bland said.

Judge Whittington said, "Overruled."

"Did the money have a smell?" Marilyn asked.

"Absolutely," Colby said. "It smelled like a marijuana field."

Marilyn nodded in satisfaction. "And did you later check to see if Mr. Ramirez had any drug-related arrests?"

She already knew the answer, of course. No lawyer likes to ask a question to which she doesn't already have the response memorized.

"Yes," Colby said, shrugging inside his suit, which fit him like the hide of the Saggy, Baggy Elephant, one of Marilyn's childhood icons. "I found out that he'd been arrested in connection with a bag of marijuana found on a bus he rode to Nashville, Tennessee."

Bland stood up. "Objection. My client was never tied to that."

"Overruled," Whittington said. "You can tell your story, Lieutenant."

"The bag was found in an overhead bin right above Ramirez's seat," Colby said. "Everyone knew he'd put it there."

"What else did you discover about Mr. Ramirez?" Marilyn asked.

Colby looked at Ramirez. "There was a piece of paper in his car. It had a bunch of telephone numbers written on it in pencil, and I ran those through the computer later. There were twenty-six numbers. Seventeen of them were the telephone or pager numbers of known drug dealers."

Marilyn thought Bland would interrupt, but he sat quietly at his table. Biding his time, Marilyn thought. She knew all too well the weaknesses he would pick on.

"Had Mr. Ramirez ever called any of those numbers?"

"Yes," Colby said, "he had."

"And when was that?"

"Well, when we catch a guy that we suspect of dealing, we check him out pretty good. Mr. Ramirez said he'd been at a casino in New Orleans, so we checked out his hotel there. He might have been to a casino, but he also made some phone calls from his hotel room. Three of them were to numbers on that list."

Marilyn could hear Bland stirring behind her, but he didn't rise to object. So she kept going.

"Could you tell us about the three numbers he called from the list?"

"All three were numbers of drug traffickers known to the New Orleans police department."

Marilyn smiled. "I have no further questions, Your Honor."

Bland stood up, rubbed his hands together, humble as Uriah Heep, and said, "Lieutenant Colby, was it ever proven that my client had ever touched that bag of marijuana found on the bus to Nashville?"

"Well, no," Colby said, "but—"

"We don't need any *buts*," Bland said. "Isn't it true that anyone on that bus could have put that marijuana there?"

"Well, yes, but—"

"No *buts*. Anyone could have put the marijuana in the overhead bin. No one saw my client put it there. No one saw him touch it in any way, and his fingerprints were not on the bag. Correct?"

"Yes, but—"

"Now, now, Lieutenant. Remember about those *buts*. Let me ask you another question: has it ever been shown that the writing on that paper you say you found in Mr. Ramirez's car was indeed done by Mr. Ramirez?"

"No," Colby said.

He was no longer smiling. He sat stiffly, twining his fingers together, and Marilyn was pretty sure he would have liked to wring Bland's neck. She understood the feeling.

"So anyone could have written those numbers, right?"

"I guess so, but they were in Mr. Ramirez's car."

"There go those *buts* again. I hope the judge doesn't have to warn you about them. At any rate, I have another question: Can you prove that my client made any of those phone calls you claim were made from his hotel room?"

"It was his room," Colby said.

"True. But could his wife have made the calls? What about the person who cleaned the room? What about Mr. Gomez? Couldn't any of those people have made those calls?"

"Well, sure, possibly, but—"

Bland waggled a finger. "Ah-ah-ah. Remember about the *buts*."

Bland was on a roll, which really irritated Marilyn. She could see her case going down the tubes, and she had a sudden vision of Ramirez happily growing old in the United States, running drugs and sending illegal dollars home to his son in Columbia.

"Your Honor," Bland said, "I don't believe I have to say any more. It's clear to me, as I'm sure it is to you, that my client is entirely innocent of everything he's been accused of."

"Would you like to make your closing argument, then?" Judge Whittington asked.

"Yes," Bland said. "My client, Mr. Ramirez, obtained the money found by the troopers in a legal manner, and the note found in his car could have been written by anyone, just as the phone calls from his room could have been made by any one of several people."

Judge Whittington said, "What about the drunk driving?"

"There's that, true," Bland said, "but who among us hasn't had one too many on occasion? It's a common failing, and certainly not one that should cause anyone to be deported."

"Gambling?" Whittington said.

"Perfectly legal in Louisiana," Bland said. "Why, I myself have been over to one of the casinos for a game of chance. More than once, in fact." He pointed to the two grimy paper bags of money on the evidence table. "My client won that money in a legal game, and it should be restored to him when he walks out of this courtroom and goes back to his wife."

Bland turned and walked back to the defense table. He gestured toward Francisco (Frankie) Ramirez and spun on his heel to face the judge again.

It would have been a wonderfully dramatic gesture had it succeeded, not that it would have impressed Marilyn in the least even if it had. But the important thing was that it didn't succeed. The edge of Bland's hand caught on his briefcase, knocking it from the table to the floor, where it fell open, causing an overpowering odor of decaying tuna to reek out into the courtroom. Even Bland's face turned a little greenish around the eyes and mouth, though Marilyn thought he should have been used to the smell.

Everyone looked at Bland, who reached for the briefcase. Just as he grabbed the raggedy handle, there was a sound from the bench.

"Meowrrr?"

Marilyn turned just in time to see Oliver Wendell Holmes emerge from beneath the bench in all his orangeness. He sniffed the air briefly, then jumped to Colby's shoulder and from there to the evidence table, where he skidded into a bag of money, knocking it off the table and sending crumpled bills flying.

Oliver Wendell Holmes was bothered not at all by the sight of flying money. It is, in fact, doubtful that he even noticed it because he, too, was airborne, gliding downward toward the fetid opening in the briefcase. Before anyone could stop him, he was buried inside it.

The briefcase bumped several inches across the floor, coming to a stop against a leg of the defense table. Nothing could now be seen of the cat except for a long orange tail that whipped from left to right.

Bland looked at the tail as if he might grab it and pull the cat out of the case, but he made no move.

Colby appeared outraged that a cat had used him as a launching pad. It was a good thing, Marilyn thought, that the trooper wasn't carrying his sidearm.

Judge Whittington stood looking down, his slit of a mouth open in what might have been horror or possibly a smile. With the judge, it was hard to tell.

Ramirez sat twitching behind the table as if undecided on whether to make a run for it or just stay where he was.

But Marilyn was looking at the money. There was quite a bit of it, scattered all around the evidence table, the bills lying on the floor in crinkled heaps. There was something about the money, and suddenly Marilyn snapped to what it was. That was when she knew that none of the money would be going to Columbia but that Ramirez would.

"Lieutenant Colby," she said, "is that the money you took from Mr. Ramirez's car?"

Colby turned his eyes to her and said, "Huh?"

Marilyn repeated her question.

"Oh," Colby said, sneaking a glance at the briefcase, from which the tail of Oliver Wendell Holmes still extended. "Yeah. I mean, yes. It is."

Marilyn had been to a casino once or twice herself. She'd won fifty-two dollars playing blackjack, not much, but enough for her to have learned something about casino money.

"Then the money in the bag couldn't have come from a casino, could it," she said.

Bland looked away from the cat. So did the judge. And so did Ramirez.

"Huh?" Colby said.

"That money couldn't have come from a casino," Marilyn repeated. "Look at it. It's old, it's crumpled, it's worn, it's been handled over and over."

"Lots of people handle money in a casino," Bland said, but Marilyn was sure she detected a note of desperation in his voice. After all, he said he'd been to casinos more than once.

"Not money like that," Marilyn said. "They don't give you old money in a casino. It messes up their machines if you use crumpled money. I'll bet you could go to every casino in New Orleans and ask them. They'd tell you that it's new money only, or at least money that's not wrinkled or torn."

Oliver Wendell Holmes's tail had stopped moving. Marilyn thought she heard the sound of purring, but she couldn't be sure. Maybe the cat was asleep. Probably was, she thought.

Judge Whittington finally took his eyes off the briefcase and said, "Is that true, Lieutenant Colby? About the money, I mean?"

Colby sighed as if ashamed of himself. "I don't know why I didn't think of that from the beginning. It's just like she says, Judge. Casinos don't want any old money. It screws everything up. They might take in a few old bills, but they never give any out. That stuff on the floor there? It's drug money, just like I told you."

Judge Whittington nodded slowly. "I do believe you're right," he said.

🐈 🐈 🐈

"So," Emma said, sipping her frappuccino, "there's one less criminally inclined illegal in the country today, thanks to you." She paused. "And a cat named Holmes."

"Oliver Wendell, not Sherlock," Marilyn said, watching the traffic. "I never thought I'd have a cat to thank for beating Roland Bland."

"What was in that briefcase of his, anyway? Tuna fish?"

"Worse," Marilyn said.

"What could be worse?"

"Canned cat food."

"Cat food? Why would anyone carry cat food in a briefcase? I mean, even Bland has to be smarter than that."

"Cats make people do strange things," Marilyn said, thinking of Judge Whittington. No one had said a thing when he'd walked down from the bench, retrieved his cat, and stowed it away in its basket.

"Yeah," Emma said. "But cat food in a briefcase?"

"Bland was feeding a cat at his office," Marilyn said. "He didn't know where it lived or where it came from, but every day it would show up at the door and cry. So he started feeding it. Sometimes, when he was in a hurry, he'd just put the empty can in his briefcase. There wasn't anywhere to throw it, and he didn't want to leave it in his doorway."

"It would have been better for him if he had," Emma said. "But you have to give him credit for being nice to animals. How did he take losing to you again?"

"Pretty well," Marilyn said.

"Did he say anything?"

"Uh-huh."

"Well?"

"He said, 'Only a mean Barbie would send a legally married man back to Columbia.'"

"What about the drug money?" Emma asked.

"He didn't mention that."

"Ramirez will probably be back here within a month, you know."

"Probably," Marilyn said.

"Maybe he'll get caught again."

Marilyn nodded. "I hope so."

"And maybe Bland will defend him. You might enjoy that."

Marilyn smiled. "Especially if I can get some help from Oliver Wendell Holmes."

Animal Sounds

Dulcy Brainard

Both had been married before, and although he was older by thirteen years, her one marriage had lasted longer than his two combined. They had in common a wariness of personal commitment, a preference for intimacy, and the internal unease that results from those conflicting inclinations. They had other things in common too—each was a native New Yorker, each had a career in publishing, and each was passionate about cats: she for, he against.

Bob Neely was a literary agent. He started out in patent law, parlaying an undergraduate degree in engineering and a J.D. from NYU to an invitation from a white-shoe law firm in downtown Manhattan. Soft-spoken and well-mannered, with a slight build, a round face, and a predilection for good grooming, Bob appeared born to the firm's paneled halls. Illness in the associate ranks his third year led him to a spot on the team representing a writer who was suing her publishing house for underpayment of royalties on a trade-paper mystery that had been made into a prime-time mini-series. Bob relished working on that case, so when the firm pointed him back to his patent desk, he declined and lit out on his own as an agent. That decision brought a quick end to his first marriage just as his wife, an investment banker at J.P. Morgan, had promised it would.

Within ten years he developed an expertise as perfectly tailored to the newly meshing media as his Savile Row suits were to his 5' 8" frame. He represented celebrity authors and lesser-known ones, capitalizing on his ability to recognize subjects that were just about to capture popular interest. His agency, which he operated by himself, thrived as the publishing industry wrenched itself into a big business and editors and authors began to move among houses much as rush-hour commuters moved among PATH, LIRR, and subway lines at Penn Station.

Next he married a client, a famous British novelist who was being sued by her previous agent. She and Bob mistook the flash of cameras in her high-profile case (she'd been sleeping with that agent too) for stars in their eyes. Their marriage was effectively over within months.

🐈 🐈 🐈

Laurie Michaels was a bookseller, owner of the Bookshelf, a small, tony store on the upper East Side. Twelve years earlier, she had inherited the shop from the founder, a crusty lesbian named Blackie who had known more about books—popular or esoteric—than any other single individual in the city.

An inch taller than Bob, long-limbed and energetic, Laurie was as full of movement as he was self-contained. She had begun work at the Bookshelf as a freshman at Hunter College. In her senior year, she accepted Blackie's offer of an escalating partnership deal, which didn't provide much more than a living wage but gave Laurie 5 percent of the business at the outset, with an additional 2 percent accruing each successive year. Blackie was a robust, cranky fifty-five at the time, and Laurie's dad, a dentist in Queens, cautioned his daughter against the deal. But Laurie loved books and the business of selling them and had only to agree to five years' employment, after which Blackie would buy back her share if she wanted out. That's less time, she told her father, than it would take to get an MBA at night school.

Three years later, Blackie was dead from heart failure. In her will she gave the store and the four-story building in which it was housed to Laurie, the only person, so read Blackie's lawyer, who had ever made her see value in being straight and having kids.

🐈 🐈 🐈

Bob and Laurie knew each other's names on the Thursday evening in April when they first met. Both were guests at the Edgar Awards Banquet. He sat at a Random House table (the incoming MWA president, a Pantheon author, was a client), and she was with St. Martin's Press. One of the latter's authors had won the Best First Mystery award for a novel set in the Bookshelf's neighborhood and featuring a blind English teacher, his grown daughter, and her very smart Standard Poodle. Laurie, who had hosted the author's first reading and sold hundreds of copies of the book, felt like the book's godmother. She stood with the ecstatic St. Martin's contingent (which had so often been a bridesmaid and rarely the bride), her face aglow, accepting kisses, high-fives, and a series of hugs as the crowd filed out of the hotel ballroom.

Bob stopped to congratulate the winner's editor, Mim Towers, a legendary figure in the genre and an old friend.

"Didn't you promise that you were never, ever going to publish an animal story?" Bob asked.

"I did," said Mim with an unapologetic grin. "But this manuscript came in nearly flawless. Plus, the heroine is an old bitch with curly white hair. How could I resist?"

Introductions were mixed in with congratulations.

"You must know Laurie Michaels of the Bookshelf. She's been a huge part in the book's success."

"Actually no," Bob answered Mim, smiling at Laurie. "I'm delighted to redress the oversight."

Laurie offered her winningest smile as they shook hands and gave in to an urge born of the moment's giddiness.

"Woof," she said brightly. "Woof."

After a moment of startled silence, everyone roared.

"Best line award," said Mim, wiping her eyes.

"Did I ask for that?" Bob asked Laurie as they moved with the group toward the escalators. "Or were you making a statement for canines?"

"Neither," Laurie answered, still trying to squelch a giggle. "Something just came over me."

They met up with Bob's client, the new MWA president, whom Bob introduced as a literary lion.

"Private joke," he said as the man began to demur. They were headed for a party being thrown by the lion's publisher. Laurie surprised herself again by accepting Bob's invitation to join them.

ᵔᶮ ᵔᶮ ᵔᶮ

The following Sunday afternoon Bob stopped in at the Bookshelf.

"I thought you'd have a shop dog," he said, nodding at the Abyssinian asleep in the afternoon sun flooding the front window display.

"That's Ffolio," Laurie answered. "There were three cats here when I got the store. Only he's extant. The one near your feet is Clause, in training for succession."

"Booksellers' school for cats?" Bob said, stepping gingerly away from the small Siamese that pressed between his legs and the walnut paneled side of the counter.

Laurie laughed and pushed her hair back from her face. Black and curly, it sparkled in the same sun that shone on the dusty gray-blue cat. Her eyes, the color of Ffolio's fur, shone with a softer gleam. She had enjoyed Bob's company at the Random party more than she'd anticipated. She'd been delighted to see him come in the door.

"I don't like cats much," he said, suddenly needing to get that straight.

"I thought it was animals in general."

"Especially cats. Too secretive. Superior." He shook his head. This woman, this really beautiful, bright woman, could not care in the slightest whether he liked animals or not.

But she did. And she had an idea of what prompted his revelation. Something was starting between them. So unexpected, this excitement. "Supposedly, we don't like in others qualities of our own," she answered.

"Are you suggesting that I'm superior and have things to hide?"

"I don't know if you're superior. And I expect that we all have some secrets."

The bell over the door rang. Laurie spoke with the customer, leaving Bob to look about on his own. He had asked a friend, director of marketing at a small Manhattan publisher, about the Bookshelf at a party the night before. Laurie Michaels had been among the first booksellers to strategically oppose the discounters, the friend had said. She had enlarged the store after taking it over and set up a big space for readings and signings. The Bookshelf was now a must-stop on any author tour, with a decent-sized audience guaranteed. Laurie lived in the top two floors of the building, alone. Her ex-husband, a high-school sweetheart who had been a long-term Ph.D. candidate in economics, had left her for an undergraduate right after the store's renovations.

A wide gallery ran along three sides of the store, accessed via a handsome curved stairway on one side. The floors and furnishings were deep walnut color, the fittings brass, the lighting subtle, abundant, and inviting. Moving backward to better see the mezzanine, Bob stepped on the Siamese. Its cry was sharp and menacing. He leapt away, his heart racing, while the cat fled to the back of the store.

"Sorry," he said to Laurie as she and the customer turned to him with concerned expressions. "I don't think I hurt it."

A pretty, pale young woman came forward with the Siamese in her arms. "Are you all right?" she asked Bob. He told her yes, embarrassed and irritated—he was the stepper, not the steppee. The woman's hair, the same color as the cat's, was absolutely straight and hung to her shoulders in one piece like a curtain.

"How's the injured party?" Bob nodded at the cat and stepped aside as Laurie returned to write up a sale.

"She's fine," answered the young woman, eyeing him through small wire-framed glasses. "Just a little put out."

Laurie handed the customer her package and turned to pat the Siamese.

"Bob Neely, Gina Bellson, my assistant and right hand. Also in line for succession."

They shook hands. "I'm going to show Bob the store and upstairs," Laurie told Gina. "Let's keep the cats down here." As they walked away, Laurie wondered whether he, like her, found the prospect of viewing the rest of the shop less compelling than the prospect of touring her apartment.

🐈 🐈 🐈

That's where they ended up that night; Bob had asked if it was presumptuous to invite her out for dinner that evening. Laurie thought fleetingly of saying she wasn't free. But the chemistry was imperative; she hadn't responded so powerfully to a man for a very long time.

"He's balding, a little bossy, probably too successful for his own good, and he doesn't like cats," she said to her father on the phone a few weeks later.

"Does he have any bad points?" asked the modestly successful former dentist who'd lost most of his hair by the time his only child was in kindergarten.

Laurie laughed. "He's intelligent and funny and he accelerates my heart rate."

Dr. Michaels had retired to Boca Raton as a widower and rarely ate dinner alone. "That's what counts, Princess. The rest you deal with."

Their romance lasted. Laurie and Bob were surprised, but not their friends, who agreed they were a natural pair and wondered why no one had introduced them years ago.

Only two problems marred the relationship. One was the difficulty of getting across town between his apartment on West End Avenue at Eighty-seventh Street and her place at the corner of Sixty-third and Second Avenue. The other was the cats. The obvious solution to the first problem only highlighted the second.

"If you're not really allergic, then you simply adjust," said David Aggrand, Bob's best friend and deputy editor of the *New York Times Book Review.* They sat at the bar in an Italian restaurant on West Twentieth Street, waiting for Laurie and David's wife.

"It's an emotional allergy," Bob answered. "As threatening as anything physiological. They jump on the bed, sleep on the pillows, make mewling noises all night long, dig their claws into my back or my butt, and shed hair everywhere. And the only way she says she'd even consider moving in is if they come with her. I hate the thought."

Finally, however, on Thanksgiving weekend, Laurie did move in, with both cats, whom she transported back and forth to the store with her every morning and night. She wouldn't allow them to stay in the store or her apartment alone. "Gina offered to take them home with her at night, but they belong to me and the store. They're part of my life."

It was an experiment, both agreed. As besotted as Bob remained with Laurie, a state he was beginning to think of as love, he was unable to reconcile himself to the cats. He recognized that part of it was a childish jealousy that they could claim her immediate, undivided attention. The only concession he'd gotten in that regard was that the cats be closed out of the bedroom when they were making love.

The week before Christmas, Laurie moved back to Sixty-third Street. Bob told Dave that the cats were an insurmountable obstacle. "It borders on the tragic. The two of us get along so well, as though we truly were made for each other. I think of her all through the day. Thoughts that warm my heart." He shrugged helplessly at Dave's incredulous look: no one expected such sentiments from buttoned-up Bob Neely.

"If you're not splitting up, where will you sleep together?" asked Dave, an acute reader.

"At her place, with the beasts pacing outside her bedroom door until the deed is done."

"Well, maybe it's not all bad. Couldn't you get used to it? Going out with her, staying over at her place when you can?"

"But I want to marry her, God help me. Not in a package though, dragging along these two creatures like meddling in-laws. I don't know what I'm going to do."

🐈 🐈 🐈

Late in the morning of February 16, Dave got a call from Bob's secretary. Bob was at Mt. Sinai Hospital. He'd fallen at Laurie's apartment and broken his leg. Would Dave please come to the hospital?

"I tripped over the old cat, the fat one," Bob said from the hospital bed. His left leg was wrapped in a massive cast, ankle to hip. His face was mottled with two days' growth of beard, his thin hair was unkempt, and his hospital gown was stained. Dave was astonished at the sight and could only nod for him to continue.

"It was about midnight. I was going home, had a breakfast meeting. I stepped on the cat right below the landing—never saw it—and slid down to the bottom of the stairs. I couldn't get any breath and was sure I'd punctured a rib, didn't even notice my leg. When the EMTs came, Laurie went to look at the cat. They were lifting me on the stretcher when she cries out, 'He's dead. He's dead!' This big bearded guy says, 'No he's not, lady. Just his leg is broke.'

"I didn't see her until late that afternoon, Thursday. She took the cat to the vet, she told me. There weren't any broken bones so she asked for an autopsy, just to satisfy her curiosity. She was going to call me back last night but she never did.

"Then this morning her assistant calls. Turns out the cat was poisoned."

"God! How?"

"Rat poison. Warfarin to be exact, in some salmon. In some salmon that I had brought."

"You brought the cat poisoned salmon?" A smile threatened to crack Dave's rapt expression.

"I brought the cats salmon," Bob said slowly. "I brought Laurie candy. It was Valentine's Day. Hell, I even brought Gina candy. I was asking Laurie to marry me. I did, in fact, and she said yes. That night. We'd been miserable since she moved back and had decided that somehow we could figure out where we'd live, what to do with the cats. There wasn't any rush; I just wanted her to marry me. I gave her a ring too, a ruby for Valentine's Day. Everything was great. But now my fiancée thinks I poisoned her cat, for which she is apparently going to sue me."

"For cat murder?"

"I did *not* intentionally harm the cat. I don't know what she can file for. All I know is I did not poison the cat, even if I might have wanted to, and that its bereaved owner won't return my calls. Apparently she's having the candy tested too."

By that evening word of Bob's accident and Laurie's accusation had polarized their friends. Those backing poor Bob were mainly successful New York City males, the majority divorced, and a lot of up-and-coming young editors. There were also a couple of cat haters, a bookseller (although his retail enterprise was made up of superstores) and everyone they knew who had ever fallen down a flight of stairs. Those taking Laurie's side were predominantly female, pet-fanciers, small business owners, and divorced women.

🐱 🐱 🐱

"Of course I didn't believe it," Laurie said to Mim early Saturday afternoon on Second Avenue. The day was sunny and mild. A strong breeze tossed Laurie's hair, increasing her air of agitation. "I didn't even think of his being involved until the toxicology report."

Mim had called Laurie that morning to ask if they could have lunch. Laurie's extra Saturday sales help was out with the flu, so they'd gotten salad at the Korean grocer down the street to eat at the store.

"But why would he need to get rid of the cat—and only one of them—if you'd already agreed to get married?" Mim asked.

"My father raised that same question. Neither of you has any idea of how much Bob really hated these cats. Gina says that Clause must have been in another part of the store when Bob was feeding the fish to Ffolio."

They walked into the store. Laurie told Gina to call her from the back if she needed help. "Plus," she added as they passed the stairway to the mezzanine, "he may have thought that this was precisely the time to do it, while I was committed and willing."

Mim scooped her lunch out of the clear plastic container onto the plate Laurie handed her. "Tell me what happened, step by step," she said, feeling like a character in a manuscript that she'd surely reject.

"It was Wednesday, Valentine's Day," Laurie said, pulling her chair up to the small oak table tucked in the corner. Scarred and stained, it had belonged to Blackie's Irish grandmother. "He came in just before closing with a sail bag full of packages. It was an awful day, remember? Rained and sleeted all afternoon. 'Great day for surprises,' he said. He pulled out a bottle of wine, gave me a huge pink-satin heart-box from Neuhaus, and handed a smaller box of Godiva to Gina. 'Nor could I forget the four-legged guardians of Manhattan's finest independent bookstore.' He had a quarter-pound of lox from E.A.T. He was super-charged, said the weather outside might be foul but for some reason his heart was as light as a summer morn.

"He must have thought he was keeping our engagement a secret from Gina, but he was so transparent, and of course I'd already told her.

"Anyway, then a man came in wanting all the short-listed fiction titles for National Book Awards. Bob swept the packages off the counter and brought them back here. I helped the customer, and Gina straightened up the children's section. She left right after closing, about 8:15, and Bob opened a bottle of cabernet. We had a drink down here, and he gave me a ring. It was lovely, a ruby with diamonds, the same color as the wine. We thought about canceling our dinner reservations at Felidia's." Laurie smiled dreamily, then frowned and stabbed at her salad. "But I was starving.

"We were back here by 10:30, and then it was after midnight. Next thing I hear is this horrible thumping. I leaped out of bed and found him crumpled up at the bottom of the stairs, making this awful wheezing sound. I called 911 from in here, propped the door open," she gestured behind Mim at the door that led to the small hall and her private stairs, "and turned on the store lights in back and waited with Bob. Then I saw

Ffolio near the top of the stairs. I must have jumped over him getting to Bob. I could tell he was dead just by looking.

"I sat up the rest of the night on the stairs, scared about Bob, who must have tripped over Ffolio, and feeling bereft. Ffolio had been with me through Blackie's dying, my marriage, divorce, every part of my adult life.

"Gina finally came, and we decided I should take Ffolio to the vet. There weren't any broken bones, so the vet said he'd do an autopsy if I wanted. I must have had some hidden suspicions. He called with the report around 8:00. Stomach contents revealed Tender Vittles, chicken and rice, smoked salmon, and Warfarin, a common rat poison."

Laurie grimaced as she twisted a strand of hair around one finger. Mim, so proud of her role in precipitating her friends' romance, was also distressed. She leaned over to stroke the Siamese as it wound around her leg. "Does this one miss the other?"

"I don't think so. Ffolio was pretty solitary, and Clause has always been independent. Gina found her on the street right after the penulti- mate of Blackie's cats died." The cat sprang noiselessly onto the table and let Laurie run a hand down its back.

Mim noticed the small refrigerator under the counter. "Was there any salmon left? Did you get it tested?"

"No, it was gone by the time I thought about that. The cleaning ser- vice came that night and did their periodic clearing out of the fridge. Gina called E.A.T. to ask if anyone had reported getting sick from the salmon, but they hadn't heard anything, or so they said. The candy tested okay."

Mim, who had picked up a thing or two from reading thousands of mystery manuscripts, was pondering motive and opportunity. "What's next?"

"My lawyer will be back from vacation Monday. I'll talk to her, find out what I can charge Bob with, and then get to it. Emotional cruelty, criminal negligence, willful intent to harm. There have to be a lot of angles. Sandra will know."

Mim stood up, lifting her coat from the old-fashioned coat rack. "I stopped in to see Bob before I came this morning. He's in lots of pain, of different kinds, I think, and not much like himself. Looks an unholy mess. He says he'd never have acted so unfeelingly toward you, and even if he had, he would not have been so stupid."

"But, don't you see? It didn't seem stupid to him! He knew what he wanted, and he went after it. You know him. It's why he's so successful, isn't it?" Laurie stood up fast, scraping her chair on the floor.

"But he's not devious."

"Well, he fooled me for quite a while, and I'd gotten to know him pretty well. Don't forget, Mim, he was caught nearly red-handed."

Mim buttoned her old reliable trench coat. "There's so much that's still unclear, Laurie. Don't you think you should get some more information before you take any big steps?"

"Are you suggesting something in particular?" Laurie challenged. She looked electric, her hair standing away from her head, long arms akimbo, one knee sharply bent.

Mim saw Gina watching them from the register and bent down to tie her sensible brown walking shoes. "No. But maybe your cleaning service could add to the store of facts. Or your veterinarian might tell you if the poison was in the salmon for sure. Ffolio might have gotten into something else somehow while you were at dinner."

They walked past the register to the door, which Laurie held open against the wind. "But Clause is okay," she pointed out. "She didn't 'get into anything.' This had to have been deliberate, Mim."

"Oh, I'm not disputing that at all," Mim said, heading down the street and leaving Laurie standing in the doorway, wondering. Exactly as she'd intended.

🐾 🐾 🐾

Never slow on the uptake, Laurie went right upstairs and called Insta-Cleen. It took fifteen minutes to convince Mr. Hameed that she wasn't accusing anyone of stealing food. She just wanted to know what happened to some food that had been in the fridge. He would call her back.

Laurie told Gina that Mim had tried to persuade her that she was overreacting.

"People who don't like cats never really understand," Gina answered quietly, keeping her eyes on the register's computer screen. Her hair was tangled. She's a mess, like Bob, Laurie thought. This business is hitting her hard, too.

🐾 🐾 🐾

Renata and Tony had simply cleaned out the refrigerator as the note had requested, Mr. Hameed's voice reported from her machine after closing. Mrs. Michaels would please call again if she thought of more questions.

Laurie poured herself a glass of wine from the bottle that Bob had brought, reminding herself that she'd safely drunk from it before. She remembered that she had left no note for the cleaners; in fact, it was usually the cleaners who left a note reminding them that they'd be cleaning the refrigerator next time. She thought about her assistant.

Gina had been different from Laurie's other staff from her first day nearly five years ago, taking to the business as naturally as Laurie had. From the beginning the two of them had worked comfortably together, as only women can. They learned to talk through problems before they escalated and, while they didn't often do things together outside of the store, their relationship extended well beyond the workplace. Blackie and Laurie had navigated the shoals of employer/employee relations as friends. She and Gina were furthering the evolution.

Lightly rolling the glass between her hands, Laurie gazed at the moving wine. It dawned on her: Bob's appearance changed that dynamic.

What else don't I know, Laurie repeated Mim's question.

She thought back to the morning after Bob's fall. "Maybe it was something in the salmon," Gina had said.

Then later, after Laurie had come back and said the vet was doing an autopsy, Gina had said she'd seen Bob feeding the fish to Ffolio.

"Hi. It's Sandy. I'm back, got your message. I'm so sorry about Ffolio. How awful of Bob! Are you holding up?" It was twenty years since they were in college, but Sandy's breathless energy hadn't diminished an iota.

"I'm all right. I thought you were coming back tomorrow."

"Got in late last night. Patrick and I had a fight, the weather was horrible, no point in staying. I can't believe it about Bob."

"Well, actually . . ."

"Listen," Sandy barrelled on. "I did some research this afternoon. Looks like you can't file a civil suit in New York for the loss of a pet. Here, this is from a ruling last year: 'It is well established that a pet owner in New York cannot recover damages for emotional distress caused by the negligent destruction of a dog,'" she read in an authoritative voice.

"You can bring a criminal charge here, based on old farming law, but it's only a misdemeanor for the death of an animal from things like overwork, neglect, or torture. Maximum fine of $1,000 and/or a year in prison, *if* you got the district attorney's office to take the case. I wouldn't bother trying. I'm so sorry. And I'm so angry at Bob. How are you standing it all?"

"I think I was wrong," Laurie answered. "I think it was Gina, not Bob."

"God, that may be worse! You haven't eaten, have you? I'm coming over. We'll go out."

♦ ♦ ♦

"So why aren't you worried about her putting something in *your* food?" Sandy asked over steamed mussels at a small Italian restaurant on First Avenue.

"Because I think it was an aberration. For years she had reason to think, with my tacit agreement, that her life would go like mine would have if Blackie hadn't died. She and I would work in the store, and one day I'd invite her to be a partner. Then last April Bob entered the picture, shaking up everyone's expectations. Hers too, I bet."

"But she could be seriously crazy."

"If she poisoned Ffolio, it's appalling, I agree. Before I decide anything, though, I want to talk to her."

"Well, I'm staying over tonight. No argument. You may be right, but she could still be nuts and plotting a crime against a higher species."

♦ ♦ ♦

"I was planning to call you again, too," Bob said. It was 7:30 Sunday morning. He had groped groggily for the phone, but the sound of her hello brought him fully alert. "I've tried to reach you, do you know?"

She told him everything, her anger at him, her regret at blaming him so readily, her suppositions about Gina.

"I'd gotten used to the trajectory of my life, too," she said. "Before you changed its course. That's why I needed to cling more closely to the familiar, like having the cats around all the time. The store, Gina, Ffolio defined me. You said, in effect, that that dictionary was out of date. It's scary. Do you understand?"

"That somebody can knock you completely off course? I think so."

"Well, I suspect it was something like that for Gina. I'm going to call her now, and get her over here before Sandy wakes up, throws papers around, and terrifies her."

♦ ♦ ♦

Gina arrived at the store twenty minutes later, the bell ringing as she unlocked and opened the door. Her face was blotchy, her hair was matted, her clothes were thrown on. Laurie didn't need to raise the topic.

"Tell me what happened," she said as they sat with coffee at Blackie's table.

"I didn't want him to die, really! Just to get a little sick, so you'd pay more attention. To the store, I thought then, but that doesn't make any sense now." She lifted her head.

"I was petrified when I saw that he had died. I couldn't let you find out it was me. The salmon just popped into my head. I didn't even think about Bob."

"What exactly did you do?"

"I got rat poison from my super, for rats in the basement here, I said. I put just the littlest bit into Ffolio's food that night, while you were in the front with that customer and Bob was in the bathroom. And then I gave him some of the salmon. I thought he'd just get a little sick and that would make things like they were again." She shook her head slowly. "It sounds so dumb. It *was* so dumb."

"What about Clause?"

"I was going to give it to her too, but I just couldn't. She's been here as long as I have.

"That's what's so awful—I know what Ffolio meant to you. I'll do whatever you want. I'll quit, you can fire me. You can sue me. I'll pay whatever you say."

🐈 🐈 🐈

"Then we talked about what's next," Laurie reported that afternoon from the chair next to Bob's bed. He had on ironed pajamas that he'd made Dave bring over. He was clean shaven and as kempt as possible under the circumstances. Laurie held his hand, tracing the lines on his palm with her thumb.

"I told her I understood what she might have been thinking. Even so, the process of rebuilding trust will be really hard. I said I wasn't bringing any charges but showed her the statute that Sandy had brought.

"In effect, she's on probation. We'll see how it goes. If this turns out to be the isolated incident I believe it is, maybe it'll all smooth over. I'd like it to work out with her. In some ways it's kind of interesting to think about not being so wedded to that place."

"Is wedded the problem?" Bob asked. His tone was light, his expression anxious.

Laurie gave him another winning smile. "Not if it's to you. If you'll still have me, I mean. Clearly, Gina hasn't been the only victim of lapsed reason."

Bob turned his hand so that he was holding hers. "I'm going home on Tuesday. I know I'll be a terrible patient, but can I ask you to spend some time on West End? Can you leave Gina in charge to make sick calls?"

"I've made arrangements already. One of the deals is that she's taking Clause home with her at the end of the day. I'm going to be your night nurse, the only animal you'll have to contend with." She drew a finger slowly down his chest, muttering a ridiculous, low growl.

Bob leaned back on the pillow and closed his eyes.

"Meow," he said softly. "Oh, meow."

The End

Special thanks to Stacy Grossman, Esq., of Legal Fiction, Inc., for research.

Blue Eyes

Janet Dawson

———————————

Ney, Jeri," Cassie Taylor said with a chuckle. "Have I got a case for you."

I cradled the phone receiver between chin and shoulder as I switched off my computer, glancing at my watch. "I can give you half an hour. Then I've got to take Abigail to the vet."

Cassie's chuckle escalated into outright laughter.

"Why is it so funny that I have to take my cat to the vet?" I asked.

"It's not. Abigail, I mean. It's just that . . ." She stopped talking as she tried to get her laughter under control. "Come on over and I'll explain."

Mystified, I locked the door of J. Howard Investigations, located on the third floor of a building near Oakland's Chinatown. The front suite of offices is occupied by the law firm of Alwin, Taylor and Chao. Cassie's the middle partner. She and I have been friends since we were legal secretaries many years ago. Cassie went to law school, and I went into the private investigating business.

Cassie was in her office, dressed as usual in one of her spiffy lawyer suits. The elegant effect of the classy navy blue wool was spoiled somewhat by the fact that she'd removed her leather pumps and replaced them with a pair of battered running shoes, which were much more suitable for walking several blocks to the Alameda County Courthouse. At the moment, however, she was leaning back in her chair with her running shoes propped up on an open desk drawer, offering a excellent view of her sleek legs.

With Cassie was her partner, Mike Chao. Short and stocky, he wore gray pinstripes, though he'd removed his jacket. The cuffs of his white shirt had been rolled up, and he'd loosened the knot on his red tie. He was sitting in one of the two client chairs in front of Cassie's desk, holding a document in his hands. I sat down in the other client chair. "What's this case that has you in stitches?"

"I'm not in stitches, Cassie is," Mike said, looking glum. "Mainly because it's my problem and not hers. And I can't very well take it to court, because the judge will toss it back in my lap. It's about a cat. And a will."

"Don't tell me some little old lady died and left her estate to her cat Fluffy."

"Sort of," Mike said. "Only the cat's name is Ermengarde."

"Ermengarde! Who names a cat Ermengarde?" I shook my head. "That's cruel and unusual punishment."

"This from a woman who named her cats Abigail and Black Bart," Cassie commented.

"Let me give you some background," Mike said. "My Aunt Mae had a friend named Sylvia Littlejohn. She was only in her early sixties, but she had cancer, and she died about ten days ago. She named Aunt Mae as executor of her will."

"I'm with you so far," I said. "When do we get to Ermengarde?"

Mike ran a hand through his straight black hair. "Mrs. Littlejohn gave Aunt Mae sealed envelopes containing her will and her funeral instructions. And she asked that Aunt Mae look after Ermengarde until the instructions in the will were carried out. So Aunt Mae's had the cat ever since Mrs. Littlejohn went into the hospital for the last time, which was the day before she died. The funeral was last week. Aunt Mae didn't open the envelope containing the will until after the service."

"So the problem is in carrying out the instructions in the will," I guessed.

"Exactly," Mike said. "As soon as Aunt Mae read the will, she called me. For the most part, the document is fairly straightforward. Mrs. Littlejohn wasn't rich, but she was certainly well off. She left a number of substantial bequests to a number of friends as well as several charities."

"I take it one of these large sums was set aside for the care, feeding and upkeep of her cat Ermengarde," I said. Mike nodded.

"It's not worded that way, of course," Cassie chimed in. "The money is left to Mrs. Littlejohn's niece, for the specific purpose of Ermengarde's care, until such time as Ermengarde departs for that great cat tree in the sky."

"So Ermengarde's rich, or rather well off," I said. "Or her caretaker is. Unless the caretaker, or one of the other beneficiaries, decides to eliminate the cat."

Mike waved the document he was holding. "Mrs. Littlejohn anticipated that possibility, and took care of it. She states in her will that if the cat dies of anything other than natural causes, Ermengarde's bequest goes to several charities, not the caretaker or the other beneficiaries."

"And if the cat dies of natural causes?" I asked.

"The caretaker gets what's left," Cassie said.

"Aha." I digested this for a moment. "So what's the problem?"

"The problem's the niece. Or rather, the nieces. There are two of them."

I frowned. "Does the will specify which niece?"

"Nope," Cassie said.

Mike leafed through the pages until he found the offending clause. "It says here that the money is bequeathed to Mrs. Littlejohn's niece, who will have full control of the money as long as it's spent to provide Ermengarde with all the comforts to which she's accustomed."

I reached for the will and read the clause, raising my eyebrows at the number of zeros after that dollar sign. "Wow. That's a lot of cat crunchies. Who the hell drew up this will anyway? A summer law clerk would have known better than to leave a beneficiary unnamed."

"For an attorney to make a mistake like that borders on legal malpractice," Cassie said, with a look that would have withered the yellow chrysanthemums on the credenza behind her desk.

I had to agree. I glanced through the rest of the will. Every other bequest specified a beneficiary by name, whether it was a person or an organization. The clause relating to Ermengarde was the only one that didn't.

It could have been a mistake. It was possible whoever typed the will had left out the name by accident. But if that was the case, the attorney— or Mrs. Littlejohn—should have caught the error when they proofread the will. Unless neither of them had read through the document. I looked at the date the will was signed. Earlier this year, ten months ago.

Somehow I didn't think the omission of the niece's name was a mistake. It smelled deliberate, not accidental.

"Aunt Mae says Mrs. Littlejohn's attorney was named Bruce Cathcart," Mike said. "She found his name and address on some other papers Mrs. Littlejohn left with her. Cathcart's also the one who notarized the will, as you'll see from the last page."

"But you can't find Cathcart," I finished.

"He's done a bunk," Cassie said. "Or so it appears. Which means we can't ask him just what he was thinking when he drafted up this will. If he was thinking at all."

"He's disappeared?" I asked.

"When I went looking for him," Mike said, "I couldn't find him. He rented an office in another law firm, Burke & Hare. When I contacted them, the office manager told me he'd left. And she claimed he didn't leave a forwarding address. But I got the feeling she wasn't telling me everything. All she would say was that he was there two years."

"What about before that?" I asked. "Was Cathcart associated with another firm? Did he have a partner?"

"According to the bar association, he was practicing solo when he rented space from Burke & Hare," Cassie said. "Before that, three years ago, he was with the Bestwick firm over in San Francisco. Nobody there will answer any questions about him. All the human resources manager will do is confirm that he worked there for five years. The bar association doesn't have a current address for him. Nor did they have any record of complaints against him. That doesn't mean there weren't any, of course, just that they didn't get reported to the bar."

"The guy definitely sounds like he's had some problems. If people don't want to talk about him, that could mean they have nothing good to say."

"That's what I thought," Mike said. "He must have had a secretary, though. If you could locate the secretary, maybe that would lead us to Cathcart."

"Worth a try," I said. "That's the first problem. I assume the nieces are the second problem. Only two so far?"

"So far," Mike said. "Aunt Mae organized the funeral according to the instructions Mrs. Littlejohn left, and she notified everyone in Mrs. Littlejohn's address book. She also put a notice in the *Oakland Tribune* and the *San Francisco Chronicle*. Both of the women showed up at the funeral, introduced themselves to Aunt Mae as Mrs. Littlejohn's nieces, and said they'd read the death notice in the *Chronicle*. Aunt Mae had never met either of them before. Neither had anyone else at the funeral. My aunt had heard Mrs. Littlejohn speak of a niece, but she was under the impression that they weren't close, and that the niece lived in another state."

"So you're not even sure the nieces are really nieces," I said. "Let alone the real niece."

"Their names are Cathy Wingate and Mary Hooper." Mike reached for a yellow legal pad on which he'd scribbled some notes. "Aunt Mae's got Mrs. Littlejohn's address book, and she says she didn't see either name there."

"And neither woman is listed as a beneficiary elsewhere in the will," Cassie added.

"Do they know about the will?"

Mike shook his head. "No. I thought it best not to bring up the matter until I was sure which one of them actually is Mrs. Littlejohn's niece. That's where you come in." He tore off a sheet of yellow paper. "Fortunately, Aunt Mae had the presence of mind to get their addresses."

I looked at the sheet. Both of Ermengarde's potential guardians lived in San Francisco. I asked Mike for his aunt's address and phone number, then I glanced at my watch, mindful of Abigail's vet appointment. As I stood up, I folded the paper and tucked it into my purse. "I'm on it. I'll get back to you as soon as I have anything."

"The sooner the better," Mike said. "I can't get this will admitted to probate until this mess is straightened out."

🐪 🐪 🐪

Abigail was not thrilled with the prospect of going to the vet. Neither of my cats are. They have been known to vanish at the rattle of a cat carrier latch. However, Abigail is old and fat, and I'm faster than she is. I scooped her up, ignoring the flailing paws and the outraged meows of protest, and wedged her through the door of the carrier. Then I strapped her into the passenger seat of my Toyota and set off for Dr. Prentice's office, with Abigail muttering imprecations all the way.

Mike didn't know how old Ermengarde was, I thought, as I watched the vet examine Abigail. My own cat was nearing twelve, and I didn't want to think about losing her, but it was hard to know how long a cat would live, even the most pampered feline. Whether Ermengarde lived another year or ten years, she was going to live in style, considering the sum of money Mrs. Littlejohn had left for her care and feeding. And the niece who administered Ermengarde's money would also benefit quite nicely.

My vet conceded that Abigail had slimmed down some since our kitten Black Bart came to live with us. That had upped the cat's exercise level, plus I'd been monitoring her diet. Dr. Prentice administered the required vaccines. That done, I opened the door of the cat carrier and Abigail retreated inside. Coming home from the vet was the only time she ever willingly got into the carrier.

"Do you by any chance have a client named Sylvia Littlejohn?" I asked Dr. Prentice. "With a cat named Ermengarde?"

"Yes, as a matter of fact, I do," the doctor said. "Why do you ask?"

"Mrs. Littlejohn died recently," I said.

"Oh, no," Dr. Prentice said. "I'm sorry to hear that. I hope someone's taking care of Ermengarde. She really loved that cat."

"Yes, the cat's being cared for," I said. "How old is Ermengarde? Is she in good health?"

"I'll have to check my records." Dr. Prentice left the examining room and came back a moment later with a file. "Ermengarde's four. And she's in excellent health. If she doesn't have any major medical problems in the future, she could live another ten to twelve years."

I took my cat home, promising her that if she stayed healthy she wouldn't have to go to the vet again for another year. Then I headed over to an address in the Oakland hills to see Mike's aunt, who was caring for Ermengarde pending resolution of the mystery of her friend's will. I was eager to meet the newly rich cat.

🐈 🐈 🐈

She had blue eyes, slightly crossed. And there was a Siamese somewhere in her gene pool. She was small and elegant, with a luxuriant, long, fluffy coat, mostly white veering into pale champagne and dark brown in places. The dark patches on her dainty pointed face had the look of a harlequin's mask. Her ears and tail were tipped with brown, and so were three of her four paws.

Ermengarde was indeed a gorgeous cat. She gazed at me, unconcerned, with those big blue eyes, rested regally on a dark blue towel on Mae Chao's sofa. I held out my hand and let the cat take a delicate sniff. I knew I'd passed inspection when Ermengarde rubbed her pointy chin against my fingers and allowed me to stroke her silky head.

I saw a white electrical cord running from under the towel to an outlet on the wall. "There's a heating pad under that towel," Mrs. Chao said.

"Sylvia always had heating pads for this cat to sit on. She said cats are like heat-seeking missiles. They always find the warm spot."

I smiled, thinking of Abigail and Black Bart, and how fond they were of my down comforter, especially in winter. I'd have to try the heating pads for them.

I'd seen no other evidence of felines in residence, the sort of evidence I saw at my own house. Mrs. Chao's sofa, dark green with a floral motif of large pink peonies, showed no signs of cat claws shredding through the fabric. The beige carpet didn't have stray bits of cat food and kitty litter, at least none visible. And I didn't see the usual buildup of cat hair anywhere else except the blue towel on which Ermengarde rested. That was covered with long white strands. Either Mae Chao wasn't a cat owner, or she was extraordinarily tidy and had extremely well-behaved cats. If there is such an animal.

"I take it you're not a cat person," I said. Mrs. Chao had made tea, and I sipped at the fragrant jasmine brew.

"Not really," she admitted. "Although I really like Ermengarde. She's such a sweet, good-natured kitty. And very well-mannered. Of course, she's been subdued since she came to live with me. I'm sure she misses Sylvia."

I looked at Ermengarde, wondering what dark secrets of feline misbehavior lurked behind those crossed blue eyes. "Ermengarde's an odd name for a cat."

"Sylvia named her after an old nanny who took care of her when she was child," Mrs. Chao said. "She said Ermengarde—the woman, not the cat—practically raised her and her sister after their mother died. Sylvia was about eight when that happened. Her sister was four or five. Their father was a wealthy businessman here in Oakland, and he traveled a lot. So Sylvia and her sister were frequently left alone, with the original Ermengarde, who was a German refugee. She came over here right before World War II."

"I wonder why the cat reminded her of the woman."

"Oh, she told me." Mrs. Chao reached over and ruffled the cat's fur. "The original Ermengarde had blue eyes that were slightly crossed. When Sylvia saw this little white kitten at the Oakland SPCA four years ago, she immediately thought of Ermengarde. Who has been dead for years, of course."

"What was the sister's name?"

"Oh, dear, let me think." Mrs. Chao reached for the cup of tea she'd set on the lamp table at her end of the sofa. "Lucille, that was it. And I believe her married name was Fanning. From the way Sylvia talked about her, I gathered that the sister was dead. And that they'd been estranged for many years."

That would explain why no one among Mrs. Littlejohn's contemporaries seemed to know that she'd had a niece, until the two women claiming kinship had shown up at the funeral.

I asked if I could look at Sylvia Littlejohn's address book, the one Mrs. Chao had used to notify people of the funeral. It was a worn leather volume that looked as though its owner had used it for many years. I leafed through the pages slowly, looking at the names listed, as well as for scribbles in the margins and bits of paper tucked into the pages. As Mike had said, neither of the purported nieces was listed in the address book.

Which struck me as odd. Presumably Mrs. Littlejohn really did have a niece. Why else would she have designated the niece as the person to look after Ermengarde?

Mrs. Chao interrupted my thoughts with a question of her own. "What happens if they're not really Sylvia's nieces?" She scratched Ermengarde behind the ears, and I heard a contented purr rumbling from the blue-eyed cat.

"I guess we'll have to figure that out when the time comes," I said. "It might be up to the probate judge."

"Well, if nobody else wants her, I'll take care of her," Mae Chao said. "I don't care about the money. But I'm getting to be quite fond of this cat."

🐈 🐈 🐈

The law firm of Burke & Hare, where Bruce Cathcart had rented an office, was located in a suite on an upper floor of a high rise near Lake Merritt. The whole building was lousy with lawyers. I was surprised the management company dealt with anyone who didn't have a *juris doctor.*

The office manager at Burke & Hare wasn't all that thrilled about discussing the missing perpetrator of Mrs. Littlejohn's will, at least not at first. But in my business all it usually takes is a little cajoling. In the end, she and the secretaries in the firm dished the dirt.

They hadn't liked Bruce Cathcart much. He was arrogant, they said, and treated the administrative staff as though they were talking pieces of furniture. The attorneys at Burke & Hare didn't care for him either. In fact, the office manager finally admitted Cathcart had been asked to leave. She wouldn't tell me exactly why, but something in the way she skated around the edge of it indicated that it was about money. Wasn't paying his bills, I guessed.

What about Cathcart's secretary? I asked. Which one? came the reply.

Cathcart had several secretaries. Several left, no doubt because of the way he treated them. Others he hired through staffing agencies, then fired before he was due to pay the agencies for their fee for finding the employee. After pulling that stunt several times, word got out and the staffing agencies refused to work with him anymore. So he'd resorted to ads in the local newspapers to find temps and part-timers, none of whom stayed for very long.

Except the last one. She'd worked with Cathcart for several months. And she'd registered on the view screen at Burke & Hare for reasons other than her job proficiency.

"They were having a thing," the office manager said. "It was more than just a working relationship, if you know what I mean."

"Office romance?" She nodded. "What was her name? And do you remember what she looked like?"

"Kay Loomis. She was . . ." She stopped and thought for a moment. "Late twenties, medium height, dark hair, blue eyes."

🦌   🦌   🦌

I went back to my office and cruised several investigators' databases, looking for information on Bruce Cathcart and Kay Loomis, as well as the purported nieces, Cathy Wingate and Mary Hooper. Cathcart seemed to have vanished completely. A look at his credit report gave ample evidence why. The attorney's finances had gone down the tubes long before he took a powder.

Interestingly enough, Loomis had dropped out of sight about the same time Cathcart had. Maybe they'd run off to a desert island together. I quickly squelched that romantic notion. It was more likely they were in this scam together. I just had to figure out exactly what the scam entailed and how they were pulling it off.

There wasn't much information on either Wingate or Hooper. It looked like they'd both surfaced in San Francisco earlier this year, just before Mrs. Littlejohn had signed that new will Cathcart drew up for her. And not long before the attorney disappeared. Wingate lived in Bernal Heights, Hooper in the Richmond District. When I dug further, I discov-

ered that both women worked as secretaries, temping for one of the
staffing agencies that specialized in legal support staff.

I had a late lunch at the nearby deli, then drove across the Bay Bridge
to San Francisco. My first stop was in the city's Financial District, which
was also lousy with lawyers. The firm of Bestwick, Martin & Smithson,
where Cathcart had worked before hanging out his shingle in Oakland,
occupied several floors in a highrise on California Street.

I took the elevator to the Bestwick reception area and worked my way
through a receptionist and an office manager before I found anyone with
an axe to grind. She was an associate in Wills and Trusts. Her opinion of
Bruce Cathcart was, in her words, lower than snail snot. But she really
couldn't go into detail, not right here in the office. She told me to meet her
downstairs in the lobby in fifteen minutes. It was more like twenty. We
went outside, then across the street to one of the espresso joints that spring
up in this part of town like weeds in a garden.

"The guy's a loser," Beth Fonseca told me, slugging down her cappuc-
cino as though she needed a late afternoon infusion of caffeine. "I'm surprised they didn't fire his ass sooner."

"They fired him? Why?"

"Misconduct, negligence, misappropriation of funds. You name it."

I asked her to name it. She was reluctant at first, but I assured her
that we'd never had this conversation. So she gave me a few examples
of Cathcart's skullduggery, the kind that could get him disbarred or
jailed.

After the attorney went back across California Street, I finished my
latte. Time to meet the nieces, I thought, glancing at my watch. It was
late enough so that even if they'd worked that day, they should be home.

I retrieved my car and headed west in the thickening rush-hour traffic. Mary Hooper lived near the intersection of Twenty-first Avenue and
Lake Street. Finding a parking place anywhere in San Francisco is always
a chore, and it took me several passes before I wedged my Toyota into a
space between a fire hydrant and someone's driveway. The apartment was
on the lower level of a house in the middle of the block, looking as though
it had been converted from a garage.

I rang the bell. No answer.

I went back to my car and kept an eye on the place until I saw a gray
Ford pull up outside the house. The driver was a man. The woman in the
passenger seat leaned over and kissed him, then got out, walking toward
the house. I jotted down the plate number as the Ford pulled away. By the

time the woman entered the apartment I was out of my car and headed toward the house.

Definitely a converted garage, now a bare-bones studio, I thought, judging from what I could see when Mary Hooper opened the door. Late twenties, medium height, I thought, looking her over. Her dark brown hair fell to her shoulders, and she had blue eyes. Just like Kay Loomis, Cathcart's last secretary. Was that Cathcart in the Ford? I wondered.

I introduced myself, telling Mary Hooper that I worked for the attorney handling her aunt's will. "He's a little concerned about some irregularities," I said. "For instance, you're not named directly as a beneficiary. There's just a reference to a niece."

"I'm surprised she mentioned me in her will at all." She poured herself a glass of orange juice, then held the carton up and asked if I wanted some. I declined. She took a seat on the end of the futon on a frame that served as both bed and sofa, and crossed her legs.

"Mother and Aunt Sylvia weren't close. I don't know why, and now that Mother's dead, I can't ask her," she added regretfully. "When I moved here earlier this year, I decided to make contact. I wish I'd done it sooner. Aunt Sylvia was really a nice lady." She sipped her orange juice. "What's going to happen to her cat? She really doted on that cat. I'd be happy take it."

I looked at her face, trying to detect signs of duplicity. I saw none, only concern for Ermengarde's fate. "The cat's being cared for. How did you know she had a cat?"

"Oh, I was over at Aunt Sylvia's house a couple of times."

"It's interesting," I said, "that you weren't listed in her address book."

"Really? That's odd. Maybe she had my number written down someplace else."

"Maybe. It was lucky that you saw the notice of the funeral in the newspaper."

"Yeah, it was," she said, smiling again. "I would have hated to miss the service."

"And it would have made it more difficult for me to find you," I said, "if you hadn't given your name and address to Mrs. Chao. Then I had to wait until you came home. Were you at work?"

She nodded. "Yeah, it's just a temp job, in a law office. I'm doing that until I find a job I like."

"More job opportunities here than where you lived before?" I asked.

"Definitely more," she agreed. "There weren't as many jobs back home." She took another swallow of juice and smiled at me again.

"Where was that?"

Her smile grew less welcoming. "Detroit. That's where I grew up. Say, what is this, some kind of test?"

It was, but at this point I didn't know whether she'd passed or failed. I'd have to go back and do some more database research to see if her story about living in Detroit was true. And I wanted to put a trace on the license plate of that Ford that had dropped her off.

I took my leave. "You'll let me know about the cat," she said. I assured her I would.

Cathy Wingate's apartment was on Cortland Avenue in Bernal Heights. When she opened her front door, somehow I wasn't surprised to see that she, too, matched the description of Kay Loomis. Late twenties and medium height, again, with blue eyes looking at me from a face fringed with short brunette hair.

I gave her the same spiel I'd given the other niece, and asked if I could come in.

"You mean Sylvia left me something?" she asked, amazed. "I'll be damned. What a sweet old gal." She held the door open wider. Her apartment was also a studio, sparsely furnished and with an air of impermanence. She looked tired, as though she'd had a rough day.

"I'm looking for a job," she volunteered, popping the top on a soda from her refrigerator. She asked if I wanted one, and I shook my head. She sat down on what looked like an old sofabed and kicked off her shoes. "I had two interviews today. I'm bushed. It takes a lot out of you."

I went right to the questions. "What do you do?"

"Legal secretary, legal word processor. Whatever I can get that will pay the rent. At least for now." She sipped her soda. "Both of my interviews today went really went well." She held up her hand, and I saw that her fingers were crossed. "Wish me luck."

"Better job prospects here than in . . ."

"Denver," she said. "I moved here from Denver, not quite a year ago. I don't know about job prospects, but the weather is sure as hell better. So, what did Sylvia leave me? I don't mean to sound greedy or anything, but at this point, an extra fifty bucks would be a godsend."

"We'll get to that. Is your family still in Denver?"

She frowned. "Why all the questions?"

"I'm just curious about why Mrs. Littlejohn would leave you something in her will."

"Well, so am I," she said with a shrug. "I mean, I'm her niece. But it's not like we were close. I never even met her till I came out here. I decided since she was in Oakland, I'd look her up."

"Why weren't you close?"

"She and my mom had a falling out, years ago. Mom didn't like to talk about it. And Mom's dead now, so I can't ask her."

"What about your father?"

"He's dead, too."

"What was his name?"

"George Cooper."

I digested this. Funny how Cooper and Loomis both had double Os. And it was a short walk from Cathy to Kay.

The phone rang. She made no move to answer it, instead letting her answering machine pick up the call. It was a man's voice. He didn't leave his name, just, "Hi, call me when you get in."

"Boyfriend?" I asked. Bruce Cathcart? I wondered, but I didn't say anything.

"Just a guy I've been out with a couple of times." Cathy Wingate set her soda on an end table and gave me a hard look. "I get the feeling you don't think I'm Sylvia's niece."

"Just exercising a little caution," I said, leaning back in my chair.

"If it will make you feel any better, I've got some old pictures that belonged to my mother. They show her and Sylvia when they were kids."

"I'd love to see them," I told her.

She got up and moved over to a desk that had been pushed against a wall. She opened a drawer and then walked back toward me, opening the flap on a large accordion folder. She rummaged in one of the pockets and drew out a handful of snapshots. She sifted through the photos in her hand, then held one out to me. "Here. That's Mom on the left and Sylvia on the right."

I glanced at the photo, a faded color snapshot showing two youngsters in frilly dresses who could have been anyone's kids. "Did you know your aunt had a cat?" I asked.

"Oh, my God," she said, concern written on her face. "I forgot about her. Is somebody taking care of her? I should have asked that Mrs. Chao I met at the funeral. Sylvia loved Ermengarde. Did you know she named that cat after her old nanny? I knew why, too, the minute I saw the cat."

"Why is that?"

She handed me another photograph, this one a larger reproduction showing the two little girls standing on either side of a seated woman in a dowdy black dress. Cathy Wingate pointed at the woman's worn round face. "Ermengarde and the cat have the same eyes."

I looked at the photo and smiled. The woman's eyes, like those of her namesake, were blue, slightly crossed.

*ᴺ *ᴺ *ᴺ

"But Aunt Mae said she thought Lucille married a guy named Fanning," Mike said. "You're telling me Cathy Wingate's father was George Cooper."

"Lucille's first husband was Tom Fanning. In fact, that's why Sylvia and Lucille had their falling-out. Tom was courting Sylvia, then changed his mind and went after her younger sister. After he was killed in a car accident, Lucille married George and they had one child, Cathy. She was in Sylvia's address book, by the way. As Mary Catherine Cooper, instead of her married name, Wingate. Sylvia never bothered to change the name."

"What happened to Mr. Wingate?" Cassie asked.

"He died of cancer last year, which is one reason Cathy decided to leave Denver for California. At the same time, Sylvia knew she was dying and wanted to make arrangements for Ermengarde. That's when she went to see Cathcart."

I smiled, this time with grim satisfaction. "I traced Cathcart from the plate number of that Ford. He was living in the Sunset District, as John Benson, a deceased client whose social security number he'd appropriated for new identification. Now that both Cathcart and Loomis have been arrested and charged, Kay's singing long and loud. Says it was all Bruce's idea. Turns out Sylvia did specify her niece Mary Catherine Cooper as Ermengarde's caretaker. After she'd signed the will, he substituted the altered page, then set up Kay in the role of the niece, Mary Hooper. What tripped them up was Ermengarde. Cathcart knew what the cat's name was. But he didn't know why Sylvia chose that name."

"So Mike gets the probate judge to sign off on your affidavit," Cassie said, "Cathy Wingate gets designated as Mrs. Littlejohn's one and only niece. And Ermengarde gets a home."

"Well, there's just one problem," Mike said, frowning. "And I don't think Jeri can fix it. Cathy Wingate's allergic to cats."

CAT, THE JURY

Catherine Dain

"If there ever was an excuse to get out of jury duty, this is it. Show me the notice again."

"Wait till we get to our table." Michael headed purposefully toward the one vacant table near the small lunch counter and grill.

Two burly, bearded men wearing Harley-Davidson vests above their swim trunks glared as Michael cut them off. He pretended not to notice.

"We shouldn't have come to the beach." Faith stopped, ready to retreat, but the two men moved away without comment.

"Of course we should have come," Michael replied. "Although next time we're going to rent one of those tables with the yellow umbrellas."

"Making reservations for the beach seems un-American. Still . . ." Faith let the sentence trail away. If the bikers had wanted to argue, they would be eating sand with their sandwiches.

The August heat had rendered West Hollywood uninhabitable. When Michael had called that morning asking Faith to cancel whatever appointments she had and join him in a trip to the beach, Faith had confessed that the two clients scheduled for the afternoon had already cancelled. She lived in an older building, with only a window unit to cool her combination office and living room, and one client had explained politely that suffocating heat was not conducive to productive psychotherapy. The other had left a message on her answering machine while she was in the shower.

Michael had read about a European-style area of the Ventura beach where yellow umbrellas had been set up near a small espresso and sandwich bar, allowing spur of the moment beach-going and instant picnics. Ventura sounded like a long drive for nothing to Faith, but since Michael was driving, she agreed to go.

Once they had walked the length of the rickety old Ventura pier and back, stopping to watch the group of fishermen at the end, she was too tired and hungry to walk down the beach to the yellow umbrellas. The lunch counter on the pier was as far as she was willing to move. Besides, the area with yellow umbrellas was packed with escapees from the city. They hadn't thought to make reservations, so they would have had to wait.

The topper was that she was almost cold. Not quite, but almost. The Los Angeles basin was well over a hundred degrees when they left. The Ventura beach wasn't even eighty, and there was a stiff breeze from the ocean. With just a light terry cloth jacket over her bathing suit, Faith wanted shelter. The pier provided it, the beach didn't.

Still, she had to admit that the Ventura beach had its charms, with its clear green water and slightly hazy blue sky. The ocean ended not at the horizon, but in an offshore mist that hid the Channel Islands from view. That was why the breeze was so cool—the marine layer.

Faith set the plate with her grilled veggie burger on the small table next to Michael's teriyaki ahi sandwich. She took a long swallow of her iced tea.

"Elizabeth is a cat," she said. "A cat can't be a juror. How did they get her name?"

"From the voter registration rolls. I bet Bobby that the system was so lax that I could register Elizabeth and no one would check. I was right. And so Elizabeth—my cat—has been summoned to jury duty."

Faith examined the summons. Municipal Court in Van Nuys. She took a bite of her veggie burger and thought about the heat. The pervasive heat, the heat that she had been wandering through malls and going to afternoon movies to get away from. The heat that they had come to the beach to escape. The heat that would be waiting for her when she returned to the city, returned to an apartment with only a fan in the bedroom and a window unit in the combination office/living room.

"I'll go," she said.

"My God! Why?"

"The courthouse will be cooler than my apartment—anything would be—and all my clients are cancelling until the end of the heat wave. I don't blame them, either. I might as well do something useful. They have an on-call system, so I don't have to go every morning. And it's for Municipal Court. That means even if I get a trial, it'll be somebody fighting a traffic violation, or petty theft, or a minor dope bust, something like that. It'll only take a few hours. I'll take a book with me and read in the jury room the rest of the time. Elizabeth will have done her civic duty, and no one will know you diddled with the political system."

"What will you use for identification? I didn't get her a driver's license, and you don't look like a six-year-old blue-point Himalayan anyway."

"The last time I was a juror, no one checked for identification. I showed up with a badge, and they took my word for it. People try to get out. They don't try to get in. If you're worried, ask Bobby to make me a driver's license. He can get something out of his computer that I could flash in a pinch."

"That's breaking the law," Michael pointed out.

Faith rolled her eyes and took another sip of her iced tea.

"I'll only have to lie about my name. The rest of it is close enough. Elizabeth is a television actress—television commercials are the art form of the new generation—and I used to be a television actress. Would you rather explain why Elizabeth can't be a juror?"

"I'll get you something that will pass."

Faith nodded. She picked up her veggie burger and prepared to enjoy the rest of the afternoon.

🦙 🦙 🦙

When the alarm went off on Monday morning, Faith awoke with a jerk that scattered Amy and Mac, her two domestic longhairs, from the bed. It took a few startled, puzzled seconds for her to remember why she had set it the night before.

"Jury duty," she muttered.

Mac stared at her, wild-eyed.

"It's for Elizabeth," she explained. "Michael's cat. A long story."

Amy headed for the kitchen, certain food would be forthcoming soon.

And Faith headed for the shower, not certain that it was going to do much good. The day was going to be another scorcher.

Even getting dressed and made-up required taking breaks in front of the wheezing window unit. She was damp before she left the building. With a book under her arm and a jacket over it, in case the courthouse was actually refrigerated, she dashed for her car, the one place in the world where the temperature was under her control.

Surely jury duty would be better than another day in the heat.

She took Coldwater Canyon over the hill, past Ventura Boulevard and on to Victory Boulevard, where she turned left toward the government complex that included two courthouses, one Municipal, one Superior. Following the directions on Elizabeth's summons, she found the jury parking lot. A young man glanced at the card and waved her through. He had waved at the car before hers, and he waved at the car after hers, too.

The new jurors were all arriving at the same time, causing quite a bottleneck, and the line of cars moving slowly into the structure meant that they would all be late.

Faith parked between the two cars that had been in front of and behind her coming in. She fell into step with the fiftyish man in a work shirt and jeans who emerged from one and the sixtyish woman in a cotton blouse and skirt who emerged from the other, as all three walked briskly across the street and right, toward the building that housed Municipal Court.

There was another bottleneck just inside the door. Everyone had to pass through the metal detector. Nobody set it off, and the guard seemed bored.

The herd moved as one to the jury room. Faith sat and waited for her name—Elizabeth's name, that is—to be called. Whoever had summoned them clearly had done this before and knew they would all be late. The public address system came to life about half an hour after she arrived.

Faith sat and waited through the orientation, first listening to a clerk explain the routine, then watching a videotaped judge explain the system. She sat and waited through a long silence. The room felt uncomfortably like a bus terminal, and she didn't really feel like reading the paperback novel she had brought. But at least it was cool. And not too cold.

Shortly before noon, the speakers came to life again, and an amplified voice called out, "Municipal Court will not be seating a jury today. Superior Court, however, needs jurors. At one-thirty, the following prospective jurors will report for duty at the Superior Court building on the other side of the walkway. If your name is not called, you are dismissed for the day. Walter Ivey, Jane Guerin, Elizabeth Haver . . ."

Faith was picking up her things, getting ready to leave, when she realized unhappily that she was now Elizabeth Haver.

The voice gave directions to the courtroom.

As ordered, Faith reported to the Superior Court building after lunching in the crowded cafeteria. No one wanted to leave the area. It would have meant exposure to the heat.

The man and woman she had met in the parking structure were among the group in the hall waiting for the courtroom door to open.

"Bad luck," the woman said brightly, nodding at Faith. The woman had short white hair and wore heavy bifocals that reflected the light from the windows.

Faith nodded in return. She didn't really want to get caught in small talk. It would mean establishing her identity as Elizabeth Haver, and she wanted to keep the lies to a minimum.

It was almost two o'clock when the bailiff opened the door and motioned them all inside.

More waiting, more listening to instructions.

And it dawned on Faith as the first twelve prospective jurors were questioned that if she were seated, and if she told them her name was Elizabeth Haver, she wouldn't simply be lying. She would be committing perjury—actually breaking the law. She thought about explaining to the bailiff that this was all a mistake, that she had to leave. She thought about suddenly becoming ill.

She imagined the cold eyes of the judge penetrating her heart.

There was no easy out, no way she could tell the truth without making things worse. Perjury it would have to be.

She tried to figure out from the questions what kind of crime the defendant was charged with. It had to be violent, and serious, or the judge wouldn't care so much which of the prospective jurors had recently been victimized.

The defendant was a woman, a grossly obese woman with a spiky halo of flaming red hair. She didn't look particularly violent, although she did look vaguely familiar. Faith had seen her face before. On television. She remembered the protruding blue eyes with the dark shadows beneath.

The voir dire questions that weren't about crime all seemed to do with belief in extrasensory perception. The prosecutor was using his peremptory challenges to get rid of jurors who absolutely believed in psychic phenomena. The defense attorney was using hers to get rid of skeptics.

The judge was excusing people who said they had seen so much media coverage of the case that their minds were made up.

Faith remembered who the woman was: Molly Jupiter, billed as the World's Greatest Psychic. A few months earlier she had been arrested for the murder of Charles Bennis, operator of a psychic hotline that was advertised extensively on late night television. Faith hadn't paid too much attention to the media coverage because too much had been happening in her own life at the time. All she remembered was the fat psychic, who had seemed even fatter on television, refusing to talk.

If Faith wanted to avoid this jury, all she had to do was tell them her mind was closed, one way or the other. Closed on psychic phenomena, certain the woman was a murderess.

Unfortunately, her mind was open on both issues. It was one thing to lie about her name, another to lie about her tolerance and sense of fair play.

At the end of the afternoon, Faith—now Elizabeth Haver—was one of twelve jurors sworn in to decide the case of Molly Jupiter.

Opening arguments were scheduled for ten the following morning.

Faith glumly trudged out of the courtroom. The white-haired woman, also on the jury, caught her at the escalator. "What do you think?" she asked. "By the way, my name is Jane."

"I think we shouldn't discuss it," Faith said. "And my name is— Elizabeth."

"Glad to meet you, Elizabeth. You mentioned when the judge was asking questions that you're an actress. Might I have seen you in anything? You do look familiar." Jane seemed determined to strike up a conversation.

"Uh, no, I don't think so. I've been living on residuals, nothing recent."

Faith was almost glad to hit the heat. Walking from the courthouse to the parking structure left both women short of breath, ending all talk.

They waved goodbye as they reached their cars.

Turning the air conditioner to maximum cool restored Faith's good humor. She considered driving until morning, until it was time to return to court.

She went home because her cats were there. And she needed to confess her crime to Michael.

"Faith, you knew it would be perjury," he said when she called.

"I didn't think. Could I be prosecuted?"

"I don't know. Probably not—or at least not unless you cause a mistrial. Are you sure you want to go ahead?"

"Forward is easier than back."

"And it's for a good cause."

"I know. You read about all these lousy court decisions. Maybe I can do something right."

"Don't flatter yourself. The cause is staying out of the heat, and you know it."

Faith sniffed. "Partly true. Besides, I want to know what happened. This was a case that got some attention. I'll tell you about it just as soon as I can."

"Of course. You don't want to add misconduct to perjury."

"That's enough. I'll call you tomorrow."

🐾 🐾 🐾

The bottleneck at the door to the Superior Court building reached all the way down the stairs. Faith was perspiring heavily by the time the guards passed her through the metal detector. And she was not in a good mood.

"Elizabeth!"

A hand tapped Faith's shoulder. Startled, she turned to see the juror named Jane, smiling at her.

"I was thinking about you last night," the older woman said. "What good experience this will be, if you're ever cast in a crime series."

Faith made a weak attempt to smile back.

"I suspect it isn't the same," she said, moving purposefully toward the escalator.

Jane scurried to catch up. "Well, we'll certainly find out, won't we?"

The crowd had thinned in the hall, but the escalator renewed the now-familiar bottleneck.

Faith realized that she would be doomed to chat with Jane for the duration of the trial. She turned, calling on all her reserves of charm, and found a smile that was almost sincere. "Yes, we surely will," she said.

She smiled through the wait in the hallway, smiled as the bailiff called them in, smiled as Jane kept talking.

Once seated in her spot as Juror Number Four, Faith began to study Molly Jupiter, who was having a whispered conversation with her attorney.

The woman could have gone straight from the courtroom to the Renaissance Fair. She was wearing several layers of dark blue cotton, including a blouse, a long ruffled skirt, and an equally long sleeveless vest. Her pudgy hands were clasped in front of her in a manner that seemed to Faith too relaxed for the circumstances. She searched for signs of tension.

As if sensing Faith's gaze, the woman glanced at her, focused the protruding eyes for a moment, eyes that seemed an even deeper blue this morning, nodded, and returned to her conversation. The attorney, whose beige tailored suit offered a striking contrast to her client's dress, didn't seem to notice the momentary shift in attention.

"All rise," the bailiff called.

The judge, a dark-haired woman with a friendly face, entered and took her place. She greeted the jurors and called for the opening arguments, and the trial was underway.

The prosecutor was a young black man who looked barely out of law school.

"Ladies and gentlemen of the jury," he began, looking each of them in the eyes, one at a time. "The defendant is charged with brutally murdering her former employer, a man who had built her professional career. Because of the nature of the crime, I will have to describe acts and show photographs that will offend some of you. Let me apologize in advance. But there is no other way."

The prosecutor proceeded to tell them how Charles Bennis had advertised in several magazines catering to those with an interest in the occult, looking for someone who could be billed as the World's Greatest Psychic. He auditioned close to a hundred psychics before hiring Molly Jupiter. Bennis set her up as star of her own psychic hotline, complete with infomercials on late night cable. The money poured in. Then Molly Jupiter decided she wanted to be in business for herself. Bennis threatened to sue. He was bludgeoned to death two days later. A piece of skin matching Molly Jupiter's DNA was found under Bennis's fingernails, and the defendant had a scratch on her arm. Plus, she had no alibi for the time of the murder.

"Circumstantial evidence, yes," the prosecutor said. "But circumstantial evidence can be convincing. Think of the light inside your refrigerator. How do you know it goes out when you close the door? Can you see it? No. You know there is a light switch, and you believe that the door hits the light switch when it closes, and the light goes out. Circumstantial evidence. But you have no doubt that the light goes out."

Molly Jupiter sat quietly, looking at her hands, as the prosecutor dramatized the story. Faith wondered again if she was truly that calm, even as the prosecutor had the jury seeing the fat woman as a murderous refrigerator door.

The defense attorney's statement was short.

"Much of what you have heard is true," she said. "One thing is not. Molly Jupiter did not commit the murder. This is a case of mistaken identity. The police arrested the wrong psychic. The real perpetrator was not Molly Jupiter but her cousin, Melinda Parris, who was passed over originally for the title of World's Greatest Psychic, and then passed over a second time when Molly left the hotline. Molly Jupiter was framed. What you will hear is circumstantial evidence. Nothing places Molly Jupiter at the crime because she wasn't there. Someone cut off the victim's light. But it wasn't Molly Jupiter."

The defense attorney looked each of them in the eyes, just as her counterpart had previously.

Reasonable doubt, Faith thought. All she has to do is convince one of us that there is a reasonable doubt. A case of mistaken refrigerator doors.

At the end of the opening statements, the judge ordered a lunch break.

"Do you mind if I join you, Elizabeth?"

"Not at all, Jane." Faith sighed. It was going to be a long trial.

🐈 🐈 🐈

The assistant district attorney took four days to present his case. First he established a motive, calling several witnesses to testify that Molly Jupiter had been struggling to survive when she had answered the ad, that Charles Bennis had saved her from certain bankruptcy, and that there had been loud, ugly arguments when she wanted to leave the hotline and go out on her own. Two psychics who worked the hotline confirmed that threats on both sides escalated when Bennis said he would sue Jupiter for everything she was worth if she started a competing service.

During cross-examination, both psychics admitted that they had trouble imagining Molly Jupiter as a murderess.

Then the assistant district attorney called the coroner to the stand and showed the promised photographs of the bludgeoned body. He was right. They were ugly. Faith was more disturbed by them than she had expected to be.

There was also a photograph of Molly Jupiter's arm, showing what appeared to be a partly healed scratch.

The circumstantial evidence tying Molly Jupiter to the crime scene was mostly built around the DNA. When cross-examined, the DNA expert had to admit that sometimes first cousins were genetically close enough to confuse the issue. No one had checked Melinda Parris's DNA.

There was a lot of hypothesizing about Jupiter going to Bennis's house on the pretext of settling differences, most of which the defense attorney objected to and the jury was told to ignore.

The defense attorney had her turn the following Monday morning.

She called Melinda Parris to the stand.

The cousins certainly looked alike. Melinda Parris was as round as Molly Jupiter, with the same protruding eyes, although she had spiky black hair and dressed in layers of white cotton. Faith wondered about the choice. It made her think of refrigerator doors again.

The testimony was short. Melinda Parris denied committing the murder.

"I had no motive," she insisted. "I was in a position to take over the hotline. In fact, if you check the phone records, you'll see that I was signed on to the computer that evening, taking calls. I have an alibi."

"One of those calls was well over an hour," the defense attorney pointed out. "You could have faked the call to yourself, which would have given you plenty of time to commit the murder."

Melinda Parris rolled her eyes. "But I didn't."

That was the entire defense. Molly Jupiter didn't take the stand.

The closing arguments were much the same as the opening ones.

The judge instructed the jury to decide whether Molly Jupiter was guilty beyond a reasonable doubt.

Faith looked again at Molly Jupiter. The woman responded to Faith's gaze almost as she had at the beginning of the trial. But this time as she met Faith's eyes, she seemed to mouth the word "meow" before she turned away.

🐈 🐈 🐈

"Remarkable," Michael said as he refilled Faith's wine glass. "But you probably imagined it."

They were sitting on Michael's deck. The late afternoon sun was obscured by smog, but the worst of the heat wave had passed.

"Of course. That's what I thought, too. Still, I had a sense of a meeting of the minds. As if she knew what I had done, that I had assumed a cat's identity, and knew at the same time that I wasn't a criminal. I believed that she was a victim of mistaken identity. And I couldn't believe the woman was a murderer."

"Oh, Faith! So you persuaded the others to agree?"

Faith shook her head. "No need. We elected a forewoman—Jane—and she suggested a preliminary vote. Twelve not guilties. We were back with the verdict in under an hour."

Michael pushed the half-empty bottle of chardonnay into the ice bucket with a practiced hand.

"Was that really doing your civic duty?" he asked. "I thought you were supposed to discuss the evidence."

"I suppose we decided that our civic duty didn't include wasting the court's time when our collective mind was made up. Anyway, that wasn't the truly remarkable thing."

Michael waited as Faith took a sip of her wine, drawing out the moment.

"Well?" he prompted.

"The remarkable thing was that as Jane and I rode down the escalator, she told me that Molly Jupiter had looked at her and mouthed 'meow.' And Jane remembered a time that the refrigerator door hadn't shut off the light because of a problem with the switch. It was her parents' refrigerator, a very long time ago, which was why she hadn't remembered sooner. Her mother discovered the cat playing with this little plastic switch that came from the refrigerator door."

"And 'meow' reminded her."

"Yes. And then Walter, who was right behind Jane, said that Molly Jupiter had looked at him and mouthed 'meow' just as he was thinking she was probably guilty. He realized that the scratch on her arm could have been a cat scratch—he said it looked more like a cat scratch than a human scratch."

"I suppose you're going to tell me nine more stories proving each juror was swayed by Molly Jupiter's eyes, and that each one took 'meow' personally."

"No. I was afraid to ask because I couldn't tell mine."

"She may not be the World's Greatest Psychic, but she has to be the World's Greatest Hypnotist."

"Possibly."

"Did it occur to you that the two women were in it together?"

"Of course it did." Faith glared at Michael, then took another sip of wine. "But I wasn't about to make that hypothetical case for the other jurors. It was up to the prosecution to prove guilt beyond a reasonable doubt, and they didn't do it."

"And you were really afraid that someone, somehow, would expose you. You wanted to end the charade, and not guilty was the easiest way to do it."

"I don't know. I rather liked being Elizabeth." Faith looked at the cat, who was curled up on the chaise a few feet away.

"Good. That means you can vote twice in November," Michael said.

Elizabeth opened her eyes, her deep blue, protruding eyes, and met Faith's gaze.

"No. I got away with it once, and I'm not doing it again." Faith shivered as she said the words. "Besides, if the district attorney comes up with new evidence, I may have to confess my misdeed. I get fifteen minutes of fame and the prosecutors get a second shot at conviction. My cat impersonation may turn out to have been a good idea after all."

Elizabeth yawned, nodded in forgiveness, and went back to sleep.

The End

The Memory Pool

Tracy Knight

My grandfather's law office was cavernous and musty-smelling, with formidable cobwebs suspended from the upper corners. He and his two best friends were seated around a card table in the middle of the large waiting room while I huddled on the floor against a wall, my arms and legs as crossed and closed as my attitude.

My grandfather, Farley Bellson, leaned back in his chair and stuck his hands down the front of his pants. Then he said to his Gang of Two, "Gentlemen, it's time for today's memory pool."

As I watched him and his two decrepit cronies nodding emptily to one another as they swallowed the dregs of their after-lunch coffee, my late adolescent body filled again with the harsh restlessness that I had felt often in recent days. It had been only three weeks since I'd arrived in Lamoine—"to show some responsibility, learn to care for someone other than yourself, and help out your family," to quote my mother—but if there was anything to be learned here in the torpid drone of my grandfather's world, it wasn't conspicuous. He didn't seem to have any clients (which didn't surprise me, given his age of eighty-seven and the Alzheimer's), and so we spent four hours a day sitting alone in his office, pretending to be comfortable around each other, staring at a telephone that rang only when it was a wrong number. The highlight of his daily existence was when his two best friends dropped in and ate lunch with him, after which they played their foolish game.

Grandpa cleared his throat as if he were preparing to give a campaign speech and continued, "Let me remind you of the rules of our memory pool, gentlemen."

He turned over the envelope he held and studied his own scrawled handwriting on the back. Obviously he'd completely forgotten what was written there. "We meet once a day, at noon," he read, "and after lunch, we each see a photo that we must remember. The photo is sealed in this envelope and secured in the possession of my recently arrived grandson, uh . . ."

"Ellery," I muttered from my place in the shadows.

"Ellery. The most trustworthy twelve-year-old boy a man could hope to have as a grandson—"

"I'm nineteen," I reminded him for the thirtieth time.

"Of course. Anyway, gentlemen, when we meet the subsequent day, we each must announce what picture we remember being sealed in the envelope. The first person to utter the correct answer is treated to lunch the next day by the other two. Everybody clear on that?"

The other two old men nodded like jostled mannequins.

"Okay, now it's time for today's challenge. Son," he said, turning to me, obviously having forgotten my name again, "please count to three."

Maintaining a dour expression I knew he didn't see, I quickly and flatly said, "One-two-three."

Larry Beckwith nearly screamed, "Sammy Davis Jr.! Right? I saw him on the *Dean Martin Show* last night. Or a few years ago. Sometime." Beckwith was an eighty-year-old bachelor, a retired pastor. He was as round as Curly Howard and even sported a haircut identical to the Stooge's. But Curly, unlike Beckwith, had possessed the sense to shuffle off his mortal coil before his appearance went from amusing to pitiful.

Nodding, Morris Tittweiler, a widower and retired veterinarian who lived two houses down the block from my grandfather's, said, "Sammy Davis. Yes. He's right. I always enjoyed the noises he made."

"They call it singing," I said under my breath. I remembered Morris Tittweiler's name easily because of his initials: M.T. Empty. And he was. Of the three, he was most deeply submerged in Alzheimer's Lake, rarely surfacing for a breath of reality.

Tittweiler proudly wiped a hand across his skeletal, liver-spotted face

as if he'd just correctly answered a Final Jeopardy question. Then he suddenly shot straight up in his chair. "One thing, Farley."

"Yes?"

"Why are we doing this? I, uh . . ."

"You forgot," my grandfather said, raising an index finger into the air.
"That's the entire point, Morris. Each of us is showing compelling evidence of encroaching senility, Alzheimer's. Having our little memory pool
every day permits us to exercise what memory we have and to commis-
erate with one another during our declining days. Interpersonal food for
the soul. Remember?"

"Oh, yeah." A vacant smile. He had no clue.

Grandfather opened the envelope and pulled out a rumpled newspaper photo of Richard Nixon. "Well, your answers were incorrect," he
said, "but at least *you* answered. I, on the other hand, had no notion
whose picture was in the envelope. It appears the decay of our memories
is continuing apace. Hmm. I guess this means I lose. I'll bring lunch for
the three of us tomorrow. I must remember to make a note of it." He
smiled, but the irony was lost on his two friends.

The office's front door opened, and in strolled the city police chief,
Bill Grandling. He wrenched his middle-aged simian face into the sem-
blance of a smile and said, "Good afternoon, gents. How are things going
today?" Then he shot me a suspicious glare that only I saw.

"Why, we're fine, Chief," my grandfather said. "Will you join us for
coffee? We'll give you the honor of selecting our target picture for tomorrow's memory pool."

Grandling dragged a chair from the perimeter of the waiting room
and sat. "You guys are still having your pool every day, huh? Sure, I'd be
happy to help out." He began thumbing through a tattered copy of the
National Enquirer in search of a photo. "By the way, you fellas locking your
doors these days?" he asked absently as he continued turning pages.

The three men laughed in unison.

"Of course not, Chief," my grandfather said. "This is Lamoine,
remember?"

Chief Grandling said, "Well, you might want to consider it. There's
been a bunch of break-ins around the county recently and—this should
be of special interest to you, Farley—in three cases people's pet cats have
been stolen. I'm starting to wonder whether the thieves are selling them
to medical labs or something terrible like that. You'd better be more careful, all of you."

"How horrible," my grandfather said. He gestured in my direction. "Will you go find Lucy for me, uh . . . ?"

"Ellery," I said. I stood up and shambled into my grandfather's private office.

I quickly scanned the pictures that hung on the walls. Seeing my grandparents as a young couple made me vow to myself that I'd never end up like my grandfather, an all-but-retired attorney who had never lived anywhere but this tiny nowhere town. I wouldn't be like him, sitting around waiting to die with nothing useful to contribute or accomplish. My life was going to mean something right up until the very end.

Lucy was asleep on my grandfather's plush desk chair. She was a sleek black cat with small splashes of white: a vest, a band at the tip of her tail, and a lopsided spot on her chin that made her look like she was sneering. I related to that.

I picked up Lucy—who immediately uttered a complaining yowl—and carried her out to my grandfather. When I dropped her in his lap, he smiled.

"I'll have Lucy sing a tune for you gents before you leave." With that declaration, he hugged Lucy close to him, closing his eyes and tipping his head to one side as he carefully listened to her thunderous purrs.

He nodded, then quickly but delicately squeezed her.

She emitted a sound much more articulated than a simple meow: two syllables, something like "Ngeeee-rowwwl!"

All four men laughed uproariously. I remained silent, but confessed to myself that if this were being done in my dorm room with a couple of buddies, it'd be hilarious. Here, with these four, it was just sad. Sad and stupid.

"It's magically harmonic, don't you think?" my grandfather said.

Two squeezes. Sure enough, Lucy released two more garbled verbalizations.

"That last one was a B-flat if I'm not mistaken," my grandfather said with a grin. He petted Lucy gently on her head and kissed her cheek. "What a good girl you are," he whispered. "You can talk and you can sing. What a talented, sweet girl you are."

Maintaining his monkey grin, Chief Grandling stood up, licked the envelope flap and handed the sealed envelope to my grandfather. "Okay, now that you've all seen it, here's your answer for the next memory pool," he said, hitching up his pants for good measure. "You fellas take care of yourselves. And remember what I said about locking your doors."

As soon as the police chief departed, my grandfather turned to me and said, "Keep this safe and secure for us, won't you, son?"

I walked to the table and, as my grandfather handed the envelope to me, I noticed the skin on his hands, how paper-thin and transparent it was. As thin and transparent as his life appeared to my nineteen-year-old all-seeing, all-knowing eyes.

I nodded impatiently. I was already bored to death with this town and the grandfather I'd visited exactly twice before being forced to move here. "I'm going out," I said, folding up the envelope and stuffing it into my back pocket.

I left the office, as I did every day at this time. A daily walk was necessary just to keep a bridle on my sanity. It was still hard to believe that I was being held hostage in Lamoine, a town of three thousand, when only a few months ago I'd been cavorting with my friends at the University of Wisconsin in Madison.

I'm not sure when I crossed the line with my parents. Maybe it was the conviction for Driving While Intoxicated when I was apprehended navigating my VW bug across a frozen pond while wearing no pants; maybe it was the fact that I was on academic probation because I missed half of my classes and slept through the other half, most likely it was the episode in which I and three other neo-hippies held a sit-down strike in the University Union to protest the high price of textbooks, then tied up the campus policeman who had been summoned to remove us.

Regardless, my parents informed me that neither their emotional nor financial support would be forthcoming for the time being. My solitary option was to live with my grandfather for a semester, to tend to him in his failing health and hopefully learn a bit of responsibility in the process. Only then would my return to school be considered.

The whole thing stank.

Trudging around the town square, I did my best to divert my attention from self-pity by examining all the old buildings encircling the square and the towering trees whose autumn leaves were only beginning to turn. I proudly basked in the double-takes of passers-by when my long stringy ponytail or the small tattoo of a dove on my Adam's apple caught their attention.

Within a half-hour, however, I tired of my walk. As I did every day. I returned to my grandfather's office.

"Who's there?" he said, sitting up in his chair and looking me straight in the eyes.

"Ellery."

"Who?"

"Ellery. Your grandson. Your daughter Ann's son."

"Of course," he said, rubbing his eyes. Undoubtedly as soon as I'd left the office they'd all fallen asleep. As they did every day.

Sure enough, Larry Beckwith and Morris Tittweiler were still sitting at the card table, heads bowed backward, mouths open, ragged snores erupting like spews from tiny volcanoes.

But something was wrong. Several chairs in the waiting room had been tipped over.

I quickly walked into my grandfather's private office. Files full of papers were scattered across the floor and all the framed photographs had disappeared from the wall.

Then I realized there was no sign of Lucy.

Returning to the waiting room, I said to my grandfather, "Who's been here?"

"What do you mean?"

"Someone was here. All the pictures in your office are gone. Lucy's gone, too."

"Lucy?" His eyes widened and he barreled into his office as he called his cat's name over and over.

By then, Larry and Morris had been restored to vague sentience, looking befuddled as always.

My grandfather said, "Did you two see anybody come in here? There's been a burglary and, more importantly, a kidnapping. Lucy is gone!"

The two old men exchanged bewildered glances, then shrugged in unison.

Soon, Morris and Larry arose from the card table like frazzled robots and mutely exited the office, leaving my grandfather and me standing there staring at each other.

His eyes were moist, and that got my attention because the rest of him looked so dry and withered. In fact, his eyes reminded me of the beagle I had as a child; it used to look at me with that same pleading expression once in a while.

He stood silently for a few moments, just like that, frozen. Then he furrowed his brow. "Who are you again?"

"Ellery Marshall. Your grandson."

"Hmm. And who am I?"

Sighing, I said, "You're just an old man who's lost his cat."

A single tear dripped down his wrinkled cheek.

🐈 🐈 🐈

"Why isn't he talking?" Police Chief Grandling asked.

We were in my grandfather's living room, steeped in dusk's lengthening shadows. Even though I'd called the police department early in the afternoon, the Chief had only now arrived. For all his talk about area cats being stolen, he apparently didn't consider my call an emergency. And by the time he arrived, my grandfather had fallen into silence.

"He just gets like this," I said. "Usually when it's getting dark. He becomes more confused and, a couple of times, it's like he's forgotten how to talk. Like now."

Chief Grandling patted my grandfather's hand. "It'll be okay, Farley. I'll keep looking for your cat."

My grandfather smiled and nodded, feigning awareness of what was going on.

"And you," the Chief said to me, narrowing his eyes to pinpoints, "you need to be taking better care of your grandpa."

My face instantly swelled with heat. That moment I wanted to empty my gut of the frustration and anger that filled it. Instead, I gritted my teeth and nodded amiably.

I walked him to the front door. Before leaving, Chief Grandling said, "This grandfather of yours has done more for this little town than anyone I know. He donated a big piece of property to the county, and they named the city park after him. He's helped more families than I can imagine who were down on their luck, lost their houses or jobs. And he treats everyone he meets with dignity and respect. He's one in a million and we're lucky he lives here. *You're* lucky he's your granddad. See what you can learn from him."

Even as I was inwardly trembling with rage at the condescending way the police chief treated me, I was equally concerned about my parents' reaction to the news. Finding out that I had allowed my grandfather's pet cat and family pictures to be stolen wouldn't exactly speak to my responsibility and competence as a caregiver.

But I still had the opportunity to show them I could handle myself like a grown man. I could take care of my grandfather. And I could take care of myself.

A half-hour later, my grandfather slowly emerged from his fog of confusion and I persuaded him to take a walk with me.

"It'll be good for you to get some fresh air," I said. "And we can go visit your friends. Maybe they'll remember something now." It was a slim

chance, but worth a try, even though there could be nothing more difficult than solving a mystery when all the witnesses had memories like
weeping colanders.

🐈 🐈 🐈

The streetlights were flickering to life and a cool breeze was blowing.
Several times my grandfather abruptly stopped in his tracks, stood at
attention and inhaled deeply, beaming like a fool, as if the wind itself had
become a sudden joy.

We walked to Larry Beckwith's, about three blocks away. When we
knocked on Beckwith's door, no one answered, even though all the lights
in the house were on.

"Sometimes he doesn't hear so well," my grandfather said. "Let me
take a peek. He won't mind."

We stepped to one side of the house and peered through a curtainless
window.

I could barely contain myself. I wanted to shout with joy, proclaim
my victory.

In the den of his home, Larry Beckwith sat in a recliner. On the coffee table in front of him sat the framed photos of my grandparents,
arranged in a perfect semi-circle. He examined them one by one, all the
time petting Lucy, who sat in his lap.

"There's Lucy!" I said. "And all your pictures! It was him!"

I moved to rap on the window but my grandfather reached up and
caught my arm so quickly it startled me. He pressed a finger to his lips
and nodded.

"We've got to confront him," I whispered.

"Very well," he responded without a hint of enthusiasm.

The front door was unlocked and we walked in. My grandfather told
me to stay put while he went in and talked to Beckwith.

As I waited, I could almost picture my parents congratulating me on
helping my grandfather to so quickly retrieve his lost cat and photos. I'd
be welcomed back at my parents' with open arms and returned to the
U of W before I knew it.

When he emerged from Beckwith's den, he said simply, "Let's go."

"Wait a minute. What about the pictures? What about Lucy?"

My grandfather sighed deeply. "Larry says they're his."

"What do you mean? That's nuts!"

He shrugged.

"I'm calling the police," I said, hoping Beckwith would hear me. "I'm not going to let you just give away your stuff I like this. We're getting it back!"

He put his arm on my shoulder and guided me out of the house.

We were silent most of the way home and, right before we entered my grandfather's house, he said, "Okay, son. If you absolutely insist, we'll do something about this dilemma. I'll make you a deal. Don't call the police. We'll resolve this in another forum."

"What's that?"

"Small claims court."

"Okay . . . but I still think you're being silly for not just walking in there and taking back your stuff. You have a right to it! I don't care if it was your friend who stole everything. It's your property!"

"At my last count, there are twenty-three important things in life," my grandfather said. "This ain't one of them."

Because we were in a county that was virtually crime-free, my grandfather was given a court date only two days after filing his complaint, and yet he still bemoaned the fact that he'd suspended the memory pool until the case was decided.

It must have been the last case of the day, since the judge (who looked even older than my grandfather) struck his gavel at exactly 4:30.

Larry Beckwith was there. Next to him was a cardboard box full of my grandfather's pictures and a carrier that contained the insistently meowing Lucy. Beckwith was leaning back in his chair, asleep.

Twice the judge banged his gavel, possibly in an attempt to wake Beckwith. Beckwith released a louder, wetter snore.

"Farley," the judge said, "I understand that you're saying Larry stole these items from you. Am I right?"

There was no reply. My grandfather stared straight ahead. He had that beagle look in his eyes again. They were moist, frightened, lost.

"Farley?" the judge said. "Are you with us, my friend?"

After several uncomfortable moments inched past, I raised my hand like I was in math class. "Sir . . . Your Honor, may I speak for my grandfather?"

The judge furrowed his brow. "You're who? Farley's grandson?"

"Yes."

"Humph." The judge didn't seem impressed with my appearance. Whether it was the nose ring or the Metallica tee-shirt I couldn't say. "Well, I suppose you can," he barked.

In a consciously polite manner I presented what I knew about the memory pool, and about how Larry plainly had stolen my grandfather's belongings after Chief Grandling had left and the others had gone to sleep.

"Do you know this as a fact? Did you see it happen?" the judge asked.

"Well, no, but—"

"You didn't see evidence of a crime yourself or talk to Mr. Beckwith, right? And, heck, you haven't been here that long. You can't even say for sure that the items belong to Farley. Maybe he was just keeping them for Larry."

"But I—"

Suddenly, out of nowhere, Larry Beckwith yelled, "My cat sings!"

The judge smiled and said, patiently, "We'll get to you soon, Larry." He looked again to me and said, less patiently, "Son, I'm going to need some testimony from your grandfather. I don't see any way around it. You're not a part in this case. You have no standing."

"Okay," I said. Then, thanks to Beckwith's inappropriate comment, a brilliant idea struck me. "Your Honor, my grandfather isn't able to speak right now, but I still think I can get answers from him. Can I do that?"

"What do you need?"

I pointed in Larry Beckwith's general direction. "I need the cat."

Astonishing me, the judge shrugged. "Well, sure, give him the cat, Larry."

Beckwith looked shocked, but he let me open the carrier and remove Lucy, who meowed even louder now, as if I were pulling out her claws one by one.

I laid Lucy in my grandfather's lap and she fell momentarily quiet.

Operating on pure instinct, my grandfather smiled vacantly while he hugged Lucy close to his body.

"What now, son?" the judge asked, coming dangerously close to picking his nose.

"Watch, Your Honor. Grandpa, listen to me. I want you to use Lucy to answer me. Do you understand?"

He looked me in the eyes and I thought I saw one corner of his mouth lift in an effort toward a smile.

"Once means 'yes,' and twice means 'no.' Understand?"

Without missing a beat, my grandfather tipped his head to one side to listen to Lucy's purring, then squeezed her quickly.

"Ngeeee-rowwwl!" Lucy said.

"B-flat!" Larry Beckwith shouted.

The judge banged his gavel. "Order!"

"That's a yes," I said to the judge. "And what's a no?" I asked my grandfather.

"Ngeee-rowwwl. Ngeee-rowwwl," sang Lucy.

"Proceed," said the judge.

Amazing. Here I was, a raging mutant who looked like he'd just stomped away from a fistfight at a grunge concert, and the judge was actually cooperating with me. More than that, he seemed to be enjoying the show.

I was the hip, gifted city kid showing the supposedly wise minds of Lamoine a thing or two about problem solving.

I asked my grandfather a series of questions. When I showed him a photo of himself and my grandmother, he squeezed Lucy once to indicate that it was him in the picture. When I asked him whether he'd had Lucy since she was a kitten, he carefully teased a "yes" out of her.

Then I asked him the central question: "Is it true that Larry Beckwith stole all these items from your office, including your pictures and your cat Lucy?"

With grandfather's help, Lucy emitted a B-flat. I slid my hands into my back pockets, mentally preparing my closing argument.

Then, to my complete surprise, Lucy released another "Ngeee-rowwwl."

"Wait a minute," I said. "You just answered that Larry Beckwith *didn't* steal the items."

A single B-flat.

"What?" My brief legal career was crashing down around me. "Grandfather, listen to me. If these items belong to you, and Larry Beckwith now possesses them, you're saying that you gave them to him."

A lone B-flat.

"That decides it then," the judge said. "They were gifts. Case dismissed!"

He pounded his gavel and left the bench.

I stood there, speechless, gazing at my grandfather, who smiled weakly and winked at me.

Larry Beckwith yelled, "My cat! She sings!"

The bailiff removed Lucy from my grandfather's lap and returned her to the carrier.

Larry carried his bounty out of the courtroom with the help of a couple of observers including Morris Tittweiler, who had wandered in late thinking he was at the coffee shop and ordered toast from the court reporter.

Within minutes, only my grandfather and I remained.

I felt my face flushing as I grabbed him by the wrist and led him out of the courtroom. I didn't know what to say.

We had just stepped out onto the courtyard when he turned to me. "I'm proud of you, son."

"What? You're talking."

He smiled. "Indeed I am."

"But I thought—"

"I had planned to stay mute and let things run their course, but I must admit, your thinking to use Lucy as a means of communication was highly creative. And entertaining, to boot."

"Why did you lie?"

He paused momentarily, then said, "I didn't lie. Even if I had, son, there's lies and then there's lies. Maybe lies that don't hurt anyone and help people realize their dreams, become more of who they are, are something different, better than ordinary lies. Wait until it's dark and I'll show you something. You'll see."

After supper, my grandfather and I walked the three blocks to Larry Beckwith's home. At this point, I admitted to myself that I was truly intrigued for the first time since I'd come to Lamoine.

"Right this way," he said, leading me around to the side of the house. He arrived at the window, peeked inside, then motioned for me to take a look.

Larry Beckwith was sitting in a recliner in his den, just like before. On the coffee table before him sat the family pictures from my grandfather's office. On his lap sat Lucy.

"Isn't it nice?" my grandfather said.

"Nice? You gotta be kidding. He's sitting in there with a roomful of stolen goods. *Your* goods!"

Grandfather shook his head. "No. He's sitting in there with memories of life."

"What do you mean?"

"Larry never married. He spent his life serving the community. With his Alzheimer's getting worse all the time, I think he found himself float-ing away. He needed something to anchor him."

"Anchor him?"

The light from Beckwith's den illuminated my grandfather's face. It looked strong and noble, almost young. "That's right, anchor him. He's sitting in there right now, son, thinking how lucky he is to have shared in a family like those in the pictures, and to have the company of a cat who loves him. He's anchored, at least for now. His life means something. He's not alone."

"What about you?"

He patted me on the shoulder. "I'm not alone either."

"But . . ." I began, but then realized I had nothing further to say.

"I must confess something, Ellery. For weeks I'd been thinking of giv-ing Lucy and the pictures to Larry. I could tell how much he wanted them. Needed them. He needed them more than I did, and even more than Morris. As bad off as Morris is these days, he still remembers his wife and family."

"There wasn't a theft. So everyone was in on this whole charade?"

"Larry wasn't. But, yes, everyone else was. It was something we wanted to do for our friend. Chief Grandling returned to the office after you left for your walk that day. He and Morris and I carried everything out to his car and Grandling took all of it to Larry's house while Morris and I messed the place up. We didn't even have to miss our naps."

"So the police didn't need to be involved? There didn't need to be a court case?"

"True. But it's perfect that everything happened as it did. We all par-took of a brief but memorable adventure and, most important of all, the town got to see what a good grandson I have."

I was still puzzled, trying to sort out everything. "So the point was . . . ?"

Still watching his friend Larry Beckwith with Lucy and his make-believe family, my grandfather said, "There are twenty-three important things in life. That, my son," he said, pointing toward his old friend, "is one of them."

🐈 🐈 🐈

My grandfather and his friends never met for another memory pool.

Two days later, Grandpa suffered a stroke, serious enough that he was hospitalized, then transferred to the nursing home.

The last time he spoke, he spoke to me.

We were in his room late one night, after the squeaks of the passing aides' shoes had become tolerably infrequent. I'd taken to bringing books to read to my grandfather when he didn't feel like talking. That night, I was reading aloud from *Venus on the Half-Shell* when I heard a sudden, sharp intake of breath.

I looked up. He had the beagle look in his eyes. He pulled the covers up to his chin.

"What's wrong?"

"Who are you?" he asked, voice trembling.

"I'm Ellery Marshall. I'm your grandson."

"And . . .who am I?"

"You're my grandpa. You're Farley Bellson."

"Ahh." He went silent for a moment, then asked, "My life. Was it a good one?"

"It was the best," I said. "You were the most accomplished and generous man around, the most amazing attorney in the world, you had the most beautiful wife and children a man could ever dream of, and you touched every person you ever met in a way that made their lives larger. There is no one walking the earth who's better than you, Grandpa."

"That's nice to know," he said, closing his eyes.

During sleep that night he had a massive stroke and, this time, he didn't return.

My parents came for the funeral, helped me pack my belongings, and took me home. I'd be re-enrolled at U of W for the next semester. Simple as that.

One day some three weeks later I found a folded-up envelope in the back pocket of the jeans I hadn't washed for months. It was the envelope from my grandpa's last memory pool.

But instead of a picture inside, there was a note.

"You're a good man," it said in my grandfather's hand. "Please don't forget us." Below the message were four signatures: Grandpa's, Larry Beckwith's, Morris Tittweiler's, and Police Chief Grandling's.

There are twenty-three important things in life, I reminded myself, placing the note in my front pocket and patting it there.

Twenty-two to go.

The Lawlessness West of the Pecos

Jan Grape

The judge was on a rampage again, throwing papers and tearing his hair and yelling. The yelling was the worst part. "Get that goldarn silly cat out of my courtroom." Judge Roy Bean had been known to cuss in two languages for two hours and never repeat himself. In all fairness, however, his Southern breeding kept him from turning the air too blue in the presence of a female.

"Your honor, this courtroom, as you call it, is that cat's home," said Sarah Jane Austin. She tried not to sound defiant but was unable to sound meek either. As the defendant currently before Judge Roy Bean, the man also known as "The Law West of the Pecos," Sarah Jane couldn't help it if Judge Bean had convened court in a barn. It certainly wouldn't be her choice. Of course, being in a court of justice wouldn't be her choice either. She'd much rather be on the stagecoach heading to California. She'd always thought she wanted to be married, but now she had many doubts.

Langtry, Texas, wasn't much of a town, but it was Judge Bean's town, and he ran it to the best of his ability. Well, he ran it with the backing of the Texas Rangers, and if he wanted his court convened in a barn, then who was Sarah Jane to argue. Especially when she was being accused of something she had not done.

Judge Bean's authority had begun with the railroad being built. The savage and barren Texas wilderness covered many square miles, but the populated region on the banks of the Rio Grande some twenty miles from the Pecos River had its beginnings as a construction camp or tent city. The saloons, sporting houses, and gambling halls were full of faro men, poker men, monte men, dice men, wheel men, and card sharks of all ilk, mingling with railroad workers, young Easterners trying to make their stake, runaway farm boys, pickpockets, gamblers, and a few foreigners. The dancehalls also nourished a few women who fought and hustled in the dives. The place was ripe for thievery, robbery, fights, duels, and plain old murder. Trouble swarmed like blue-tail flies buzzing an aggravated cow. The region was often called "Hell on Wheels" by right-thinking folks.

Several citizens of Langtry were law-abiding. Ranchers, cattlemen, soldiers, railroad workers, salesmen, and preachers—the general makeup of most small Texas towns, good people who would do anything for you. But the ruffians were the ones who made the loudest noise and caused trouble. They were the ones who gave Judge Bean his opportunity to be "The Law West of the Pecos."

Since the nearest hall of justice was in Fort Stockton, two hundred miles away, the governor sent a troop of Rangers hoping to keep problems to a minimum along the migratory towns until the railroad was completed. Roy Bean, saloon owner and profiteer, the nearest thing to an honest man in those early days, had been appointed a justice of the peace by the commissioner's court on the recommendation of Captain Oglesby and General King.

Judge Bean didn't hear Sarah Jane's remarks regarding the cat, or if he did, he was not about to admit it. All the judge cared about was having this trial over with, sentencing this bar-room floozie so he could finish off the new bottle of fine Kentucky whiskey a lady mule skinner had left for him just this morning.

A lady mule skinner. If that didn't gall your gullet then nothing would, thought Judge Bean. A dadgum female trying to drive a supply wagon out here in the desert, where some of the wildest men who ever rode worked and lived. Woman must be crazy.

Now where did that stupid cat go? Bean drew his revolver and began searching for the cat. "Here, kitty. Here, kitty."

"Judge Bean," Sarah Jane said. "Judge Bean?"

The judge finally looked at Sarah Jane. "What is it, child?" He looked down at the gun in his hand. "Awww. I ain't going shoot the cat, just gonna scare her a little."

He put the gun away, sat back down and focused squinty eyes at Sarah Jane. "Don't you realize you're on trial for horse thievery here? How dare you keep interrupting this court."

Sarah Jane knew she had to pacify the man or there was no telling what he'd do. "I'm terribly sorry Your Honor, sir. But the cat you are looking for, Tinta, lives here in this barn. I wouldn't be surprised to discover she's recently had kittens. She's only upset because she's not used to people being in her barn disturbing her babies."

"*Tinta*? Means 'ink' in Spanish, don't it?" the judge asked, ignoring the rest of the girl's explanation.

"Yes sir. Ink or inky. I named her that for obvious reasons—she's black as midnight."

"Well, she's going to be one dead cat if she doesn't quit squalling."

"Maybe Your Honor can finish this trial up over at the Jersey Lilly, and Tinta can go back to her babies." Sarah Jane patted her blonde hair back into place and smoothed her blue gingham dress. She was eighteen years old and too innocent looking for this dry, dusty country.

"Look, young lady. Mr. Conrad says you stole his horse from this here barn. Your attorney sent word that I needed to ass—er—tain," he stumbled over the long word. "Ascertain that you'd been out here before. Like if you knew your way around and such."

"Well, Judge. You know I've been inside here many times. I've worked in here, cleaning stalls, feeding the animals because I'm engaged to be married to Mr. Conrad."

"Which doesn't prove a single thing in my book," a contralto voice spoke up from the doorway.

Judge Bean looked up and blinked as the bright morning sun suddenly streamed in, nearly blinding him. When he could focus again, he saw a vision of loveliness. She had dark hair and was wearing a high-fashion dress of green brocade and a hat with two white doves on one side. "It can't be. Can it? Miss Langtry? Darling Lily, I knew you'd come one day. . . ."

"Judge Bean, I'm not Lily Langtry. I'm Dallas Armstrong, and I represent Miss Austin. Is her accuser in the courtroom?"

"Miss Armstrong. Ahem, uh . . . I thought you were a drover—a mule skinner. I had no idea you were a lawyer, too." Judge Bean kept looking at her. She looked so much like the picture he had hanging on the wall of the Jersey Lily. His own true love, the British actress, Miss Lily Langtry.

"I am, but I've also read for the law—although I've not taken the bar examination."

Judge Bean banged the gavel. "Court's taking a ten minute recess." He uncorked a bottle of whiskey and poured a hefty slug in his cup. "And what are you doing in Langtry?"

"I'm employed by Mr. Allen Pinkerton."

Roy Bean nearly choked on the bourbon. "The detective agency?"

"Yes. While I was vacationing in San Antonio I heard of Miss Austin's plight. Her mother asked if I'd help." She smiled sweetly at Judge Bean. "And where is her accuser?"

"Mr. Conrad had business elsewhere this morning," said the judge.

"In that case, may we have a few hours? I need to confer with my client and have time to verify her story."

"All right. Court's dismissed until tomorrow morning." The judge banged on the makeshift table and jumped up. He was only too happy to bring matters to a close for the day. He wanted to finish his bottle of whiskey and try to figure out how Miss Lily Langtry had slipped into town disguised as a mule skinner and lawyer. Of course, she is an actress, he thought, as he walked outside, got on his old dun horse, Bayo, and rambled toward town.

Sarah Jane called to the cat, "Tinta. You can come in now. That nasty man has left." The cat jumped into the young woman's arms and began purring. "Thank you, Miss Armstrong." Sarah Jane breathed into the cat's fur. "You and Tinta may have saved my life. If Tinta hadn't upset the judge in the first place, I'm sure he would have found me guilty and hung me right here on the spot."

"Well, he doesn't have the authority to do such a thing. All he can do is arraign you."

"What does 'arraign' mean?"

"It just says you will be bound over for a trial. Most likely one of the Texas Rangers would take you to Del Rio."

Sarah Jane began crying.

"Oh, merciful heavens. Don't do that. There's nothing to cry about. I don't think either the judge or Mr. Conrad thinks you're guilty, so we've just got to prove you're not." Dallas looked at the girl closely. "You're not, are you?"

"Not what?"

"Not guilty."

"Oh gosh. No. Mr. Conrad is only mad because I wouldn't go to the big dance with him over to the King Ranch."

"You mean Mr. Conrad is just a frustrated beau?" The young girl nodded. "Why did you refuse to go to the dance with him?"

"Because he can't dance. Who wants to go to the dance with some old cowboy who can't even dance?"

"Who indeed," said Dallas. It must be the heat down here, she thought. They're all addled by the hot sun. The girl's remarks made no sense at all.

"Come on," Dallas told Sarah Jane. "Let's go to my camp. I need to figure out a plan of action."

"Okay. Can I bring Tinta with me?"

Dallas looked at the black cat snoozing peacefully in the girl's arms. "I thought she had babies to take care of."

The girl laughed. "No. They haven't been born yet, but I was hoping to get Judge Bean's mind off of shooting her." The cat had her own agenda however; she jumped down, scrambled up a pole, and jumped to the floor of the loft.

"Pretty good. You're a quick-witted young lady."

Sarah Jane smiled at the compliment and started to climb into the back of Dallas's wagon, but Dallas told the girl to sit up front with her. "You'll get bounced around too much back there."

"Tell me what you're doing out here in this God-forsaken country. Where do you live, by the way?" Dallas clucked her tongue and the mules started walking slowly in the direction of Langtry.

"I'm boarding at Mrs. Shaw's right now. After Mr. Conrad fired me, I rented a room with her and got a job at the general store. I plan to apply for the schoolteacher's job in the fall."

"What did you do for Mr. Conrad?"

"Kept his books."

"Business or household?"

"Both. Say, did my mother hire you to bring me home?"

"Not exactly." Dallas looked at the girl. "She just wanted me to be sure you were okay. She'd had word you were in trouble out here—all on your own and. . . ."

"Well, you can just stop this wagon and let me out. . . ."

"But that's no solution."

"You let me out right now. Stop."

Dallas stopped the wagon and Sarah Jane jumped down. "I thank you for the few extra hours of freedom. But I'm perfectly capable of taking care of myself, and I don't need help from you or my mother." The girl took off walking.

Dallas followed along for about a mile and kept trying to persuade the girl to get back into the wagon but finally gave up when Langtry appeared in the distance. Dallas turned the mules in the direction of her campsite, but she watched until Sarah Jane had reached the outskirts of town.

Wonder what the full story is there. Why is this pretty girl out here in this wild territory with all these hard-nosed ruffians? Mrs. Austin had not been very forthcoming when she hired Dallas.

❧ ❧ ❧

"Miss Armstrong?" the slender, pale woman had said. "I've received word my daughter is in serious trouble. She's going to be tried for stealing a horse from her future husband."

Dallas could have corrected Mrs. Austin by saying she was a Mrs. instead of a Miss, but didn't want to explain how she actually was a widow. "Has the man accused her?"

"Not only that—it's possible she could be found guilty."

Mrs. Austin had contacted the Pinkerton agency and had been given Dallas Armstrong's name and informed that Agent Armstrong would call on her in due time. When Dallas received the telegram from the agency, she had gone directly to the Austins' home.

Dallas had made arrangements to leave immediately for Langtry, and Mrs. Austin didn't explain how her daughter had managed to get herself to the area in the first place other than the mention of marriage plans.

"See if you can bring her back," Mrs. Austin had pleaded. "I would like to have her home again. Back among civilized people instead of those barbarians where she is now."

"I'll ask her, but if she's as headstrong as you've said, that will be all I can do. She is a grown woman after all. I won't force her to come back here."

❧ ❧ ❧

Dallas packed her wagon, hitched her horse Vinegar to the back, and found herself several miles down the trail when the sun had set. Some people actually liked this wilderness, but Dallas didn't think she could ever feel completely comfortable here.

The canyons *were* beautiful, though, she thought, gouged out by the Rio Grande and the Pecos, but the endless miles of nothing gave out such a sense of desolation. That and the constant wind blowing and blowing, sometimes gently but more often shrieking and screaming out of the arroyos and canyons.

The wild animals—coyotes, foxes, bobcats, and mountain lions—didn't bother Dallas too much. They stayed away from people the majority of the time. Even the rattlesnakes and the lizards didn't bother her much. She usually left them alone unless a snake got too close—Dallas was a pretty good shot with her old long-barrel .38 Colt—but the prickly pear cactus and other harmless-looking bushes with hidden spines and thorns drove her crazy. She hated stepping or sitting on something that looked so innocent and getting stuck in unmentionable places.

Dallas had to admit March was a nice time of the year. Spring brought color to the desert: even the prickly pear had wonderful yellow blossoms, and the yucca sent up tall spikes that turned into pillows of white bell-shaped flowers. An occasional scarlet patch of some minor little cactus pincushion showed up on a hillside along with the greenery, softening the landscape somewhat. You did have to keep alert, however, because danger often lurked around the corner of this boulder or that mesquite tree.

Dallas noticed the dust the two horses stirred up long before the riders appeared. She poked her campfire and set the coffee pot back on the flame. Earlier, she had changed into her riding clothes—pants, shirt, and jacket—packing away her dress and fancy hat. She double-checked the Colt before placing it in the holster under her jacket. She finished eating her rabbit stew and was ready for the coffee when the men arrived. She liked the fact they stopped a little distance back and both took off their hats.

"Miz Armstrong," the older man said. "I'm Ira Conrad and this is my son, Lucas. May we join you for coffee?"

"I've only got one extra cup, so if you're packing a cup or can share, you're welcome to what's left in the pot. Have you eaten? It's rabbit stew."

The men dismounted, and both pulled a cup out of their bedrolls. "We have eaten, thank you." Both men were lean and tall. The older man had gray hair and a gray and black moustache.

Dallas poured the coffee and watched as the men settled down. She waited for them to begin.

"Miz Armstrong," said Lucas, the younger man. He was more attractive than his father, with startling blue eyes and light brown hair. "I'm sorry to have troubled you to come all this way. Sarah Jane is a very head-strong young woman, and sometimes she needs a firm hand. When that doesn't work, I have to resort to drastic measures."

"Such as accusing her of stealing a horse?"

"That's about it."

"But that's a bit harsh, and the accusation could get her hung."

"Not in Roy Bean's court. He's only a justice of the peace. He has no authority to hang anyone," said Ira.

"We all know that, but people in San Antonio don't know it," said Dallas. "The word got to Sarah Jane's mother, and naturally she became quite upset to think her daughter was in imminent danger."

"But she never was," said Lucas. "It was only to scare her a little."

"Of course, but you understand Mrs. Austin's perception." Dallas wondered what these two really wanted. Everything they were saying could just as easily have been said tomorrow in town.

"I have instructed Sarah Jane to write a note to her mother explaining how it was all a misunderstanding. I hope you will take that letter back to Mrs. Austin when you leave tomorrow." Lucas held an envelope out to Dallas. "You are leaving tomorrow, I take it?"

Dallas didn't answer, but he obviously took her silence for an affirmative answer.

"I will pay for your time, of course, and also for your expenses in coming all the way out here. It was simply my fault. Since Sarah Jane and I are to be married, I shall have to find other ways to persuade her—to counteract her bullheadedness." Both men stood.

Dallas stood also, took the envelope he handed her, glanced at it, and placed it in her jacket pocket.

"We are looking forward to a wedding in June," said Ira. "Sarah Jane has high hopes that her mother will be able to travel by then." The older man had not said too much, obviously preferring to let his son state his case.

"Mrs. Austin's health seemed poorly, but perhaps she will be better by June," Dallas said.

"We do thank you for the coffee," Ira said. "Shall I give you payment in paper or in gold coins?"

Ah, thought Dallas. Papa is the one controlling the purse strings. "I would not take money from you, Mr. Conrad. Mrs. Austin has already paid my fee, and I shall be happy to take Sarah Jane's letter to her mother for no charge. It's part of the job I was hired for."

"And what exactly were you hired for, Mrs. Armstrong?" asked Lucas as he put his hat back on his head.

"Normally that information is strictly confidential between my client and myself, but since you are part of the family, as it were . . . I was hired to be sure Miss Austin received a fair trial and to escort her back to San Antonio if she wished to go. But she's already made it clear she wants to stay here, so my job is finished."

"And you'll be leaving tomorrow morning?" Ira said, mounting his horse.

"As soon as things are clear with Judge Bean that Miss Armstrong won't be tried for horse thieving." Dallas forced a small smile and wondered why they seemed so anxious that she leave. "You will talk to Judge Bean first thing tomorrow?"

"Yes indeed," said both men in unison. They tipped their hats and rode back towards town.

"What was that all about?" Dallas wondered aloud to Vinegar. He huffed air through his nostrils and shook his head as if he understood. "I never saw two men so antsy about me staying someplace. We might just have to hang around a bit to see why."

The next morning Dallas rode Vinegar into Langtry. When she reached Judge Bean's saloon, she almost fell off her mount as a mountain lion let out an eerie sound. That's when she noticed all the cages in front of the Jersey Lily. Each had an animal in it: a coyote, a fox, a mountain lion, and some type of black cat that must be a panther. She got off Vinegar and tied him to the hitching rail. A large bear chained to a pole came shuffling around the side of the building just as she stepped onto the porch. She let out a soft scream until she realized he couldn't reach her. "He must be tame," she whispered.

A horrid smell reached her nostrils as she neared the door, and she stopped immediately.

Smells like someone died in there, she thought. She stood in the doorway and peered inside, looking down a long hallway, unsure of what she'd find. On her right was a big room, and as her eyes adjusted to the dimness she saw a pool table with a young man laid out on it. "My stars and nightgown," she said. "Somebody did die."

But the young man moved and rolled over, opening one eye as he did so. "And just who are you, pretty darlin'?"

"That there is Miz Armstrong, son." Judge Bean walked out of a room on the left of the hall and out onto the porch. "She's a mule skinner and a lawyer and not someone you want to even think about tangling with."

"I thought from the smell he had died," said Dallas. Then she realized this establishment obviously was also Roy Bean's home. "I am sorry; I don't mean to sound rude."

"No, ma'am, you're quite right. The odor coming from a drunk often smells like death and my Sam usually smells like a cantina this time of day."

Judge Bean's huge stomach poked through his vest, showing his red longjohns. His shirt-tail hung out in back, and his hair and beard looked as if they'd not been cleaned nor combed in days. The man didn't smell like a lilac himself, but Dallas tried not to show her shock. He certainly had not looked so unkempt yesterday. An evening of drinking didn't set well on him.

She asked if the Conrads had spoken to him about dropping the charges against her client.

"Yes. They did. She's free as a bird."

"Judge Bean, you and I both know that young lady didn't steal a horse. What do you think is going on there?"

"Miz Armstrong, I wouldn't dwell on it too much. The Conrads are almost as rich and powerful as the King family. You don't want to cross 'em."

A young boy came running up, interrupting, "Señor Judge, Señor Judge!"

"What is it, Manuel?"

"They found a woman's body out in Meyers Canyon," said the boy.

"Do they know who it is?" the judge and Dallas asked at the same time.

"Somebody said it was that lady that works at the General Store."

Dallas gasped and turned away quickly as she felt nausea rise up.

"Oh migo . . . uh, er . . . uh, my good gosh," stammered the judge. "Let me get the buckboard."

"May I go with you?" Dallas asked. "I must know if it is Sarah Jane."

🦙 🦙 🦙

When they arrived at the canyon, they found that the railroad men had brought up the young woman's body and wrapped her in a saddle blanket. Judge Bean pulled the blanket back and took a quick look. "It's Sarah Jane Austin all right."

"Did anyone see anybody around?" asked Dallas.

The railroad workers shook their heads.

One of the men stepped forward and removed his sombrero. "Nothin', Judge. We were the onliest ones out here this mornin' I think."

The second man spoke up. "I just saw that piece of blue material flappin' in the breeze, and something told me we needed to look closer. I climbed down and could see it was a body."

"So you men got her out?" asked Dallas. "Was she shot?"

"I couldn't see no bullet hole," said the second man. "Back of her head is smashed like a gourd."

"And have either of you men ever seen Miss Austin before?"

The first man spoke up. "I knowed she worked at the general store, but I didn't really know her."

"This here is Ramon Rodriguiz," said Judge Bean. "He's a good man. And over there is his brother-in-law Pedro. Both are hard workers and honest men."

"You 'cusing me?" asked Ramon. "I didn't do nothin'."

"No, no," said Dallas. "I'm just wondering what happened."

"Well, we best get her loaded into the wagon and back into town," said the judge.

In a few minutes the men had Sarah Jane's body loaded into the wagon, and they started their three-mile journey back into Langtry.

Once in town the men took Sarah Jane's body to Mrs. Shaw's house. Normally Judge Bean, also the coroner, checked the bodies at the Jersey Lily and made a ruling or determination of the cause of death. But it wasn't in him to treat Miss Austin's body in that crude manner.

After a thorough examination—which included consulting with Mr. Shaw, who had had some medic training during the Civil War—Judge Bean ruled that Sarah Jane Austin had fallen off the bridge at Meyer's Canyon—suffering a severe head injury, and it was death by accident.

When he told Dallas his ruling, she was furious. "Judge, how can you say her death was an accident?"

"You want me to rule it what it actually is, a suicide? That's too harsh and would be devastating to her poor mother."

"*No.* She was killed."

"And just what makes you think somebody killed her, murdered her? Do you know anything that could make me change my ruling?"

"No. But I know as sure as I'm standing here that she didn't kill herself, nor did she have an accident. The only thing left is murder."

"And may I deduce you think Lucas Conrad is guilty of something?"

"Look, he accused her of stealing his horse for no more reason, she said, than she refused to go to the dance with him. Doesn't that strike you as pretty dumb? Why did she lie to me? And then the Conrads, both father and son, rode all the way out to my campsite to try to pay me to leave Langtry immediately."

Dallas paced the floor in front of Judge Bean's desk in his office inside the Jersey Lily. "Judge Bean, why did the Conrads want me out of town? I think it was because they didn't want me to be here when Sarah Jane's body was found."

Judge Bean looked thoughtful. "Miz Armstrong, you could very well be right, but there is no proof. Bring me some proof, and I'll make a different ruling."

"You can bet that's exactly what I will do—find you some proof." Dallas turned and practically stomped out of the Judge's saloon.

When she reached her wagon, she remembered the letter Lucas Conrad had given her to take to Mrs. Austin. She got it out and opened and read it without any qualms:

Dear Mother,

The court thing was only because of a silly argument between Lucas and myself. He only meant it to make me stop and think how I might be hurting him. I'm sorry you heard about it and got worried. I did not need nor want an attorney, but I'm thankful Mrs. Armstrong is willing to bring this letter to you and tell you herself how happy I am. I am looking forward to my wedding in June, and if you are unable to travel—well then we shall come to San Antonio to be married.

Always,

Your loving daughter, Sarah Jane

The letter was bland and pointless. It really didn't say much, but reading the letter gave Dallas the idea for a plan of investigation.

Dallas stopped in at Mrs. Shaw's house. "Has anyone notified Sarah Jane's mother?"

"Yes," said Mrs. Shaw. "Judge Bean sent a telegram. He expects to hear something back before long."

"Do you mind if I look in her room? She said she would give me a letter today to take to her mother. If I can find it, I'll see that Mrs. Austin gets it. It might be of some comfort to the poor woman."

"Of course. It's the first door on the left upstairs. Oh my, oh my." Mrs.

Shaw wrung her hands and wiped her eyes. "I just can't believe this poor girl is gone."

Dallas entered the room where Sarah Jane had lived. She didn't know what she thought she'd find, but she felt compelled to look at the dead girl's things.

She searched through the tall oak wardrobe and found nothing except the girl's dresses and shoes. A large chest of drawers stood on the other side of the bed next to a wash basin. On top was a Bible and a photograph of a woman and man. The woman was Mrs. Austin, and presumably the man was the girl's father, Mr. Austin.

Dallas pulled open the top drawer and found several letters written to Sarah Jane from her mother, two copies of *Harper's Weekly* magazine, and a small sewing kit holding two needles stuck in a pin cushion and two spools of thread—one black and one white—and a thimble.

A little box was hidden under a pair of kid gloves and a scarf. Dallas opened it and found a ring with an opal stone, several pins, two necklaces, and three hat pins with jeweled topknots. She poked her finger through the jewelry, and just as she was ready to close the lid she spied a tiny key. She picked it up and looked carefully at it. She couldn't be sure, but thought the key might open a small jewelry or music box. Since she found the key in the girl's jewelry box, Dallas reasoned the key might fit a music box. Maybe the girl had hidden a letter or some papers inside that could explain things. Nothing made sense to Dallas, but the girl was dead. That part was real. Maybe it *had* been a tragic accident, but why had the girl been out at Meyer's Canyon anyway? It was a lonely spot, and not a place a young woman would go all by herself, especially in the evening.

Dallas searched the room thoroughly and could find nothing the key might be used for, but she wasn't ready to give up on the matter. She heard masculine voices downstairs and thought one sounded very much like Judge Bean. She slipped the key in her pocket and hurried downstairs.

"Hello, Judge. Do we know yet what to do about poor Sarah Jane's body?"

"Here's the telegram I just received." He handed her the paper.

AM TOO ILL TO TRAVEL STOP CAN MRS. ARMSTRONG HANDLE BURIAL? STOP LUTHERAN CHURCH PLEASE STOP HOPE TO VISIT THERE ONE DAY STOP —MRS. SAM AUSTIN

"Of course I'll take care of things. How sad not to be at your child's funeral," Dallas said. "And sadder still for her to be buried so far away, but I guess it can't be helped."

Mrs. Shaw sniffed in the background. "Did you find a suitable dress for her?"

Dallas nodded, thankful that Mrs. Shaw came up with a likely reason for Dallas to have been upstairs in the girl's room. "She has a lovely dark blue silk that will be perfect."

Judge Bean left after offering to take care of things with the Lutheran preacher. "I'll be back soon as we have a time set."

Dallas started back up the stairs then stopped to ask Mrs. Shaw, "Did Sarah Jane have a wedding dress being made?"

"Yes. Claire Lenander is the town dressmaker. I think Sarah Jane had something being made there. Or she bought a dress in San Antonio and Claire was fitting it. I'm not sure of all the details."

Dallas couldn't imagine that Sarah Jane would leave an important box at the dressmaker's, but maybe she had had no other place to hide something.

After bringing down the burial clothes for the woman, Dallas excused herself and headed to the dressmaker's shop.

Claire Lenander said that, yes, Miss Austin had a dress on order and had planned to have it fitted at her shop when it came in. Claire was also making the going-away dress for the honeymoon trip. But, no, nothing had been left there for safekeeping.

Dallas could only think of the general store where Sarah Jane worked as the last resort. Surely the girl wouldn't leave something important out at the Conrads' ranch. Maybe she only had sentimental things that she didn't need to hide from her future husband.

She wasn't sure how to ask the Conrads about it.

Dallas made a quick trip out to her campsite to get a dress and hat to wear to the funeral, and on the way she remembered when she first saw the girl—out at that barn where Judge Bean was holding his court. Sarah Jane had mentioned something about being out in that barn often, doing chores, and she knew all about the black cat—how the cat was expecting kittens.

Could she have hidden something there? It didn't seem likely as the barn did belong to Lucas Conrad, but Dallas didn't have any other ideas. Could she do any serious looking in that barn without getting caught?

Dallas rode out to the barn and had a cover story ready when she arrived. She decided not to go up to the ranch house but to talk to a ranch hand instead. One cowboy looked to be in charge of the bronco-busting going on in the nearby corral, so she approached him.

"Hi," she said, when he turned to her. "I'm Dallas Armstrong, and I was here the other day for the court hearing? I think I lost my favorite hat pin here. Do you think anyone would mind if I look?"

After the cowboy's initial shock at seeing a woman at the corral, he was quite cooperative. "Mr. Lucas is over at his father's place today. His father is in Galveston awaiting a cattle shipment, but I'm sure Mr. Lucas won't mind. It's okie-doke by me. Can I help you look?"

"Oh goodness, no. I don't want to take you away from your work. I won't be long, I'm sure."

He nodded and turned back to the horse training.

Dallas walked into the barn and looked around. "Where would a good hiding place be?"

"Meooow."

Dallas looked up and saw Tinta standing at the edge of the loft. "Well hello, Missy. Have you had your babies yet?"

Tinta stretched, scampered down the nearest pole and hopped into Dallas's arms. Dallas thought of her own cats who had been expecting throughout the years, especially one years ago who had had kittens on the Fourth of July and spoiled an evening out with her husband-to-be, Hank Armstrong. The night had not been wasted, however, as the two young people fell deeply in love that evening. She decided if Tinta *was* expecting, it was way too early to tell because her tummy seemed completely unchanged.

Tinta kept looking up at the loft, and Dallas wondered, could Sarah Jane have hidden something up there?

You'll never know until you look, she thought, and climbed the ladder to the loft.

Tinta, purring and dancing, led Dallas to a snug little alcove hidden behind several huge bales of alfalfa.

Dallas noticed a nest Tinta obviously had made, but the cat had not pulled out fur to line it yet, so it probably was for sleeping not for birthing. Dallas also spotted a saddle blanket nearby and what looked like an old milking stool, as if someone had made a place to sit and daydream or contemplate her life.

It's Sarah Jane's hideaway, thought Dallas. She began searching further, and back in the corner where the wall and the roof beams came together, Dallas felt the rough edges of something hard. She pulled it out. It was a book. More specifically, it was a diary. And it had a lock.

Dallas took the key she'd found in Sarah Jane's jewelry box from her pocket. The key fit. Dallas opened the diary. It only took a few moments of reading to realize what had gotten Sarah Jane killed. Cattle rustling. The Conrads were stealing cattle from nearby ranches and selling them to Europe for three times the going price. Sarah Jane wrote that Lucas Conrad said he would kill her and her mother if she ever told anyone what she had found out. She knew he would do it, too. She was afraid to tell anyone the truth—even when she went to court.

Dallas heard a slight noise and looked up.

Lucas Conrad was at the ladder, his head and shoulders already above the loft floor.

"Mrs. Armstrong. So you found it?"

Dallas had laid the diary on the old stool before she stood up. "Found what?"

"Sarah Jane's journal."

"So you did have a reason to kill her. You knew Sarah Jane had found out about the cattle rustling?"

"Of course. That's why she broke our engagement and why she threatened to turn me over to the Texas Rangers due here next week."

"So you accused her of stealing a horse in hopes she would be sent to jail over in Fort Stockton. That way she wouldn't be around when the Rangers came. That's when you threatened her too. When it all backfired you had to get rid of her."

"Well, she did know too much, and she claimed to have written everything down in case something happened to her. But I didn't believe her. And I looked everywhere last night for any place she could have hidden her journal."

Lucas Conrad's face turned ugly then, and Dallas felt fear as he pulled a gun and pointed it at her. This man had killed one woman already and wouldn't hesitate to kill again. She glanced to her right and then to her left for a way past him.

"You can't get around me. But even if you do, I'll chase you down."

Lucas laughed and the sound was cold, sending shivers down Dallas's backbone.

Suddenly, a loud "meooow" startled the man.

He turned and looked behind him.

That was all the distraction that Dallas needed. She rushed toward Conrad with both her arms out straight and rigid.

Tinta meowed again, dancing around, and Conrad tried to sidestep her. Dallas's outstretched hands shoved against the man's body.

He tried to keep his balance but couldn't, then staggered and went over the edge of the loft, screaming as he fell and landed with a thud.

Dallas hurried down the ladder and over to Conrad. He was breathing, but he was knocked out cold. She darted outside to her horse and grabbed a lariat from her saddle. Conrad was trussed up like a calf when he woke up, both legs tied to his right arm. His left arm was broken, or it would have been tied up also.

Dallas had worried that the cowhands would come running to Conrad's aid when he woke up and called out, so she had gagged him with his neckerchief. She pushed and pulled until she got him inside a grain storage room. "You can just stay there until I get Judge Bean. Looks like he'll be holding justice court out here once again."

Conrad moaned and tried to talk but the gag did its job. "You better lie still and rest while I go to town for Mr. Shaw. You could have internal injuries."

Conrad groaned again.

She ignored him and closed the door. She climbed back up to the loft to get Sarah Jane's journal and to check on Tinta. The cat was calmly cleaning her face. "You yelled at just the right time, little miss Tinta."

Tinta jumped into Dallas's arms and began purring. "And what's this story about you having babies? Was it just a false alarm? It better be, 'cause I'm taking you back to San Antonio with me."

Tinta put one paw up to the woman's face and purred extra loud.

🐈

CATNIP

Dick Lochte

1 was sitting in my favorite chair in the den, going over my notes for the Donna Seaton trial—the most important trial of my short, heretofore undistinguished prosecutorial career—when a tall redhead of uncommon beauty walked in wearing a gorilla suit. She was carrying the gorilla head in one furry hand, a wooden box in the other.

"I'm bored, Billy," my wife Jenny said, flopping down on the over-stuffed sofa.

I continued staring at her.

"Oh, this old thing?" She pointed to the gorilla suit as if she'd forgotten she was wearing it. "I found it in the attic. Found this, too." She held up the wooden box. "What the heck is it?"

It was about half the size of a good tool kit, with screen mesh windows on either side and a metal door at one end. "My turtle box," I said. "My grammar school buddies and I used to have turtle races. Line up four or five boxes. We stole the remote clickers from our parents' TVs, and Guy Terriot, this incipient electronic genius who's now working for Bill Gates, rigged the doors so they opened on the click. First turtle to crawl out of the box was the winner."

"Sounds like you boys were pretty starved for entertainment," Jenny said, pulling the metal door open. "Clicker's still inside." She reached in and found it. "These were inside, too." She withdrew a pack of pink envelopes held by a rubber band. "The hottest, wildest mash notes I've ever read, written by somebody named Tara to somebody named Wild Willy."

"Wild Willy, huh? Can't imagine who that might have been."

"They're addressed to William Quinlan, this house, New Orleans, Louisiana," she said, accusingly. "Wouldn't that be you?"

"My uncle William," I replied, employing the guile that comes naturally to members of the legal profession. "I was named for him. He lived with us for a few years around the time I was at Tulane. Dashing bachelor type. The ladies loved him. Can't imagine how his letters wound up in my turtle box." Not for the first time, I questioned the wisdom of moving back into the family home on Henry Clay Street.

My intention had been to sell the old place, unused since my mother's death two years before, and buy one of those nice, clean, all-amenities-included condos along St. Charles Avenue. But Jenny wouldn't hear of it. "This house is hurricane-sturdy and mortgage-free," she'd argued. "It's completely furnished, Billy. Think of the money we'll save. Remember, I'm not working anymore."

So I agreed. But the ambiance was getting to me—sleeping with Jenny in my parents' big bed, for example. And having her root mercilessly through my past.

"I assume this is a Mardi Gras costume," she said, indicating the ape suit.

"No. The whole family had 'em. Saturday nights we'd put 'em on and dance around the back yard in the moonlight."

"I wish that were true," she said. "We've only been in New Orleans for eight weeks and already I sense you're turning conservative on me."

"Me? Conservative?"

"One of us is still wearing his tie from work."

With a sigh I lowered the lid on my laptop and placed it on the floor where an assortment of manila folders formed a druid's circle around my chair. "Why don't I go slip into my biker leathers? We'll get out the chopper and zoom through the Quarter terrorizing tourists."

"You're kidding, but I'd love to. I'm bored, Billy," she repeated. "I've been a good girl for nearly a year. But that was in L.A., where there were other things to do. Here, I just loll around, reading books on local lore and remembering the excitement of my old life."

I met Jenny at a large cocktail party held at the sprawling estate of the mayor of Los Angeles. I was one of the up-and-coming deputy district attorneys tapped for attendance. Trying to stay out of everyone's way, I walked into our host's study and found the most beautiful woman I'd ever seen perusing his honor's bookshelf.

It was lust at first sight.

Not until Jenny was certain the lust had firmly congealed into a love stronger than civic duty did she confess to me that she'd crashed the party. She'd been looking for the mayor's wall safe when I stumbled into the room. She preferred stealing from politicians, she said, because there was always a little something you could find in their safes that amounted to a "Get Out Of Jail" card.

The discovery that my one true love was a professional thief caused quite a bit of anxiety on my part. I was, after all, an officer of the court. I won't bore you with the arguments that ensued, encompassing such dreary topics as good and evil, crime and punishment, male chauvinism and female rights to an occupation of one's own choosing. Let it suffice to say that, four months after that fateful meeting in the mayor's study, Jenny agreed to hang up her burglar tools, make several handsome anonymous donations to local charities and become my bride. In that order.

When New Orleans District Attorney Timothy Mathern, a friend of my late father, offered me a job in my hometown, I leapt at it. I envisioned it as the ideal way for both of us to start our married life relatively afresh. But the slow pace of the city had only succeeded in giving Jenny more time to recall the joys of burglary.

"Why don't we go somewhere for a drink?" I suggested.

"What about your trial prep?"

"I'd rather spend time with my beautiful ape girl."

She shook her head, red tendrils whipping her face. "No-no-no. I know that look on your face, Billy—that pinched, beetle-browed, squinchy combination of frustration and panic. You're in trouble on this one."

"No trouble. The case just isn't as strong as I'd like."

She moved in front of me and offered me her back. "Unzip me while you fill me in," she said. "I'll give you the felon's perspective."

"How much do you know?" I asked, digging through the fake ape fur for the zipper.

"Well," she said, emerging from the costume in her bra and panties, "I know that it was a gross murder with lots of blood. Ritualistic. The carved-up victim was a not very pleasant old lady named Laura Denecheaux, one of the richest women in New Orleans. Petroleum, I guess. Inherited from her father."

"And grandfather," I amended, admiring her lithe figure as she began folding the ape suit.

"The point is she was loaded, and she had this house tabby that she dearly loved."

"That would be Lulu, an extremely rare black Burmese," I said.

"Rare, huh?" Jenny asked. "How would that translate into U.S. currency?"

"Usually anywhere from several hundred to several thousand dollars. But if you're talking Lulu, about $40 million," I said. "Regardless of whether the jury finds Ms. Denecheaux's ward, Donna Seaton, guilty or innocent, Lulu still inherits the bundle."

"A forty million dollar cat," Jenny said. I wasn't happy with the way her green eyes were glistening.

"You ever engage in dog- or cat-napping when you were working?" I asked.

She sat on my lap and began to remove my tie. "I stuck to strictly inanimate objects," she said. "But a forty million dollar cat . . . Anyway, if the cat is the heir, why did Donna Seaton sic some maniac slasher on Ms. Denecheaux?"

"She'd been set to take over Lulu's legal guardianship in the event of the old lady's death. But, according to the lawyer for the estate, Maurice Fortier, Laura Denecheaux was about to change her will, dumping Seaton in favor of one Louise Hendry, the president of People For Animals."

"Uh-oh," my darling wife said. "People For Animals. Scam alert!"

"I think it's legit," I said. "They've got veterinary clinics in three southern states, offering their services free to those who can't afford them. I know these things because I had a long chat with Ms. Hendry, who seems like a genuinely dedicated woman."

"Don't tell me. In her thirties, blonde, wears glasses she doesn't really need and even with them on manages to curl your toes."

"Absolutely wrong," I said. "She's myopic. Needs the glasses."

"And I bet she's taking care of little Lulu while the nasty trial goes on."

"Well, yes," I said, feeling oddly defensive. "Somebody has to care for the heiress. Lou . . . Ms. Hendry has fixed up a nice room for the cat at her home."

"So," Jenny said, pretending to study my hair and pat down little errant tufts, "why would Donna Seaton want the ordeal of caring for a forty million dollar cat?"

"It's a matter of naked ownership and usufruct rights," I said.

"According to Ms. Denecheaux's will, Lulu has the naked rights, that is, the house, the stocks, the bonds, the various holdings. She owns them, but being a cat, she can't really do anything with them. As guardian, Seaton has the usufruct. Which means she can use and enjoy the forty mil to make life comfortable for herself and the cat. She just can't sell, lease or dispose of it."

"That's okay, but is it worth murder?" Jenny asked, running her fingers through my hair.

"Lulu's nine years old. When she goes to cat heaven, assuming she dies a natural death, Seaton gets both naked ownership and usufruct. The inheritance will be hers, free and clear."

"Why did Ms. Denecheaux want to change her will?"

"The lawyer says she 'overheard' one of Seaton's phone conversations with, in her words, 'an obvious member of the demimonde.'"

"Now you're talking," my wife said, snuggling closer. "They were discussing her gruesome death?"

"Not at all. They were discussing sex. Pretty steamy stuff, according to Ms. D. She was shocked that this woman who'd been under her roof for nearly six years could be so 'brazen.' She told lawyer Fortier she wanted to fire Seaton on the spot but was canny enough to consider the possibility of a wrongful termination suit. She requested that Fortier hire a private investigator to secure proof of Seaton's lack of moral turpitude."

"I love that kind of talk. Moral turpitude," Jenny said, wiggling closer. "Were there pictures, Billy? The kind you guys snigger about down at the D.A.'s?"

"Nothing even vaguely snigger-worthy, I'm sorry to report. The sleuth, a colorful gent named Lou Cronin, who speaks like something that just crawled out of an all-night forties movie festival, took some shots of Seaton in the company of a thug named Joe Gordon."

"Thug?"

"A lower echelon rackets guy. Anyhow, Cronin had shots of Seaton and Joe Gordon necking up a storm."

"Shocking," my wife said, adrip with sarcasm.

"It wasn't exactly the kendo chop Ms. D. had been hoping for, but she believed that because Gordon was a wiseguy, she had reason enough for the dismissal. Lawyer Fortier thinks she must have made the mistake of confronting Seaton, possibly giving her notice, before she had the chance to change the will."

"And Seaton got the wiseguy to carve up the old lady?"

"That's the problem. She and Gordon were seen at a cheesy casino in Bay Saint Louis at approximately the time Laura Denecheaux was meeting her fate. But, only a few days before, Cronin the private eye followed them both to an establishment on Magazine Street named Le Bistro Voudou, where they chatted up the owner, Henri Lebord. Cronin identified Lebord as an associate of thieves—"

"Look who's talking," my wife whispered against my neck.

"—and murderers," I completed my statement, trying to ignore the way my neck was tingling. "Cronin's snitches told him that Lebord has, in the past, acted as buffer for a hit man known as The Reverend. The Rev is a knife artist who really loves his work, as is evidenced by the remains of Ms. Denecheaux."

"The lawyer knew in advance about The Reverend?" she asked, nuzzling my ear.

"Yep. But when he relayed Cronin's information to Ms. Denecheaux, suggesting she might be in danger, she called him a melodramatic idiot."

"Well," Jenny whispered softly into my right ear, "She was concentrating too much on Seaton's hot phone call. She wasn't thinking murder; she was thinking sex."

"I know precisely how that feels," I said, straining every muscle in my body to stand with her still in my arms. Having passed that hurdle, carrying her, staggering, to the big bedroom was a snap.

🦌 🦌 🦌

Eventually, we got back to our discussion of the Seaton trial. We were in the kitchen where I used to eat my Cream of Wheat every morning before biking off to Holy Name of Jesus grammar school. We were sipping hot cocoa, cozily wrapped in thick terry robes from the Ritz in Paris where we honeymooned. (To this day Jenny thinks we stole them, and I would never dream of ruining her fun by admitting I had them added to the bill.) "So what was it that convinced Big Tim to indict Donna Seaton?" she asked, watching her marshmallow melt in the liquid.

"Well, we've got the lawyer's statement about the will. We have Seaton's bank records indicating a withdrawal of thirty thousand dollars three days before the murder. That transaction was in cash, according to the bank manager, and Seaton refuses to explain what she did with the money.

"Then we have Cronin's photos of Seaton and Gordon and Henri

Lebord. Plus, and this is a big plus, the P.I. overheard the lady make the comment to Lebord, 'It has to be done Tuesday night.' That was the night of the murder."

"Any hard evidence?" Jenny asked, zeroing in on the big problem. "The knife the Reverend used? The Reverend's prints in the house? The Reverend himself?"

"Haven't found the weapon. There was a windowpane removed from one of the French doors at the side of the house, which is how the Reverend has been entering his victims' homes. That's how he did it in Metairie last summer and in Baton Rouge a year ago. Both deaths were just as bloody as Laura Denecheaux's. As for locating the guy, the cops are clueless."

"But Big Tim thought you had enough to go to trial." Big Tim being my boss, the District Attorney.

"Big Tim was being pressured by lawyer Fortier, a man of influence in this city."

"Who's defending Seaton?"

"A pit bull named Gene Bethune. He destroyed poor old Lou Cronin on the stand. He translated all his old-fashioned hard-boiled slang for the jury, as if the guy were speaking Hindi. I objected, but Judge Bascombe Seymour, who has more than a touch of sadism in his Southern soul, said he was having trouble understanding the witness, too.

"Then Bethune mumbled a question, and before I could object Cronin asked him to repeat. And Bethune shouted, 'Are you sure you heard Ms. Seaton's comment in that noisy bistro correctly?'"

"Ouch."

"Thanks for your sympathy," I said.

"No weapon," she said. "No killer. But you still have the missing money."

"As Bethune has pointed out to the jury, it's no crime to withdraw money from a bank. Not even in cash. And if his client wanted to, say, make ten or twenty anonymous donations to various church poor boxes throughout the city, it is entirely within her rights to do so."

"This Bethune is an evil man, isn't he?"

"I've put his number on my speed-dial," I told her. "In case one of us should ever need the services of a criminal lawyer."

She sipped her cocoa, licked away a bit of residue with the tip of her pink tongue and said, "What've you dragged out of the boyfriend, Joe Gordon?"

"His name, address, and phone number. He denies any association with this city's criminal element and would have us believe that he's an entrepreneur. He says he and Seaton are engaged and will marry as soon as this annoying little trial is over."

"Unless I've miscounted," Jenny said, "that leaves only restaurateur and hit man agent Lebord. Why's that name sound familiar?"

"Don't know, honey. But he's joined our team. The cops tossed his establishment and found several cases of booze without any kind of tax stamp on them. In return for our forgetting to notify the Alcohol, Tobacco and Firearms folks, Lebord has agreed to tell the jury that Seaton asked him to arrange for an introduction to the Reverend."

"He admits fronting for a hit man?"

"No. He says he told Seaton she'd made a mistake, that he had no connection whatsoever to the Reverend."

"You believe that?" she asked.

"Not for a second. But that's all he'll give us. I'd love to put this Reverend away, but right now I'll settle for him telling the jury that Seaton was shopping for an assassin."

"Her Rambo of a defense lawyer is going to go after Lebord with tooth and fang. How reliable is a guy who peddles illegal booze?"

"He claims he doesn't know how those cases of whisky got in his locker. He thinks they may have been put there by a previous owner."

"Like your uncle Will's love letters," she said.

I sighed.

"He's a liar, Billy," she said. "No telling what he'll say or do on the stand."

"A wild card is my Lebord."

"I'd love to see how you play him," she said. "When are you going to call him?"

"I'm not sure."

"Of course you are, Billy. When?"

"Tomorrow."

"Please, oh please, can I come?"

It was the first time she'd ever asked to watch me prosecute a case. "I'd rather you saw me on a day when I felt more confident. . . ."

🐱 🐱 🐱

But she was there in the packed courtroom the next afternoon when Henri Lebord took the stand. The jury was a pretty cosmopolitan collection of truth-seekers, but I'm not sure they were ready for Lebord. He was an odd duck, five-six or so, with long braided black hair and a face white as whey, made even paler by his preference for black clothing. Black long-sleeved shirt. Black trousers, held together on his wiry frame by a unique snakeskin belt. His sockless feet wore scuffed sandals. A variety of items were pinned to his shirt, including several little cloth bags, a bright yellow feather, and a hank of hair. When we'd met in my office to discuss his testimony I'd suggested he leave the decorations at home before taking the stand. Wasted breath.

He sat bent forward nervously in the witness chair while responding to my introductory questions. Yes, he was Henri Lebord, owner of Le Bistro Voudou on Magazine Street. Yes, he recognized the defendant, Donna Seaton.

"Have you ever spoken with Ms. Seaton?" I asked. I expected his response to be, as it was in my office, "*Oui*. On the night of April 17 of this year, Ms. Seaton entered my *taverne* with a man I know slightly, Joe Gordon, to ask me to arrange a meeting with someone called 'The Reverend.'"

What he said, after a moment's hesitation, was, "*Oui*. On the night of April 17, Ms. Seaton entered my bistro with a man known to me as Joe Gordon. He stopped by to tell me they are engaged to be married."

Feeling my stomach and lower bowels lurch unpleasantly, I said, not too desperately, I hope, "Didn't Ms. Seaton have a particular request?"

"Objection. Leading the witness."

"Let me restate," I said. "Was there any other reason for Ms. Seaton's visit?"

A frown creased Lebord's forehead, fingers fondled the objects pinned to his shirt. "*Non*. Not as I recall. We just discussed their good fortune."

"Do you know the man who calls himself the Reverend?" I asked.

"I know *of* him. I read about him in the *Times-Picayune*. They speak of him on television."

I indulged in a short fantasy of choking Henri until his eyes popped out. "Did you not say to me, in the presence of two New Orleans police officers, that Ms. Seaton told you she wanted to contact the Reverend?"

"If I say anything like that," Henri Lebord said, "it would not be truth. Maybe you misunderstand me, sir." He was not being cute or smart-alecky. He seemed uncomfortable, tense, obviously not enjoying himself. That made two of us.

I turned to Judge Seymour, who was grinning at me. A sadist, like I said. "Your Honor, in light of Mr. Lebord's, ah, confusion over statements he has previously made, I'd like to request a brief recess to gather—"

"Your Honor," the pit bull said, rising from the defense table, "Mr. Quinlan has had more than ample time to prepare his witness and himself for this trial. There are at least another two hours left in the day. I owe it to my client to request that we use them."

"Ah am inclined to side with Mistah Bethune on this point, Mistah Quinlan," Judge Seymour drawled, happy as a clam. "Please carry on."

I saw my beautiful wife leave her chair and move to the bar, shoving a slip of paper at my clerk, Jay Hodel. "That being the case," I said to Judge Seymour, "I'd like to designate Mr. Lebord a hostile witness."

"Soun's lak a fine idea."

"Hostile?" Lebord asked. "I am not hostile."

While the judge explained the term to the creepy nerd, I moved quickly to the prosecution table and glimpsed Jenny's note. *Has he been in Denecheaux's house?* it said.

Lebord avoided my eyes as I approached.

It was the worst sort of situation for a lawyer. One of the prime rules of the game is that you never ask a question unless you already know the answer. From this point on, I was flying blind, working with a flopped witness who didn't mind lying under oath. A prudent prosecutor would have stepped back and turned Lebord over to his new friend, Bethune. But I wanted to rattle his cage a little first.

"To your knowledge, have you ever told me a falsehood, Mr. Lebord?" I asked.

"I . . . a falsehood . . . ?"

"A lie, then. Yes or no?"

"I, uh . . . *non.* I do not recall doing such a thing."

"And you don't recall saying anything about Ms. Seaton wanting to get in touch with the Reverend?"

"Asked and answered, Your Honor," the pit bull objected.

"Sustained. Gettin' all this, mah deah?" His "deah" was a sixty-year-old court steno.

"Do you sell illegal merchandise in your tavern, Mr. Lebord?" I asked.

"*Non.* Not to my knowledge."

"Didn't the police find cases and cases of untaxed whisky stacked up in your liquor locker?"

"*Oui.*" His fingers were hopping from one little pinned bag to another. Very distracting. "But, sir, I do not know where the bottles come from. I do not put them there."

"You're trying to tell us that behind your back, somebody snuck into your bistro and loaded up your locker with cases of smuggled scotch and bourbon?"

"Your Honor," Gene Bethune squawked. "Mr. Lebord's not on trial here. The legality or illegality of alcohol found on his premises has no bearing on this case."

"Goes to credibility of this witness, Your Honor."

"Ovah-ruled. You may continya, Mistah Quinlan, but don't press yoah luck, son."

"Mr. Lebord," I said, "how close a friend are you to Mr. Gordon?"

Henri frowned. "We talk a few times."

"More of an acquaintance?"

"*Oui.* I guess."

"You ever work with Mr. Gordon?"

"*Non.*"

"For Mr. Gordon?"

"*Non.*"

"So this guy you know slightly made a special trip to come to your place to tell you he was getting married?"

"Asked and answered!" Bethune shouted.

"Okay," I said and was about to let Bethune sing his duet with Henri when I remembered Jenny's note. "Mr. Lebord, did you ever see Ms. Seaton at some location other than your bar?"

"Huh?"

"Have you ever met with her where she lives, at the late Ms. Denecheaux's home?"

"*Non.*"

"Ever been inside the Denecheaux home?"

He hesitated before replying, "*Non.* Why would I?"

I didn't have the foggiest idea, not having had the opportunity to ask my wife about it. Fortunately, lawyers don't have to answer witnesses' questions. Instead, I told Judge Seymour that I was temporarily finished with Mr. Lebord but might have some other questions for him at a later time.

Ms. Seaton's pit bull stood and said, "I have no questions for this witness, Your Honor. Mr. Quinlan's done my job for me."

Judge Seymour dismissed Lebord and called it a day.

Jenny was waiting for me.

"I bet I know who could use an Old Fashioned right about now," she said.

"Were you just guessing or did I miss something?" I asked.

"About the Old Fashioned?"

"No. About Henri Lebord being in the Denecheaux house."

"Drink first. Then a nice filet mignon at Chris' Steak House. But no more talk about the case until we get home tonight. Then I'll tell you what you missed. You're so lucky to have a wife with a devious mind."

🐈 🐈 🐈

At nine-thirty, weary and woozy from beef and bourbon, I sat on the too comfortable sofa in the den, watching my devious-minded wife through rapidly lowering lids as she made a selection from the wall-length bookshelf. "Shouldn't've let you talk me into that last shot of whisky after dinner," I said. "You know too much booze puts me to sleep."

"It relaxes you," she said. "And after the day you've had, you need a little relaxation."

"Yes, indeed," I said. "Come on over here."

She remained where she was. "Billy, why do you suppose Lebord did his flip?"

"I imagine Bethune and Company outbid us somehow."

"Exactly," she said. "But if he'd gone along with you, his tavern would stay open, and he'd avoid a lot of trouble. What could Bethune have offered? Money? What's money when you're facing Treasury hounds? They're notoriously bad news."

I liked what she was saying, but I was feeling weary and unloved. "Couldn't we talk about this in bed?"

"You know we don't talk in bed," she said. "Right now I have a point to make."

"You could make it sitting here next to me," I said, patting the cushion.

She remained where she was. "I think Bethune is holding something heavier over Lebord's head than the illegal sale of alcohol."

"I agree one hundred percent. Now come over here."

She approached, but only to hand me a book.

I blinked at it. *New Orleans Voodoo,* by Michel Beauchamps. Then I blinked at her.

"That thing I knew and you didn't," she said. "It's in there."

I flipped through it. "Three hundred and twenty pages," I said.

"That's the nature of books," she said. "Lots of pages. I know. I've got so much time on my hands, I've been reading one of these every day."

"Even if I were sober and not two-thirds asleep, it'd take me hours to leaf through this. Give me a little hint."

"Think Reverend, mister," she said, starting for the door.

"Whoa. Wait. Where're you going?"

"Just to the kitchen for some cocoa."

I stared at the book. *Reverend.* Great. I started flipping the thin pages, blinking at the tiny type. I was having trouble focusing. That one drink too many. I was squinting at the beginning of a chapter on Marie Laveau, the Voodoo Queen, when my eyelids turned out the light and I went to sleep.

🐈 🐈 🐈

What sounded like the cry of a baby woke me at a little after one. I felt vaguely hung-over and sweaty. Mouth full of damp, ill-tasting, moist lint. The book had fallen to the floor.

Yawning, I left it there and dragged myself up to the bedroom.

The bed was pristine. Empty. No wife anywhere.

I retraced my steps to the top of the stairwell and called Jenny's name. No response.

On the main floor, I called her name again.

The door to the downstairs bathroom opened and she emerged, smiling. "Hi, honey," she said. "Feeling refreshed after your cat nap?"

"I heard a baby cry," I said.

"That's so sweet," she said. "You're dreaming about babies. Could be a sign."

"I don't think I was dreaming about babies." But I couldn't remember dreaming about anything. I started for the bathroom. "Aspirin in there?" I asked.

"Kitchen," she said, taking my arm. "Any luck with the Voodoo book?"

"Luck? No. It put me right out. Look, I feel like hell, and in another eight hours I'm going to have to walk back into that courtroom like Samson with a buzz cut at lion-feeding time."

"It was Daniel with the lions," she said. "But you get points for buzz cut."

"If you've got something I can use in court, please let me have it."

She stopped off in the den to get the book. Then she led me to the kitchen where she presented me with a glass of water and two aspirin. I swallowed the pills and asked, "Why are you feeling so chipper?"

"Because I didn't have two Old Fashioneds before dinner, one with dinner, and three straight shots of bourbon after. Anyway, the section you want is the one titled 'Fit for the Morgue.'"

It was the seventh chapter in the book. It told the gruesome story of a follower of the infamous voodoo Dr. John who, at the end of the 1800s, began performing blood rituals on fresh, unclaimed corpses purchased from corrupt morgue attendants. When the venal attendants were booted out and his supply of dead bodies dried up, the witch priest turned to living creatures—women in the main, though not exclusively, for his ceremonies.

The oddest thing about the man was that, in addition to his bloody voodoo sacrifices, he performed more conservative religious services in his own chapel in what would eventually become the uptown area of New Orleans. His name was Reverend Claude Lebord.

"Reverend Lebord," Jenny said when I closed the book. "What do you think?"

"A great-grandfather of our Henri?" I asked.

"If not then at least a role model," she said.

"A little thin," I said.

"Think about it, Billy. Lebord isn't just a front man for a paid killer. He is the killer. And the defence crowd knows it and that's how they got him to join their team."

"I like it," I said. "But it's all mush. Nothing solid. What can I do with it?"

"You're the lawyer."

I mulled it over. It seemed just this side of hopeless.

"When you recall Lebord," Jenny said, "get him going on his name."

I tried to imagine Bethune sitting still for that. "What's in a name?" I asked.

"Have faith," she said. "Recall the maniac to the stand."

"Dr. Boudreaux's up first thing in the morning." Boudreaux was the coroner. "I could probably pull Lebord back in the afternoon. You're convinced he's the Reverend?"

"Does a horsefly eat Spam?" Jenny replied, as if that were an answer.

"Well, we can check his alibis for the nights of the Rev's murders. But the bag of tricks is really empty. No fingerprints worth noting. No witnesses. Just probabilities."

"Some of my best friends have been convicted on circumstantial evidence, Billy."

"Well, I'll do my best," I said. "Speaking of which, shall we go to bed now?"

When the phone woke me at seven the next morning, I was alone. I grabbed the receiver from the nightstand and grumbled, "Yeah?"

"You hear the news?" my boss, Tim Mathern, asked.

"Not really," I said. "What's up?"

I heard him inhale and exhale and knew he was smoking. It probably wasn't his first of the day. "Somebody stole the damned black cat," he said.

"Come again?"

"Lulu, the forty-million dollar feline," Big Tim said. "Somebody broke into Louise Hendry's home in the Garden District last night and made off with the animal. The cops say it probably wasn't the Reverend, mainly because Hendry's still intact. Also, whoever did this was a real pro. Just a scratch or two on the rear door lock. Hendry was asleep in her bedroom right next to the room with the cat. She didn't hear a thing. Didn't know the puss was missing until this morning."

I didn't like any of it. I particularly didn't like the fact that Jenny, who usually slept in until nine or ten, seemed to be missing. "Any idea what time the theft occurred?" I asked.

"Hendry says she went to bed at ten-thirty. Give her another half-hour to nod off, I suppose it could have happened any time after that. They're set up at her place to tape and trace any ransom call. But my guess is the Seaton woman arranged for the catnap just like she arranged for Miss Denecheaux's murder. That the way you see it?"

"Right," I lied.

"This going to impact on the trial, do you think?"

"Hard to tell," I said, sitting on the edge of the bed.

"Well, give 'em hell today, podnah," he said.

"Will do." I was staring at the black, rubber-soled shoes lying on the carpet. Part of what my wife used to call her neo-Ninja nightwork outfit.

"Give Jenny a big, wet kiss for me," Big Jim said before ringing off.

🐾 🐾 🐾

I left home thirty-five minutes later. There'd been no sign of Jenny. No sign either of the cat whose cry I had mistaken for a baby's the night before. But I did find shiny black hairs on the rug in the downstairs bathroom and a toilet paper ring that had been gnawed on.

Edgy, anxious, dehydrated, and despondent, I drove to the Crescent, a tavern not far from the Criminal Courts Building. There, I joined Officer

Ray Ponetta, some twenty pounds past the NOPD guidebook for a man barely six feet, who was at a table eating something brown and messy while sweating through his shiny, lime-colored sports coat. Ray was in charge of the Denecheaux murder investigation.

"Hey," he said, good-naturedly, "how about that cat gettin' snatched, huh?"

I dispensed with the amenities and moved directly into the reason I was there. Lebord had told us he was working the night of the murder. I wanted Ray to check that out and let me know the results before court convened at two that afternoon.

"I'll get right on it," he said. "You hungry, you oughta try some of this gree-ards an' grits."

"I, ah, already ate," I said. "Is that warrant you used for Lebord's bistro still good?" When he nodded, I asked if it included his residence. Again a nod. "Perfect," I said. "I want you to check out both places for every knife with a serrated edge you can find."

"What's this all about, counselah? You p.o.'ed at the man for jackin' you up in court yestaday?"

"Yeah, I am," I said. "But I'm not just doing this for spite."

"You figyah Lebord's the Reverend?"

"Maybe, but let's keep that our secret for a while."

*

I spent a little over an hour of the morning session taking the coroner, Dr. Boudreaux, through information from his autopsy and various other elements of physical evidence. Then I used up another twenty minutes comparing the fatal cuts on Laura Denecheaux's body with the wounds of other victims presumed to have been dispatched by the Reverend. Dr. Boudreaux, a very serious, slow-talking man, nearly put the jury to sleep. But they perked right up when Judge Seymour, over Bethune's objection, allowed us to flash a few grisly crime scene photos of the victims. The three murders, Dr. Boudreaux concluded, had been performed by the same hand.

Bethune didn't use much of the hour and a half I'd left him before the noon break. "Dr. Boudreaux," he asked, "have you discovered any physical evidence, any blood, incriminating fingerprints, anything at all to suggest that Ms. Seaton had anything whatsoever to do with the murder of Ms. Denecheaux?"

Boudreaux took his time before replying. But it didn't change his answer, which was "No."

🦙 🦙 🦙

I was working on my notes and an oyster po'boy at my desk when Ray Ponetta showed up. "Man, they was knives grammaw at both them places. We picked up twenty-seven. They's another twenny-five or so steak knives at the bistro, but you didn't want them, too?"

"Maybe," I said. "But let's see what the lab can do with the ones you did grab first."

"Man, there wuz all this spooky stuff at his place, too. Dragon's Blood. Goofah Dust. Devil's Shoestrings. Gambla's Luck. Voodoo stuff. Ah doan like to be in the same room with some o' that junk. Lebord is one serious voodoo."

"He around when you were going through his stuff?"

"Naw. The day man let us in the bistro. The buildin' managah opened up the apawtment fo' us. I'm sorry, cap, but I let ya down about Lebord's alibi. I got nuthin' for ya. Couldn't find the night bawtenda and he don't come on 'til fo'. I'm gonna drop by the bistro then, tawk to him an' the regulah boozahs, see what they can remembah."

"Okay. And after you're through, hang a padlock on the place and we'll notify the ATF about the illegal booze."

He chuckled. "Teach the weasel not to renege on a deal."

"How quickly can the lab get us some results on those knives?"

"Usually they're like molasses in wintah," Ray said.

"I'll call over there and see if I can thaw 'em a little," I said. "And thanks for the fast work."

He smiled. "Feels good to run a little. Build up an appetite."

🦙 🦙 🦙

The afternoon session was to begin at two o'clock. My clerk, Jay Hodel, and I arrived a little early, just in time to see my wife on a waiting bench outside the courtroom, sitting thigh to thigh with Henri Lebord. He was chattering away like a Paris magpie.

"Isn't that—" Jay began.

"I'm afraid so," I said.

She spotted us headed their way and moved her head in a quick "no" gesture.

Annoyed and a bit dismayed, I took my confused clerk and led him quickly to the closed courtroom door, which was still locked. We were five minutes too early. I spent the time talking to Jay about nonsense, just to keep both of us from gawking at my wife while she flirted with a man who was probably wondering how she'd look with her throat slit.

The hall was filling up by the time the courtroom door was unlocked. Jay and I were the first in. As we approached the prosecution table, we both noticed the pink envelope at the same time. Jay picked it up. "It's for you," he said, frowning. "But it's old. And it's postmarked eighteen years ago. Damn, this is a weird afternoon."

I snatched it from him. It was one of the envelopes Jenny had found in the attic. But instead of one of Tara O'Neill's damn fine love letters, it now housed a slip of white paper on which my wife had written: *Ask Lebord about Lulu.*

"How'd it get in here?" Jay asked. "The door was locked."

"For every lock there is a key," I said, turning to watch the spectators file into the courtroom. *Ask Lebord* what *about Lulu?* I wondered.

Gene Bethune bounced jauntily to his table, where he stood sneering at me until the jury began to file in. Then he immediately exchanged his sneer for a warm and confident smile and sat down.

Judge Seymour entered, robe aflutter. As the call for order came, I took another glance at the crowd. My reckless wife had found a spot five rows back at the far right of the room. She smiled at me and gave me a wink.

At the sound of my name, I turned to find Judge Seymour looking at me expectantly. I told him that I wanted to recall Mr. Henri Lebord to the stand.

The voodoo had lost some of the sparkle he was showing Jenny out in the hall.

"Mr. Lebord," I said, "Yesterday you mentioned that you'd heard of the homicidal maniac who calls himself the Reverend. Is that correct?"

"Heard of him, *oui.*"

"Where do you suppose he got his nickname?"

Lebord shrugged. "I imagine he thinks it makes him soun' *un type cool.* You know, like a cool guy."

I smiled at his rather quaint usage. "So you think he gave himself the name?"

"*Oui,* I suppose."

"You don't think it was something the media came up with?" I said.

"They're the ones who usually invent a name for serial murderers. The Bayou Strangler. The Kissing Killer."

"Maybe they did. I dunno."

"No. You're right," I said. "He gave himself the name. At least, according to a couple of the Reverend's competitors who're now behind bars."

Henri stared at me.

"You think the name's cool, huh, Mr. Lebord?"

"It is . . . different."

"Can you think of some underlying reason why this murderer might have selected that particular nickname?"

"Object, your honor," Bethune complained, "What's the point of all this?"

"Gentlemen, would you both gathah 'round the bench?" the judge requested.

When we'd done so, he said, "Care to explain what you're up to, Mistah Quinlan?"

"Your honor, we've heard from various experts, including our coroner Dr. Boudreaux and Officer Ray Ponetta, that it's relatively certain Laura Denecheaux was murdered by the man known as the Reverend. It's the people's contention that Donna Seaton hired him to commit the murder. What I'm hoping to do here is clarify that connection."

"Mr. Lebord has already stated under oath that he knows nothing about the Reverend," Bethune said.

"Mr. Lebord owns a popular bistro," I said. "I assume that means he hears a lot of things about a lot of people. Perhaps he knows more about the Reverend than he thinks he does. That's all I'm trying to find out."

The judge gave me a mildly skeptical look. "Let me remind you about hearsay evidence, Mr. Quinlan," he said. "Okay, son, I'll give you another few casts of yo' line. Then you're gonna have to find yourself a different pond to fish in."

As I turned back to Lebord, my eyes caught something odd and yet familiar on the floor against the rear wall. Not twenty feet from where I was standing was my old turtle box. And through the screen side I could see there was something inside it. Something moving around. I suddenly realized what Jenny had in mind.

A chill went through me, prompted by the sheer outrageous, *I Love Lucy*–ness of her scheme. Maybe I could avoid it by taking another tack. "Mr. Lebord, I've been wondering about your use of language," I said. "You were born *here,* were you not?"

"Yes."

"Then the accent, the occasional use of French words, are, what . . . affectation?"

"It is the way I speak. *En Français* with friends. In English, when I must."

"Did your parents speak French?"

He nodded. "Parents. Gran'parents. We have been here for generations, but we have always maintained our ties to France."

"Any of your ancestors members of the religious community?"

He smiled and his eyes sparkled, but he remained silent.

"I was thinking of Claude Lebord. Was he your great-grandfather, by any chance?"

A slight nod of the head.

"Could you please answer yes or no?" I asked. "For the stenographer."

"*Oui.* Yes."

"That would be the *Reverend* Claude Lebord?"

"*Oui.*"

"The Reverend Claude Lebord who performed ritual sacrifices involving the bloodletting of his victims?"

"Object, your honor," Bethune wailed. "Mr. Lebord's ancestry is not at issue here."

"Mistah Quinlan," the judge faced me, smiling, "we can all see where you're headed. I'd be happy to let you continya, if you've got something concrete to put into evidence."

Would that I had. "No physical evidence, your honor. Not at this time."

"Well then I guess you been wastin' the aftahnoon so fah, because we're jus' gonna have to strike all those questions about Mistah Lebord's lineage from the record. You finished with this witness?"

"Just one or two questions more, your honor."

"They bettah be more appropriate than the last."

Not in this lifetime, I thought. "Mr. Lebord," I said, "yesterday, you stated you'd never been inside the Denecheaux home. Right?"

"This is true."

"What about Ms. Denecheaux's cat, Lulu? You ever come in contact with the cat?"

"Of course not."

"Somebody stole it this morning," I said. "It wasn't you, was it?"

Bethune objected, of course.

Judge Seymour frowned and shook his head at me. "That washes you up, Mr. Quinlan," he said. "From here on . . ."

His sentence trailed off as his attention drifted to something happening to the left of me.

I followed his line of sight. A few feet in front of my now-open turtle box, a lovely, long, and muscular cat was enjoying her sudden freedom by stretching luxuriously. Lulu's face and body and legs were a satiny black, but her rather large pointed ears were a dark brown. She made a little "brrrrr" sound and moved her small rounded head from side to side, her wide-apart bright golden eyes surveying the courtroom. She was a handsome animal, all right. Not worth forty mil, maybe, but handsome.

It was not until she took a step in our direction, her shiny coat glistening as if it were liquid, that I noticed the effect she was having on Lebord. Maybe it was some voodoo thing—Marie Laveau the voodoo queen assuming feline form. More likely it was simple guilt. In any case, he was petrified, unconsciously drawing back as Lulu approached.

I heard Judge Seymour yelling "Somebody get that damn animal outta mah courtroom."

Lulu moved closer to Lebord. Sniffing him. She lifted her right paw and placed it on his leg.

With a yelp of *"le chat noir,"* he leapt from the witness chair.

"Get the damn cat," the judge was shouting. "Grab him, Quinlan."

I didn't bother to correct him on the sex of the cat. And I certainly didn't grab Lulu. Instead, I turned to the stunned members of the jury and shouted above the increasing din, "Mr. Lebord, are you trying to tell us you've never seen this cat before? That you've never set foot inside the Denecheaux home? That you didn't murder Laura Dene—"

I was interrupted by something very sharp entering my back near the left shoulder. A pain more intense than any I could recall shot down my arm. I staggered, tripped on the stenographer's chair, and fell head first into the court clerk's table.

When I awoke, lying on my stomach in a bouncy ambulance, a paramedic gave me a shot of something. Before it did its job, he told me Lebord had been carrying a long thin knife in an ankle sheath. He drew it to use on the cat, but Lulu had been too swift for him. So he settled for me.

"My wife?" I asked. "Is she . . ." I looked around the vehicle.

The paramedic seemed a nice, empathic guy. "Some ladies would rather not ride with us. I'm sure she'll show up at the hospital."

🐜 🐜 🐜

She was there when I awoke the next day. "How're you feeling?" she asked.

"About like your average knife victim." I was lying on my side in a hospital bed, trapped in some foam rubber device that kept me from rolling back on the wound, which my doctor had said was deep but not devastating.

"I'm sorry it got so crazy," she said. "It seemed like such a good idea at the time. Henri Lebord would say he'd never had contact with Lulu, and then out she'd pop to head straight for him. Maybe hop up on his lap. It's the kind of image a jury would remember. No matter what the judge instructed them, they'd be certain the cat knew him. I just didn't dream that Lebord would freak like that."

"It made for an interesting session."

"But," she said brightly, "now the jury has that image of him stabbing you, which is even more damning."

I nodded.

"The *Picayune* says they found traces of several blood types on the knife. Yours, of course. And Laura Denecheaux's. So we were definitely on the right track."

"I feel a little dizzy," I said. "Think I'll go back to sleep."

"Oh, Billy, according to the morning news, Judge Seymour is calling some sort of hearing about how Lulu got into the courtroom. I imagine you'll be invited."

"All I can do is tell them the truth: that I didn't have anything to do with stealing the cat or putting it in the courtroom. I suppose I could pass a polygraph, if they insist. Though if they ask me about the turtle box. . . ."

"Don't worry about that," she said. "With the bailiff and Lebord wrestling over the knife and those policemen charging into the room and everybody screaming and yelling, I managed to hide the box behind the judge's bench. He'd vamoosed by then. I wanted to be with you in the ambulance, but the box could have been a problem. It's now back in the attic where it belongs."

She is sort of amazing.

"What happened to Lulu?" I asked.

"One of the jurors caught her. The big man with the square head who looks a little like the Frankenstein monster."

"Claude Appleton," I said.

"Whatever. Your girlfriend at People For Animals says she's going to reward him handsomely as soon as they retry and fry Donna Seaton."

"Well, I suppose a new trial was in order anyway."

"I don't feel good about Louise Hendry having the dear cat back in that amazingly unsafe apartment of hers. You know, Billy, I rather liked having Lulu around. And we have our big old house."

I glared at her.

"I didn't mean Lulu," she said. "Any cat. A pound kitty."

"It's not the impossible dream," I said. "Jenny, something's been bothering me, as I lay here in my delirium and pain. I can see how you broke into the courtroom at noon and planted Lulu. And how you used the old remote clicker to set her free. But what made you so sure, out of all the people there, the cat would seek out Lebord?"

"Good Lord, Billy, what in the word did you think I was doing with him on that bench? Flirting? I was slipping catnip into his pants pocket."

"You never cease to amaze me," I said.

"I hope not. Oh, aren't you just too lonely in that nice bed? Wouldn't you like a little company?"

"We're in the Hospital of the Sacred Heart of Jesus, with nuns popping in here with pills and prayers every ten minutes. I've got a serious back wound and a possible concussion and I'm stuck in this rather limited position." I stared at her and could feel my heart start beating faster. "But, yeah, I would like a little company."

She smiled, sat on the side of the bed, then swung aboard, moving close. "You're *my* catnip," she said.

The End

ꓓOSKIN'S CAꓔ

Shirley Rousseau Murphy

The Greeley courthouse rose just above the false-fronted store buildings that crowded along three blocks of Main Street. The courtroom was on the second floor of the hundred-year-old granite landmark which housed, as well, all of Farley County's offices. Folks came there to renew drivers' licenses, apply for hunting permits, and settle land disputes. The atmosphere was casual. Men appeared in court wearing bib overalls, coming directly from the fields. On hot summer days, dogs wandered the halls looking for a cool spot in which to nap. The town was small and clannish, everyone knew everyone, and all stores were closed on Sunday, which was rightly reserved for God and a big dinner; everything about the town was old, much of it unchanged since the War Between the States except for its bright new pickups and tractors, and computers in all the stores.

Hidden within the courthouse walls and ceilings was a warren of old, abandoned air ducts and peculiar niches from various remodelling projects over the years. Here generations of mice had proliferated, their colonies becoming so bold and clever that they sprang the janitor's traps and would not touch the little yellow packets of poison bait he distributed. The week before the Bobby Hoskin trial, Judge Blane, sick and tired of mice chewing his desk blotter and his papers, ordered George Figley, who took care of maintenance, to procure some cats from the volunteers at Animal Rescue and set them on the mice. He then forgot about the matter as he prepared for Hoskin's trial. Three cats were duly obtained, good mousers all, and were housed in the courthouse basement and given the run of the building.

Bobby Hoskin had shot his mother and father with a twelve-gauge shotgun and had blown away his two small brothers at the same time. The town of Greeley took swift action. Within an hour of the 911 call, Hoskin was in jail on suspicion. Within seventy-two hours he had been arraigned and charged with murder. Judge Blane didn't consider moving jurisdiction to another town: Hoskin lived in Greeley. Hoskin's family was murdered in Greeley. Hoskin would be tried in Greeley by his peers and neighbors.

When Ada Whitney was selected as a juror, she could hardly wait to convict Bobby. Of course, she didn't divulge this to the defense attorney when he querried prospective jurors. She simply said she was capable of being fair. Though Ada had never served on a jury before, she felt she was very fair.

There was no motel in Greeley, so the jury was to be sequestered two miles from town in the small, simple bedrooms of the Christian Retreat. Ada cancelled her housecleaning jobs for the next three weeks, bought some frozen dinners so her husband Carl wouldn't starve, and packed her suitcase. As jurors were allowed to choose their roommates, Ada and Lithecia Flowers naturally roomed together, they being neighbors and members of the same church.

Ada, sun-browned and sturdy, made the younger woman seem as white and insubstantial as gauze. Poor Lithecia was not a happy juror. She quaked at the prospect of hearing the gory details of the case, but she felt that serving on the jury was her civic duty.

Bobby Hoskin had shot his father in the blue and white family kitchen at eleven-thirty on a Saturday morning as John Hoskin was making a grilled cheese sandwich. After Bobby blew away his father, smattering Nell Hoskin's pretty kitchen with gore and bone, Bobby turned off the stove and went in the living room, where he sat on the couch and waited for his mother and two little brothers to return home from the Piggly Wiggly. James was ten, Billy seven. Bobby, at twenty-seven, was a strapping, handsome lad and a major stud around Greeley. He was quiet and mannerly, though, until he got a few beers in him. The morning he killed his family he had not been drinking.

When Bobby's mother and brothers entered the house just before noon through the front door, loaded down with Piggly Wiggly bags, Bobby rose from the couch. He fired five rounds into them, emptying his shotgun and scattering bits of iceberg lettuce, hot dogs, white bread, paper bags and blood across the living room ceiling and the flowered wallpaper. The new damask couch and matching loveseat that May Hoskin had got on sale at Sears and didn't have to pay for until next summer were not in returnable condition.

With three members of his family dead in the living room and his father's body sprawled bleeding in the kitchen, Bobby stepped outside to his '94 Ford pickup with the killer wheels and roll bar and drove twenty miles north. Parking beside the Worley River, he threw his good shotgun into nine feet of water and watched it sink down through the river silt.

Driving back to town, he made several conspicuous stops at local stores then drove home where he "discovered" the bodies and called 911.

The sheriff, arriving with two backup cars, found Bobby standing by the phone still holding the receiver, weeping and weakly cursing whoever had done this terrible thing. When Bobby saw the sheriff, he looked up at the ceiling and shouted at the Lord to strike down the killers.

Bobby's gun was found three days later when an alert twelve-year-old boy fishing along the river came upon fresh, oversized tire marks, grew suspicious, and called the newspaper—the papers were full of the murder. Jury selection began the day Bobby was indicted.

Ada Whitney was accepted for the jury only after she swore she had not known the Hoskins well, had known them only to speak to, and after reiterating that she was capable of being totally fair. She did not say that she was determined to fry Bobby; she considered that convicting Bobby of first-degree murder was extremely fair. If she could have drawn and quartered him, or pilloried him like in the old days to die of thirst in the summer sun she would happily have done so.

She did tell the judge that after the Hoskins were found dead and Bobby was taken off to jail, their tomcat, with nothing to eat in its deserted home, found its way to her place half a mile up the road, where she'd fed it with her cats for a week then put it in a box and carried it to her friend who ran Greeley Animal Rescue, so they could find it a new home. The judge didn't think her short relationship with Bobby Hoskin's cat would prejudice her judgement.

The cat had in fact been the only one in the Hoskin family to whom Bobby had shown any affection. He ignored his parents and his two little

brothers as if they were pieces of furniture. But you'd see Bobby sitting in
the front yard on a rusted lawn chair taking a break from working on his
truck, and the cat would be winding around his feet or on his lap. Or
you'd see it, a huge red-tabby tomcat with big balls and one white foot,
sitting on the truck fender as Bobby tinkered under the hood. Ada had
heard people say that when Bobby whistled the cat would come running
to him just like a dog.

The jury convened on Monday the seventh of June. The jurors had
left their suitcases in the sheriff's bus. The day was hot and all twelve
jurors were dressed in summer cottons, the women in sleeveless dresses,
their fleshy arms still pale from the winter. But Judge Blane kept the air-
conditioned courtroom so cold that the women all sent home for
sweaters, which were duly deposited in the sheriff's office by their hus-
bands or one of their children. The first night after court, the jurors ate
supper together at a long table in Donna's Family Cafe with a sheriff's
deputy sitting at each end to guard them and keep them from talking
about the case. Later, Ada and Lithecia were getting ready for bed when
Lithecia began to cry.

"What's wrong?" Ada said, pulling off her pantyhose.

"It's so terrible. Those poor people, his own parents and those pre-
cious little boys. All this talk about blood and the—remains. How can
you stand to listen?"

"It's what we're here for, Lithecia. If we don't know the facts, we can't
make a judgement."

"Well you read mysteries all the time. You're used to those terrible
things. I just feel all shaky inside." And Lithecia wept so hard that Ada
wondered if the younger woman would get through the trial without getting physically ill. Then Lithecia began to pray aloud, beseaching God for
His guidance. She kept on until Ada had to snap at her to make her go to
sleep.

But Lithecia received her sign from God quickly.

Word from God, in fact, reached her the very next morning.

The jury had been sent out of the courtroom while Defense conferred
with the judge. The jury room, where they waited, was a twelve-by-
twelve cubicle that hadn't seen paint since Sherman burned Atlanta. The
windows were so filthy you could hardly see out, and hard wooden chairs
surrounded a wooden table around which the seven men of the jury sat
smoking. There was one dinky bathroom shared by men and women,
with just a thin door separating the toilet from the gathered jurors and no

soap in the basin. Ada complained about the soap until the bailiff put in a bar of Ivory. She'd used the facilities, trying not to make a tinkling noise, and had washed her hands and come out, when she glanced up at the air return above the table where the seated men were talking baseball and saw, through the air grate, two eyes looking back at her.

She made out a big red cat with one white paw. That was Bobby Hoskin's cat crouching behind that vent as big as a terrier and glaring twice as bold.

She could see that the vent grid was loose, and after a while the cat, evidently wanting human company, leaped down, banging the grill behind him, and trod smiling across the table. All but two men ignored him. Will Breen from the barber shop scratched the cat under its chin, and the cat waved its tail and purred. Maybe it missed Bobby. She wondered if it was looking for Bobby. She wondered how it had found its way here.

"That'll be one of the cats Millie Sayers brought," Lithecia said. "From Animal Rescue. For the mice, you know. She brought three cats. I saw her in the drugstore before we came on jury duty. The maintenance man takes care of them in the basement."

"Well isn't that the limit. Bobby Hoskin's cat ending up right here in the courthouse where Bobby's being tried."

"That's the Hoskins' cat?"

"Sure is," Ada said. "I'm the one took him to Animal Rescue. Couldn't see him go hungry. Five cats of my own is enough."

That night when they were alone in their room, Lithecia prayed again, and this time she thanked God for giving her a sign.

"What sign?" Ada asked.

"Why the cat, of course. Bobby Hoskin's cat." She turned to look at Ada. "God sent that cat. It's God's sign, sure as you're sitting on that bed. You may have taken the cat to Animal Rescue, Ada. And Millie may have brought it over here. But that's how God works. The cat," Lithecia told her with a level look, "is God's sign. The Lord sent Bobby Hoskin's cat to intercede. Sure as the nose on your face, the Lord wants mercy for Bobby."

Ada looked hard at Lithecia. But she kept her mouth shut. Lithecia seemed near the edge after the second day of gory details and was probably in no state to be reasoned with.

🐾 🐾 🐾

They didn't see the cat again until the fourth day of the trial. Sheriff Larsen was on the stand, testifying that Bobby's fingerprints were on the shotgun his department had pulled from the Worley River, and Bobby's prints were on the shell casings they had found at the scene. Ada thought it amazing that Bobby hadn't picked up the casings. During the sheriff's testimony, the cat entered the courtroom from the back hall. Walked in bold as you please, waving his tail, and padded toward the judge's bench. Laughter rippled through the courtroom.

When Bobby Hoskin, sitting beside his lawyer at a table between the judge's bench and the jury, saw the cat, his face lit up in a huge smile.

This was the first expression of any kind that Ada had seen on Bobby's face. The young man, for four days, had sat as still and expressionless as a stone, staring down at the table as if he heard nothing of the testimony. As if he'd gone into some kind of trance. Lithecia said he was grieving for his murdered family.

But now, seeing the cat, Bobby's entire being seemed to brighten—as if his only friend in all the world had come to comfort him. He looked so much younger suddenly and so open and boyish that Ada felt a pang of pain for him.

Beside her, Lithecia was weeping. Snivelling and blowing her nose. Ada could just hear what she was thinking, that God had given his sign, that God in his wisdom had sent this innocent animal to intercede for Bobby Hoskin. That God had sent Bobby's small, helpless friend to show how gentle Bobby was. To show that he, God, wanted the jurors to be merciful. And Ada realized that Lithecia had begun to make her nervous.

At the judge's amused nod, one of the deputies scooped up the cat and deposited it back in the hall and shut the door. The courtroom quieted. The next witness to take the stand was the checkout girl at Piggly Wiggly who testified that May Hoskin and the two little boys had bought hotdogs that Saturday morning, had paid in cash, and had not seemed disturbed or upset in any way.

That night at supper, which was served family-style with big bowls of vegetables and meat filling the center of the long table, the two deputies, both hearty eaters, sat packing in the groceries and laughing about the cat.

"I wondered," Deputy Harn snickered, "how long it'd be before that tomcat came in the courtroom. That animal's all over the building, bold as the devil. Not about to move if it wants to sit on your desk. Looks you right in the eye, daring you to make it jump down." Harn grinned. "Seen it twice in Judge Blane's chambers. Sitting right there on his papers lashing its tail. Judge seems to get a kick out of it."

Judge Blane was an elk hunter and a skilled fisherman. There was nothing soft about him. If he took a liking to a cat, which was typically a woman's animal, no one could call him a sissy.

"It keeps the mice out of his desk," Deputy Green said, helping himself to mashed potatoes. "I hear the judge talking to it, and the cat just winding around him and purring away." He grinned, his mouth full of potatoes. "That cat's a real piece of work."

Lithecia hung on their words—as if everything about the cat had special meaning. Ada was growing impatient and short-tempered with Lithecia. She wanted to ask the deputies if the cat visited Bobby Hoskin in the holding room where he was confined during court recess, but she didn't want to give Lithecia any more ammunition in the matter.

That night when they were alone, Lithecia went on about God's sign until Ada turned on her.

"God," Ada snapped, "wants Bobby Hoskin to fry. Use your brain, Lithecia. Bobby's fingerprints were on the gun. The way forensics figured out the tire marks in the Hoskin yard, Bobby was there when his mother and brothers got home. He left after they were dead, and came back later to find them and call 911." She was nearly shouting. She glanced at the thin walls and lowered her voice.

"His mother's blood was spattered on his shoes and pants, Lithecia, that the cops found in that Dumpster north of Worley. His mother's blood was flecked on the floor mats of his truck."

Scowling, she held Lithecia's gaze. "If God has his way, Lithecia, Bobby Hoskins will fry like a fly in a bug zapper."

"God *saves* souls," Lithecia snapped. "He doesn't burn them."

It was against the judge's instructions for the jurors to discuss the case between themselves, same as discussing it with anyone else. But Ada's patience was gone. Sure as piglets squeal, Lithecia was building to a vote of not guilty. It would take only one dissenting vote to hang the jury and set Bobby Hoskin free.

Well it was bad enough being shut up in that pokey little jury room thick with cigarette smoke, with her bowels out of order because she wasn't getting any exercise sitting in the jury box all day and then eating huge meals at night. Now, to top it off, she had to listen to Lithecia's crazy theories. When Bobby wept on the stand, mourning his departed family, Lithecia wept. When Bobby gave his emotionless testimony, describing his supposed actions on the fatal day, Lithecia listened wide-eyed, believing every word: that he left the house that morning after his mother had used his truck to run over to the Laundromat because their washer was broken, that she had cut her sandaled foot on those sharp rocks in the Laundromat drive. That after she had gotten home he'd gone to run some errands, had returned home to find his parents and his two little brothers brutally murdered. He told it all with a fake look of pain twisting his face like a painted mask.

Lithecia was so riven with pity for Bobby that she practically wrung her hands. She stared at him with those big, pale eyes until Ada felt her stomach go sour. And when the cat appeared again two days later, strolling directly into the jury box to rub against the jurors' ankles, Lithecia glanced at Ada with a look of pure vindication: This time, God had sent the tomcat intimately among them. God intended his message to rub off and cling to them just like the red-tabby cat fur that clung to Ada's stockinged ankles.

She didn't know how Lithecia could be so foolish. The testimony against Bobby was overwhelming. No other suspect had been implicated. No other scenario seemed possible but that Bobby Hoskin had brutally murdered the four members of his family.

She'd wondered more than once why the defense hadn't gone for temporary insanity. Seemed to her, that was the only way to win this case.

But she had her own theory about that. She thought maybe this court-appointed lawyer found the crime so horrible that he meant only to go through the motions, that he'd be happy to see Bobby Hoskin fry.

🐈 🐈 🐈

The cat did not appear again until the ninth day of the trial as the prosecution cross-examined Bobby for the last time before the jury was sent out. Again the beast entered the courtroom, striding boldly, and again when Bobby saw his cat his blank expression exploded into such wild joy that it wrenched even Ada's heart. Bobby must be terrified for his life; and he had no one, no family now, only this big, scruffy tomcat.

Reaching out over the witness stand, Bobby softly whistled for the cat, as if he expected the big tom to leap into his arms and cuddle against him.

The jurors didn't take their eyes from the small, intimate scene. The gallery sat hushed. Defense council, seeing the courtroom drama shaping in Bobby's favor, remained utterly still.

The district attorney and the assistant D.A. glanced at each other and began to fidget. Ada could see them wondering how many of these jurors would convict a man of blood-cold murder when one of God's helpless creatures loved and trusted him—loved Bobby so much that it had found its way from Bobby's home five miles south of town directly to the courthouse, just to be with him.

If a cat trusted him so completely, how could Bobby Hoskin be capable of this chilling murder?

Bobby whistled again and made a faint clucking noise. The cat, sitting on the carpet before the witness stand, looked up at him for a long time.

Then it turned and leaped onto the judge's bench and sat staring intently into Judge Blane's face. The judge looked back with interest until the cat turned and fixed his gaze on the jury, his eyes blazing into the jurors' eyes.

Lithecia cast a sharp *I-told-you-so* look at Ada. As if to say that God's final word was, at this precise moment, being transmitted for each juror to understand. The pale woman looked so certain that Ada wavered; she wasn't sure what to think.

Had God led her, Ada, to take the cat to Animal Rescue so the beast would end up here at the courthouse? *Had* God meant for the cat to find Bobby and save him? *Could* Bobby Hoskin somehow be innocent? Could his soul not, after all, be filled with cold malice?

Or, she wondered, even if Bobby had done the bloody deed, was he, as Lithecia claimed, not deserving of death? Would the jury, if they convicted him, kill a young man desperately in need of another chance at life?

She kept going back to the coincidence of the cat. If the cat was not a direct messenger, if there was not a divine purpose for his being here, then his timely arrival at the courthouse, and his insistent appearances in the courtroom, added up to a mighty strange set of events.

She had, she decided, been around Lithecia too long. She shook her head, trying to clear it, and glanced at Lithecia again. Lithecia's gleam of righteousness was contagious, Lithecia's arguments were, despite Ada's own good judgement, beginning to make sense.

From the bench, the cat continued to stare deeply into each juror's eyes—until Judge Blane picked him up and dropped him gently to the floor. The judge said not a word. No one rose to remove the cat. The beast sat down at the foot of the judge's bench and began to wash his paws. The judge nodded impatiently to the prosecutor, who proceeded with questioning Bobby Hoskin.

It was after the prosecution presented its closing statement and court recessed for lunch—or dinner, as she and Lithecia and most everyone else called their noon meal—that Ada noticed the change in Lithecia.

The younger woman sat at the lunch table as white and frail looking as ever but now, beneath Lithecia's palor, Ada saw something different.

Lithecia's features had hardened. Were rigid with a taut determination. As if the young woman was preparing to do battle.

But not until after lunch, after the final plea by the defense, during which Bobby's court-appointed lawyer actually wept, did the cat make his move.

Just before the jury was instructed and sent out to decide their verdict, the cat began to pace the courtroom, swaying boldly between the bailiff's box and the jury, between the judge's bench and the tables where sat the prosecution, the defense, and the accused. Circling the courtroom lashing his tail, swaggering with all the importance of a practiced trial lawyer, the cat held the audience captive. He was so full of himself that he seemed to have grown larger and broader, to have grown considerably in stature.

Bobby watched him, his eyes widening.

Lithecia clasped her hands together and directed her look at the ceiling where, presumably, God was looking down.

As the defense wound down its plea, the cat leaped to the rail of the bailiff's box. While the jury was formally instructed and court was adjourned, the cat sat unmoving.

Bobby Hoskin rose to be led back to jail. There was expression in his eyes now. A thin gleam of triumph—overlaying the look of a trapped beast. And suddenly the prisoner, in one violent lunge, had a choke grip on Deputy Green's neck, had jerked the deputy's gun from its holster and cocked and pointed it at Green's throat.

The courtroom was still. At Bobby's nod, the other four deputies stepped back. At his command they laid their guns on the rail of the bailiff's box and retreated to the far wall.

Pressing his hostage ahead of him, Hoskin started for the back door, the four-inch barrel of Green's .38 jammed so hard into Green's throat that the deputy choked for breath.

At the same instant, from the rail, the red tomcat rose and in a flying six-foot leap slammed straight into Bobby's face, clawing so wildly that Bobby dropped the gun screaming, snatching at the cat with both hands.

Jerking the cat free—and ripping his own skin in the process—he heaved the cat above his head and threw it hard at the wall. Bobby's face was a bloody mask of hatred and cold rage.

The cat hit the wall hard and fell. It lay still at the feet of four deputies as they grabbed Bobby.

There wasn't much of a scuffle. They had him on the floor and in cuffs when the cat rose again, shook its head, and began to stalk Bobby Hoskin.

No one moved. The cat swaggered across Bobby's prone, manacled body and dove for Bobby's throat.

A deputy said later that if they'd shot the cat, they would have shot Bobby. And no one, not even the Sheriff's finest, had the nerve, or the heart, to grab that cat and pull him off. Ada didn't see the expressions on the deputies' faces. She couldn't take her eyes from the cat and what he was doing.

The cat finally turned away, his whiskers gory, and stalked out of the courtroom. Three deputies knelt to try to stop the bleeding and save Bobby, and as the amubulance siren screamed down Main Street, Ada looked at Lithecia.

A terrible change had come over the younger woman. Beneath the shock of reality, Lithecia had crumpled; she looked thinner and smaller— as insubstantial and white as if she were indeed made of gauze. All her religious verve seemed to have drained from her. She appeared, now, to be looking only inward.

God had spoken, just as Lithecia predicted. Trouble was, Lithecia got the message wrong.

The End

MISSING the CAT

Mat Coward

I've only been up in court once in my life, and that was mainly because of a dog.

For about three months in the summer of 1979 I was going out with a Cuban girl called Jay, which was short for something or other Hispanic which I've now forgotten. She was a student at London University, and the fact that I can remember neither her full name nor what she was studying perhaps suggests that I was not as in love with her as I thought I was. She was amazingly beautiful, though, and sexy, and generally excellent company—that much I do remember.

Her sister was also living in Britain then, and the sister had a boyfriend, Mahmood, who worked as a kitchen hand at a restaurant not far from Leicester Square. Although by the time I met him, he wasn't actually working there anymore because he was on strike.

"Conditions in the catering industry are unbelievable," Jay told me one night in a pub in the Charing Cross Road. "Literally unbelievable! What is London—a great capital city, or a third world sweathole?"

"A bit of both, I suppose," I replied. "That's how it is with capital cities." Not that I was really arguing with her. The catering industry was notorious for long hours, low pay, and an immense shit-eating requirement. The employees were mostly new immigrants, too scared to stand up for their rights.

Mahmood and his pals must've been made of sterner stuff than most of their fellow sufferers, because they joined a union and attempted to open negotiations with management. Management responded in the time-honored fashion of sacking them all and replacing them with a fresh lot of semi-slaves. Two months later, Mahmood and the boys were still holding that picket line, living on strike pay and fresh air and the enriched vitamins that are contained in the substance known to science as Human Dignity.

Quite how I came to be standing alongside them, one warm Friday night in late August, is still a matter of some confusion to me. Certainly I had never stood on a picket line before, nor ever expected to, being myself the sole employee of a dingy, unprofitable second-hand record shop in Kentish Town. Put it down to being in love, I guess.

"Put this round your neck," said Mahmood, plonking a sandwich-board over my shoulders.

"What does it say?" I said, trying to read the placard upside down.

"Same as these," said Mahmood, handing me a sheaf of poorly dupli-cated handbills. "It says 'On strike for the right to join a union. This restaurant staffed by scabs. Please eat elsewhere. Thank you for your kind support.'"

"It says that?" Maybe I needed glasses. All I could see was squiggles and gibberish.

"In every known tourist language," said Mahmood. "German, French, Arabic, Spanish—"

"Not English?"

Mahmood frowned. "If they're English, you can employ the spoken word, no?" He put a hand on my arm. "That is why we are so grateful for your help tonight, Malcolm. Some of the fellows here don't speak English too well, so you will be of great assistance. I can see why Jay is so fond of you: you are a young man of courage and conviction."

Courage? I didn't like the sound of that: *courage*. . . . On the other hand, I was too scared to ask Mahmood what he meant.

🐈 🐈 🐈

After about half an hour, I was feeling a lot calmer. Nothing particularly alarming had happened. Five parties of tourists had been successfully turned away, while one group of Englishmen in suits had slipped past the blockade, despite my most eloquent efforts.

"Look, gents, would it actually kill you to eat somewhere else, huh?"

"Yes," said their spokesman. "It would actually physically kill us." His friends' chins wobbled as they laughed.

"In that case," I said, "could you at least read this before you go in?"

The spokesman glanced at the handbill. Turned it over. Frowned. Turned it over again. "This is crap," he said, sounding quite affronted. "It's total gibberish." He screwed it up and tossed it over his shoulder.

They entered the empty restaurant, to be met by a manager who appeared to be in training for the World Fawning Championships. I heard the words *all lies, gentlemen, I assure you* before the door swung shut behind them. The "gentlemen" made the arrogant tactical error of choosing a table right by the window, where they were treated to the sight of me scratching my bottom with unnecessary vigour and thoroughness throughout their first course.

All in all, I felt I was getting the hang of this "Solidarity with the Proletariat" lark. It wasn't skilled work. It didn't require courage. All it required was an ability to do what one was told by beautiful girls from Latin America, which was well within my capabilities. Plus, it provided a rare opportunity to be terribly rude to posh bastards in a good cause.

Yup, I was beginning to enjoy myself. Which was when a guy walked straight up to me out of the blue and gave me a cat. Just like that.

I started to protest, but by the time I got the words out, the silent man had vanished back into the early evening crowd from whence he'd sprung.

Odd, I thought, holding a cat in my arms, where previously there had been only handbills. *Most people just drown 'em in buckets.*

The policeman arrived about thirty seconds later.

🦙 🦙 🦙

Bow Street Magistrates Court, for all its leather and mahogany, its ancient dusty air, and its echoing corridors, was not a grand palace of justice. More like a conveyor-belt system for dealing rapidly with minor offenses.

In answer to the charge of obstruction, I pled not guilty. I'd been taking part in a perfectly legal protest, I insisted, obstructing no one and nothing. I had no idea why I'd been arrested.

Police Constable Arthur Groyne was happy to explain. "The matter of obstruction, sir, arose due to the fact that the accused was accompanied by a large and fearsome dog, the presence of which was a clear deterrent to persons entering the restaurant situated at—"

"I didn't have a dog," I said.

"Mr. Hurst," drawled the chairman of the bench. "Please be quiet. You will have your say in a moment."

"But I didn't have a dog," I said. "I've never had a dog."

"This police officer says you did have a dog, Mr. Hurst. Are you calling him a liar?"

I wasn't falling into that trap. Twenty years ago, you did not accuse cops of lying under oath. "No, sir, but I believe he was mistaken. There was no dog."

"Certainly was a dog," said P.C. Groyne.

The chairman gave me a look that said, *You see? There was a dog, the nice policeman says so.*

"But there was a cat," I blurted, and immediately cursed myself. I hadn't intended to mention the cat—didn't want to complicate matters—but all this nonsense about a dog had disoriented me.

"A cat?" said the chairman, as if the word were unfamiliar to him. PC Groyne, I noted with interest, was blushing behind his beard. The chairman turned his mildly offended gaze upon the officer. "The accused says there was a cat, Constable?"

"It was a dog," said P.C. Groyne. "I have been a police officer for fifteen years, sir. I know the difference between a dog and a cat."

The magistrates conferred for a moment in whispers, and then the chairman spoke. "Can you describe this dog, Constable?"

"Certainly, sir. With pleasure." P.C. Groyne produced his notebook from his tunic pocket. "If I may refer to my contemporaneous notes, sir? The aforementioned dog was a large animal of canine demeanour, black with a white muzzle, four-legged, with a short tail, a dog-like face, and large teeth."

"And fearsome, I believe you said?"

"And fearsome, sir, indeed. A dog of a most fearsome nature."

Having elicited such incontrovertible testimony, the chairman did not bother to hide his sneer as he turned to me. "Doesn't sound much like a cat, does it, Mr. Hurst?"

"Doesn't sound much like the animal in question, sir," I said. "Which, for the record, was small, quite young, predominantly ginger, with a distinctive double kink in its tail."

"For heaven's sake, this is intolerable," the chairman muttered. He conferred once more with his colleagues. "Mr. Hurst. Can you produce this alleged cat?"

"No, sir. The cat ran off at the moment of my arrest."

"Most convenient, Mr. Hurst."

I pointed at the policeman. "OK, then—can *he* produce the dog?"

This brought a smug shake of the head from the chairman. "It is not up to P.C. Groyne to produce or not produce the dog, young man. It is not, after all, his dog. It is your dog."

"But I haven't *got* a—"

"I trust you have a license for this fearsome dog of yours, Mr. Hurst," said the Chairman, clearly enjoying himself now. "Otherwise you may be fined, you know." P.C. Groyne gave an appreciative chuckle.

I sighed and surrendered. I felt angry, frustrated, and even embarrassed, but most of all I felt stupid. Everyone knew that Bow Street magistrates always sided with the police, rarely troubling themselves with such trivia as evidence. I had to be an idiot, wasting my time arguing about cats and dogs with this bunch of asses. It was Saturday, for heaven's sake, and the pubs were open.

"If I admit the charge, sir, can we get this over with?"

I was fined three pounds—roughly the price, back then, of a reasonable weekend's pubbing.

Having handed over my beer money, I went to the Gents, where I found myself standing next to P.C. Groyne. Keeping careful rein on my temper, I asked him: "Just as a matter of interest, Constable, what was all that about?"

He didn't answer until I was washing my hands at the basin (he didn't bother washing his; probably thought it an effeminate affectation). "People like you," he growled, grabbing the lapels of my suit coat in his surprisingly small, pink fists, "are ruining this country. Do you know that? You don't even work at that bloody restaurant; you're just a professional trouble-maker! Well listen, sonny—I won't forget your name."

I won't forget yours either, I thought. But then, to be fair, anyone would have a hard time forgetting a name like Groyne.

🦌 🦌 🦌

Mahmood didn't drink alcohol. Instead, in a dark corner of a crowded pub, he sipped a tiny bottle of alleged orange juice which cost more than my Guinness.

"Yes, Malcolm," he confirmed, "this policeman, Groyne, we know. He does not arrest us so much, but if he sees white people supporting us, this angers him. Yes, he has played this trick before."

"The trick with the cat?"

Mahmood's orange juice paused at chin level. "Cat? You mean dog, yes?"

Don't you start, I thought. "Cat, dog, whatever. You didn't see me being given the animal that evening?"

"I saw nothing, sorry to say. We had a rush of customers at the other entrance. First I have known of it is when P.C. Groyne is arresting you."

"OK, but can you describe the man who usually dumps the cats?" I held up my hands. "Sorry, Mahmood—I meant dogs."

"Ah. The Dog Man. No, I only ever snatch a glimpse. He moves fast, you have seen yourself."

"True enough. But it's definitely not P.C. Groyne?"

"No, no. Him I know, only too well. He's in very thick with the management, as probably you have guessed. But the Dog Man is a similar looking man, I can say. Quite big, made of both fat and muscle together, you know? Mostly bald, though not old. A big face, as if made of dough."

Well, that narrowed it down a bit. To half the adult male population of London.

🐈 🐈 🐈

My brief picketing career was over, perforce. I didn't dare imagine what treats P.C. Groyne might arrange for me if he saw me there again. But that wasn't the end of it for me, because I just couldn't get that cat (the one that wasn't a dog) out of my mind.

I like cats. I like dogs, too; I'm not prejudiced. I suppose it's just that cats remind me of happier days. The first cat I ever knew, a black and white named Tricksy, had been given to my mother as a birthday present when she was seven. Mum was twenty-eight and divorced with two children when Tricksy died on her lap, purring to the end. Imagine that: twenty-one years. And my mother's bereavement was long and deep, let me tell you. This'll sound crazy to anyone who doesn't know cats and cat people, but the truth is I don't think Mum ever fully got over Tricksy's death. It marked a kind of turning point in the life of our family, certainly. A bad turning.

I felt that I ought to make at least a token effort to find out what had happened to the missing cat after it leaped from my arms when I was arrested. I had to fear the worst. There was lots of traffic in the West End of London . . . and, with all those restaurants, lots of rat poison.

Jay agreed, which, I admit, was another factor in maintaining my determination. "This poor cat is as much a victim of the slave bosses and their tame police as are the strikers," she pronounced, in that erotically serious way of hers. "Yes, Malcolm, you must search for the cat who is missing."

"Missing"—not a bad name, I thought, for a nameless cat. Fine. But where to start?

Assuming the overzealous cop and his bulky-but-swift accomplice usually used a dog for their frame-ups (probably as a kind of furry insurance policy against the unlikely presence of passers-by naive enough to offer themselves as witnesses for the defense), then why had they employed a cat on this occasion? Presumably their regular dog was ill or dead or working another gig. So the accomplice had, at the last minute, substituted a cat. A stray, I guessed: easily available and unlikely to hang around long enough to contradict P.C. Groyne's story.

Knowing—or guessing—all this did me no good at all. I had no leads, so to speak, on the Dog Man. Which left just one option: prowling around the back alleys at night after the restaurants had closed, jangling a can opener against a tin of smelly sardines, in the hope, however forlorn, that Missing might still be in the area.

I had to be careful. This was P.C. Groyne's patch, after all, and I soon came to know his routines: which restaurants and bars he liked to pop into for a friendly chat and free refreshments.

On the third night of my vigil, I was loitering in the shadows of a rubbish skip, waiting for Groyne to emerge from a steak house on the edge of Leicester Square. There'd been no sign of Missing: I'd met a couple of hedgehogs, many pigeons, and a fox, but no cats at all. The pointlessness of my quest was becoming more obvious with every minute.

I hated the thought of quitting. I felt a kind of connection to that cat which even now I can't fully explain. (Two strays thrown together by chance in a big city? Nah, too corny. Forget it.)

Groyne eventually left the steak house, burping his appreciation. I shrank further back into the shadows, but the sweat froze under my T-shirt as Groyne seemed to look right at me and then started marching towards my hiding place. My trousers were saved from ruin, though, when Groyne stopped some yards away and spoke some words I didn't catch. From the shelter of another skip there emerged, sheepishly, a man of roughly the same size and shape as the cop.

The Dog Man: it had to be.

"You prat, Vince! What the hell are you doing here?" Groyne gave the Dog Man (Vince, apparently) a clip round the ear, the sort you sometimes see mothers giving to kids they regret owning.

"I'm sorry, Arthur, honest! I was only—"

"Get away home, you moron," Groyne snarled, and this time Vince took a flat-handed slap to the face hard enough to raise a bruise.

P.C. Arthur Groyne strode off in the direction of Trafalgar Square.

"Excuse me mate, I'd like a word."

Vince jumped. He hadn't heard me come up behind him; he hadn't been meant to. But it was obvious he recognized me the instant he saw my face.

"This is all your fault! Arthur won't pay my rent, thanks to you. You and that cat."

"It's the cat I'm interested in," I reassured him. "Not you—just the cat."

Vince wasn't listening. "Clint was poorly that day; he had a chill. I couldn't take him out like that, could I?"

"Clint?"

"Dogs are same as us, yeah? They got a chill, you got to wrap 'em up with a hot water bottle."

Clint. "So you used a cat instead."

"Arthur says I made him a laughing-stock down the nick. I don't think that's fair. It's all your fault. If you hadn't been making trouble for Arthur's friends outside their restaurant, none of this would have happened, and Arthur wouldn't have hit me."

Vince looked to be on the verge of tears. Outwardly, sure, he was off the same shelf as P.C. Groyne. But he lacked the swagger, the confidence.

"Listen, mate, I never meant to get you in trouble with Arthur. He often hit you?"

"Sometimes," the big man sniffed.

"I am sorry, honest." I was, too. Almost. "Thing is, Vince, I just need to find that cat. That's all. If you can remember where you got it from, or what happened to it—"

Vince sprang away from me. "I never touched it! I never hurt it, I swear, I never. I wouldn't!"

And he was off. That Dog Man, he truly could move, for a big guy.

Even if I could've caught him, what was I going to do? Beat the truth out of him?

It was only on the journey home that a somewhat pertinent question entered my skull. What had Vince been doing there, that he didn't want Arthur Groyne to know about? Answer: same as me. He was looking for Missing.

Which raised several other questions, of course, but I was tired and fed up, and I tried to put them out of my mind. For the next twenty years, I tried to put them out of my mind.

🦌 🦌 🦌

Twenty years later, I was still working in the record shop and still living alone in the small flat over the shop. My life was good enough. Plenty of friends, a few lovers, no serious illnesses. A warm place to sleep: us strays don't ask for much more.

Jay and Mahmood and poor, scared Vince remained only as half-forgotten walk-ons in my mental biopic. But I still worried about Missing, every now and then. That might sound daft—after all, I'd lived a life full of loose ends. But most of those ends were ones I'd left dangling deliberately. Missing the Cat was one I'd tried, and failed, to tie up.

Realistically, there was nothing more I could do, following my confrontation with Vince. Realistically, with each month, and then each year that passed, the likelihood that Missing was still alive faded. Street cats are not noted for spectacular longevity. But still, some lonely nights, into my mind would drift unbidden a picture of that double-kinked tail. "Realistically," after all, is just a word frightened humans use to shield themselves from their own hearts.

I forgot, and didn't forget, and then, about five years ago, I met a girl called Sammy who worked as a clerk at Bow Street Magistrate's Court, and I had an idea. Only a small idea, a little token of an idea, really.

The Metropolitan Police Service had changed some during those years, and cowboys of the Wild West End like P.C. Groyne were no longer quite so welcome in its ranks. Plus, Groyne was an unusual name.

"If you ever hear of a man named Groyne being brought before the courts on any sort of charge," I asked Sammy, when I thought I knew her well enough, "let me know, would you?"

And she did. She didn't forget, and last month, after all these years, she rang me. *Well,* I thought, *this is nothing to do with a stray cat any more, but still I'd like to be there. For auld lang syne.*

There had been no press present when I'd had my day in court, but there were one or two journalists at Bow Street that morning. I sat behind them on the public benches and waited for the accused to be led in. When he appeared, I got the shock of my life.

Vincent Groyne, unemployed decorator, pleaded guilty to the manslaughter of his brother, retired police sergeant Arthur Groyne, and was committed for trial at Crown Court. Committal hearings are brief, anti-climactic affairs, but this one did have a small, pathetic moment of excitement at the end, as the prisoner was being taken from the room.

Turning to the Bench, that big, sad man cried out: "Please, who's going to feed my cat?"

"Cat?" I said aloud, though no one heard me above the scraping of chairs and the clasping of briefcases. "Don't you mean dog?"

🐈 🐈 🐈

Two hours later, I arrived at the address given by the accused in court—a small, paint-peeling, semi-detached house in the middle of a long, tedious road in the working-class suburb of Leytonstone.

"Are you a friend of Vincent's?" asked Mrs. O'Donnell, Vince's landlady, as we sat in her clean, under-furnished living room.

"It's some years since I'd seen him," I told her. "I was sorry to hear about what happened."

Mrs. O'Donnell looked away, as if ashamed of what she was about to say, but determined to say it even so. "I'm only surprised it didn't happen long ago. That brother of his treated poor Vincent like a slave. Worse than ever since Arthur retired from the police." The way she said *retired* suggested there might be a story there, but if so, it wasn't the story she was telling today. "Then when Arthur announced he was moving in here with Vincent—he'd been thrown out of his last place for drunkenness, I happen to know that for a fact—well, that was the last straw. There was a fight, and . . . I'm sure Vincent didn't really mean to hurt him. But Arthur said he'd have to get rid of the cat—he'd always hated it."

We sipped our tea in respectful silence for a moment, and then I got to the point. "About the cat—" I began.

"Will you take her in? Oh, bless you! I'll fetch you a box to carry her in. I can't keep the poor thing, you see. She doesn't see eye to eye with my budgie." She leapt to her feet and led me to Vince's room, which was almost empty except for a dirt tray, a feeding bowl, and a bed, upon which snored an ancient, ginger cat. "He had a dog, too, when he first moved in. But that's long gone."

"Does she have a name?" I asked.

Mrs. O'Donnell smiled, sadly. "He just called her Sweetie. She was a stray, you see, originally."

The cat on the bed stretched, and I got my first good look at her. "She had her tail amputated?"

"It had been damaged in a fight, the vet thought. Or by a car, maybe," said Mrs. O'Donnell. "I don't suppose she'll be a burden to you for long. She must be twenty years old if she's a day. You're doing a kind thing, God bless you."

"Not really," I said. "It just so happens I've been thinking lately that my life has a cat-shaped hole in it. Yes, indeed, Mrs. O'Donnell, I've been thinking that for quite a while."

I'd never know for sure, of course—not really. But I didn't care. She was a fine, friendly old cat in need of a home. And for whatever reason, I was in need of her.

As I carried her home on the bus that day, speaking softly to calm her in her box, I said to her, "Well, Sweetie, whoever you are, one thing's for certain. You're not Missing any longer."

PRINTS

Ann Barrett

Gordon McKay cast a sideways glance at his client and sighed. Or rather, yawned then sighed. He'd been up half the night mulling over how to avert what he feared was a foregone but unfair verdict. But there had been no 2 A.M. flash of brilliance.

Besides, court-appointed cases disheartened him. While McKay was the lead proponent of his firm's carrying out its share of community service—his partners had nicknamed him "Good-do Gordon"—the overly complicated lives of his non-paying clients typically gave him insomnia. The more lucrative side of his business seemed a degree insulated from their legal tangles. And Shays, McKay and Crimmons, Attorneys at Law, had a reputation that appealed to the blessedly endowed. Money cushioned. Money also afforded McKay enough emotional distance to view his endeavors as a game. A game he mostly won.

But this case, *this* case. . . . Light from a low winter sun streamed through the courtroom windows, making the sweat on his client's forehead shine. Joe Richards was a tall man, thirtyish, with abundant dark hair and a muscular build. Handsome but hapless, thought McKay, reflecting that Richards's goods looks were unfortunately unaccompanied by mental prowess. McKay had had to explain every legal detail at least three times, with a confused stare Richards's typical response.

And worse, handsome was a sinker this time—in a murder rap. An obviously premeditated murder rap, to boot. Richards's girlfriend had been found stabbed. Several witnesses were slated to testify about conflict in the relationship—make that cat fights, rather, from what McKay knew. And Richards had been off camping by himself in the White Mountains the weekend she was killed. No alibi. And no hope.

But still, McKay believed him. He'd seen plenty of lying and evasion before, and this was different. Richards seemed bewildered at his predicament and, more importantly, genuinely unmoored by the loss of his girlfriend. He'd even depleted McKay's supply of Kleenex.

McKay had gone through the tissues, too, but from allergies rather than tears. The back of Richards's only sport coat carried a dusting of white fur that McKay knew, from the tickle in his nose, had originated from some cat. He was beginning to sniffle now. Should have suggested Richards have it cleaned, he thought, reaching for his handkerchief.

McKay was stifling a sneeze as the prosecution began questioning their first witness, the police detective. Peter Shribman peered from the stand through rimless glasses that magnified his brown eyes. The compactly built man sat, hands folded in his lap, with a stillness that seemed at odds with the violent details of his testimony.

"Mr. Shribman," asked Alfred Gomes, the district attorney, "on September second of last year, did you have occasion to investigate apartment #352 at 48 Rock Street in Lowell, which had been occupied by Miss Anita J. Olney?"

"I did."

"And what did you find there?"

"A murder victim, identified as Anita Olney."

Gomes paused to allow the words to acquire weight, then looked toward the jury. McKay had always thought that Gomes, who was a frequent courtroom rival, had been cursed with a vaguely rat-like countenance. Gomes's small but protruding black eyes, set above a long nose and unfortunate chin, rarely blinked as they fixed upon a witness. His handlebar mustache didn't help matters either. While it was a judgment that McKay expected to pay for with a few additional moments in purgatory, he suspected that Gomes thought even worse of him. McKay had prevailed in all but a few of their encounters, and Gomes's pique had turned personal. He now generally refused to negotiate settlements with McKay and forced most of their cases to trial. Not that there had been any wiggle room in this one, anyway. It was either acquittal or murder one. And McKay was afraid that this was the case that might even Gomes's score.

Gomes turned back to the witness. "Please describe for the jury the scene as you came upon it in Miss Olney's apartment."

"Well," Shribman began, "the victim was lying facedown on the kitchen floor. She had sustained multiple stab wounds, primarily in her back and neck. She had been dead approximately twenty-four hours. There was blood surrounding the body—on the floor and on one of the walls. Some blood had also been tracked into the living room by an animal, apparently the victim's cat. Two kitchen chairs were overturned, and objects knocked off the counters."

"Your Honor, the prosecution submits to the jury photographs of the crime scene."

"Any objection, Mr. McKay?" asked the Honorable Gareth Simmons, glancing over half-glasses poised at the end of his nose.

McKay shook his head no and the projector whirred on, lighting a yellowed, slightly torn screen. The first slides were as Shribman had described. What had been Anita Olney lay crumpled. Masses of blond hair streamed away from the slight figure, contrasting vividly with blood pooled on the floor. McKay noticed two men on the jury averting their eyes. Another juror, an elderly woman, covered her open mouth with her hand. McKay thought fleetingly of his own daughter and suppressed a shudder.

The last slide displayed a baseball cap. A smear of dried blood stained the top of the blue hat and half-obscured the letters "G. E. I." emblazoned on the front. McKay stared at the screen for a long time. Something was off about that hat.

Gomes cleared his throat. "Mr. Shribman, where was Mr. Richards employed?"

"At Grady Enterprises, Incorporated. As a mechanic."

"Did you determine that the hat belonged to Mr. Richards?"

"His prints were all over the visor."

"And you found it next to the body?"

"Yes. It—"

"Tell us about the locks in the apartment," Gomes cut in.

"The door was set to automatically lock. The windows were also locked and unbroken."

"No sign of forced entry?"

"No."

"Mr. Shribman, in your opinion, how could the perpetrator have gained access to Miss Olney's apartment?"

"Well, he would've had to have had a key. Or been let in."

"He would have had to have had a key, or been let in," repeated Gomes with gravity. "Thank you, Mr. Shribman. Your witness, Counselor."

McKay unfolded his rangy frame from his chair. His legs were stiff as he approached the stand. I'm feeling this case in my bones, he thought, as he ran a hand through his graying hair.

"Mr. Shribman, did you test the blood found in Miss Olney's apartment?"

"Yes. Everything originated from the victim."

"And where were those samples taken from?"

"From the floor next to the body, and also from splatters on the wall."

"Nowhere else?"

Shribman looked at him blankly. "That's where the blood was—the floor and the walls."

"But you said that there were also animal prints."

"Oh. Yes, well—"

"And you didn't test those prints?"

Shribman shrugged. "They were tracks from the body."

"So you didn't test *all* the blood stains, did you?"

The detective squirmed slightly. "No."

"And you said these tracks were in the living room. Did they extend all the way to the body?"

Color drained from Shribman's face. He held McKay's eyes. "Oddly, no."

"Yes—very odd, isn't it, Mr. Shribman? Odd unless the blood in those prints came from someone else, correct?"

"Objection. This is ridiculous, Your Honor!" Gomes cut in.

"Overruled, Counselor. The witness will answer the question." Judge Simmons absently touched a crystal statue of a curled and sleeping cat, which he always placed on his bench. Attorneys had long debated the significance of this cat after hours, and it had prompted an enterprising few to send the judge Christmas cards graced with pictures of cats or kittens. The statue had evolved into something of a courtroom talisman: Supposedly, its placement on the left side of the bench favored the prosecution; a right side orientation meant sympathy for the defense. McKay noted that the statue's current position was dead center in front of Simmons.

Shribman regained some composure. "I can't see how that's possible."

"But it *is* possible, is it not?"

"Yes. But unlikely."

"Now, sir, tell us about that baseball hat. Where did you find it?"

"About four feet from the body."

"Did you find it right side up?"

Shribman's eyebrows rose. "Yes, I did."

McKay rubbed his chin. "If a hat just accidentally fell off someone—say if it were knocked off, or if the person bent over—how would that hat most likely land?"

"I suppose upside down. But that depends—"

"And how would you characterize the bloodstain on the hat?" McKay interrupted.

"The top of the cap was stained."

"In what manner?"

"A solid stain. It was a smear."

"Now, if a garment worn by a killer during a knifing were blood-stained, what form would that stain usually take?"

Shribman paused, then pushed his bangs back with the palm of his hand. "Probably a splatter."

"And where would the splatter be?"

There was another moment of silence. "In the front."

"Now again, Mr. Shribman, how would you characterize the blood-stain on Mr. Richards's Grady Enterprises cap?"

"A solid smear on top of the cap." Shribman's voice was quiet but clear.

"A solid *smear* on *top* of the cap," McKay repeated. "And the cap right-side up, too. Mr. Shribman, that hat looked placed to you, didn't it?"

Shribman was silent.

"Mr. Shribman?"

"Yes."

Gordon McKay's eyes were briefly lit from within. "Thank you, Mr. Shribman."

As he returned to his chair, McKay reflected that Anita Olney had been near the age of his own daughter, Clarissa, whom he had met for break-fast that morning. The pictures had gotten to him because Clary had hair like that. In the restaurant he had admired his daughter's long golden curls when she turned around to signal their waiter. She had her mother's hair. And her mother's eyes, smile, and laugh, he thought wistfully—at least the way he remembered them. They'd lost her so long ago.

But Clarissa, a lawyer like her father, was alive and spirited and most likely arguing a case that very moment. She was engaged to a man McKay thought highly of, and he knew they both looked forward to children. McKay vicariously savored their anticipation of the future. What, he wondered, would Anita Olney's future have been?

🐈 🐈 🐈

Gomes called his next witness. Cameron Elliot Westfield, a tall, slim man wearing a charcoal Hart, Shafter and Marks suit, strode purposefully to the stand. Reflections of the brass ceiling lights glinted off Westfield's shoes.

"Mr. Westfield, would you tell us how you knew Anita Olney?"

Westfield cleared his throat. "I am president of the Lowell Bank and Trust. Miss Olney had been my secretary for approximately six months."

"And did you ever observe Miss Olney's interaction with the defendant?"

"Yes. Mr. Richards occasionally visited her at our office."

"And how would you characterize those interactions?"

"Hmmm. . . ." Westfield straightened his yellow silk tie. "I'm afraid she was always slightly fearful of him. She often looked worried. Eventually I asked if anything was troubling her."

"And what did she tell you?" Gomes paced in front of the witness stand, hands balled in his pockets, his nose elevated as if sniffing the air.

"She confided in me, but only slightly. She said that things weren't going well at home—er, with Mr. Richards. But she didn't elaborate. I assumed that it was a garden-variety relational problem. That is, until she came to work with a black eye—"

"Objection, Your Honor! Conjecture!" McKay half-rose from his seat.

"Overruled, Mr. McKay," replied Simmons. "We need to follow this. Continue please, Mr. Westfield." Simmons unconsciously fingered the crystal cat and moved it a few centimeters to the left.

Westfield shrugged his shoulders. "Well, she didn't want to talk about it. She seemed embarrassed—understandably, I guess. She said something about falling down the stairs." He stopped to smooth his close-cropped graying hair. "I took her explanation at face value until I actually saw the fellow in action—screaming obscenities at her right in our office."

"I never!" The shout came like a shot.

McKay put a hand on Richards's shoulder. "Mr. Richards . . ."

"But he's lying!"

Simmons gaveled the rumbling crowd into silence. "Once more and you're in contempt!" he snapped. "Go on, Counselor."

Gomes cleared his throat. "Mr. Westfield, did you discern the reason for the altercation that you witnessed between Miss Olney and Mr. Richards?"

"As I said, I walked in in the middle of it. But I gathered that it involved jealousy. I distinctly remember that he called her a 'slut.'"

Gordon McKay imagined one hundred pairs of eyes burning the back of Richards's head, boring into what was prejudged to be his black, evil soul. He studied the frowns on the faces of the jury—mostly middle-aged or elderly women, with a smattering of well-scrubbed young men who looked to him like recent graduates of a seminary. One woman was clutching the varnished rail of the jury box, shaking her head.

"Your witness, Counselor," said Gomes. His mustache twitched above a slight smile.

McKay leaned back in his chair and folded his hands behind his head. He took a long breath before speaking.

"Mr. Westfield," he began, "you never saw Mr. Richards lay a hand on Anita Olney, did you?" He noticed that the man took a long time to meet his eyes.

"Well, we were in a bank—in an office environment."

"You never saw him hit her."

The witness coughed. "I saw the aftereffects. Other employees at the bank did, too."

"But you just said she never directly told you that she was struck by Mr. Richards."

"She was embarrassed about it."

McKay rose and moved toward the stand. "But it's true that she never specifically said Mr. Richards hit her?"

Westfield turned and spoke directly to the jury. "She was afraid of him. I saw her bruises. I heard him scream at her."

"Answer the question, sir."

Westfield shifted in his seat. "I wouldn't have expected her to. Battered women . . ."

"Yes or no, sir."

He paused for several seconds, considering.

"No."

"Thank you," McKay replied, adding "sir" as he turned toward his chair.

Clary had remarked that morning, as they sipped coffee, "People are rarely what they first appear to be. Many of my clients, many of the people I see in court, have 'fronts'—or projections. The truth, if you ever find it, is buried in layers. A trial's a little like peeling an onion." She paused to bite into a muffin, then giggled. "And sometimes it makes you cry."

McKay had laughed, then rejoined, "And it smells stronger the more you unpeel!"

McKay reflected that this one was beginning to stink.

🐈 🐈 🐈

The next witness, Ellen Doyle, had been Anita Olney's neighbor. She was a plump woman who wore a too spring-like flowered dress that billowed above too-high pink sandals. She sashayed rather than walked. Ellen gave Gomes a bright smile that faded quickly. She just remembered she's in a courtroom and not a garden party, McKay thought.

"Miss Doyle," Gomes began, "how long had you and Miss Olney been neighbors?"

"Oh, neighbors two years. Friends almost as long. The way I met her was, when our building lost its power one winter and I had *fifteen* pounds of steak—that's prime rib, not chuck, mind you—in my freezer for a party, and I was just beside myself. Well, Anita had a balcony, so—"

"Did Miss Olney confide in you?" Gomes cut in.

"Oh definitely! Poor girl had no family left. And that's another story—you just wouldn't believe how her Mom suffered with her cancer. Just about took over her uterus and—"

Gomes raised his palm in front of the witness. "Miss Doyle. Miss Doyle, please!" Ellen stopped and stared blankly at him.

"Were you observant of the relationship between Miss Olney and Mr. Richards?"

"I should think so! I had dinner with them at least a couple times a month. Anita and I both loved to cook, see, and we'd taken this Chinese cooking class—" McKay could see that Gomes was trying to keep from rolling his eyes.

"And how would you characterize their relationship?"

Ellen sighed. A little longer than necessary, thought McKay.

"Well . . . definitely rocky, I'd say. Anita was frequently upset. She'd come over to my place after they'd had a spat."

Gomes's eyes glistened. "They argued frequently?"

Ellen for the first time looked hesitant. "Yes."

"About what?"

"Of course I don't know the *whole* story. But Joe seemed jealous a lot. And I know they had a lot of conflict about her new job."

"Why? It was an excellent position. Executive secretary to a bank president was a significant step up for her. Would you say," Gomes asked as he smoothed down the lapel of his suit, "that Mr. Richards felt somehow threatened, or undermined, by her advancement?"

McKay sprang to his feet. "Objection, Your Honor!"

"Sustained. A bit more slack, Counselor."

Gomes took a step back, folded his arms, and smiled. "Yes, Your Honor." He turned back to Ellen. "Miss Doyle, were you aware of specific issues involving Miss Olney's position that resulted in conflict between her and Mr. Richards?"

Ellen shrugged her plump shoulders. "Well, maybe the hours."

"Mr. Richards objected to her not being available?"

"That, and I gathered Joe didn't go for Anita's boss—and him so good to her! Anita got a pay raise after only three months. And Mr. Westfield's so nice. Took such an interest in her career! You know, he'd give her rides home, too, so she wouldn't have to deal with the bus—and he'd even drop by to pick up work so she wouldn't have to carry in so much in the morning." McKay suddenly stared hard at Ellen. His scalp tingled. "I always told Anita she was lucky to work for someone who cared. I could tell you stories about some of the bosses *I* had. There was this one—"

"Thank you very much, Miss Doyle. Your witness, Counselor."

McKay's chair scraped against the wood floor as he backed away from his table. He paused in front of Ellen Doyle for several seconds, during which he noticed the ticking of the clock over Judge Simmons's head. He crossed his arms before speaking.

"Miss Doyle, why would you suppose Joe Richards objected to Mr. Westfield?"

Ellen shrugged. "I just can't imagine. He was so wonderful to Anita."

"And in your opinion, Miss Olney appreciated Mr. Westfield as a boss?"

"Oh yes! It was always 'Cameron this' and 'Cameron that.'"

"They had a close working relationship?"

"Anita would've *slaved* for Mr. Westfield."

"And exactly how often did you see Mr. Westfield at Anita Olney's apartment?"

"Objection—"

"Your Honor," McKay cut Gomes off, "I'm pursuing an avenue of questioning that the prosecution itself introduced."

"I really don't see the relevance, Counselor. Sustained," Simmons said gruffly.

McKay sighed. "Miss Doyle," he began, "I understand that you were the one to alert the police after Miss Olney was murdered. Tell us how you came to determine that there had been an attack."

Ellen looked suddenly solemn. "Well, the cat, actually. I found Casper wandering around the hall, meowing pitifully—and Anita never let him out of the apartment. I thought he'd just been shut out, so I knocked but got no answer—which was odd for a Sunday morning. Anita liked to sleep in and then cook a good breakfast. Often, I'd join her."

"What did you do?"

"I took Casper into my place and gave him some food. The poor kitty's still with me. Then, all day, I knocked to see if Anita'd come home. Toward night, I got a funny feeling that something was wrong. Anita had left a key with me the last time she went away on vacation—with Joe," Ellen sniffed and wiped at a tear underneath her eye, "so I could go over and feed Casper for her. She said to keep it for the next time—or in case she locked herself out or somthing."

McKay crossed his arms and looked down at the floor before continuing. "Miss Doyle, did you hear anything, see anything, *notice* anything strange the weekend that Miss Olney was murdered?"

Ellen held his eyes for a long moment. "Let me think. . . ."

"Did you see anyone go into or come out of her apartment that weekend?"

"Only Mr. Westfield."

🦌 🦌 🦌

Murmuring filled the courtroom. McKay whirled around to glance at Westfield, whose face was white, then turned back to the stand.

"Mr. Westfield was in Anita Olney's apartment the night she was murdered?"

"I ran into him Saturday evening, leaving with a sheaf of papers. He told me Anita'd been typing an important document at home. . . . Oh!" Ellen's hand flew to her mouth.

McKay turned to the bench. "Your Honor," he began in a resonant voice, "I move for a suspension of this trial pending an investigation of an additional suspect who has just been determined to have been at the scene of the crime, Mr. Cameron Westfield."

"This is an outrage!" Westfield shouted.

"Order! Order!" It took five strikes of Simmons's gavel to silence the crowd. "Bailiff, remove the jury! Gentlemen, in my chambers immediately!"

McKay and Gomes followed Simmons's billowing robes through the courtroom doors and down the hall. The judge swept into his chambers and abruptly turned to them, arms akimbo. He fixed Gomes with a wide-eyed glare.

"Counselor, I expect this to be the last half-baked case I see in my courtroom! You have more work to do."

🐐 🐐 🐐

McKay parked across the street from Joe Richards's building and picked his way around mud-streaked snow banks to reach the front steps. The day was nasty. Wind-driven sleet seemed to aim for the half inch of exposed neck between his hat and scarf. He stepped through the door quickly, then tried to ignore the urine stench permeating the foyer.

He was tired. The call from the D.A.'s office had awakened him from a sound sleep that morning. He'd groggily punched at his alarm clock, mistakenly believing that it was the source of the offending ring, then wrestled with his sheets as he hurried out of bed. He had just entered the living room as the message was ending, and he caught the words ". . . results implicate a third, unknown party." There had been no going back to sleep.

McKay searched through the names printed on bits of masking tape stuck next to the line of doorbells and pushed the one marked "Richards." The inner door buzzed immediately. He climbed one flight of steps and found Richards waiting outside his apartment, holding a fluffy, loudly purring white cat.

"Hello, Joe. New roommate?" McKay immediately felt an itch gathering in his nose.

"Hey, Gordon. Meet Casper. He was Anita's, remember?" Joe rubbed the top of Casper's head. "Damn cat always followed me around when I visited and glued himself to my lap. Figured the furball would be company."

"I thought he was with Ellen."

"Yeah, well. I guess Ellen had to let him go. She's allergic. In fact, I found him outside her place, stuck in a tree—he started meowing when he saw me. Come on in and sit down."

The only furniture in Richards's living room was a sofa, television, and small dinette set. But the room was clean and neatly picked up, except for a dish of cat food that trailed several Friskies nuggets. McKay peeled his coat off and sank onto the couch. "So, you've seen Ellen?"

Richards smiled and colored slightly. He put the cat down and sat. "She keeps calling me. Telling me how sorry she is about Anita and about all the shit I've been through. Things like that. And, she started bringing dinner over. And—well . . . in fact, she's coming by this afternoon."

"Joe, I came by to tell you that Westfield was let go. The DNA results didn't match. Those paw prints were human blood that wasn't Anita's or yours, or Westfield's either. So the case is still open."

"God, I hope they find that bastard. You know, I suspected all along that Anita and 'Mr. Pinstripe' were carrying on, but—"

"They were. He admitted it."

Richards's jaw tightened. "Yeah. Well."

"And, while we can't prove it, I suspect that he may have found her—I mean after she was killed—when he came by that day. Found her and didn't say anything. He's married. He's prominent. He's not supposed to have a key to his secretary's apartment."

"And Anita wasn't worth going to the police for," Richards muttered bitterly.

"Worse than that, I think. Joe," McKay leaned forward and clasped his hands, "was your G.E.I. hat in Anita's apartment before the murder?"

"She had one. I'd given her one a while back."

McKay nodded slowly. "Westfield might have also tampered with the crime scene. He may have been worried that someone knew about his relationship with Anita, so he placed that hat."

"Asshole!" Richards stood up. "Why can't you do something about that?"

McKay sighed. "Because we can't prove anything, Joe. We don't know. I'm just trying to piece things together in my own mind." They looked at each other for a long minute.

The doorbell startled both of them. "Ellen," Joe said and got up to buzz her in. He opened the apartment door.

She arrived a few seconds later, flinging her arms around Joe's neck as she walked into the apartment. Joe briefly patted her back then released himself.

"Ellen, Mr. McKay's here."

Ellen looked around, startled. It took a second for her to compose her face into a tentative smile. "Why hello, Mr. McKay." She walked over to shake his hand. "How nice to see you."

"You too, Ellen. Actually, I was on my way out."

"Why don't you have dinner with us?" Richards asked. "We have plenty of the spaghetti sauce that Ellen made. Please stay."

Ellen noticeably blanched, then smiled weakly. "Yes, Mr. McKay. Joe appreciates what you did so much." She slid out of her coat and handed it to Richards, then reached up to remove her hat. The left cuff of her dress sleeve was unbuttoned and the fabric fell away from her wrist.

"Oh, thank you, but I—" McKay stopped when he noticed the four parallel scratches running the length of her forearm. "Well sure. I'd like that. Thanks."

She quickly buttoned her sleeve. "Joe, do you have any wine? I could really use a—"

Ellen was interrupted by a low, unearthly growl from the floor. Casper stood facing her with his back arched and fur on end. The cat hissed, baring his teeth. Ellen took a step back.

"Casper! Be nice!" Joe scooped the cat into his arms. "I don't know what gets into him when Ellen's around. He's so friendly with everyone else."

Ellen's hand shook as she smoothed her hair. She gave a brittle laugh. "I guess I'm just not a cat person. So tell me, Mr. McKay, is the case sewn up yet?"

McKay rubbed his chin. "Well no, Ellen, it's not. But I don't think it will be long now. Not long at all. . . ."

MR. BIGGLES FOR THE DEFENSE

Matthew J. Costello

The phone intercom produced a soft tone that made Ernest K. Thorp stop doodling on his Palm Pilot 5 with its expanded memory and never-used 33.6 kps modem.

"Yes, Connie?"

Connie was actually Conseula Romero, wife to Antony, spelled thusly, with a giant emphasis on the 'An'. Whenever Consuela—Connie—referred to her husband by name, her jaw opened wide as if she were about to engulf a hoagie with the works.

Or something.

And old An-tony Romero made periodic visits to the office, to scarf up his wife's check or just lurk in the outer office for a few minutes, marking his territory. He was big, solid, a Latino tank of a man; one would not want to get old Antony mad by hitting on his pretty, petite wife.

Besides, she was a good secretary and budding paralegal. His other paralegal, Molly, was—Ernest imagined—president of the local Harley and Jack Daniel's shooters club. But she, too, was more than competent.

Competence was good. Made the wheels of enterprise roll. Kept the bucks flowing into Ernest's small but growing practice in criminal law.

"Mister Thorp, I have the County Jail on the line."

Except, despite her competency, Connie pronounced it "Meeester Thorp." Someday, when Antony wasn't around, he'd have to suggest to her to get some elocution or diction lessons. Lose the accent. Play a little Pygmalion with the bright-eyed lady from the Dominican Republic.

"Thanks, Connie. I'll pick up."

Ernest knew the man on the other end of the phone. When he had been with the prosecutor's office, he had had lots of dealings with James Tidyman, County Jail Supervisor. It paid to be nice to old Jimbo since he could make life a piece of cake—or hell—for any of Earnest's clients.

And the current request on the table was . . . definitely one for the books.

"James, thanks for getting back to me."

James grumbled something in reply, something that sounded like, "Sew rye, Urn."

As in, "It's all right, Ern."

"So have you run our request through the powers that be?"

While Jimbo processed the question, Ernest brought up the handy-dandy calendar on his Pilot. Tomorrow afternoon was clear, had been wiped clean in anticipation of getting the green light for his little court-approved experiment on behalf of his client.

"Well—" Ernest heard the word *whale*—"there's one little problem. The D.A.'s office doesn't rightly mind you taking Mrs. Jerryman out of the jail—as long as you have two of my deputies with you."

Why, thought Ernest? Did they imagine that petite Mrs. Jerryman would make a getaway and head south? Pick up a dinghy to Castro's Cuba and ask for political asylum? *I murdered my husband with his claw hammer. Can I stay here please?*

"So, what's the problem, Jimmy? We'll bring the deputies along."

Jimmy grunted. Not exactly a grunt, but some sort of primal sound that represented a *problem*.

"Well you see, Ernie . . ." Another *whale* sighting. "We have this *problem*. Gotta take the two deputies. And that's time away from jail, maybe, Ern, even overtime, plus the bookkeeping. What I'm trying to say here—"

What he's trying to say, Ernest knew, was . . . where's the beef? Or at least the grease to make this little road-show work. Money makes the world go around, and nowhere more so than in the court system of this great country of ours.

"Oh, is that all? Don't you worry about that, Jimmy." As in, take the damn gun from my head, the cash is coming. "I'm sure Mrs. Jerryman can

cover the expense of the deputies and, of course, your own personal overtime dealing with bookkeeping."

A bit of hesitation on the other end of the line. Ernest guessed that
Jimbo was wondering if he should nail down that figure right now. But
Jimmy must have thought the better of it.

"Alrighty then, Ern. We're all set." The "we" of the "we're" was a pig-
calling sound. Ernest could picture the man's mouth widening to a big
satisfied grin. "You can come by this afternoon and take her to her house.
Just one question, Ernie, about your little plan."

Ernest wanted the call ended. He needed to call the judge's office to
get a court observer to meet them at the jail.

"What's that, James?"

"Well . . ."

There she blows.

"I was wonderin' . . . will you pick it up, or should I send one of my
deputies?"

Ernest was half listening, scrolling through his phone numbers until
he reached the one for Judge Pillbord's office.

"Pick up?"

"Yes, the cat, the kittie? Want us to get it?"

Ernest laughed. The cat. The creature at the center of this whole little road trip.

"No, James. Don't worry. I'll take care of that."

Yes, Ernest would pick up Mr. Biggles from the kennel on the way to
the jail. After all, Mr. Biggles was about to be the defense's star witness!

🐈 🐈 🐈

Ernest waited on the street by the side exit to the County Jail. The sun
was blistering, and he wondered if he should have waited in the car. But
he had a whole entourage with him: the two officers of the jail and the
court reporter. It was a regular little circus train heading to the house
where William Jerryman was murdered with a claw hammer by—it
would seem—his petite wife.

It fell to Ernest Thorp to disprove that claim.

The side door of the jail opened. Mrs. Linda Jerryman walked out,
blinking in the sun. She wore a green county-issue jumpsuit that did little to hide the fact that, though she was small, she was more than an
attractive package. Obviously the sixty-two-year-old Mr. Jerryman must

have thought so, bringing her back from a business trip to Las Vegas, already married.

Linda Jerryman came up to Ernest and grabbed his hand.

"Ernie, did you get him?"

Ernest nodded. "He's in my car, Mrs. Jerryman, meowing like crazy."

Linda Jerryman ran to the car and opened the back door. Ernest could only see the small tufts of orange sticking out, but Linda draped herself over the carrier.

"Mr. Biggles, mommy's missed you soooo much!"

In response, Mr. Biggles produced a long, soulful meow. The meaning, Ernest imagined, was probably less "glad to see you, too" than "get me the hell out of here."

Linda turned back to Ernest. "Can I take him out?"

Ernest shook his head.

"No. Not till we get to the house. Then you can"—he looked at her two guards and the court observer—"show us everything you told me about."

Now Linda stood up, all business. She sniffed as if the reunion had overcome her just a tad. "Right. Well, you'll see. You'll all see. Mr. Biggles will show you. Then," she said with a big smile, as big as the yawning emptiness of the Great Plains states where cornfields stretch from Omaha to Mars, "everything will be fine."

Right, Ernest thought. *Maybe.* Though not too fine for Mr. Jerryman, who was already six feet under with a nasty hole in his forehead. Fine was a word Mr. Jerryman had left behind forever.

"We better get going," one of the guards said. This test wasn't supposed to take too much time.

Ernest nodded. Mr. Biggles was in the car, and now they were ready to see how cute little Linda's defense all boiled down to one mangy, orange cat.

🐈 🐈 🐈

As they pulled up to the house, Ernest glanced over at the two guards to catch their reaction to the size of the mansion. He could see from the expressions on their faces that they suddenly had a deeper understanding of who it was Mrs. Jerryman was accused of killing.

The victim, her hubby, had major bucks.

The house resembled a giant cruise ship, a mammoth boat of a mansion that only went up two stories but occupied an entire block, shrouded by tall palm trees dotted with tropical pines. It was all but invisible from the street, but once through the electronic gates, everyone in the car was treated to an unobstructed view of one mighty big house. In fact, the only place Ernest could compare it to, at least in the environs of Miami, was the castle occupied by Al Pacino in *Scarface*.

Come to think of it, he ended up getting whacked too.

Anyone who came to kill Mr. Jerryman would have to get past the electronic gate, then past the house's own security system, then—God!—somehow find the billionaire in this expansive warren of rooms.

Didn't seem worth the effort.

Especially since, in this case, the murderer didn't steal anything.

All of which made it doubly, even trebly, worse for Mrs. Jerryman's case.

Only one person stood to gain from Mr. Jerryman's sudden and violent demise—pert Linda Jerryman.

"Whoa—"

That was the reaction of one of the beefy guards to the house.

Linda made a derisive noise in response that sounded like the last belch of air escaping from a popped balloon, as in—"*You* try to keep it clean!" But Ernest was more than sure Linda Jerryman never had to deal with the day-to-day running of this stucco Tara.

They pulled up to the front. The shiny ribbon proclaiming a "Police Scene" rustled in front of the giant double-door entryway.

On cue, Mr. Biggles spoke up. Another long, low disgruntled meow filled the car.

"Oooh, Mr. Biggles," Linda purred. Then she turned to Ernest. "See, he knows." Then, nodding to the guards and then Ralph, the court-appointed observer, she said again, "See, he knows." And one more time for good measure, lest anyone missed the point. "He *remembers*."

The car stopped. The guards got out first and stood by the door while Linda got out, holding the cat carrier. Ralph was sitting beside Ernest in the front. He slid out and, Ernest noticed, began his official observing. A sworn court officer, his testimony about what happened during the next few minutes would be vital to the case.

Linda Jerryman turned to the entourage.

"I don't know if I can stand it."

Ernest nodded. Linda was undoubtedly talking about being overwhelmed by her memory of discovering hubby with the claw hammer buried in his forehead.

"It's okay," Ernest said. "We'll be out here." Then, in case she needed some honest encouragement, "You have to. For your case."

Was there ever any real doubt that she'd do it?

Do monkeys fly?

She took a deep breath. Everyone watched the intake of breath and its results with barely guarded appreciation.

"Okay," she said. "I'll go in now." She looked down at the cat. "Are you ready, Mr. B? Such a good kitty."

The words seemed almost to be a cue. But then how many times has this woman walked into a crime scene?

She walked to the giant double doors, entered the monster house, and shut the door behind her, while the guards, Ralph, and Ernest waited outside under the hot mid-summer Miami sun.

ﯫ ﯫ ﯫ

The ride back was quiet. Ralph took notes on a large yellow pad documenting what had just transpired inside the house.

Mr. Biggles, about to be returned to the pound, was also subdued, though based on what they had just witnessed, Mr. Biggles wouldn't be doing much more time in the feline slammer. Nor would his owner be incarcerated much longer.

Hard to believe, thought Ernest, *I may actually win this case.*

He looked over at Ralph, writing furiously on his fourth page of legal-sized yellow lined paper. Ralph was the court's eyes and ears on what happened. Then the jurors would decide.

He looked back at Linda, sandwiched between the two guards.

She smiled at him.

And, thought Ernest, *if I get Mrs. Jerryman off there will be no question that I'll get paid. None at all.*

He smiled back.

Not that he was such a great lawyer. But that was one hell of a cat. As the court was about to learn.

ﯫ ﯫ ﯫ

The downtown courthouse was stifling hot despite being sealed and air-conditioned. Perhaps so many bodies were overwhelming the cooling system. The tabloid "media"—if you could call those parasites by that name—were all over this story, grabbing pictures of Linda. The Internet had pictures of the murdered Jerryman only hours after the crime, though no one knows how the official photos got released. The pictures were extraordinarily grisly, but the murder mavens on the Web gobbled them up.

The Internet is so *educational!*

The courthouse was packed, obviously fueled by the day's testimony. Ernest looked around at the noisy crowd and thought, *they'll get their money's worth today. That's for sure.*

Ernest's assisting lawyer, a sleepy-eyed woman who knew criminal law like most people know their social security number, was ready to deal with all of the prosecution's expected objections.

The prosecution had the report from Ralph. They knew what was ahead. They didn't look happy.

Finally, the bailiff entered and asked the noisy assemblage to stand for Judge Pillbord. The judge, an unattractive woman with dark hair, bore a surprising resemblance to Judge Judy. So far during the trial she had kept a tight rein on what could have been a runaway freight train.

After everyone sat down, Judge Pillbord looked at Ernest, then at the prosecution team, and then she signaled that she'd like to talk quietly to both sides.

Ernest hurried up.

"Look, I don't want this turning into a circus today," she said, snorting a slight lateral *S*. Ernest nodded. "We're going to deal with this . . . evidence . . . the same way we've dealt with everything else about this trial."

She looked at the lead prosecutor to make sure he understood exactly what she was saying.

The prosecutor nodded. "Your Honor, I'd like to reserve a challenge to—"

Judge Pillbord held up a hand. "Your time to challenge has passed. You agreed to this test, you have the—" she waved some typed pages in the air "—documentation. It's up to the jury now, and what they make of it."

"But—"

"Let's get going!" Pillbord barked, her sloppy *S*'s kicking up spittle as she sent the opposing lawyers back to their desks.

Well, that was good, Ernest thought. *The state will have to sit there and take it.*

"Counselor?"

Ernest sprung to his feet. "The defense calls Ralph Guttentag."

The audience spun around to watch the short, squat man make his way down the aisle to the witness seat. After being sworn in, Ralph sat back, smiled at the judge and looked right at Ernest.

"Mr. Guttentag, would you please tell us in what capacity you serve this court."

Ralph cleared his throat. "Yes. I am a court-appointed, legally bonded impartial observer."

Another smile.

"Yes, and in that capacity you do what?"

"Oh, I observe or note things for the court, provide depositions—"

"And in general, act as the court's eyes and ears?"

"Exactly."

"Objection." The lead prosecutor was starting his attempt to stem the tide of the upcoming testimony.

Pillbord looked right at him. "Your honor, Mr. Guttentag's testimony is still subject to interpretation. He can't suggest that his observations represent fact."

"Overruled," Pillbord said.

So much for that objection, and probably any more to come. Ernest smiled at the prosecutor. *Suck it in,* he thought, *because you're going down.*

"Now, Mr. Guttentag, would you please tell us what you saw on the thirteenth of this month, just yesterday."

"Yes, it's in my report, but I will tell you." Ralph started in by describing the trip to the Jerryman house, with the cat in tow.

"If it please Your Honor, the defense would like to produce the just-mentioned cat, Mr. Biggles, as defense exhibit A."

The prosecutor jumped up again but was again waved away by the judge, who gave the order for Mr. Biggles to be brought in and placed on an evidence table. In moments, the cat carrier, with Biggles's yellow fur sticking out of the holes, was part of the show in the courtroom.

"It was this cat that went with you, isn't that right, Mr. Guttentag?"

Guttentag leaned forward as if trying to see more of the cat in the carrier.

"I assume so." He smiled. "I mean, if that's Mr. Biggles."

In response to its name the cat meowed, and the courtroom burst out in laughter. It *was* funny, but Ernest had to keep a firm hold on the proceedings, otherwise the absurdity of it all would get in the way of the defense.

"Now, if you'd tell us what you saw yesterday?"

A deep breath. "Well, Mrs. Jerryman entered the establishment with Mr. Biggles while we waited outside."

"We?"

"Yourself, Mr. Thorp, me, and the two guards."

"And can you tell us why we waited?"

"Yes, I can," Ralph said. "The point was to demonstrate what would happen when an intruder entered the house."

"An intruder?"

"Yes, someone who didn't belong there."

"I see. Go on please."

"Well, we waited—I don't know—about five minutes, and then we walked up to the front door."

"With you in the lead?"

"Yes."

"And could you tell us what happened then?"

"Sure. I entered the house."

"Using a key?"

"Yes."

"So you didn't make any big noise, nothing alarming or disruptive?"

"Oh no, we entered very quietly."

"And then?"

"Well, I knew Mrs. Jerryman had gone to her room just as she had the night of the unfortunate encounter—"

"Objection, Your Honor, to the witness' terminology. It's not an 'unfortunate encounter,' it's a murder. Cold blooded. Bloody, a—"

"Sustained." The judge turned to Ralph. "The witness will be directed to call the 'encounter' a murder."

Ralph nodded. "Y-yes, Your Honor."

Ernest looked at the beleaguered prosecutor and rolled his eyes. Is that the best he could do—hairsplitting over terminology?

"Mr. Guttentag, would you please continue?"

"Yes. We entered, me in the lead."

"And you didn't see anyone?"

"Didn't see anyone . . . except for the cat, Mr. Biggles."

Ernest walked over to the cat carrier. "Your Honor, may I?"

Pillbord nodded. Ernest opened the carrier and pulled out the fluffy orange cat.

"You saw *this* cat?" Ernest gave the cat a little scratch under its chin.

The cat arched up, obviously starved for affection after his time in the pen.

"And tell us what happened then."

"Mr. Biggles was there, at the foot of the stairs, and as soon as we entered, he started hissing, howling . . . it was weird. Like he was some kind of alarm cat."

"Obj—"

"Overruled. Continue, Counselor."

I'm on a roll, Ernest thought. *Everyone wants to hear what old Mr. Biggles did.*

"Continue, Mr. Guttentag."

"Yes. Mr. Biggles hissed and growled, and then he hacked up this giant, reddish hairball."

"Really?"

"Yes, and in a flash, after more hissing, another."

The courtroom grew quiet.

"Two hairballs? Right there?"

"Yes . . . and then one final one, all in a row. It was some kind of reaction to strangers, I guess."

"Objection, Your Honor, Mr. Guttentag is simply interpreting what could have been—"

The judge hesitated. Sustain it, and she'd have to tell the jurors to ignore what had been said. Overrule it, and then Ernest could deliver the *coup de grâce.* Courtesy of Mr. Biggles.

"Overruled. The witness is simply providing what he saw to be happening at the time. Mr. Thorp, continue."

Swish! He shoots and scores. Ernest looked back at Mrs. Jerryman, who looked pleased, mighty pleased. In fact, from the twinkle in her eyes, *way* more than pleased.

"Thank you, Mr. Guttentag. You may step down."

Ralph left, hairball testimony delivered, while Ernest turned to the judge.

"Your Honor, I would like to re-admit to evidence the crime scene photograph, enlarged, as defense exhibit B." Ernest went to the side of his desk and produced a poster-sized enlargement of the crime scene.

It was a cropped close-up, showing a portion of Mr. Jerryman's head, which looked like a disfigured moon of Jupiter with an erupting volcano gushing red lava.

The vision of the head was horrible, so enlarged as to be unreal but revolting nonetheless. But the little circles behind the head were what Ernest wanted everyone to see—the three clumps that, as could be confirmed in the official detective's report, were three reddish hairballs in a line.

Mr. Biggles had this odd response to strangers. Soon as they came in the house, he'd hack up fur . . . right in a line.

He did it the other day, and he did it the night Mr. Jerryman was killed. And he left the evidence right there, at the foot of the stairs for everyone to see. Some stranger killed Mr. Jerryman.

And as they say: case closed.

🐈 🐈 🐈

A week layer, Ernest was once again back at the Jerryman mansion, this time sitting cozily on a couch with the widowed mistress of this lavish domain—and all the money attached to it.

She handed Ernest an envelope.

"Thank you," she said, pressing the envelope of cash into Earnest's hand. She smiled, and the room felt a bit on the warm side.

Mr. Biggles meowed, a jealous lover, and wandered in. He hopped up beside Ernest and gave him a steely-eyed stare.

"Hope he doesn't—" Ernest laughed and made a gagging gesture.

Mrs. Jerryman didn't laugh. "Don't worry, he wouldn't. Not without my permission." She hesitated. "After all, you're not a stranger, and I don't want you to be."

The temperature climbed another few degrees.

Mr. Biggles growled again. Mrs. Jerryman made a cooing noise.

"Ohh, Mr. Biggles, you're upsetting Ernest." Then she made a little whistling noise, and Mr. Biggles literally leaped off the couch and jumped onto an empty chair like magic.

Ernest laughed. "Some trick."

"Oh, Mr. Biggles knows lots of tricks!" She made another whistle, and this time Mr. Biggles threw himself into the air and turned 360 degrees around.

Ernest gasped. "That's amazing. You should do a show."

Mrs. Jerryman's smile broadened. "Oh, but we did do one."

Ernest nodded. And he had a funny feeling, like when you've eaten something that you know won't agree with you. But the trouble was still mere moments ahead.

"A show?"

"Yes. In Vegas. 'Mr. Biggles and Linda.' We did the lounges. That's, where I met my—" she took a deep cleansing breath "—husband."

"A show." Now Ernest took a breath. "What kind of show?"

"Mr. Biggles did tricks. Lots of tricks."

"Lots?"

"Yes. There wasn't anything I couldn't teach him, isn't that right, Mr. B?" On cue, the cat spun around in the air again.

"Could teach him anything, could you?"

Mrs. Jerryman smiled broadly. "Anything."

Ernest looked over at Mr. Biggles. He was tempted to ask the question about what exactly were the limits of Mr. Biggles's performing talents.

But the trial was over.

The verdict was in.

Besides, maybe Mr. Biggles could learn to stop growling at him.

After all, he can learn to do anything!

FAMILY TIES

Richard Chizmar and Barry Hoffman

1

A couple years ago, my momma told me about the one and only time she saw her daddy cry. It was a very long time ago at his youngest brother's funeral. Uncle Bobby was her favorite uncle in the whole world, Momma said, and he'd got himself killed at the factory. Momma told me it broke her heart to see her daddy that way. Felt like something inside of her was dying, like her heart was just ripping apart.

That's how I felt when they brought Jason into the courtroom.

Like something inside of me was dying.

He seemed so small. So scared. His arms looked so skinny in the handcuffs. And he wouldn't look at me.

He hadn't been the same big brother for a long time now, that's for sure, but the old Jason still lived inside my head. The way he used to wink at me and laugh when he was up to no good or fooling around teasing Momma. The way he used to take charge of a bad situation out on the street and turn it around. Or the way he could look at you with those big brown eyes of his and make you believe you could do almost anything, even fly if you wanted to. I was his Little One, and he was my big brother. Always so strong and sure of himself.

Now, sitting up there on the witness stand, as the lawyers and the judge asked him questions, he mostly just stared at the floor in front of him. Nodded his head every now and then. And when he did look up, it was like staring at a stranger. Like someone you passed on the street corner and never thought twice about.

A tear rolled down my cheek, and before I could wipe it away with my shirt sleeve, Momma did it herself with a balled-up Kleenex. "You okay, honey?" she whispered.

I nodded and tried to smile.

Momma knew I wasn't okay. She'd been through this before—a couple of times with one of her nephews—but this was my first time inside a courtroom. It sure looked different than on television. Everything was so big and the ceilings were so high and the furniture didn't look all shiny and pretty. And there weren't a lot of fancy-dressed people running around yelling and screaming like on television either. Just me and Momma and Jason, the judge, and a bunch of fat lawyers and policemen. And some lady with curly red hair who was typing everything that was being said.

It was cold too. Real cold. Didn't they have heat in a place like this?

I hugged myself and shivered. It all made me feel so small. Like a little girl. Much younger than fourteen years old. It all made me want my big brother even more.

"I'll always be there to watch your back, Little One," he used to tell me. "Try not to worry so much. I'll take good care of you."

And he had. Up until six or seven months ago. Until everything changed. . . .

2

Jason had been more than just a big brother to me. He'd been my father, protector, teacher, playmate, my best friend in the whole world. He and Momma were everything to me. Our daddy had taken off soon after I was born. Left one morning for work and never came back, Momma told me. Rumor was he moved down to Baltimore with some other woman. Jason was three at the time. I saw a picture of my daddy once. It was old and wrinkled and faded, but he didn't look a thing like Jason or me. Just some stranger is all.

From the time he was old enough, Jason took care of me. Took good care of me, too. Making sure I was dressed for school on time and had some breakfast. Making sure I did my homework before watching television. Teaching me to read better than anyone in my class and how to write cursive. How to wash my clothes and help keep the apartment clean. Always checking on me after school and making sure I wasn't smoking cigarettes or hanging around with what he called "the bad kids."

Momma did the best she could with both us kids. And her best was pretty darn good. We started out in the projects. Rats, roaches, brown water, and a whole lot worse. But Momma worked two jobs all day long and took in some baby-sitting whenever she had a couple of free hours. When I was six, we moved three blocks north to a two-bedroom apartment. It was still pretty cold in the winter—heck, I've never lived anywhere where the heat works the way it's supposed to—but we had hot food on the table and store-bought clothes on our backs. No more food stamps or charity for us. Momma was a proud woman, and she taught us kids to be the same way. Most nights, she'd come home from her first job, shower, grab a bite to eat or squeeze in a nap, and then she was gone to the bus stop and her night job. Seven days a week it was like that. Sometimes we teased her and called her the Phantom.

"It won't always be like this, kids," she'd promise us. "It'll keep getting better and better. Just you wait and see."

And we believed her, too.

In the meantime, it was up to us to take care of ourselves. But it wasn't all work either. We had fun together. Lots of it. We'd play board games when it was raining outside and watch movies on television. Jason even pretended to like to watch cartoons with me. Sometimes we'd play Stratego or Monopoly or cards at the kitchen table and bake chocolate-chip cookies or cupcakes. I can still see Jason now, walking over to check on the cookies and me pretending to sneak a peek at his game pieces. He'd give me one of those I-know-exactly-what-you're-doing looks and wink at me. He never once yelled or got mad because he knew I wasn't really cheating; just teasing him and trying to get a rise outta him.

The summer I turned ten years old, Jason taught me how to play basketball. How to dribble and pass the ball. How to shoot and play good defense. He was a great teacher; he was real patient and hardly ever got mad, even when I didn't listen to him. And he was tough with me, too. Didn't treat me like a sissy or anything. Later, when I started playing rec ball at the YMCA on Saturday mornings, he came to every game and sat in the stands with his friends from school. I could tell he was proud of me.

And, of course, it was Jason who brought Simon home three days before my twelfth birthday.

Simon was a skinny little runt of a gray kitten. The first time I laid eyes on him he looked more like a baby beaver than a cat. Jason had found him inside a Dumpster behind the Laundromat meowing away in a rainstorm. Said he was afraid the poor thing might've drowned if he hadn't come along. Figured the kitty could keep me company when he was at basketball practice after school or working down at the video store. That evening, we went down to Fisher's Pet Store, and he bought me a collar, a food and water dish, some cat food, and a place for Simon to use the bathroom. He gave me a big hug out on the sidewalk in front of Fisher's and wished me an early Happy Birthday. That's how I like to remember my big brother.

A few months later, when I started whining that Simon liked Jason more than me, he really surprised me and brought home another kitty. A girl this time. He named her Samantha—after the mom on *Bewitched*—and we made a return trip to Fisher's Pet Store. Simon and Samantha took to each other like brother and sister, and Samantha grew to be as fond of me as Simon was of Jason. Some nights she would sit on my lap for hours and watch television, and she slept at the foot of my bed every night, curled inside the covers.

It was around that time that Momma got her promotion at the store, and she was finally able to quit her night job. Good thing too, because before long she was busy at the store every night until eight or nine o'clock. She usually came home about an hour before my bedtime. *But just wait and see, kids,* she told us a few weeks into her new schedule. *It'll be worth it. It comes with a good pay increase and a lot of responsibility.* My God, we were so proud of her. I remember we celebrated with dinner at Pizza Hut and a movie afterwards. Jason gave a toast at the restaurant, and Momma started crying and laughing at the same time, and then I did, too. Jason said we were both crazy ladies and acted all embarrassed.

So things were good for all of us—no, they were great—for about a year after that. We both kept on missing Momma, but Jason and I understood why she had to be gone so much. And we still had each other. It was probably the happiest time of my life.

Then, just like that, things started to change.

Jason started to change.

It was little things at first. I noticed he didn't smile as often as he used to. He wasn't as funny as he once was—not as many wisecracks or practical jokes or silly faces. He didn't spend as much time hanging around with me either—watching television, playing games, or playing with

Simon and Samantha. Some days after practice he went right to his bedroom and stayed there until dinnertime. Some mornings I had to wake him up for school, when it had usually been the other way around.

And then it got worse. He went from being a little moody to downright grumpy. Some days he was mean to me; other days he just ignored me. I couldn't believe it. I hadn't done anything at all to make him act this way. Some nights we'd sit at the kitchen table eating dinner and not say a word to each other. It was like living with a different person.

I talked to Momma about it, and she told me it was probably just "girl trouble." That's exactly what she called it—*girl trouble*. Promised me that she would talk to him. Said all teenagers went through it, and you just watch and see, he'll be back to his old self before we know it.

But she was wrong. It kept getting worse.

Soon I started noticing other things. Jason didn't shower as often as before. Sometimes I could smell the sweat and the stink on him all the way across the room. And his clothes were always wrinkled and dirty. For someone like Jason, this was a big deal. In the old days, he used to be such a sharp dresser, so handsome and cool; all my girlfriends used to say so.

And then there was school. Once basketball season was over, he started missing classes. Some of my friends would tell me they saw him leaving school early, or once in a while, he would tell me he was sick and for me to leave without him in the morning. He would promise that he was coming in late, and then he'd never show up at all.

I tried to tell Momma what was going on, but she was real busy at work, and Jason always had an answer for her anyway. He was good like that; he always had it covered.

One of the worst things of all was how Jason started treating Simon and Samantha. First he just ignored them. He didn't feed them anymore or clean their litter boxes when it was his turn. He didn't play with them. He pretty much just pretended they didn't exist. That was bad enough, but then he got mean. He started pushing them away when they slinked over to him for attention. He tried to kick them when they got in his way. That kind of thing. I couldn't believe he could do those things, but he was like that pretty much every day.

Then, one day, I found out his secret. His dirty little secret.

I came home early from practice one Saturday afternoon and walked in on him in the bathroom by accident. The door wasn't locked, and I didn't even know anyone was home. Jason was bent over the sink, smoking a little glass pipe. His face was all red and sweaty and his eyes were wild and glassy. I knew what he was doing right away—smoking crack cocaine. I ran into the kitchen crying, and he followed me, the pipe still in his hand. I was hysterical, screaming and crying. Jason sat me down at the table and calmed me down, but first I made him put the pipe away; I couldn't even stand to look at it. We talked for almost two hours that night, and this is what he promised me:

He said it was only a phase he was going through. Kind of an experiment. Everyone was doing it at school, and he wanted to try it. But he knew it was stupid, and he'd already decided that it wasn't for him. Today was only the third or fourth time he'd tried it, he swore to me. So, no problem, he would stop. He didn't like the cocaine, and he certainly didn't need it. He would stop. It was as simple as that.

I wasn't sure if I should believe him or not, but he was so convincing. So much like the old Jason. God, it felt so good to see and hear him like that and to be able to talk to him again. He wasn't at all like the stranger I'd grown to know.

So by my bedtime that night, Jason agreed not to take drugs ever again. And I agreed not to tell Momma anything and to trust him. We were sister and brother again, and we watched television—Simon and Samantha on our laps—until Momma came home from work. I thought things were going to be better from that night on. This time it was my turn to be wrong.

Things were better for about a week.

But then came the next couple of months—Jason losing so much weight and quitting his summer-league basketball team; Momma complaining that money was missing from her purse and a necklace was gone from her top dresser drawer; Jason quitting his job at the video store. . . .

Call me stupid but I never thought it was the drugs. People got hooked on dope all the time—especially in my neighborhood—but not my brother. He was too smart for that, for goodness sake. I just thought Jason had changed. That happens lots of times, you know. Plenty of my friends were close to their sisters or brothers when they were younger and then as soon as they reached a certain age, they drifted apart. I just thought that's what was happening with Jason and me.

It all came to a head a few days after Jason's seventeenth birthday. I came home from school and found him sprawled on the kitchen floor. His face was a bloody, swollen mess, and his arm was bleeding. The kitchen table was overturned, and a chair was broken. Samantha was going crazy in the corner behind the trash can, meowing and whimpering louder than I had ever heard her.

Jason refused to go to the hospital, so I wet a washcloth and started cleaning his face. I kept asking him over and over again what had happened but all he would say was: "I'm sorry. I'm sorry. I'm so sorry. . . . "

I was just finishing with his arm when suddenly a sick feeling came over me and I asked him: "Where's Simon?"

He shook his head and started crying.

I felt the panic in my stomach. "Jason, what happened to Simon?"

"I'm sorry. . . ."

Louder this time. "Jason, where's Simon?"

And that's when he broke down and told me everything: about the drugs and the money he owed. About how they warned him this would happen. How they were waiting for him inside the apartment . . . and finally, about what they'd done to poor Simon, as his final warning to come up with the money or else.

My hands were shaking. I couldn't believe this was happening. Happening to us. Inside our own apartment. I picked up Samantha and walked into the living room. Sat on the sofa and cried for a long, long time. Poor Simon. God, I was going to miss him.

Before Momma came home, we cleaned up the mess and made up another story. I never asked exactly what happened to Simon; I was afraid to.

And, of course, Jason promised to stop again. He owed the men two hundred dollars. I loaned him all the money I had—just over forty—and he swore he would make good on his debt and never do drugs again. He swore he would borrow the money from his friends and get his job back at the video store and repay me. He promised me and I believed him. He was my best friend in the whole world.

Two weeks later, money wasn't a problem any more. But he wasn't working at the video store. Instead, he came home one evening, and I noticed the changes right away: a fancy gold watch on his right wrist, a thick bracelet on his left. A beeper clipped to his belt. A new jacket and boots. And a swagger to his walk that hadn't been there before. He walked up to me, pulled a wad of bills from his front pants pocket, and peeled off two twenty dollar bills and handed them to me. Walked into his bedroom without saying a word and closed the door.

I knew the truth then. He was never going to stop. Never. He was dealing now. Out on the street to pay off his habit. Using was bad enough, but dealing. . . .

For the next few days, I tried to think of how to tell Momma without breaking her heart. She was working so hard and was so proud of us, I couldn't bear the thought of telling her, of disappointing her. But she had to know.

That weekend, Jason brought home another cat for me. He had a gold-studded collar and a fancy gold tag that read *SIMON 2*. I kept the cat but threw away the collar and tag. I named him Jordan, and by Monday he and Samantha were old friends.

Jason had no problem flaunting his newfound wealth in front of me, but Momma was another story. If he knew she was going to be home, there was no jewelry, no flashy new clothes or pager on his belt. To Momma, he was still the old Jason, a little more distant maybe, a little more grown-up, but still her baby boy. He still came home every night, but he'd started sneaking out after Momma fell asleep.

One night, when I knew he was gone, I heard a story on the news about a drive-by shooting over on Madison, two blocks north from where we live. The man on the news said it was drug-related and three young men were killed. I cried myself to sleep that night with worry, and when I saw Jason the next morning in the parking lot in front of our apartment building, getting out of the passenger side of a shiny new Jeep Cherokee, I was relieved and furious at the same time.

I ran up to him and hugged him as the truck drove away.

"Oh my God, Jason," I cried. "I thought you were one of those men on the television, the ones that got killed—"

"Hey, hey, Little One. It's okay," he said, wrapping his arms around me. "It's okay. I ain't never gonna be the one, so you just stop your worrying."

I looked at him, at his glazed eyes, his crooked smile. He was high as a kite.

I hugged him as tight as I could, and he hugged me back. I kissed him on the cheek and said, "I love you, big brother," and I walked to school.

A couple days later, on a Sunday afternoon, it finally happened. Three policemen knocked on our door. They had their hands on their guns and a search warrant. There had been a middle-of-the-night robbery at Hardesty's Pharmacy, where Momma worked, and evidence at the scene pointed to Jason: a spare key, which was evidently used for entry, was found there, and the serial number was registered to Momma. And a wallet with Jason's identification was also found on the floor.

Although it was almost noon, Jason was still asleep when Momma let the officers into his bedroom. He was in handcuffs before he was fully awake. The policemen discovered five stolen watches and several baggies of cocaine underneath the mattress of his bed.

Jason never said a word when the officers walked him out of the apartment. Not to Momma, not to me, and not to the policemen.

3

Even Jason's voice sounded strange to me. The courtroom was so big and empty that it echoed off the walls. Or maybe it was the microphone, but he sounded like an old man, not my seventeen-year-old brother.

I listened to him talk:

"I didn't steal no watches."

"I wasn't in no fool store."

"No, sir, I don't know where they came from."

"No, Your Honor, I don't take drugs. Never have, never will."

I could tell he was trying to sound strong and smooth and in control—like the old Jason—but his voice reminded me of that afternoon when I found him beat-up and laying on the kitchen floor. Right before he'd started to cry and tell me how sorry he was.

I reached over and took Momma's hand. I gave it a little squeeze, and she did the same.

Twenty minutes later, with Jason sitting next to his lawyer, the judge pronounced Jason guilty and shook his head sadly as he handed down his sentence. "You leave me with no choice, young man. The evidence was found at the crime scene. You were caught with stolen property and crack cocaine in your bedroom. Yet you refuse to take any responsibility for the crime. I've taken into account the fact that you are a first-time offender, but . . ."

And then the judge sentenced Jason to a juvenile bootcamp upstate until his twenty-first birthday.

I heard Momma start to cry. I squeezed her hand again. I knew how hard this was for her.

"Removing you from this environment may be the best thing for you," the judge continued, and for the first time Jason met his eyes. "It's still not too late to turn your life around. There are people in this courtroom," he said, pointing to Momma and me, "who are counting on you. You've let them down. And now you have three and a half years to straighten yourself out and become the man you think you are."

And just like that, the judge banged his gavel and walked out of the room.

Suddenly the room was full of conversation and activity. The sound of shoes on the hardwood floor. Lawyers chattering away and shuffling papers. Briefcases being closed. Police officers huddled together talking. In a matter of minutes, Jason was headed for a side door, on his way out of the courtroom. He looked over his shoulder at us. There were tears on his face.

Momma stood on her tip-toes and waved and cried, "I love you, baby! I love you!"

And then he was gone.

We hugged right there in the courtroom. We hugged tight and for a long time, searching for hope in each other's arms. And then we headed home on the subway.

Three and a half years wasn't forever. And then we would be a family again. In the meantime, it was just Momma and me, and Samantha and Jordan. Just the four of us, waiting for Jason to come home again. Waiting for things to be the way they used to be.

All the way home, I thought about Jason. I thought about only the good times. Back when we were kids, playing those silly games and watching television for hours. Running around the apartment chasing Simon and Samantha. I thought about that smile of his and how he used to wink at me. How much he used to love me and Momma.

And I knew I had done the right thing. Stealing Momma's key from her purse and sneaking into the store that night. Taking those watches and hiding them under Jason's mattress. Leaving his wallet behind.

That night I fell asleep on the sofa with my head in Momma's lap, and I dreamed about my big brother coming home again.

For the Benefit of Bootsy

A John Francis Cuddy Short Story

Jeremiah Healy

Let me get this straight," I said to the man sitting in the client chair on the other side of my desk. "You're being sued by a . . . cat?"

Oscar Mudge squirmed a bit, the reverse stenciling of "JOHN FRAN-CIS CUDDY, CONFIDENTIAL INVESTIGATIONS" on my office door arching over his head. "No, Mr. Cuddy. I've been served with process by Dana Jeffers, who is in charge of a trust for the benefit of . . . Bootsy."

"Which you told me is a cat, though."

Mudge squirmed a little more, now seriously stressing the old chair, since he went about two-fifty on maybe five-eight of height. Well past forty, Mudge wore a gray tweed suit that looked a good ten years out of style, even with my limited appreciation of fashion trends. His tie was regimental, the black, straight hair parted slightly to the right of center, which I'd bet would parallel the man's politics as well. Boston's weather can be raw in November, and Mudge kept leather driving gloves on his hands.

He said, "Perhaps I should explain a little further."

I leaned back in my swivel chair. "Perhaps you should."

Mudge squared himself, and wood squeaked against torqued screws and glue. "For years I represented Felix Felber. Does the name ring any bells?"

"Textile magnate. Got out of the mills before they went south, then moved to Brookline and began doling out his money to various charities." I tried for more, but all that came back was, "And he died recently, from a fall, right?"

Mudge pursed his lips. "Quite good, Mr. Cuddy. Felix passed from us a week ago, but he allegedly executed a codicil to his will a week before that. A codicil drawn up by the Jeffers woman."

Allegedly stuck in my ear. "So Ms. Jeffers is a lawyer?"

"Yes, though rather a young one. And the amendment she drew provides that the bulk of Felix's estate goes to one legatee."

Uh-oh. "Not . . . Bootsy?"

The current expression on Mudge's lips would curdle the cat's cream. "Absurd, isn't it?"

"And you think that therefore Mr. Felber might not actually have . . ."

"It would have been so out of character for him, it's beyond absurd."

I stared at Mudge for a moment. "I think you need a lawyer."

His eyes closed and opened once. "Mr. Cuddy, I *am* a lawyer."

"Oh."

"One who is being sued for alleged malfeasance in the prior management of Felix's investments."

"You were his investment advisor?"

"Investment *manager,* actually. I had handled things for him ever since he had suffered a partial stroke three years ago."

"What about the attorney who did the original will?"

"I handled that as well."

"But Mr. Felber didn't ask you to do the amendment."

"No. In fact, in his last weeks, he never even mentioned the possibility to me."

"Why do you suppose that was?"

"Because," said Mudge portentously, "I don't believe the codicil's valid."

"Now it sounds like you need a handwriting expert."

"No. No, it's Felix's signature, all right." Mudge wrung his gloved hands, the leather making almost as much noise as my poor chair. "I've seen it affixed to hundreds of documents. To be sure, though, I did run the codicil by an expert against the possibility of tracing, and so forth. The signature is definitely the handwriting—even the pressure of pen—that Felix would have applied since the stroke."

"And so your theory is . . . ?"

"Felix couldn't have known what he was signing."

"And you want me to substantiate that this codicil therefore is fraudulent?"

"Yes. Two individuals allegedly witnessed the execution, Jeffers herself and the man who kept the grounds."

"Meaning the gardener?"

"Yes."

I reached for a pen of my own. "And his name?"

"Warren. Suh-*dell* Warren."

"Spelling?"

"S-e-d-e-l-l. One of their made-up names."

"Their?"

"Warren is a black, Mr. Cuddy. As is Dana Jeffers."

I put down my pen. "And because they're both of the same race, you automatically think they're in cahoots somehow?"

Mudge made the chair creak more than just squeak this time. "That, and the fact that Ms. Jeffers's mother, Lorraine, was Felix's housekeeper and cook."

"Lorraine Jeffers worked in the house, too, but didn't witness the signing of the codicil?"

"I imagine *law*-yer Jeffers didn't think *ma*-ma Jeffers would be suitable for that task."

I was about to ask Mudge to take his business elsewhere when he said, "You see, Mr. Cuddy, Bootsy the feline—legatee to an estate of nearly seven million dollars—belongs to Jeffers Senior."

"Oh."

A smug smile. "So, you appreciate my predicament. I feel responsible as Felix's long-term steward and confidante to prevent this preposterous fraud from being carried off, yet now that Jeffers Junior has sued me—*me*—for malfeasance, I must defend myself in the public's eye and in court against . . . against . . ."

"A cat."

Even the smug smile disappeared. "If you'll promise to stop repeating that," said Oscar Mudge, "I'll increase your daily rate by 10 percent."

🐈 🐈 🐈

I knocked on the door to an office in one of the older buildings fronting Massachusetts Avenue near Beacon. The painting on the exterior needed a major overhaul, and neither the lobby nor the elevator had impressed, either. But when a female voice on the other side of the fourth-floor door told me to enter, I saw an interior painted a bright and pleasing yellow, with hanging spider plants and a vase of tulips centered on the desk. The only woman in sight was African-American, late twenties, with corn-rowed hair bunched behind her head with a scrunchy. The hair band picked up one of the minor colors in her print dress and matched the polish on her nails.

She smiled, one gold incisor among the otherwise gleaming white teeth. "Can I help you?"

"Dana Jeffers?"

"Yes?"

"My name's John Cuddy." I opened my identification holder so she could read the laminated copy of my license. "I'm here about the estate of Felix Felber."

Jeffers took her time reading, the greeting smile fading. Then she looked up. "Maybe you should have a seat."

Her client chairs were more modern than mine, with chrome struts supporting caned seats and backs. I took the one to her right as she sat down in a padded judge's chair.

Jeffers said, "You're working for Oscar Mudge, I imagine."

"That's right."

"And what did he tell you?"

"Client confidence, counselor."

"Let me guess, then." Jeffers smiled again, but more like a predator sensing prey. "I'm aiding and abetting my greedy mother, who somehow snowed the late Mr. Felber into moving his millions."

"Are you?"

A blink. "Am I what?"

"Aiding and abet—"

"Mr. Cuddy," said Jeffers, coming forward in her chair and planting her elbows on the desk as though she wanted to arm wrestle. "Oscar Mudge thought he ran that poor old man's life. And I guess in a lot of ways—on account of the stroke—somebody had to. But Felix's *quality* of life jumped off the scale thanks to my mother's cat. Apparently, when he was a young boy, he loved Felix the Cat cartoons because 'Felix' was his name, too. And, as an old man, he just took a shine to Bootsy, and Bootsy to him. I visited Mama often enough in that house, I should know."

"And on one of those visits, you witnessed Mr. Felber signing the codicil you drafted."

"Sedell Warren and me, both."

"And Mr. Felber knew what you'd put in front of him?"

Jeffers stiffened. "I had him read it out loud, then explain it in his own words. He even talked about the cartoon stuff. Then Felix signed, without any coercion and in his own house."

"Does your mother still live there?"

Jeffers seemed a little thrown by the change of pace, the braided hair shimmering behind her like a beaded curtain. "Until Mr. Mudge tries to kick her out. But he won't, because somebody's got to keep everything looking nice for the Realtor to sell it."

I processed that. "My client is still the executor of the estate?"

"Of course he is. I do mostly criminal stuff, including that DNA case you might have read about last week?"

The *Boston Herald* had done a piece on a defendant getting off because his lawyer—apparently Jeffers—had matched some hair found at the scene of a murder to a suspect the police had overlooked. "But you felt competent enough to do the codicil?"

"Simple paragraph incorporating a simple trust. In one sentence, Felix left most of his estate to Bootsy. The proceeds of the house'll still go to Mr. Mudge's charities."

"*His* charities?"

"He didn't tell you?" A triumphant smirk. "Well, then, let me. Mr. Mudge is the 'investment manager' for every one of the charities named in the will. Which is fine with me."

"I thought you were suing my client for malfeasance in handling Mr. Felber's money."

"Look, Mr. Cuddy," Jeffers angled back in her chair, "the original will was done before Felix suffered his stroke. If he wanted to leave Mudge in charge of the charity things, that's fine with me. I just need an accounting for the trust of what's supposed to be in the estate, and Mudge won't give it to me. What else could I do but sue him?"

"How much did your mother receive under the original will?"

"Felix had provided for Mama to the tune of two hundred and fifty thousand dollars."

Pretty nice melody. "So you're saying she wouldn't need the other seven million?"

"I'm the trustee for Bootsy, not my mother."

"And who inherits when the cat dies?"

Another predator smile, the gold tooth glinting. "Maybe you should ask whoever's trying to kill it."

"What?"

"Same night that Mr. Felber took his header down the stairs, somebody nearly clawed Bootsy to death."

"Clawed?"

Dana Jeffers extended the three middle fingers of her right hand, curving them so that the polished nails seemed to be talons. "With one of those three-tined things, like you use in the garden?"

🐈 🐈 🐈

Brookline is a lovely town that borders Boston on the west. Though it's been civilized since the seventeenth century, some of the settlers must have thought they'd reached the Rockies, because I've never seen any other relatively flat topography sporting so many switch-back roads.

The Felber place occupied a cul-de-sac at the end of one of the switchbacks, with probably a commanding view of the city from its third-story windows. There were white pillars, red bricks, and cement cornices over every window, to the point that you might have mistaken it for an Ivy League dormitory.

I left my old Prelude in the circular drive and pulled a fob on the massive, paneled front door. The woman who answered a minute later was black and stolid. She wore a polka-dot blouse, denim skirt, and running shoes with white socks. Her hair was buzzed short, hoop earrings dangling from each lobe.

And she didn't look happy to see me.

"Mrs. Jeffers?"

"My daughter told me you'd be coming around."

"Did she tell you why?"

A scowl the older Jeffers might have learned from Oscar Mudge. "Said you thought we was stealing from Felix."

"That might be what my client thinks, but I'm trying to keep an open mind."

The scowl stood down a notch. "Suppose you'll be wanting to see things for yourself."

"That would help."

"Well," said Jeffers with a huff, "come on then."

I followed her through a high-ceilinged foyer that ended at two internal arches flanking a staircase to the second floor.

"These the stairs?"

"Where Felix fell down?"

"Yes."

"Uh-unh. The cellar ones."

"Cellar?"

"For his wines and such." Another huff. "I'll show you."

When we reached the kitchen, a cat was curled up on the sill of a small bay window, taking in the weak November sunlight. His head perked up, maybe at my unfamiliar step. He was all black, except for a white nose and four white paws and the three nasty scabs that ran longitudinally along his back where the fur had been shaved down to his skin.

I said, "Bootsy."

The cat rose to its feet and hissed at me.

Jeffers crossed the room to her pet. "Ain't nothing wrong with your instincts, Boots."

"I don't want to upset him any more, but I would like to get a look at his wounds."

She picked the cat up tenderly, then brought him over toward me, Bootsy growling all the way. "He don't like for you to touch him," she said.

I didn't, but Bootsy snaked a front paw at me anyway.

"You should teach him not to lead with his right," I said.

"Don't matter much. He don't have but two claws on his whole body."

"Two?"

"I got him as a stray. The people at the animal-shelter place didn't know how he got like that, except maybe somebody abused him. But he set you up with that little powder-puff right, then he cut you to the bone with the claws on his left."

I advanced my hand, Bootsy giving me the one-two and nearly grazing me with his dangerous paw, those remaining claws separated by a missing member. "You keep him indoors, then?"

"Try to. Once in a while, though, he escape, don't you, Boots?" The cat stopped growling at me and looked up at Jeffers. "Yes, that time the other cat got you, and you wouldn't come out even for food?"

I saw a door off the stove area. "That lead to the cellar?"

"Uh-huh." Jeffers put Bootsy back on the sill. "You can open it, you want."

The knob was old glass, and the steps below looked even older. Some were swayed in the middle, others listed a bit to port or starboard. No railing on either side.

I said, "Seems like it would have been kind of tricky for Mr. Felber to negotiate these."

A grunted laugh behind me. "Felix, he growed up in this house. Took those stairs two at a time till his stroke, when he got kind of frail and tentative." I went down tentatively myself. Ten degrees cooler, but what you really noticed was a stain on the cement floor at the bottom.

"That's poor Felix's head blood, where he landed. I tried to wash it out, but once blood comes, it want to stay, make you remember whose it was."

"What time did Mr. Felber fall?"

"Round ten at night, best as I can figure."

I moved toward the wine bottles stacked in columns of diamond-shaped boxes standing a foot from the cellar walls. "You didn't find him right away?"

"Not till the next day. Sedell and me went to the movies, and when we got back around ten-thirty, we was real quiet so's not to wake Felix. But come morning, I went to bring him breakfast, and his bed was empty."

Nice collection of wines, mostly reds and many of those Californian, with a sheet of stainless steel over the floor beneath them and some wooden blocks that matched the boxes to keep the lowest wines above any minor basement flooding. "Did it look like Mr. Felber had been sleeping in his bed?"

"That's what I mean about when he must've fell. Felix, he went upstairs to sleep every night at ten sharp to get his eight hours in. And I know he didn't fall after we got home, or one of us would've heard."

"Where were you and Mr. Warren?"

No hesitation before a firm, "I was in my room, and Sedell was in his."

"Were you present when Mr. Felber signed the codicil to his will?"

Jeffers hesitated a moment this time, then said, "I was there, alright, in the den. But Dana didn't want me signing, too. Just her and Sedell done it so everything be all legal."

I was about to ask for confirmation on Felix Felber reading and explaining the codicil aloud when I heard a rattling noise to my left. Turning, I was blinded by a blazing light that might have come from heaven itself.

"Sedell," said Lorraine Jeffers above me, "You close those doors before you let every bit of heat out of this house."

🦌 🦌 🦌

"I'm kind of dirty for sitting in the parlor."

Pointing to the left, I said, "That bench over there would be fine."

Sedell Warren led me toward a stone bench in the middle of a proud garden humbled by November's frosts. Reaching the bench, I saw a fat cherub carved in the middle of the top, seeming about to spit from its puffed cheeks.

"Puffed" didn't apply to Warren, though. Maybe six feet tall, he was so wiry that every bone his work clothes didn't hide seemed covered merely by skin and not by flesh as well. Pushing the bill of a stained John Deere ballcap off his forehead, Warren eyed me warily from sunken sockets. I said, "You know why I'm here?"

He nodded. "Lorraine's girl called her. I don't know one thing about what happened to Mr. Felber."

Both the Jeffers women had called him "Felix."

I said, "Actually, I'm more interested in what happened to Bootsy."

Warren frowned. "The kitty-cat?"

"Why would somebody attack him?"

A cracked and leathery hand rubbed a stubbly chin. "I know that's what Lorraine thinks, but could be he just run under one of my tools."

"You don't keep them hanging up?"

"I do, but Bootsy, he kind of a devil."

"How do you mean?"

Warren gestured with both hands. "He all the time getting into things, and whopping at them with his little feet, even though he don't have but the two claws left." Warren finished in a flourish of fists, like a boxer windmilling the speed bag. With authority.

I said, "You ever in the ring?"

A sheepish smile. "Some, back when I was a boy. Fight game ruint a lot of my friends. I got lucky, though. All's it did was knock some sense into me. I learned about flowers and plants." Warren sighed. "Mr. Felber, he just loved this garden to pieces."

"Back to Bootsy," I said, "you think he pulled one of your tools down on top of himself?"

"That's what I told Lorraine." Another sheepish smile. "Her and me, we been keeping company, if you get my drift?"

"That's what she told me, too."

"All right, then. When Lorraine and me come back from the picture show that night, I thought I heard something in my shed."

"Your shed?"

Warren waved his hand over beyond a clump of trees. "For Mr. Felber's garden. Well, I don't like for nobody to be messing around there, so I walked over before I went to bed. And one of my tools was off the hook."

"Off the . . . ?"

"Off the hook I hang it from. Was my 'claw-fork,' I call it. On the floor, and with blood dripping from the pointy parts. Must've been Lorraine's kitty-cat, whopping away with his paws till that claw-fork fell down and scratch him."

I thought about the wounds I'd seen on Bootsy's back. "Kind of deep and even scratches."

Sedell Warren gave me a wise smile this time. "Us peoples ain't ever gonna know all the things God's creatures can do."

I asked Warren if he'd walk me to the shed. Its door swung inward, so Bootsy could have pushed his way through. And the "claw-fork"—maybe twelve inches long including its wooden handle—was hanging low enough that the cat could have knocked it off. But the tool was also too low to build much momentum falling toward Bootsy, and I had trouble seeing how the wounded cat could have exited the shed without somebody holding the door.

🐾   🐾   🐾

Back in my office, I sat behind the desk and stared out my window at the Massachusetts statehouse across Boston Common. Most of the trees had dropped their leaves, and except for the capitol's gold dome, the scene looked as bleak as the Felber case felt.

Which is when it struck me that I thought of it as the "Felber" case instead of the "Mudge" case.

Opening a drawer, I pulled out some three-by-five notecards and started writing down the impressions I'd acquired. Oscar Mudge appearing so indignant in coming to see me; Dana Jeffers, the criminal specialist, seeming stubborn in her law office about the codicil and trust she'd drawn for Felber; Lorraine Jeffers projecting discomfort in speaking with me but defiance in defending her cat; Sedell Warren opining that Bootsy might have hurt himself on a gardening tool.

And then I tried to write down everything I'd learned about the late Felix Felber. His reliance on Mudge for investment management; his interest in the garden Warren maintained; his frailty from the stroke; his partiality to the housekeeper's cat.

Finally, I listed everything I'd learned about Bootsy himself, which made me think of a question I hadn't asked.

Picking up the phone, I dialed the Felber house. When Lorraine Jeffers answered, I said, "This is John Cuddy again."

"What you want now?"

"When I was over there today, you told me that Bootsy had once been in a fight with another cat?"

A pause before, "That's right."

"And you also said something like 'He didn't come out for days.'"

"Boots be licking his wounds, account of that other—"

"Mrs. Jeffers?"

Another pause. "Yeah?"

"Where was Bootsy hiding?"

🐈 🐈 🐈

"What in the world?"

Oscar Mudge stared at the two of us as I closed his office door behind Dana Jeffers. He struggled to rise from the other side of a large, mahogany desk, but I don't think his effort grew out of courtesy for us as visitors.

I said, "I think you ought to sit down, Mr. Mudge."

"How dare—"

"Maybe lie down," said Jeffers as she took a red-leather, brass-tacked armchair herself, the corn-rowed pony-tail flogging the back of it.

I settled on her seat's mate as my "client" plopped back into his, Mudge's left hand reaching for the telephone. "I'm calling the police."

I gave him my most ingratiating grin. "I have the direct number for the Homicide Unit, you want to save everybody some time."

Mudge froze with the receiver halfway to his face. "The Homicide . . . ?

Jeffers nodded. "Or you can talk to us."

The phone was still hovering when I said, "We've figured it out, Mr. Mudge."

Very deliberately, he put the receiver back in its cradle, then folded his left hand over his right and across the broad stomach. "Cuddy, you're supposed to be representing *my* interests."

"As I recall, you asked me to find out if Felix Felber knew that he was signing a significant amendment to his will. He did, but then, you were already aware of that."

"I was?"

Jeffers said, "Felix told you."

Mudge looked at her. "What a preposterous—"

"He told you," I broke in, "and you immediately went to 'visit' him."

"Only you stopped by Sedell Warren's shed first," said Jeffers.

I nodded. "To pick up a little 'friendly persuasion,' in the form of a claw-fork."

Mudge's cheeks burned. "This is ridicu—"

"Problem was," I added, "for all his frailty, Mr. Felber wasn't about to die without a fight. Or at least without running.

"Toward the cellar," said Jeffers. "Where he figured you wouldn't dare try to follow him, what with those bad stairs and your . . . body type."

"I want you to leave now. In fact, I *order* both of—"

"Except that you got to him at the door from the kitchen, and gave him a shove, so you didn't need to use the garden tool after all."

"At least," Jeffers interjected, "not on Felix."

Mudge began to seethe. "Now look here, you little—"

I said, "But you hadn't counted on the cat."

He turned to me. "What?"

"Bootsy. He'd taken a real liking to Mr. Felber, and when you chased after the old guy with that claw-fork, the cat pitched in to help him. And Bootsy got you with his two remaining claws."

"Nonsense."

I said, "When you came to see me, you were still wearing driving gloves. I chalked it up to the weather at the time, but I notice you're not wearing them now."

Mudge seemed to steel himself so his eyes wouldn't wander downward. "What I wear, and where I—"

Dana Jeffers said, "We also found your blood."

He turned to her, baffled. "My . . . ?"

"Blood." She waved her hand, the gold tooth peeking out from between her lips. "Just a little, of course, but it was right where my mother told Mr. Cuddy it would be."

"You're both . . . insane."

I said, "Bootsy has a favorite hiding place after battle, Mr. Mudge. Under one of the wine racks in Mr. Felber's basement. On top of a stainless steel sheet beneath it."

Jeffers's turn to nod. "We found a paw print of your blood from where Bootsy scratched you. That stainless steel and cool temperature preserved enough of it for the DNA analysis."

Mudge's voice quavered as he repeated, "DNA?"

"Yes," I said. "They can do wonders now, Counselor. And it'll take just a tape measure to show the scratches on your right hand are exactly the same distance apart as Bootsy's own rather distinctive claw pattern."

Mudge's face fell, and he actually raised his right hand to his eyes, seeming to study the back of it.

Jeffers lowered her voice an octave. "You found out about the codicil, and you couldn't risk an independent investigation into your handling of Mr. Felber's money."

"No," said Mudge, still studying his hand. "No, I couldn't."

I spoke quietly now. "I've checked the records on your 'charities' filed at the state offices. You control all of them."

"And steal from each of them," said Jeffers.

"Felix . . ." Mudge cleared his throat, starting again. "Felix had always trusted me, and it was only just a little . . . dipping at the beginning, just enough to carry me through a lean month here and there. But the lean months started mounting up, so I couldn't get even with the board. And then came the stupid codicil Felix felt he *had* to let me know about. Which would have . . . which did provoke. . . ."

". . . you to kill him," I said. "And to hire me to try and bluff Ms. Jeffers off."

"I didn't know what else to do! Until Felix's house sold and I could get at the proceeds, I barely had enough money to pay for a private investigator, much less the retainer any substantial law firm would require to litigate the malfeasance case. And another killing would have looked so . . . strange."

"Even the cat's?"

"I meant that stupid creature no harm! He was the one who attacked *me*, and I simply lashed out with the claw-fork."

"In self-defense," I said.

"Yes."

Dana Jeffers smiled grimly. "Jury's gonna love that."

"You don't understand." Oscar Mudge looked from her to me before trying to take in both of us at once. "If it weren't for that accursed feline, I'd have been set for the rest of my days."

I said, "And thanks to that 'accursed feline,' you still will be."

Dana Jeffers stood. "At least, that's how my clients doing life look at it."

The End

IN THE LOWLANDS

Gary A. Braunbeck

Do you know how a hobo feels?
Life is a series of dirty deals
Except for a kind word, a cup of coffee
And the song of the wheels . . .

—Anonymous message scrawled on boxcar wall, Kansas City, 1934

There's an old superstition among hoboes—especially those whose camps are made near the switch yards—that a 'Bo's death is mourned by the whistles of two passing trains; the sounds meet overhead in the night and, though each might be a bit mournful when heard by itself, they combine to create a pleasant song of welcome for the 'Bo's soul as he takes himself that last, great freight to Heaven.

When you hear that sound, you're supposed to remove your hat (if you wear one), close your eyes, and wish that fellow's soul good travel to the Pearly Gates, then say a little prayer that the body he left behind finds its way to the Lowlands—that is, that some good soul will see fit to give it a proper burial and not just leave it where the fellow shuffled off the ole mortal coil.

A second blast of the dual train whistles serves as a message to let you know that his soul found its way home and his remains have been properly sent to the Lowlands. That's about the best a 'Bo can hope for when he leaves this world.

Fry Pan Jack told me about that legend right before the TB finally overpowered his body and he passed on, leaving his cat, Billy, in my care. I heard the trains cry for him that night. And I put his remains in the Lowlands myself, reading a passage from Jack's Bible after I finished tamping down the soil.

Now I've got to stand trial for my life before a jury of my peers.

All of this in the same week.

It happened like this:

It was as good a jungle as a 'Bo could hope for in that spring of 1933: On the sunny side of the hills, within walking distance of a fairly clean creek, and not too far from a couple of switchyards and coal bunkers; a thick patch of trees offered shelter from the chilly night winds, and the town dump was within spitting distance and ready for scavenging. Add to that the friendly atmosphere that greeted a fellow upon his arrival— sometimes just getting past the railroad bulls was cause for major cele- bration on the parts of all residents—and, well, you'd be crazy to think you could do better.

Billy and I had decked a rattler—that is to say, rode spread-eagle atop a passenger train—for about the last half-hour before we jumped. (I did the actual jumping; Billy just sort of curled himself up into a ball inside my pack and hung on for dear life.) My landing was nothing to write home about—in fact, I thought I might've twisted my ankle (not the case, I'm pleased to tell you)—but luckily we were far enough away from any yards or stations that I didn't have to worry about any bulls seeing me.

Not that I've got anything against railroad police, understand. Most of them are fairly good sorts, but there's always a couple wherever you go who make sport of cracking open a 'Bo's skull. Seems those types can't tell the difference between a bum and a hobo—and believe you me, there's a difference. As Jack used to say: "Bums loaf and sit; tramps loaf and walk; but a 'Bo moves and works and he's clean."

Even on the road there's a hierarchy—and I learned myself that word from a dictionary Jack gave to me. "Nothin'll catch folks off-guard quicker than a 'Bo with a good vocabulary, son; shows 'em you got brains, and folks're more likely to give a decent meal to a man with some brains who's willing to work than a moron."

Add to that formula a hungry pet—like a cute cat—and you're hardly ever turned away.

I suppose that's one of the reasons Billy and me found ourselves so welcome at this particular jungle that evening.

There were a couple of fellows standing watch over a pot of Mulligan stew in the center of the camp; they were the first to spot me. They'd been talking up 'til then, but once they got sight of me their conversing stopped and they just stared at me.

One by one, the other men in the camp took notice of their silence and had to have themselves a look at what was going on.

Every man there was staring at me as I walked toward the fire and the pot.

"Evenin'," I said, tipping my hat.

"Where you coming from, stranger?" asked one of the Mulligan Stew Boys.

"Michigan way. Found a couple days' work helping to unload coal at the River Rouge auto plant."

"Was they still needin' workers when you left?"

"That they were."

He considered this for a moment.

I knew what was going through their minds: *Is he on the level or is he a damned yegg?*

A *yegg* was any one of a number of disreputable fellows who posed as a 'Bo but didn't want to be bothered with actually *earning* his keep, and so made his way by robbing an honest traveling laborer. A yegg wouldn't think twice about beating up or even killing a 'Bo for whatever the man had on him.

I set down my pack and untied it—not enough that Billy could stick his head out and attract even more attention—but enough so that I could reach inside and remove a potato and an onion, which I offered to the Mulligan Brothers. They were more than happy to take it.

You never, ever walk into a 'Bo camp and not offer something to go with the evening's meal if you can help it. That's part of the code. Not that they'd let you go hungry—if there's a meal being cooked up in a camp, then that meal is for everyone there and anyone who might happen by. Just because there's a code, that in no way means that fellow 'Bos would let a man starve.

The camp warmed up to me fairly quickly after that, and when I later pulled out some recent newspapers and detective magazines that I'd managed to pick up along the way, well, you'd have thought I was one of the Permanents there. The three things you can have in your pack that will

always make you welcome in any camp are coffee (or tobacco), food, and
something for the fellows to read. Life on the road is lonely—that's a
given—but it can also be boring as hell, and a recent newspaper or a story
magazine can offer a man something to occupy his mind with besides the
worry of where his next job and meal might be coming from.

It was only when we were sitting down to dinner that Billy woke up
and started raising a ruckus inside my pack. I reached in and pulled him
out, and from the way the rest of the camp reacted, you'd have thought
I'd produced a wad of greenbacks.

"Well, damn my eyes," said the bigger of the two Mulligan Brothers—
who went by the name of Cracker-Barrel Pete (you never use your real
name in a camp and never ask a man for his)—"Why didn't you tell us
you had yourself a little fur-ball with you?"

"He was sleeping when I got here, and he doesn't take kindly to being
woke up from his beauty rest." The fellows laughed at this.

"You know, don't you," said Pete, "that there's a couple restaurants in
town that'd be happy to give a day-old fish to a cat like your, uh—he got
a name, your cat?"

"Billy."

Pete nodded. "Yessir. Never fails to amaze me, human nature, that is:
Folks who wouldn't give you a slice of moldy bread would hand over
something small and fresh for a hungry cat."

I knew that to be true enough. Many was the time when Jack and I
almost met with the business end of a proprietor's shotgun until they
caught sight of Billy; then we almost always left with a tin of sardines or
tuna. A can of tuna, mixed with some crushed cracker, sometimes lasted
the three of us a couple of days.

Pete's words did not go unheard by the others.

"Say," he said, leaning over and refilling my coffee tin, "think you and
Billy there might be up for a little excursion in the morning? Might find
yourself a decent day's work, plus old Billy there might snag us some special goodies for tomorrow's dinner."

"Don't see why not," I said, letting Billy get comfortable in my lap. I
picked a small square of potato from my stew and fed it to him. Billy liked
potatoes—onions, too, which often made his breath a holy terror. "Folks
seem to take a quick shine to him."

"Then it's settled," Pete said just loud enough that the others would
know I was more than willing to do my share. "First thing tomorrow,
we'll go into town with Billy and hit the bakery there, see if we can't

get ourselves some day-old bread or pastries—he like pastries, does he?"

"Billy's a pastry fool."

Pete laughed. "Ain't that something? A cat that likes pastry!"

We all had ourselves a good laugh then at Billy's expense, but he didn't seem to mind; an animal of sweeter nature you'd be hard-pressed to find.

I couldn't help noticing, though, that the other Mulligan Brother—a thin reed of a fellow calling himself Icehouse Willie—wasn't laughing like the rest of us; oh, sure, he was chuckling away so's to fit in, but I caught something in his eyes as he looked at Billy that didn't sit right with me.

Maybe I'm just tired, I thought, and would not allow myself to think unkindly of anyone in the camp that night.

I read a few news articles to some of the men who couldn't read themselves, then we passed another hour or so passing around one of the detective magazines, taking turns reading serial chapters (and a juicy one this yarn was, too!), then, long about ten, with the stars above us in abundance, we found our spots for the night and got as comfortable as the ground would allow.

Just before I dozed off, with Billy's terrible breath on my cheek on account he'd decided to sleep on my arm, I heard a train whistle in the distance, echoing low and lonely, and I closed my eyes, wishing Jack a good night, as well.

As if to echo my sentiments in his own unique way, Billy sneezed in my ear, yawned, then dug in his claws and conked out.

🐾 🐾 🐾

Long about three in the morning (I checked the position of the stars, something Jack had taught me to do, in order to guess about the time) I woke up and pulled Billy off my arm, sitting him down next to me. He gave a grumpy, sleepy-faced look—*You'd better have a damned good reason for this*—then sat back on his hind legs and stared.

"Shh," I whispered so as not to awaken anyone nearby. "Just . . . just stay right there."

I reached into the bottom of my pack (which I'd been using as my pillow) and pulled out a small piece of smoked salmon wrapped in tinfoil— a little treat I'd bought for Billy with some of my Michigan wages at a Japanese place in Cedar Hill, Ohio, the day before. I would've offered it to put in with the stew, but Billy had been a little out of sorts lately—Jack having only left us a week ago—and I figured the fellow would enjoy a little late-night treat.

That's when I heard the cry.

It wasn't so much a scream—it had been strangled in the throat before it could get to that point—but there was enough panic and under-lying misery in the sound to let me know that whoever had made it was either being killed or in the middle of a right terrible dream.

I took a quick look round the camp and saw Pete a few yards away with the other Mulligan Brother, Icehouse Willie, the one who'd been looking at me and Billy so strangely. Pete had Willie's head pressed against his chest and was covering Willie's mouth with one of his hands. Willie was crying fiercely, deep, body-wracking sobs, his eyes closed tight, his face getting redder and redder, and as I gently put Billy down and started over to see if there was anything I could do to help, I saw that Pete was rocking his buddy back and forth like he would a baby and all the time whispering, "It's okay, Willie, there you go, there you go, no fires, okay? It's a nice, cool night, and you're out here in the open with me and you're okay, shhh, there you go, it's okay. . . ."

It took a few more minutes of this before the other man finally fell back to sleep.

I hoped for his sake that it was a peaceful slumber.

Another quick look-round showed me that the man's cries had awak-ened a few of the residents, but they acted as if they were used to it and simply rolled over and went back to sleep.

Pete came over to me, shaking his head. "Sorry about that. Guess we should've told you about Willie."

He gestured toward the far end of the camp and we set off walking. When we were almost to the edge of the camp he stopped for a moment, a sad look crossing briefly over his face. "I don't mean to sound cold-hearted, but Willie, he's . . . he's not quite right in the head, understand? Lost his wife, Carol, and his little girl, Sandy, to a boxcar fire about a year ago when they were riding to Chicago. I was riding that same train, only I was in a different car. Terrible thing. He tried to get to them, but they were in a hay car on account the train was hauling a lot of cattle, and the flames . . . well, you get the idea."

"Yeah . . ." I whispered.

"Sometimes he talks about 'em like they're still alive." He reached up and squeezed the bridge of his nose. "Damnedest thing, though. The folks who were ridin' in that car . . . well, shit, you just *know* better than to light any kind of match in a hay car. I mean, light's a bad idea in the first place on account it can tip off the bulls, but in a *hay car!*" He shook his head. "We had just pulled out from a stopover when the fire broke out, understand? And most of the people in that car had been asleep. Willie and his family, they were sitting way in the back of the car so's they'd face everyone."

"Best way to protect a family, under the circumstances."

"That may well be, but I heard later from a couple of the folks who got out that a bull set that fire—just came running up alongside and tossed in a match. Someone hadn't closed the door all the way." He shrugged. "It happens. Them cars, they can get damned stuffy." He looked back to where Willie was sleeping quietly, then looked at me and lowered his voice. "Just between you and me, though, I always thought Willie must've gotten a look at the bull who done it, and maybe part of what makes him . . . not quite right anymore is that there just ain't enough room in him for both his grief and his wanting to get revenge on the sumbitch what set that fire."

By now we'd started walking back into camp. I looked at Pete and grinned. "It's really decent of you . . . I mean, taking him on like you have."

Pete grinned back. "That obvious, is it?" A shrug. "What the hell else was a God-fearing man supposed to do? Couldn't very well leave him to his own devices, not in the shape he's in. Yeggs'd make a meal of him and not even leave bones for the dogs. And lately—hell, ever since we came to this camp three, four weeks ago—he's been gettin' a lot worse. Not just the dreams, those're bad as ever, but he's . . . he's acting less and less . . . uh . . ."

". . . rational?"

"Yeah, that's the word. He's been actin' less rational when he's awake. Scares me, y'know? Man's been a good traveling companion, and I think of him as a friend, but if he gets to the point where I can't handle him no more. . . ." He let the words and thought trail off. He knew I didn't need to hear him complete that sentence.

"How'd he come to be called 'Icehouse' Willie?"

Pete told me, and his answer damn near broke my heart.

I stopped by my sleeping spot where Billy was still sitting impatiently, waiting for his late-night treat.

"Cute little bugger, ain't he?" said Pete.

"Not so loud. He's full enough of himself as it is."

Pete smiled, reached down, and petted Billy's head, then gave me a tip of his hat and went back to his spot beside Icehouse Willie.

I laid back down and got as comfortable as I could, then peeled away the foil wrapping Billy's treat and placed the chunk of salmon in front of him. "There you go, pal, enjoy yourself."

Billy sniffed at it, decided it was to his liking (why he always made a show of deciding whether he wanted to eat something I could never figure out), then dug in, savoring every bite.

I had to admit it looked sort of tasty and made my mouth water slightly—and it wasn't as if I'd never shared Billy's meals before—but I figured he deserved this special treat all to himself.

I stroked the fur on top of his head. "You're a good traveling companion, Billy."

He sniffed once in mid-chew as if to say, *Yeah, yeah, yeah, I'm a prince and so're you, now can I please get back to the business at hand?*

I laughed under my breath, then rolled over and fell back asleep.

The last thing I remember thinking was how I hoped that Willie could sleep the rest of the night without hearing the cries of his wife and daughter.

Damnedest thing, really, the trouble that little secret snack of Billy's caused later.

🐈 🐈 🐈

Jack was an old-timer on the road (he admitted to being "in spitting distance of seventy, but I ain't gonna tell you in what direction"), and many was the night he'd regale me with tales of his adventures on the road before I hooked up with him.

One of his favorite memories was of a house in Portage, Wisconsin, he'd spent time at a few years back.

"The mother there, her husband had died a year or so before, and what with a family to care for, she had to find a way to make herself a respectable living. She took in washing, cooked meals for others, and baked up something like forty or fifty pies a day for a little restaurant called the Pig-n-Whistle. All that pie-cooking, it took a powerful lot of stove wood.

"Now, her children couldn't keep up—poor woman had to have at least five long rows of stacked wood that needed to be split—so she was more than happy to offer a 'Bo a job splitting the logs. You could earn yourself a fine, fine meal splitting wood for her. The jungle we lived in was just a few hundred yards from her back yard, on the other side of the rail yard in a grove of trees by Mud Lake. 'Bos tended to hang around that jungle for a good long while, not just because of the work and meals this lady'd provide us with, but because if it was your birthday and her kids got wind of it, she'd bake up a little cake and send it over, and her kids . . . well, they always managed to come up with some sort of present for you, a magazine or book or old toy. Yessir, it was a good place. Many's the night, after the wood had been split and the pies baked and the evening meal served, she'd invite any 'Bo who wanted to come over and sit on her porch and listen to the radio. She always served something to drink on those nights. I remember her lemonade best, on summer evenings with the radio playing and the train whistles calling in the distance.

"Yessir, that's my idea of Heaven. In fact, that's where I first found old Billy here. He was one of a litter of kittens that someone tossed in the river one night, all tied up in a bag. If me and this other fellah—can't recall his name now—but if we hadn't been where we was and seen this happen, all them kittens would've drowned. Terrible thing, the way people treat their pets."

"What about the way they treat each other?"

He looked at me and shook his head, grinning. "You expect too much of others, son. Take my advice: If you expect no kindness, then you won't be disappointed when none is given; but, Lord, are you all the more grateful for it when it is!"

🐈 🐈 🐈

I was awakened from my pleasant dream of Jack and the Pie Lady when someone slammed a steel-toed boot into my hip. I came awake with a shout, grabbing my pack and spinning around on the ground, ready to swing at whoever'd done that to me, when I found myself staring up at one of the most unpleasant-looking bulls I'd ever seen. He stood there, big as life and three times as ugly, holding his club in his hands and looking all-too-ready to open up my skull.

And if he wasn't up to messing up his uniform with my brains, one look at the younger fellow with him told me *he* was ready.

A little too ready, from the glint in his eyes.

The big bull stared down at me. "Understand you came in here around six, six-thirty last night, that right?"

"Yessir," I said, looking around for Pete and the others. They were gathered together near the cooking area, trying not to be too obvious about looking at me.

I looked around quickly myself, wondering where Billy had wandered off to.

"Look, officer," I said, "I don't want any trouble. If you'd be so good as to tell me what this is all about—"

He snapped the business end of his club forward and thrust it into my chest. I took this as a request to shut up and listen.

"There's been rumors about a yegg moving through these parts," the bull said to me. "Don't get me wrong, boy: I got nothing against the likes of 'Bos, but last night—early this morning, actually, around four-thirty, five—someone from this camp broke into a couple of stores and stole themselves a bunch of food, liquor, and a little bit of money."

He squatted down to get his face close to mine, still keeping the club in my chest. "Reason I know they were from this camp is because it wasn't enough for them to be happy with the stores. No, they had to go and break into some folks' *homes*." He made a quick sideways gesture with his head. "Pete over there told me you're the only new fellah what's come around here lately. Sorry to say, but that makes you—"

"—your best suspect, yessir."

He studied me for a moment. "The only reason I don't have the sheriff out here with me is because, one, I didn't think you'd be stupid enough to come back here and, two, I think it would sit better with the folks who were robbed if I could go back and tell them that the 'Bos took care of the problem in their own manner . . . if you read my meaning."

And I did, all too clearly.

You live in a camp, you don't rob from another hobo. You live in a camp, thievery of any kind was to be avoided outside the camp as well— or at least kept to a minimum: a pie lifted from its cooling spot in an open bakery window every now and then, some vegetables hurriedly snatched from a garden, or an old shirt clipped from an outside line, that was acceptable if the circumstances warranted thieving, but if it could be avoided, you did so. Townspeople were your only source of jobs and handouts, and you did not—repeat, *did not*—do anything to anger them. One dirty yegg could muck it up for everyone in the camp, and a good camp near a good town—especially one where the bulls didn't run you off on a regular basis, as this one seemed to be—well, that was to be respected in the same way people respect the church they go into every Sunday.

The bull looked at his partner and said, "Watch him while I search his pack, Carl."

Carl's idea of watching me was planting one of his feet right into my chest and pressing down. Hard.

"*Carl,*" said the other bull. "What'd I tell you about that?"

"Bastard broke into *my house,* McGregor."

"I know that your place was one that he hit, but until we find something of yours or one of the other folks'—" He stopped, then looked down as he pulled a half-empty bottle of whiskey from my pack. He followed that with some bread, cheese, and a couple emptied cans of salmon.

None of which had been in my pack the night before.

"Looks like we got our man, Carl." Then McGregor pulled out an envelope with some writing on it. He read it, looked at me, then his partner, and handed the envelope to Carl.

"What's this?" asked his partner.

"You tell me. It's got your name on it."

Carl glared at me—now I was sure there was a craziness barely hiding behind his eyes—and snatched the envelope from McGregor, tore it open, and removed the letter inside.

He tried to control it, that I could see, but whatever was written on that page rattled him something fierce.

"Well?" said McGregor.

"Huh? Oh—it's, uh . . . it's just a letter I got from, uh . . . my granddad." He folded the paper up in a hurry and stuffed it into his pocket. "You piece of—" he said to me, pulling back his foot to kick me.

"Carl!" snapped McGregor. "This ain't that Illinois rat-trap you moved here from. We don't strike a man without bein' provoked."

"I can't help it! It's bad enough to break into a man's house and steal his food and whiskey, but what the hell kind of yegg steals a man's personal *mail*?"

"The kind we just caught."

McGregor stood up and gestured that I should do the same. As soon as I was on my feet Carl spun me around slapped handcuffs on me—none too gently, I might add—then marched me into the center of the camp and sat me down on an old tree stump.

"One way or another," Carl snarled in my ear just low enough so only I could hear him. "One way or another you're going to the Lowlands."

My mouth went dry. The violence in his voice was like nothing I'd ever heard before, and there was no doubt in my mind that Carl wanted to kill me with his own bare hands . . . and whatever was in that letter was the reason.

"Okay, fellahs," said McGregor loudly enough to get the camp's attention. "My shift ends at five. I got three other guys from the yard who're willing to sit on the jury. I'll stand in as bailiff. You got until then to pick out the other nine jurors."

Pete stepped up and said, "You be the one who calls Judge Carson?"

"I'll take care of it—and I'll make damned sure the people in town know that you fellahs are gonna take care of this problem. I'll offer apologies, if it's all the same."

Pete nodded. "And if it's all the same to you, McGregor, I'll be defending our friend here."

"Ain't no friend of mine." He turned to me real quick and said, "Nothing personal. If you're innocent, I'll apologize to you. Until then, you're as good as a crook in my eyes." He grabbed up a small coil of rope someone had scavenged from the dump and ordered a couple of men nearby to tie my legs and ankles to the stump.

"Be seeing y'all this evening," he said, tapping the end of his club against the brim of his hat.

Carl walked by me real slow.

Real slow.

Not blinking.

One way or another . . .

Everyone in camp watched the two bulls make their way over the hill and back toward the rail yard. Then Pete put a hand on my shoulder and said, "You know what the penalty is for that kind of thieving, don't you?"

I nodded my head.

If found guilty, they were bound by the code to either kill me or exile me.

You exile a 'Bo by marking his face; that way, he'll not find himself welcomed in any camp he comes across thereafter.

I have seen such marked men in my travels. Burned faces, faces missing an eye, an ear, a nose . . . a simple scar would be treasured as a symbol of mercy. But mercy was something you rarely found under these circumstances. Not only was a marked 'Bo not welcomed in a camp, damn few people will give him work or a handout.

Death or marked exile; wasn't much of a choice, when you got right down to it.

The rules of the road can be brutal when a bad element threatens to ruin it for the innocent.

I looked up at Pete. "You seen Billy?"

"No, I ain't. And that's how come McGregor went right for you."

"Beg pardon?"

"Whoever broke into them places had a cat with him. A couple of witnesses saw it. Guess the guy stole a fish or two from one of the markets to feed it."

"Oh, brother. . . . There were a couple of empty cans of salmon in my pack."

"Not yours, I take it?"

"No."

"Now let me ask you something."

"Anything."

"Am I the only one who's noticed that Willie is conspicuously absent this morning?"

I looked at his face and knew there was no need for me to answer.

🐈 🐈 🐈

The trial got under way a little after four P.M.

It didn't help my chances much that Eastbound Earl, the prosecutor, dumped the contents of my pack onto the ground to reveal the evidence that McGregor and Carl had found there.

It also didn't help much that Billy finally put in an appearance a few minutes before the trial started, his breath stinking of fish. He bounded right up to me and jumped into my lap, rubbing himself against my coat.

"I have to say in all fairness," whispered Pete, "that this does not bode well for your, uh . . . your—"

"Acquittal?"

"I was going to say something a little more colorful—mentioning a particular point on your anatomy—but 'acquittal' will do. Look, we both know full well that Willie's the one who snatched Billy up and took him into town when he did all that stealing. I *told* you he ain't been actin' like himself since we got here. Probably figured things would go just like they have up to this point. Hell, wouldn't surprise me one bit if he actually made an effort to be seen."

"He knew that any witness would remember the cat more than his face?"

Pete nodded. "If there was even enough light for them to see his face."

"Yeah," I whispered.

"Don't get me wrong. He's the one who did this, but the rules don't allow for his, uh, condition to be taken into account. Thief's a thief, and that's all there is to it."

We both searched the crowd of faces until we found Willie, standing way in the back of the spectators and looking for all the world like a man who was walking in his sleep.

"We'll hear the defense's arguments now," said Judge Carson, a hard-looking older gentleman whose voice sounded like he gargled with moonshine three times a day. Pete told me that Carson had ridden the rails once himself and had been treated well by the hoboes he encountered and so always oversaw these trials. "He's as fair as you're going to find."

"Pete," said McGregor, our bailiff.

Carl stood off to the side, trying to look like he didn't want to slit my throat.

"If it please the court," said Pete, standing just a bit taller than usual, "I would like to call Mr. Icehouse Willie to the stand."

There was a murmur among the spectators, and when Willie didn't come forward right away, McGregor, our inspiring bailiff, said, "All right, Willie, let's . . ."

And that's when Pete pulled me to my feet and led me up to the witness chair.

McGregor stopped and stared but said nothing.

He knew damned well—as did every other resident of the camp—that I was not Willie, but no one said a thing.

"What the hell're you doing?" I whispered.

"You remember our talk last night?"

"Yeah . . . ?"

"Just try and follow my lead. And remember that Willie stammers."

I glanced in Willie's direction; he gave me a nervous, almost apologetic look as Pete started in on his questioning.

"Okay, Willie, why don't you tell us why you—"

"Thief!" someone shouted.

The camp crowd reacted with appropriate shock.

Judge Carson banged his gavel, calling for order.

"Would you please tell us," said Pete, "why it is you're called 'Icehouse' Willie?"

I was never much for play-acting, but I gave it my best try; can't rightly say why, but I trusted Pete. "Ah, hell, Pete . . . what's that got to do with—?"

"Answer the question, please," said Judge Carson.

"Pete here, he g-gave me that name."

Judge Carson stared at me, then at Pete. "I'm gonna assume here that this has some kind of bearing on the case?"

"It does, Yeronner; it might not seem, ah . . . uh . . ."

"Evident," I whispered from the side of my mouth.

"Evident right away," said Pete, "but it will come to bear on things."

Carson sighed and nodded his head. "Just don't go off on any tangents, understand? My daughter's bringing my new granddaughter over for supper tonight, and I'll be damned if I'm gonna miss seeing them."

"Understood, Yeronner." Pete turned his attention back to me, but not before making a quick gesture with his head and eyes that told me I should look over at Carl.

I did so, and saw a 'Bo offering the bull a bottle of beer. Carl accepted—not gratefully, big surprise—and had a little trouble getting the top off. While he struggled with the bottle opener, the 'Bo who'd given him the beer brushed back behind him—

—and slipped something from his pocket.

I looked at Pete to let him know I'd seen it. I'd told him about the letter earlier that day. Evidently he'd taken it upon himself to obtain the thing without Carl's cooperation, Carl being so warm-hearted toward hoboes as he was. It probably would have seemed like taking advantage of the man's good nature to ask him for it.

I went on, remembering as best I could what Pete had told me of Willie's story last night. ". . . and after the fire, the bulls put all the bodies in this here icehouse near the yard. I . . . I, uh . . . I w-w-went in there to find my Carol and Sandy, and after I f-found 'em I wanted to sit with 'em awhile, y'know? Sandy, she don't like to be left alone when she's sleeping, and Carol, sh-she'd give me h-h-holy h-hell if I went off while they was resting." I made up this last part, which might have been stupid, but by this time I found I was enjoying playing this part—so much so that I felt a tear slip down my cheek. It wasn't hard to muster tears at the thought of how terrible Carol's and Sandy's last moments had been. Then I simply sat there, staring at the ground and shaking.

"Go on," said Pete, softly.

"Then you come in there after a bit and made me leave before I f-froze to death." Then I remembered something Pete had told me Willie once said: "Sometimes I wish I had. Least then we'd all still be together."

Judge Carson slammed his gavel against the wood tabletop that served as his bench. Someone had scavenged the table from the dump earlier; it smelled of old and rancid food and decay and probably accounted for the pained expression the Judge's face had been sporting since things got under way.

"All right, Pete, that's enough," said the Judge. "Whether or not this has any bearing on your case, I don't care. It's damned depressing, and I, for one, will not sit here and be made to listen to a man relive something as terrible as losing his family."

"May I ask one more question, Yeronner?"

"Best make it a good one."

I saw Pete glance over in Carl's direction; that glance was not lost on McGregor, who, for the rest of the proceeding, kept looking from Carl to Pete to me to Willie, then back again.

"Willie, did you see the man who set that fire in your boxcar that night?"

Carl froze, blanching.

I shot a quick glance in Willie's direction; he looked straight at me with one of the most lonely, scared, and pained expressions I've ever seen deform a man's face, then gave a short, sharp nod of his head.

"I'm a bit deef these days," snapped Judge Carson. "You're gonna have to actually *say* something."

"Oh, yeah," I said. "I saw him real good."

Carl looked about ready to dump in his shorts.

I had just a moment before I figured out what was in that letter and who had written it.

What I didn't understand was the why of the rest of it.

"O-kay," said Judge Carson, slamming his gavel once again, "that is more than sufficient for my tastes. We are here to try this man," he snapped a liver-spotted hand in my direction, "for thievery and breaking and entering. I must be gettin' soft in the head, lettin' you pull a stunt like this."

"But, Yeronner—"

"But *nothin'*, Pete." He looked directly at me. "Are you guilty of the crimes of which you're being accused?"

"N-nosir."

Carson smiled. "All-righty, then." He glared at Pete. "Now, we have heard the prosecution's arguments and seen their evidence, I have the statements of the townsfolk whose businesses and residences were broken into, so now it's your turn. That's how this works, Pete, it's called a *trial*. They go, then you go, I listen to all pertinent statements. Dull, I know, but I *like* dull. So . . . do you have any witnesses to call who might actually have something to say about the case that I'm supposed to be hearing, or should we just go right to the closing statements?"

Pete looked at me, then Carl, then Willie.

"One moment, please, Yeronner," Pete said.

"What the . . . ?" I whispered to him when he came over to me.

"You a gambling man?"

"I don't—"

"Shh, hang on."

The 'Bo who'd picked Carl's pocket came up to Pete and handed him the letter. Pete made a fairly big show of accepting the letter, opening it, reading it, then considering what he'd just read.

"Yeronner," he said, "I have no other witnesses to call, but I would ask a favor of the court."

"Oh, *hoo-ray*," muttered Carson. "What is it?"

"A twenty-four hour recess."

Carson mumbled curses under his breath, then said, "If I ask you why, is the answer going to upset me?"

"Probably."

"I should've retired last year like Mildred wanted." A sigh, then: "All right, why do you want a recess?"

"Some new evidence has just come to light which might prove my client's innocence."

Carson was silent for several moments, then said: "You're kidding."

"Afraid not, Yeronner."

"The man was discovered with several of the stolen items on his person. Not only that, but several of the stolen items were either fresh or canned fish—and *don't* think I didn't get a whiff of his cat's breath earlier. Between its breath and the smell on its fur, it could knock a buzzard off a shit-wagon."

"It looks bad, I know."

"This is such a help," I said under my breath.

"We're talking not only about the thieving here, Yeronner, but a man's life, as well. I'm willing to personally vouch for my client. Twenty-four hours."

Carson looked at his pocket watch. "No, but I'll give you some time. It's just right now six. Even though it's gonna have Mildred spittin' nails at me, we will reconvene at this same spot at nine A.M. tomorrow morning. Is that sufficient time for you to gather and examine your new evidence?"

Pete's smile was almost evil. "That'll be more than enough time, Yeronner."

I looked back to where Carl had been standing.

He was long gone.

One way or another . . .

And Pete, with more than a little help from Willie, had just turned me into bait.

"Nine A.M.," repeated Carson. "But after that, new evidence or no, some sort of action has to be taken, understand? If someone isn't punished, the town's gonna want me to have McGregor and his friends bust up this camp and send all of you on your way. I'd hate to see that happen. I know a lot of you fellahs—if not by name, then by sight—and find you a decent sort for the most part.

"Until nine A.M., then," he cracked his gavel against the table top, "this court stands in recess."

Pete looked at me and winked.

"*Please* tell me you know what you're doing."

"I sure hope so."

I looked down at Billy, whose expression seemed to say, *Me? I wanted to keep going, but you just had to stop and make some new friends, didn't you? If Jack was here, he'd hit you on the head so hard you'd have to unzip your pants to blow your nose.*

"Next time, I'll listen," I whispered to him.

Then Billy yawned. Easy to do when there's no chance your body'll be in the Lowlands come this time tomorrow.

🐾 🐾 🐾

It was close to midnight, and I was freezing.

Billy lay curled up in my lap, fast asleep.

I had been moved outside the camp, to a special "holding area" that McGregor and one of the jury bulls had set up according to Judge Carson's instructions before all the law boys had left for the night.

I was still in handcuffs, though my legs had been untied so I could at least stand from time to time and stretch. McGregor and the jury bull had taken a group of 'Bos down to the dump and hauled back a couple of discarded railroad ties which they proceeded to set upright into a portion of soggy ground. The mud pulled the ties down about two feet before the things hit solid rock and stayed in place. Then one of the cuffs was opened and my arms were stretched behind my back and cuffed again behind the two ties, both of which extended a good three feet above my head. I didn't have a lot of room for moving, but at least it wasn't so tight that I couldn't relax my shoulders a little.

But only a very little.

Pete and Willie had made themselves pretty scarce after I was secured, and for the better part of the last four hours it'd just been me and Billy, sitting in the cold night air with little more than cricket-song and starlight for company.

Trees still surrounded me, in places pretty thick.

A man could hide himself pretty well in those trees.

I had a feeling I knew what was going to happen, and why it was that no one in the camp—McGregor included—had spoken up to say that I wasn't Icehouse Willie.

It was all a crapshoot, and while I don't discourage a fellow from taking himself a big leap of faith every once in a while, it feels a bit different when a possible snake eyes will come attached to a real snake of sorts, one filled with venom and ready to end your life in a heartbeat.

I looked down at Billy's sleeping form and jostled him with my legs.

Nothing.

I tried once more.

Billy made a little mewling sound in the back of his throat, dug his back claws in just a little bit deeper, but still didn't wake up.

"Wish to hell I could sleep like you," I said to him. "You have any idea how that used to burn Jack up when you was on the road together? He used to say that you could probably sleep through a train wreck that was caused by an earthquake that took out an iron bridge." Then I laughed. "There were times he wondered whether or not you were deaf."

"What happened to your stammer, Willie?"

I snapped my head up just in time for my eyes to meet the business end of a .38.

"You should've known better than to try and catch a free ride on any line I worked for, Willie," said Carl, looking crazier than even before. He gave me the once-over, then stepped back and gestured with his gun for me to stand up. "I don't like the idea of killing a man who's not on his feet, even though you goddamn tramps barely qualify as men, you ask me."

I thought that last remark should be left unanswered, so I shimmied myself up into a standing position, much to Billy's chagrin; he finally let go of my leg and dropped onto the ground, stretching, yawning, and hissing.

"Cute cat," said Carl.

"I get a lot of compliments on him, thank you."

Carl stepped forward again and pressed the barrel of the gun to the middle of my forehead. I was amazed that I didn't wet myself, I was so scared.

"Tell me one thing," he said.

"Anything to keep the conversation goin' as long as possible."

A smile slithered across his face like a worm. "Good that you can crack wise right now. Be a good idea if you kept a pleasant thought in your head."

In the distance I heard the whistle of a train.

Far off, from the opposite direction, it was answered—though not yet joined—by the cry of another train.

"How'd you see me, Willie? I mean, I was pretty fast on my feet and that door wasn't opened all that far. I just ran up and tossed in the lit book of matches. How'd you get a look at me?"

"I d-don't quite r-r-remember." The stammer this time wasn't play-acting on my part; I was scared right down to the ground.

Carl considered this for a moment, then shrugged, pulling back the hammer. "So I didn't get everyone in the boxcar. I guess I can live with that."

Billy had by now wandered over down by Carl's legs and was rubbing himself up against the bull's steel-toed boots.

Carl kicked out a bit, but that didn't deter Billy; once he decides he's going to rub up against you, you just resign yourself to it and that's all she wrote.

"Dammit to hell!" Carl snapped, looking down and giving Billy a more insistent kick—

—and that's when the gun slipped away from my forehead, a little off to the side—

—and that's when I heard a voice yell, "Duck!" from somewhere in the nearby trees—

—and then there was a blast from somewhere that sparked right above my head and sent Carl to the ground cussing and flailing and blew away a good foot of railroad tie above—

—and before I knew what was happening, I felt someone toying with the handcuffs.

"Don't make a sound," said Pete, who was in front of me.

"Who's messing with the cuffs—?"

"Willie," Pete replied. "Did I forget to mention that he used to be a locksmith?"

I twisted my neck so as to look beside me. "That true?"

"B-bad locks in t-t-town," said Willie, working the cuffs open with some sort of pin. "Bad and ch-ch-cheap, easy to break in, easy, easy, easy."

The cuffs came off, and I took my pack when Pete offered it.

Carl still lay on the ground a few feet away, cradling his right hand against his chest. There wasn't any blood, but his hand looked to have been burned pretty good. The cylinder of his .38 gleamed in the moonlight pooling near my feet. I looked around and saw the rest of his gun a few feet beyond that.

McGregor came walking up to Carl, holding a mean-looking pump-action shotgun in front of him.

"Helluva shot, ain't he?" said Pete.

"A true marksman," I replied, shaking so much I thought I was going to drop.

Trailing behind McGregor—and looking for all the world like the most cantankerous so-and-so you'd ever want to meet—was Judge Carson. Two sheriff's deputies flanked him.

I looked at Pete. "And . . . ?"

"Okay, okay, sorry. Look, me and Willie, we been keeping close to Carl ever since Chicago. We figured it was only a matter of time before he wound up transferred to some little 'burg like this and we'd have time to . . . well, see if we couldn't do something about what he done. The trick was being able to stay in one place long enough to get the trust of the camp."

As he spoke, I noticed the other residents of the jungle, awakened by the gunfire and yelling, shuffling toward us from down below.

"They had a helluva time convincing me," said McGregor over his shoulder. "I know Pete and Willie here fairly well, and I knew when Pete pulled a stunt like he did earlier today—you know, calling you up to testify like you were Willie—I figured something pretty serious must be going on."

I nodded. "That's why you didn't say anything?"

"That's why no one who knows the two of them didn't say anything. 'Course, that letter of Willie's that Carl had on him was a pretty convincing piece of evidence. That, and what he just now tried to do to you."

Carl was still, evidently fascinated by the barrel of McGregor's pump-gun.

"I'm real sorry that we did this to you," said Pete, putting a hand on my shoulder. "But we had to distract ole Carl's attention there in order to have time to convince McGregor and the Judge that Carl here's the fellah that set that fire in Chicago."

"Twelve people died in that fire," said Judge Carson. "Be they hoboes or not, it was murder. Some parts of this country still look poorly upon that."

"Judge," I said, nodding my head.

"That was quite a performance you gave this afternoon," he said. "Mildred's going get herself quite a laugh out of it when I tell her."

"How was dinner?" I asked.

Carson shuddered. "Oh, it was great, seein' my daughter and grand-daughter, but my wife still can't make a decent gravy." He put a hand to his belly. "I was already up when McGregor came by with Pete and Willie. I figured even if this turned out to be a bust, I'd at least be out in the open when that gravy made me start sounding my horn, if you get my meaning."

The judge and McGregor, along with the two deputies, hauled Carl to his feet and cuffed him with the same cuffs he'd used on me. I'd be lying if I said I didn't get a certain amount of enjoyment out of seeing that.

I looked at Icehouse Willie. "Why'd you have to take Billy?"

"Sandy likes cats, that she d-d-does. Likes 'em a lot. Was always asking me for one. Her mother, though—" he whistled quick and low "—can't stand the things. M-m-make her sneeze something terrible."

He was crying as he told me this.

"No one's g-g-gonna burn today, nosir, not while I'm around, nosir. No one's gonna burn. The Lowlands aren't g-g-gonna take anybody today, nosir."

Pete slapped my back. "C'mon, we got to get the hell out of here."

I heard the cry of the approaching train whistles.

"Where's Billy?"

Willie opened his coat. "S-snug as a bug."

Billy was nestled comfortably in one of Willie's massive inside pockets.

Judge Carson looked at us, then toward the train whistle. "You know, this here's gonna draw a lot of attention from folks for a while. Me and McGregor and the deputies, we all heard Carl's confession. The rest'll be fairly easy." He came up to Willie. "Justice will now be served, Willie. Your Carol and Sandy, they can rest easy now. So can you."

And with that, they hauled Carl away.

I turned and looked at the rest of the camp. They had stopped several yards away and were now making their way back to their beds, cricket-song and starlight accompanying them.

Life on the road is hard, but sometimes you make new and good friends.

"You in the market for a couple of extra traveling companions?" Pete asked.

"The more the merrier," I said as the four of us took off up the hill and over the rise toward the tracks.

We decked the rattler just outside the switch yard, disembarking a few hours later just a few miles from the Canadian border. From there we caught a lumber car.

We've been a team ever since.

Some nights Willie wakes up from his bad dreams about his wife and daughter. That's when Billy helps the most, soothing his night terrors while I tell him all about Heaven, as Jack saw it. Then we smile at each other, finding peace in the thought of Jack and Sandy and Carol all sitting on that back porch under a summer night sky and sipping lemonade while the radio plays on. A good end to a good day's labors.

And no train whistles mourning.

The Lowlands can't touch us here.

—end—

Author Biographies

Parnell Hall is the author of the Puzzle Lady crossword puzzle mysteries, the Stanley Hastings private eye novels, and the Steve Winslow courtroom dramas. His books have been nominated for the Edgar and Shamus awards. A former private detective, Hall is also a part-time actor, and he has appeared in summer stock, regional theater, and interactive dinner theater events, as well as motion pictures. He lives in New York City.

Dulcy Brainard is the Editor for the Lifestyles and Mystery sections of *Publisher's Weekly*, the leading trade magazine of the publishing world. She lives in New York.

Janet Dawson is the author of a mystery series featuring Oakland, California, private Investigator Jeri Howard. Her first book, *Kindred Crimes,* won the St. Martin's Press/Private Eye Writers of America contest for best first private eye novel and also garnered nominations for the Shamus, Macavity, and Anthony Awards. Other Jeri Howard cases include *Till the Old Men Die, Don't Turn Your Back on the Ocean, Where the Bodies Are Buried,* and *A Killing at the Track.*

Catherine Dain is the creator of the Freddie O'Neal series, including the novels *Lay It On the Line* and *Lament for a Dead Cowboy,* both nominated for the Shamus Award. After receiving her graduate degree in theater arts from the University of Southern California, she worked as a television newscaster before turning to mystery writing. She has also edited non-fiction books on leadership and global business for the university's Business Education and Research Center. She lives in Ventura, California.

Tracy Knight is a psychologist who uses elements of his work to write stories with keen insight into the human mind. Other fiction of his appears in *Cat Crimes Goes on Vacation, The UFO Files, Werewolves,* and *Murder Most Delicious.* He lives in Macomb, Illinois.

Jan Grape is a co-editor of *Deadly Women: The Female Mystery Writer.* She also has short stories in anthologies ranging from *Deadly Allies I & II, Lethal Ladies I & II, Feline & Famous,* to the recently released *Vengeance Is Hers.* Her non-fiction articles appear in *The Mystery Writers Sourcebook, The Fine Art of Murder,* and *How to Write a Private Eye Novel.* A regular columnist for *Mystery Scene* magazine, she also writes for the British publication *A Shot in the Dark.* She edits the Private Eye Writers of America newsletter and is the vice-president of that organization. Along with her husband, she owns the Mysteries & More bookstore in Austin, Texas.

Dick Lochte is the creator of Leo Bloodworth and Serendipity Dalhquist, who have appeared in several novels, including *Sleeping Dog* and *Laughing Dog.* He is also the creator of Terry Manion, a New Orleans–based private eye. He has been a promotional copywriter for *Playboy* magazine, a film critic for the *Los Angeles Free Press,* and a book columnist for the *Los Angeles Times.* Recently he teamed up with former L.A. prosecutor Christopher Darden to co-author a new mystery series beginning with the novel *The Trials of Nikki Hill.* He lives in Southern California.

Shirley Rousseau Murphy is the author of seven feline mystery novels, *Cat on the Edge, Cat Under Fire, Cat Raise the Dead, Cat in the Dark, Cat to the Dogs, Cat Spitting Mad,* and *Cat Laughing Last.* She lives in Carmel, California.

Mat Coward is a British writer of crime, science fiction, horror, children's, and humorous fiction whose stories have been broadcast on BBC Radio and published in numerous anthologies, magazines, and e-zines in the United Kingdom, United States, and Europe. According to Ian Rankin, "Mat Coward's stories resemble distilled novels." His first non-distilled novel, a whodunit called *Up and Down,* was published in the United States in 2000. Short stories have recently appeared in *Ellery Queen's Mystery Magazine, The World's Finest Crime and Mystery Stories, Felonious Felines,* and *Murder Through the Ages.*

Ann Barrett primarily writes non-fiction, food-related technical articles, but has also won second place in a contest sponsored by the National Academy of Poets and had her work published in an anthology of the contest winners entitled *A Delicate Balance.* In addition, she has received honorable mention in a contest sponsored by the *Writer's Journal.* She lives with her family and two cats in Needham, Massachusettes.

Matthew J. Costello is the author of more than sixteen novels and numerous non-fiction works, including collaborations with F. Paul Wilson and Craig Shaw Gardner and film novelizations. His articles have appeared in publications ranging from The *Los Angeles Times* to *Sports Illustrated.* He scripted *The 7th Guest,* the best-selling CD-ROM interactive drama, and its sequel, *The 11th Hour.*

Richard T. Chizmar is primarily known for his work in the horror field, most notably as the editor of the World Fantasy Award–winning magazine *Cemetery Dance,* a showcase of dark fantasy and horror fiction. The best of the magazine's run was recently collected in *The Best of Cemetery Dance.* His short fiction, which has appeared in *White House Horrors* and *Cat Crimes at the Holidays,* is both poignant and disturbing. The best of his short stories was collected in the anthology *Midnight Promises* in 1997.

Barry Hoffman's short fiction has appeared in *Return to the Twilight Zone, Werewolves,* and *A Horror Story a Day: 365 Scary Stories.* He lives in Springfield, Pennsylvania.

Jeremiah Healy, a graduate of Rutgers College and Harvard Law School, was a professor at the New England School of Law for eighteen years. He is the creator of John Francis Cuddy, a Boston-based private investigator who has appeared in more than a dozen novels. He was president of the Private Eye Writers of America for two years and is currently the president of the International Association of Crime Writers. A lecturer on mystery writing, he has attended mystery conferences in New York, London, Spain, and Austria.

Gary A. Braunbeck is the acclaimed author of the collection *Things Left Behind* (CD Publications), released last year to unanimously excellent reviews and nominated for both the Bram Stoker Award and the International Horror Guild Award for Best Collection. He has written in the fields of horror, science fiction, mystery, suspense, fantasy, and western fiction, with over 120 published works to his credit. His work has most recently appeared in *Alien Abductions, The Best of Cemetery Dance, The Year's Best Fantasy and Horror,* and *Dark Whispers.* He is co-author (along with Steve Perry) of *Time Was: Isaac Asimov's I-Bots,* a science fiction adventure novel praised for its depth of characterization. His fiction, to quote *Publisher's Weekly,* "stirs the mind as it chills the marrow."

Copyrights